The Golden Lantern

by

Vicki D. Thomas

The Relics Adventures, Book 2

The Golden Lantern

Cover Art by *Jennifer Greeff*

The Wild Rose Press, Inc.
PO Box 708
Adams Basin, NY 14410-0708
Visit us at www.thewildrosepress.com

Publishing History
First Edition, 2023
Trade Paperback ISBN 978-1-5092-4806-3
Digital ISBN 978-1-5092-4807-0

The Relics Adventures, Book 2
Published in the United States of America

Unable to pull air into his lungs, Ivan's heart beat fast like the rush of water in the creek. The silver Ratling jumped off and rolled his prey over with his claws. Just as Ivan struggled forward on his belly, trying to grab The Challenger, sharp teeth sank into his side. Powerful jaws snapped several ribs and then shifted its victim's body over to take another bite.

Ivan shrieked. Unbearable pain raced through him. Blood pumped out, saturating his skin and clothing. He struggled to escape, but the Ratling held him to the ground, its teeth going deeper. Its claws dug into Ivan's right arm and sent shocks of pain through his system. Something frothy bubbled from Ivan's lips and dribbled down his chin.

Darkness edged around him. He had to stay alert—his very life depended on it.

Praise for Vicki D. Thomas

The Long Dark Cloak #1 was released May 11, 2022.

"I was so impressed with this author in book one, The Long Dark Cloak, that I am excited to see a sequel. Not only has Ms. Thomas shown the ability to develop unique characters, she draws stimulating plots and uncommon settings that feel fresh and exciting in a young adult fantasy novel."

~ Cindy Davis, www.cindydavisauthor.com
(editor and author)

"I was on the edge of my seat as I read Book Two in the Relics Adventures series. In this story, fifteen-year-old Ivan Kimble again ventures into the West Forest searching for his older brother, who failed to return to their farm as promised. Author Vicki D. Thomas did not disappoint in *The Golden Lantern*."

~ Sunny Marie Baker, author of
Western Themed Romantic Suspense novels
www.sunnymariebaker.com

Dedication

This, as well as future books in this series, is dedicated to my parents.

Although they have both passed, my mom and dad are the best examples and inspirations in my life. They instilled the value of perseverance, hard work, and the importance of following your dreams. If you have a dream, grab hold and make it happen.

I'd also like to add my gratefulness to our critique group authors: Sunny Marie Baker, Sandra Masters, and Beth Jones, who have dedicated themselves unselfishly to each other's success.

Chapter 1

Home
1947, Southern England

Ivan left the West Forest in the light rain of late afternoon, riding Bounty, his chestnut horse, with two beagle dogs following. He made steady progress across the farmland that bordered the forest on the west side. Ahead, his family's three-hundred-year-old limestone house came into view. Behind it stood a barn, where the roof sagged, and the exterior had weathered to dirty gray.

The warmth of familiarity rushed through him. *I'm home.*

Peter, his older brother, promised he would return soon, and Ivan was sure all would be well again. Together, they would work the farm, just as they once did. They'd have milk fights in the barn, race their horses through fields and open meadows, and they would someday visit far-off places.

For a moment, Peter's negligence made Ivan angry.

Why doesn't he come home now? It's been four years since he left to go to war. Doesn't he know how lonely I've been?

He couldn't stay mad at his brother for long. Peter was the only family he had. Ivan felt abandoned and lonely with no one to celebrate his return home. He mourned for his mother and father, who had died in a train accident two years ago. Without family, it seemed his loneliness deepened with every passing year. Ivan was sure his emptiness would disappear when Peter finally returned and joined him on the farm.

He stretched his aching back. After his long journey through the forest, he was weary, and his stomach growled.

"There, Bounty, look ahead!" Ivan said, patting the horse's shoulder. "Your stable is waiting for you, warm and dry. And I want my supper as much as you do." Alfred and Canute, brother beagles, barked and sped away, happy to reclaim the comforts of home.

A spire of smoke twirled from the chimney.

A boy stood on the front porch, where he leaned against the wooden railing. He stared at the stranger riding up the gravel road. His light brown horse, tied at the hitching post, danced nervously from side to side. Before Ivan left to visit the forest, Mueller McKay, his neighbor, had recommended Dan Jacobs as a dependable helper. As Ivan rode closer, he figured Dan was about his age, maybe a few years younger.

"Hey!" The boy called and waved at the stranger. "I'm Dan Jacobs. Lookin' after things while Mr. Kimble is away." He bounced a fork between his fingers and thumb. "I think he'll be back sometime today."

"*I am* Ivan Kimble."

"Oh." Dan's eyebrows lifted. "I thought you'd be older—about Mr. McKay's age. You run the farm all by yourself? How long have you lived here? Mr. McKay said you went to find your brother in the West Forest. I don't know anyone who'd dare enter that horrible place." He swept his long, straight bangs to the side, but they slipped back over his eyes.

"Yes, I take care of the farm, but Mule McKay helps when he can. My parents bought it in 1924." Ivan rushed his answers, unsure which question to address first or why it should matter to him.

"Thanks for letting me stay here while you were gone. It saved a lot of time riding between your house and mine."

"It was Mule's suggestion. Cows need to be milked early morning and about the same time each evening." Ivan felt foolish for telling Dan what he already knew.

"Yeah, I know." He rested his hands on the railing. "Did you find your brother?"

"Yes. Peter's coming home soon."

"I've heard frightening stories about the forest." Dan's eyes grew large, and his eyebrows lifted. "Like wild wolves that change into men, and witches that cast spells on you, turning you into a troll. I don't know if it's true, but I would never go there to find out."

Canute jumped and barked at Dan. Alfred woofed and ran between Bounty's legs. The horse sidled and reared, snorting into the air.

"Whoa, boy." Ivan stroked Bounty's neck and shoulders.

When he raised his front legs again, his left hoof came down hard on the edge of the porch step breaking the corner. Ivan groaned, seeing yet one more chore he'd have to do.

"What's the matter with him?" Dan stepped back on the porch a few paces.

"You're a stranger, and he's tired and cranky," Ivan replied. "It's been a long journey."

"Well…" Dan hesitated. His attention stayed on Bounty. "I-I did the milking and fed the chickens. I've

3

eaten the last of the eggs—except one, you can have it. Do you want to come in for supper?"

"Sure." Ivan dismounted and tethered the reins over the hitching rail. It was the first time a stranger had ever invited him to eat in his own home.

Dan led the way, pushing the front door open, allowing Ivan to enter. When Ivan walked in, he gasped. His experience in the forest had so profoundly changed him that the surroundings seemed strange. He felt older, like a different person. In the forest, everything was uncertain, so his senses were sharpened, his reactions alert to the odd creatures, peculiar rules, and unreal things.

Yet, they were real—and many were very dangerous. There was always the worry about whether he'd leave the forest alive.

Now he was safe.

"Anytime you want me to help out, let me know." He reached for his jacket and shoved his arms into the sleeves. "I have to hurry before it gets dark."

"Hold on a minute." Ivan drew his thick eyebrows together. "I'll pay you for your services." Though he had almost no money, he went to his bedroom and opened the top bureau drawer. His ears suddenly felt warm. *How much should I pay him, and do I have enough?*

"You're joking, of course," Dan called and laughed. "I've already been paid—and generously, too. Thank you."

"Wh-who?" Ivan stepped back into the kitchen, his eyes open wide.

"Yeah. Some stiff-legged fellow in a black jacket and a fancy red bowtie. He paid me this morning, said you'd probably be back today."

"Eustace," Ivan mumbled.

"I don't know." Dan bunched his shoulders. "Not sure he told me his name."

"That's fine then." He nodded, feeling relieved and a bit dumbfounded.

"Oh." The lad swung around after he'd moved outside. "Are you going to the Saturday Social at the Graydon Town Center? It's a fundraiser for the Graydon Hill School. That's where I go. A good school, but a little snooty. That's what I think, anyway."

"We're not snobs at the Graydon Village School, but we do have some rough characters." Ivan grimaced, knowing that was about to change.

"My sister will be at the social. Well, I call her my sister, but she's not really," he said under his breath. "It just worked out that way."

Ivan's brow rose. Good manners kept him from asking personal questions, but it didn't mean he wasn't curious. *Why does he call her his sister, but she isn't?*

"She came to stay with me when Phillip, my brother, got killed. You remember?" His lips twitched. "Fell off a tractor, and it ran over him. Still doesn't make sense to me."

"I didn't know your family, but Peter visited many times, I believe."

"Yeah, he did." Dan continued excitedly. "You'd like her. She's real pretty—nice, too. She's helping Mrs. McKay set up the food tables for the fundraiser. Maybe you'll come to the event?"

"We'll see." Ivan wasn't interested in meeting another girl since it seemed Dan hinted at this. Ivan's heart and promise belonged to a beautiful goddess.

He'd met the goddess, Anna-Iza, while traveling

through the forest, searching for his brother. Sebastian, the spirit in the Long Dark Cloak, was by Ivan's side, looking surprised and delighted at the goddess and her retinue's arrival. Ivan admitted she'd captured his heart at once. Her sparkling blue-green eyes met his and seemed to see through him. *Does she detect my cowardliness?* He wanted to justify his fear to her and explain that only moments ago, he'd slain the vicious male Swamp Dragon, but standing there, baring a naked chest, he didn't feel so bold. Muttering a weak greeting, he bowed to her.

"I must stable Bounty and have my supper." Ivan thanked Dan for his help when he was needed.

"Sure." Dan nodded. "I have to get on home and do my homework." He mounted his horse. "Thanks again, Ivan. Nice to meet ya."

Leaning against one of the rough posts on the porch, Ivan waved to the boy and eyed the road that led from his farmhouse. If only it were Peter coming instead of Dan riding away.

Before Ivan left the forest, Peter promised to come home in a few days, insisting he needed to resolve several details before he was free. Ivan understood this, but how long would it be? Combing fingers through his dark, thick hair, he stood there watching until Dan disappeared from sight.

Now that they'd found each other, Ivan was anxious for his older brother to be home. A trace of worry crept over him. *What if Peter didn't want to return*? Ivan knew Peter didn't care for the dull life of a farmer. He was accustomed to living free and unencumbered at the South Castle in the forest. And yet, Peter's affection for Ivan was sincere, which was evident when they embraced and spoke from their hearts. Ivan sighed. *Will my life ever be free of loneliness?*

Ivan led Bounty to his stable and gave him an extra handful of oats. "You weren't the most cooperative animal." He shook his index finger. "But we made it back alive." He patted his horse's cheek and neck, feeling sadness rush through him. His life suddenly felt empty and without meaning. *Is it my attraction to the kindhearted goddess that causes me to feel this way?*

He exhaled slowly, not knowing the answer. *If Peter were here, he'd explain it.*

The last egg that Dan saved for Ivan was cold and unappetizing. Even a warm piece of toast and a large glass of fresh milk didn't improve the taste or his reflective mood.

The next morning, Ivan said to Alfred and Canute, "Sorry, boys. I'm going to school, and you must stay home and watch the farm."

As he tucked his schoolbooks into his saddlebags, something small and round thumped against the bottom. It was an acorn with its cap still attached. He rolled it between his finger and thumb and slipped it into his shirt pocket. Touching the acorn caused an empty feeling in his heart. "Zephyrus, Master and Peacekeeper of the Forest," he whispered in awe.

"Come on, Bounty. There's no telling how much I've missed since I've been gone. Mrs. Hambuckle will be worried." His horse shook his head and snorted loudly. Taking a deep breath, Ivan mounted and patted the animal's neck for reassurance. "It's all right, ol' boy. There's no reason for us to return to the forest again. We're safe here at home."

Chapter 2

Graydon Village School

After half an hour, Ivan rode into the Graydon Village Schoolyard, where Bonnet, his classmate, charged out the front door, her unkempt hair flying. She scratched her head vigorously, and Ivan concluded she still had lice. He vowed he'd keep his distance from her.

"Ivan. Ivan," she called, waving. "Where have you been? Mrs. Hambuckle is beside herself with worry. Are you all right?"

He slid from the saddle and draped the reins over the hitching post in front of the schoolhouse. "Hi, Bonnet." He grinned at the girl, welcoming her enthusiasm.

Bonnet reached for his arm. He jerked it away and pretended to cough into his palm.

"Where have you been?" she asked again.

"On business." Ivan turned to stroke Bounty's shoulder.

"And what would that be?" A frown narrowed her eyes. "You're too young to have any business."

"Excuse me, I'll be late." Ivan shifted his books to his other arm and walked briskly toward the school building. Bonnet dashed ahead and pushed open the door. She entered and held it for him.

"Ivan," Mrs. Hambuckle shouted. "I've—we've been very worried about you. Have you been ill?"

"I'm fine, ma'am." He was surprised at how calm he was in front of his classmates. In the past, shyness kept his head down, eyes on his desk, and his mouth closed.

"He was away on business." Bonnet stuck her nose into the air. "Very mysterious stuff." She rolled her eyes and wiggled her fingers mid-air on both hands.

"Well, lookie who decided to come to class," Dirk jeered. His cousin, Gussy, snickered.

"You are on very thin ice, young man." Mrs. Hambuckle scowled at the troublemaker. "Do not provoke me today." For a moment, Dirk lowered his head in a gesture of submission. His jaw tightened.

"It's nice to have you back, Ivan." His teacher cleared her throat. "Please take a seat. I'll speak to you after class about catching up with your assignments."

"Yes, ma'am." He bowed and sat down.

Dirk shot Ivan a smoldering glare.

Ivan ignored him.

"Look. I have a split lip," little Mercy said in a shrill voice. "It really hurt and bleeded a lot. He did it." She pointed at Dirk. "He knocked me down in the schoolyard. He's mean as a mad bull."

Their teacher picked up a piece of chalk. "You can tell Ivan about it later, okay, dear?"

Mercy's blonde curls bobbed up and down, and tears wet her pink cheeks.

Returning to the blackboard, Mrs. Hambuckle wrote several dates.

Bonnet whispered behind her hand, "Dirk-the-Mackerel didn't have you to bully, so he picked on Mercy. She bawled like a banshee. Poor Mrs. Hambuckle was so mad. I thought she would throw Dirk down the outdoor toilet hole."

"Things are different now," Ivan said quietly. The remark left a puzzled look on Bonnet's face.

Taking a deep breath, it appeared their teacher had pulled herself together. "Bonnet, would you please see me during first recess? We have a health issue to discuss."

Looking up, Bonnet blinked. "Yes, ma'am."

"Your history lesson for today is Chapter Three of the Norman Conquest," Mrs. Hambuckle continued. "I hope you've read it. I'll give a test based on the four questions listed at the end." She moved to her desk, looking distractedly at her notes. Ivan knew his teacher was lost in her thoughts about Aaron, her missing husband since the war, and he felt her emptiness. Perhaps that would change real soon since Ivan had met Aaron while in the forest. He was anxious to tell her all about it.

"Remember, William the Conqueror invaded our country in 1066," she said in a softer voice. "He decreed the West Forest as his new hunting grounds, and no one was allowed to kill or capture any of the animals by penalty of death. These brief facts should help nudge your memory."

There were several moans from the older students, reacting to the surprise test. Ivan was certain he could remember enough to pass. He usually read far in advance of the assigned lesson simply because it filled the lonely hours after the chores were done.

Bonnet rotated in her seat toward him and mouthed, "I can help you."

Shaking his head, Ivan hoped he'd made it clear—he wouldn't need her help with the test.

"Here! Mrs. Hambuckle." Dirk shot from his seat. "I caught them whispering. Ivan's going to cheat and get answers from Bonnet. I heard them clear as anything."

"I haven't even passed out the test yet." Mrs. Hambuckle frowned.

"I tell you, Bonnet's going to give him the answers. You never see anything *he* does wrong, 'cause Ivan's your pet. His stupid bowing and, yes ma'am, no ma'am." Dirk sneered and mimicked. "Makes me sick."

Ivan slowly stood. His nostrils flared. A powerful charge rose from his belly and traveled to his chest, swelling his arms. All the students stared, eyes wide and mouths opened. In the back row, his neighbor Mueller McKay's oldest boy sat straight in his seat. Max's lips spread into a long grin. He brought his hands together in a silent clap.

"Dirk," Ivan said between grinding teeth. He glared, paused, and kept his words strong and even. "You owe Mrs. Hambuckle and the class an apology."

"Ha! I don't apologize for something that's true. You can go chase a shittin' goose."

"Dirk Mackle! That kind of talk will not be tolerated in this classroom." Their teacher rapped her knuckles on the desk. "Enough now. Let's get on with our lesson."

"We'll settle this outside where no one will be hurt." Ivan moved toward the front door, turned, and said, "Except you, Dirk."

His teacher's eyes widened, and she gave a slow nod. A small smile turned the corners of her lips.

"You'll be sorry, you rotten Russian spy." Dirk's face flushed, his cheeks puffed out.

Without looking back, Ivan left the room and walked into the schoolyard. His shoulders squared, his steps sure and confident. *After all my battles in the forest, this should be easy.* He saw the students rush to the windows, their excited faces pressed against the glass.

Today, Dirk would be humbled before his classmates and roughneck friends. Every step the bully took reminded Ivan of the vicious Black Knight, Burtack, with his arrogant, haughty attitude. Reluctantly and with great fear, Ivan fought and killed the knight during his visit to the forest. Now was the time to wipe that smug look off Dirk's face before he became like all the other tyrants in the world.

Ivan's jaw muscles hardened with determination. He held his arms to his sides and scrunched his fists. Dirk no longer wore a proud look, but instead, his squinty fish eyes were strained as far as they would open.

In a moment, Ivan heard his mother's cautious words from when he was a little boy, *Ivan, don't cause us troubles. We are foreigners and must keep quiet and not stand out. Do you understand?* He didn't. Not when he was young—and not now.

Dirk slowly crossed the yard, and when he drew closer, his hands quivered.

Can this be? When challenged, did bullies become scared that quickly? Ivan inhaled a deep breath and waited for his opponent to either back down or show aggression. *Will he fight like a man or flee like the coward he is?*

"Say…maybe we can work this out." Dirk glanced around. His cheek muscles jerked. "We don't have to bloody each other over this."

"It's not me that will be bloodied," Ivan replied with a steady voice, glaring at him.

"Wait. Let's talk about it." Dirk raised the flat of his

hands, and saliva foamed at the corners of his mouth. He was trembling like the leaves on the surrounding trees.

Ivan made a fist, ready to take the first punch. His biceps tightened. "You knocked a little girl in the dirt and split her lip. Did it make you feel like a big man?"

Dirk's mouth quivered.

"Answer me!" Ivan screamed and took a step closer. *This isn't me*, he realized through his boiling anger. *I don't behave in this way.*

"Well, no. I-I didn't mean to knock the brat down," Dirk said. "It was all her fault."

Ivan rushed forward, grabbed Dirk's collar, and twisted, pushing him backward. The boy gulped and stammered, struggling to jerk away. Ivan wrenched tighter, his teeth grinding. His right arm rose, and his fist hardened. In a second, he would rearrange Dirk's facial features. Teach him a lesson, make him eat mud. *If I land my first punch just right, I could split Dirk's upper and lower lip at the same time. It would be the perfect revenge.*

"Hold it." Dirk held up one hand, choking. There's—there's someone coming. A-a horse with a rider. Behind you. I swear."

A trick? Ivan paused to listen. Head cocked, he heard hoof beats and snorting. He suddenly wondered if it were Peter who would know to find Ivan at school.

"Quite the fighter there, Ivan Kimble," someone spoke.

It wasn't Peter, but Ivan knew the deep voice. A soldier in uniform from the West Forest's Army, under Commander Simon's jurisdiction, sat atop a light chestnut horse. With Dirk's shirt collar in a tight hold, Ivan turned. His fierce rage simmered. There was no mistaking the man with copper red hair and a full beard, a sword sheathed at his side, looking down with a grin. Ivan threw back his head with full-throated laughter. "Aaron Hambuckle. Welcome home!"

"If I were you, young man"—the soldier narrowed his eyes, glaring at Dirk—"I'd back out of this fight. Might lose your pride, but you'd keep your life."

A large area on Dirk's front trousers and down his legs quickly changed color.

"Well, now, this is quite fitting," Ivan mocked and released his grip on Dirk. He gave him a rough shove. "I know you peed in my lunchbox. Now, we're even."

Dirk massaged his neck, coughed, and backed away. He didn't utter a word, only blinked tears and glowered at his opponent. Stumbling toward the school's stable, Dirk's shaky legs scarcely held him upright. The students and Mrs. Hambuckle had left the schoolhouse and stood on the lawn watching the encounter. They clapped and cheered, adding to Dirk's humiliation.

Little Mercy stuck her tongue out and spit in Dirk's direction. "Serves you right," she taunted.

Aaron swung his leg over the saddle and dropped to the ground. "Trouble seems to follow you everywhere you go, doesn't it, my friend?" He embraced Ivan and gave him several pats on his back. "Good to see you again."

"It's good to see you, too." Ivan grinned. He took a breath and refilled his lungs to help his anger subside.

"Who's the bloke?" Aaron jerked his thumb at the boy who'd just wet his pants.

"Another bully. Like Burtack and his brother, Kruse Hays."

The soldier nodded with quick understanding.

"I…I don't think I ever thanked you for saving my life." Ivan placed his hand on Aaron's shoulder. "You killed an enemy soldier who was about to do me in during the Forest War."

"Ah, yes. I do recall. You'll have to tell me one day how you happened to be part of our war. I don't believe Zephyrus would have authorized it."

"I'm not exactly sure." Ivan stared into the distance, trying to remember the frightening details. "All of a sudden, Bounty was pushed into the thick of fighting by the other horses. It was a dreadful position to be in."

"Well, I'm just as frightened about meeting Mrs. Hambuckle. Did you tell her you discovered me in the forest? That I'd lost my memory during the war? Heaven's sake. How will she ever love a rough-looking soldier like me?" Sweat collected on his forehead, and he wiped it away with a quick stroke of his calloused hand.

"I haven't had the chance." Ivan shook his head. "First thing this morning, I had to deal with *that* rodent in the schoolhouse." He half-turned to see the lone horse and rider race through the yard and down the road.

"Do you think he learned his lesson?" Aaron's brow lifted.

Ivan shrugged his shoulders. "I don't know."

"Will you reintroduce me to my wife?" The soldier sucked in a deep breath and exhaled. A muscle twitched just above his eye.

Grinning wildly, Ivan nodded. "Why don't you stay here? I'll go tell Mrs. Hambuckle someone is waiting for her. In that way, you'll have a chance to be together in private."

"Right." Aaron clapped Ivan's back. "That's a

sensible suggestion. I wish I could stop my hands from shaking. I feel like a schoolboy myself." He gulped. "Maybe she won't recognize me—my beard. I think I was clean-shaven when we were married. What if she doesn't love me anymore?"

"You'll be fine." Ivan softly punched the man on his arm. "Pretend you're fighting the Dark Army. Be strong. Be courageous."

"Quite. I'll get a hold of myself," Aaron said. "Wait. What's my wife's name?"

"Mary."

"Mary," he repeated. "Yes, that's beautiful."

"I did tell you this before I left the forest, but I don't believe you heard me."

"No. I don't recall hearing it."

Ivan ran toward the schoolhouse, where he saw eager faces on the steps and students jumping up and down on the lawn. They cheered and applauded. Lowering his chin, Ivan's neck warmed. Now his teacher could stop worrying about her missing husband. They would be reunited this day.

Aaron had come home.

Mrs. Hambuckle met Ivan at the bottom of the steps. Her gaze darted past him, and her voice quivered. "Can it be? Is that my Aaron?"

"Come with me, and I'll introduce you." Ivan turned and started in that direction until he realized his teacher wasn't following. "What's wrong? Don't you want to see him?"

"I-I—it's been so long. I don't know if I—if we…" Ivan reached and took her chalk-dusted hand. He smiled. "This is what you've been waiting for."

Glancing ahead at the soldier, her eyebrows arched.

Then she took a deep breath and followed. As they approached, Ivan introduced them. "Aaron Hambuckle, this is your wife, Mary Hambuckle." Ivan swept his hand with a graceful arc of introduction and bowed. He watched their faces as they stared and took a few steps back, allowing them space.

The couple moved toward each other, caught up in the reality of a miracle. Aaron laughed and grabbed Mary at her waist. She squealed. He held her tightly and swung her around. Leaning back, he whooped with joy.

"Aaron, Aaron," she yelled, tears sliding down her cheeks.

"Stay as long as you'd like," Ivan said with a grin. "I'll take over your classes."

"Yes. Oh, yes. That would be fine." His teacher didn't turn to look at Ivan. She only nodded. The couple kissed. Aaron buried his face in her neck and whispered something into her ear.

Their happiness brought a deep feeling of pleasure to Ivan.

He returned to the schoolhouse to fulfill his promise.

Chapter 3

School Social

Ivan walked toward the house from the barn holding a half-pail of fresh milk to use in the kitchen. His free hand waved to his neighbor, who approached on horseback.

"Aye. When did you get back?" Mueller McKay asked from atop his mount. His curiosity had gotten the best of him that morning, he confessed, and he decided to pay Ivan a brief visit.

"Late yesterday, just after Dan finished eating supper."

Alfred and Canute greeted their neighbor with wagging tails and happy yips.

"The lad do a good job?" Mule slipped from his horse, looking worried. "I want to be sure, since I recommended him."

"I was pleased. Although, he nearly ate me out of house and home." Ivan chuckled. "He only left one cold egg for my supper."

Mule snorted. "Sounds like my four boys. They keep us busy and broke just trying to feed 'em." He swiveled on his heel and glanced at the farmhouse. "Well, where is he? Where's Peter?"

For a moment, Ivan felt helpless. He shrugged. "I did find him—in the forest like you said."

"Whoopee!" Mueller threw his arms into the air like an excited child. "That's the news I wanted to hear. Having his breakfast, then, is he?"

"Well, he had things…details that had to be taken care of before he left the South Castle." Ivan felt he should explain more fully but decided he'd said enough.

"South Castle, eh? That's mighty impressive."

"Yes, it is. Peter is in good health and plans to return soon. He asked about you, Emma, and the boys."

"He should high tail it home and help you out on the farm." Mule eyed him with a serious stare. "The job is too big for a young lad like you. But I'll be here to give a hand whenever I can."

"Thanks, I know." Ivan nodded slowly, remembering all the help Mule and his boys had volunteered in the past. "Peter promised to be here in a few days."

"Sure." Mule didn't sound convinced. He looked a bit sheepish and blurted, "One more thing. Emma asked if you would take us to the Saturday Social in your buggy. It looks more respectable than ours. Another fundraiser for the Graydon Hill School. Don't know why they can't stay on budget like our village school."

Ivan had corrected Mule several times that it was a carriage, not a buggy, but his neighbor didn't seem to remember this. It certainly wasn't fancy, parked in a remote part of the barn, collecting dust and rodent droppings. Solid black, it had no embellishments, four wheels, and a box seat. Ivan hadn't yet decided if he would go to the social. He'd only heard about it the previous evening from Dan. Now, it seemed, the decision had been made, and he'd have to pull the carriage out tomorrow and clean it from top to bottom.

"Oh, Dan told me Emma's expecting again," Ivan said. "Congratulations."

"I should've known," Mule sputtered. "That woman can't keep anything to herself. Four boys now. She says if she doesn't get a little girl this time, she's going to throw me out of the house." He laughed. "It's not my fault, is it?"

"I hope Emma gets her wish." Ivan extended a warm smile.

"Well…" Mule scratched his ear and paused. "What about all the stories we've heard happening in the West Forest? Are there really talking trees and dragons—witches?" His brow rose high. In some ways, Mule was still like a little kid, believing tall tales, which in this case, were pretty much true.

"Ridiculous," Ivan said, quoting Mrs. Hambuckle's favorite word about such rumors. He figured he was safe enough without actually telling a lie.

Mule's face dropped, but Ivan couldn't betray a trust or reveal too much. It wouldn't be good to have yet more rumors circulating about the mysterious forest.

"Then we'll see you on Saturday. Emma says come by any time after the chores are done." He grinned. "Now, maybe she'll stop torturing me about getting you to the social."

Why is it so important?

Shortly, his neighbor said goodbye and rode down the long driveway, turning right toward his farm.

Two more days passed, and still no Peter. "Maybe he can't get away," Ivan said, groping for an excuse. "Or, maybe Lord Graydon refused to let him leave until all his spying duties were completed."

****

Ivan combed his wavy black hair and donned a crisp white shirt. A bit too snug, he left several buttons undone at his neck, throwing his only tie back into a drawer. It surprised him when the suit jacket he wore for special occasions was also tight around his shoulders. He had nothing else to wear, so it would have to do for the evening.

"I'm going out tonight," Ivan said to Alfred and Canute as he closed the front door behind him. "Be sure to look after the place, and don't chase Ebony. That's probably why the cat has been gone so long."

Canute plopped onto the porch waiting for a further lecture.

Ivan felt nervous about being around so many people at a social gathering. But it was a fundraiser, after all. "A worthy cause," he added for assurance. "And I should help Emma in her condition." Maybe she'd give birth to a little girl, just like Mercy.

Do I remember how to dance? The students were forced to learn during one of Mrs. Hambuckle's classes. Wiping his sweaty hands on his trousers, Ivan recalled he didn't enjoy the lessons very much. "Well, it's too late to worry about that now." He had to fetch Emma and Mule.

Ivan stared down his gravel driveway as he gently slapped reins against Bounty's rump. No one was riding his way. *Where is Peter?* He sighed, feeling disappointed and worried. *What if something happened to him? Maybe his horse threw him into a ravine, and no one knows he's there crying for help.* Ivan massaged the back of his neck and shook his head.

"Let's go, Bounty. I plan to enjoy myself and help Emma."

By the time he guided Bounty and the carriage into Mueller's farm, he was feeling happy and quite satisfied. He thought about Mrs. Hambuckle and Aaron's reunion a few days ago, and he grinned. *Will they be there at the fundraiser?*

Ivan maneuvered his rig into McKay's yard, where their dog, Dixie, barked and howled at Bounty. His horse, not to be bullied, snorted and pawed the ground.

As Ivan stepped down from the box seat, Mule came out to meet him and clapped him on the shoulder. "Aye, Ivan. You look and smell like a fine gentleman. I won't be able to keep the young ladies away from you." He roared with laughter, pressing his hands against his stomach.

Ivan eyed him and wondered what was so funny. *Did his neighbor have something up his sleeve?*

"Em will be out in a moment. She's puttin' little Elmer to bed." They moved toward the lit porch and stood waiting. "I gave Max orders on what to do while we're gone. I don't know where that boy's head is at. Always dreamin' about something."

"You and Emma should get out more," Ivan said. "Then Max would learn and have some experience looking after his brothers."

"Don't count on it." Mule huffed. "He wouldn't recognize a board if it hit him on the side of his head."

"You're too hard on him. Give him a chance to grow up and take hold of the world. He's just confused— hasn't found his footing yet."

Pulling back, Mule's eyebrows rose high.

Ivan realized he'd never spoken to his neighbor in that manner before or offered his advice when it came to raising his family. He lowered his head and looked at the ground, wishing he hadn't said anything.

Mule opened his mouth in reaction to Ivan's comment when Emma struggled out the door carrying a double pie holder.

"Goodness me," she exclaimed. "Sorry to keep my carriage waiting. Elmer is bawling his head off."

"It's a simple buggy, Em," Mule said grumpily. "Only fairy tale princesses rode in a fine carriage."

"You look splendid, Ivan," Emma teased. "You might meet a nice girl tonight."

"Don't meddle where you don't belong," Mule shot back at his wife.

She huffed.

So, that's it. His neighbor had someone picked out for him. Ivan should've known something was odd.

"For you, M' lady." Ivan took the pie holder and bowed regally, and then opened the carriage door for her.

"Oh, go on with you." Emma laughed and hefted her stout figure into the front seat. It was clear she enjoyed the special attention. "Thank you, Ivan, kind sir."

"My pleasure. Always ready to assist a lady into her pumpkin carriage." He chuckled. Emma chuckled. Mule didn't seem to follow the remark at all.

"You sure are, ah…different," Mule said as he pulled himself up onto the box seat next to Ivan. "What happened in that forest, anyway? Did you sniff something powerful?"

Ivan wiggled his eyebrows and grinned, lifting the reins in his hands. He couldn't explain the change in words, but he knew he was different somehow.

Max stepped onto the porch. "Next time, Pa, can I go to the social with you?"

"Yeah. For sure, son. Next time."

The boy gave a weak smile and waved.

The carriage rolled along Wool-loom's Street in the main village. Bounty didn't make a fuss, which was surprising for his disagreeable temperament. Ivan clicked his tongue and gave the reins a gentle slap against his horse's rump. "Good boy."

They passed the *Rouster*, Mule's favorite pub, and a variety of other shops came into view. Bounty turned onto Graydon Street. Ye Old Antiques Shoppe appeared, nestled close to a pastry and teashop called Cookie's Crunching Crumb. There was nothing remarkable about the chestnut trees that lined both sides of the street. They showed no eyes or mouths like the trees in the forest, and Ivan was sure they couldn't speak.

Beyond The Ol' Shoe Repair Shoppe, a couple of rowdy boys were striking the store windows with broken tree branches, laughing and swearing. Their unsteady movements indicated they were drinking ale or something stronger. Ivan pulled back on Bounty's reins, bringing him to a halt near the boys. "The both of you, go home. Don't cause trouble in town."

The tallest of the boys, who Ivan suddenly recognized as Dirk Mackle, pointed the branch at Ivan and swore. "Well, if it ain't Mr. High and Mighty, Ivan Kimble. Someday I'm going to get even with you—pig!"

"Anytime, Dirk. But not tonight," Ivan said boldly. "Now, get off the street and take your cousin with you."

Dirk swore again and bent to the sidewalk, searching for something to pick up and throw, but there was nothing there.

"Blimey, Ivan. How'd you get so brave?" Mule's eyes grew large. "What happened to you in that forest, anyway?"

"He's a boy in our school who causes trouble with no end to his bad behavior. A bully that pushed a little girl to the ground to show how tough he was."

"Yeah." Mule nodded and turned around to see if the boys were following with their menacing sticks. "I recognize the name, Mackle. A family of good-for-nothins…lives a couple miles north to me. His dad's a drunk, and no one knows where the ma went. Too bad. Looks like that boy is followin' his pa's footsteps."

"What's going on?" Emma opened the carriage door and stretched her head out.

"It's okay, Em." Mule leaned to his right from where he was sitting. "Ivan here took care of it. We have a fundraiser to go to."

For a moment, Ivan felt remorse. Now, he could understand why Dirk was a troublemaker, wanting attention. He wondered if he could make it up to him in some way.

Music drifted from the Graydon Town Center. It sounded like several fiddles and the faint attempt of a flute warming up. Lights were ablaze. Lanterns hung in the trees or on posts. A long white banner stretched over the Village Center's entrance that read: Graydon Hill School Social and Fundraiser.

Guiding Bounty into an open space, Ivan pulled back on the reins and jumped off the driver's seat, giving his horse a pat of satisfaction. They paid their fee at the door and pocketed their tickets. It was the last of Ivan's money. Not a sixpence left in the bureau drawer. *What will I do tomorrow when I need to fill my larder and pay the mortgage?*

Mule opened one of the double doors while Emma turned sideways to squeeze into the room carrying the pie holder. Pausing, Ivan stopped to study the dragon image carved into the center of each door, along with a giant oak tree painted gold. *Very curious.* Had the artist seen these things in the West Forest, or had he simply imagined them? Regardless, they were astonishingly accurate.

The main room was expansive, with rough-hewn floorboards and a high wooden-beam ceiling. It appeared that most of the villagers had already arrived and clustered in noisy groups.

"Let's take the desserts to the back where the tables are," Emma said over her shoulder, leading the way with hurried steps. "I'll cut them into small pieces, and that way, they'll bring more money." Emma turned and hollered at Mule, "Where are you going?"

He pointed to the pub area. "A little drink to warm me." Jostling to the right, Mule pushed through the crowds.

"I should've expected that." Emma snorted. "This way, Ivan."

He followed and took the pies from Emma, setting them down on a lace tablecloth next to a large tray of various cheeses and homemade sausages.

"The desserts go over here," a sweet voice directed.

Chapter 4

Meeting Coreena Filmore

Ivan stared into the brightest, turquoise-blue eyes he'd ever seen. Pale, smooth skin and long, shiny blonde hair with bangs swept to the side. She tipped her head and gaped at him. Her pretty full lips parted, surprised. They gazed at each other, not moving. Finally, Ivan forced a "hello" but forgot to bow. When the girl greeted him in return, he recovered, and his shyness began to disappear.

Emma made an introduction. "Coreena Filmore, this is Ivan Kimble. I believe I mentioned him to you on several occasions." She winked at the girl.

"Y-yes," she stammered. "You have, indeed."

"The Kimble farm borders ours and the West Forest," Emma said. At the mention of the West Forest, Coreena winced. Ivan wondered what had caused her reaction.

Bowing, he made a show of respect—and delight. It came easy and natural to him, as it had for his father, who'd been royalty in Russia.

Coreena giggled. She appeared to enjoy Ivan's display of good manners. "I've heard a lot about you," she said and fluttered her eyelashes.

The way she addressed him made him feel strong and wise. Thankfully, neither Coreena nor Emma knew of the dumb things he'd done while in the West Forest. Ivan wiped perspiration from his forehead and hoped she hadn't seen the gesture.

She wore a high-neck, pink lace blouse with full, gathered sleeves. The color matched her delicate lips. Her long, beautifully shaped fingers held a plate of biscuits. "Would you like one?" She gestured with a tip of her head.

"No, thank you. Sweets make my teeth hurt." He turned away, feeling foolish for such a childish remark. Why would she care about such a thing?

Ivan realized Coreena was nearly his height. Being the tallest in his class made him even more aware of this. There were few girls who could match his stature. Enchanted with her large eyes and thick lashes, he was unable to look away, afraid her beauty would suddenly fade. Inhaling deeply, he hoped his dizziness would disappear.

Coreena smiled. "Are you all right?"

Before he could answer, someone rushed his way. "Hey, Ivan. It's me."

"What?" Ivan jolted to life, breathing again, wondering how long he'd stared at her.

Dan Jacobs towed a pretty girl with chunky arms and ample hips by the hand and moved in Ivan's direction. Looking quite put together, Dan wore a clean, starched shirt, pressed trousers, and combed hair that seemed to stay in place.

"I see you've met my sister." A sly grin pulled at the corners of Dan's lips.

"Your—this is *your* sister?" Ivan opened his mouth and gasped. "B-but…you never told me her name." He was certain a dumbfounded look froze on his face.

"Danny…" Coreena sighed. "You must be clear about our relationship."

Hiding his embarrassment, Dan glanced away for a minute. "I did explain it to him," he mumbled faintly. "Told him about Phillip and that you came to stay at my house after my brother died. And that we worked out a good solution for both of us. Didn't I tell you?" He abruptly changed the subject. "This is my girlfriend, Francine Kinsley. She's very pretty, isn't she? I mentioned her to you, eh, Ivan? Said I was bringing the prettiest girl in all of Graydon Village."

Francine gave him a playful bump with her hips. "Stop this silliness." A blush appeared on her round cheeks, but it was clear she liked the compliment very much.

She was pleasant to look at. Her brown hair hung nearly to her waist. Her eyebrows arched high over hazel eyes.

"Nice to meet you, Francine." Ivan bowed.

"That's real elegant of you, Mr. Kimble." The girl curtsied.

Coreena seemed anxious to clear up any misunderstanding. "Phillip and I were good friends. Then, he died in a farming accident. With my family far away and no one to look after Danny, I moved into their home—and stayed. Now, we take care of each other. It's a good arrangement." She nodded several times.

"I'm very sorry about your loss," Ivan said in a whisper.

Although Ivan did recall the accident since the whole village talked about it for months, he hadn't known the Jacob family, but Peter did since he was about the same age. Farm chores tended to keep Ivan busy and often isolated, so he avoided gossip and village stories. He wondered where Dan's parents were, but he thought it impolite to ask right then. It was tragic enough that Phillip died at such a young age, unexpectedly, leaving his younger brother all alone.

Dan grabbed Ivan's forearm and pulled him forward. His other hand cupped his girlfriend's elbow. "Come on. Francine's parents are here. I want you to meet them."

Glancing back at Coreena, who seemed abandoned, Ivan frowned. She smiled sweetly. "Go with Danny," she called in her lovely voice. "Emma and I have things to do here."

"This way." Dan dragged the two through the noisy crowd while pushing dancers aside. They ran into Mueller, who tipped his hat as Ivan passed. It appeared he suffered the effects of too much ale in too short a time.

Somehow, Ivan avoided knocking anyone over.

Francine rolled her eyes and twisted her lips. "Slow your pace and show good manners," she said to Dan.

"This is Mr. and Mrs. Kinsley." Dan stepped aside and added, "Mr. Kinsley is Graydon Hill's banker. You must know him, Ivan."

They exchanged greetings. Francine stood next to her father, smiling up at him. The banker *was* suddenly interested and squeezed Ivan's hand tighter. "Ivan Kimble? It's been some time since I've laid eyes on you, my lad."

"It's been a while." Ivan winced at the word lad.

"I'm sorry about your folks. Hellish train wreck." The banker shook his head. He was a large man with a heavy face.

"Thank you, sir."

"What keeps you on that farm of yours?" Mr. Kinsley pulled on his tight vest, sucking in his breath.

"The same that holds most men farm-bound," Ivan answered with a polite smile. "Too many chores for too little daylight."

"Good answer." He laughed and clapped Ivan on his shoulder.

Ivan squirmed and stretched his neck to spot Coreena in the back of the room. He hoped she needed his help so he could excuse himself and leave Mr. Kinsley's company.

"Tell me…" The portly man moved closer and dropped his hand. "Just what are you producing on your farm that has fattened up your bank account so quickly?"

"B-bank account? What do you mean?" Ivan flinched.

"Filled it right up. Several days ago," Mr. Kinsley bellowed.

"Graham. For heaven's sake." His wife came to her husband's side and jabbed him in the ribs, looking embarrassed. "This is no place to talk private business."

Brushing away his wife's remark, the man said, "We've never seen this kind of increase in the Kimble account before. I thought I should take a ride out to see you. Have you come into some kind of inheritance? Perhaps a rich Russian relative has died?"

Ivan stammered, at a loss. He felt foolish but didn't want to appear uninformed. "Who was the draft from, again?"

Mr. Kinsley leaned even closer while Ivan pulled back, smelling alcohol on the banker's breath. "Tell me," he asked in a quieter voice, "who is Zephyrus W. Barkay of the West Forest Corporation? Is that *our* West

Forest?" The banker wagged his finger in that direction. "I didn't think they had any industry in that godforsaken place except spreading silly rumors."

"Daddy, enough business. We're going to dance." Francine reached for Dan's hand and dragged him onto the floor, merging with the others.

"Investments, my lad. We've got to think about investing that money so it will grow for you." The man's eyes gleamed brightly. "With the war over, we've got a lot of rebuilding to do in England. You see my meaning?"

Seizing the opportunity, Ivan thanked Mr. Kinsley for his advice and spun around to follow Dan and Francine. Mrs. Kinsley reprimanded her husband for his unforgivable rudeness toward a possible good patron.

Zephyrus had kept his word. Ivan grinned with surprise and joy. A draft was actually deposited into his account to help with his expenses while he was in the forest. *How much did Zephyrus deposit? Enough to pay my mortgage?*

After his conversation with the banker, Ivan realized the subtleness of speaking to adults. He was more confident and assured. The answer came in a flash.

It was because of his extraordinary experiences in the West Forest, his deep friendship with Sebastian, Commander Simon, and Zephyrus. All of them. Jerking his shoulders back, he straightened his spine.

He made his way to where Emma and Coreena were selling food at a rapid pace. The lovely girl nibbled on a biscuit with jam in the center. "This is just delicious," she announced to Ivan and rolled her eyes. "I could eat sweets all day."

Ivan grinned at her, enjoying the gleam in her eyes.

Coreena wiped a crumb from the corner of her mouth. "Would you like to dance with me?"

Ducking his head, Ivan admitted, "I'm not very good at it."

She blinked and gave a slight nod.

Ivan accepted this as her willingness to take a chance, and they moved to the floor. He stepped closer, timidly taking her into his arms.

They began slowly and a bit awkwardly at first. Ivan tried to recall which direction his feet were to move and how to avoid hers. Then, something magical happened. Ivan suddenly remembered the steps that Mrs. Hambuckle laboriously taught them during their dance class. Though he hated them at the time, now he was overjoyed to make practical use of the lessons.

The music became louder. They were caught between people in the crowded area. Ivan guided her, found their space, and soon they were having a merry time, keeping pace with the lively tunes.

"You are generous to help with this event, what with losing Phillip." Ivan steered her away, yet again, to avoid being jounced by another enthusiastic couple.

She pulled back her head to meet his eyes. "It's been several years, but I do still miss him. Although I find it helps to be with others and contribute instead of feeling sorry for myself."

"I hope I'm not too impolite, but what happened to Dan and Phillip's parents?"

"Oh," she said and gazed into his eyes, looking a bit surprised. She lowered her face and pressed her fingers into Ivan's left shoulder. "Well, that's a sad story."

"You don't need to tell me if it's too—" he hesitated "—personal."

33

"It was well-known to the village and townspeople." She took a breath. "After Phillip died in the accident, their mother died of a broken heart, having no will to live. He was her favorite son, and she didn't want to go on living without him."

Ivan brought his eyebrows together and blinked. "And their father?"

"The village talk was that their father couldn't bear the grief of losing the two of them, and so he left, abandoning poor little Danny."

"I'm so sorry." Ivan searched the crowd, trying to spot Danny, and feeling deeper sympathy for him.

"He's a good boy. We get on very well together. I sometimes teach at the Graydon Hill School when our teacher is away, and that brings in a little extra money. Danny does chores and errands around our neighborhood. That's how he happened to work for you while you were away."

"It worked out just right for both of us." Ivan moved closer to Coreena with his arms tightened around her and his cheek pressed against hers. She seemed to like his closeness.

She stumbled. "Oh, sorry." Ivan gasped. "That was probably your toes."

"It was, but not to worry." She laughed. "I've had them stepped on many times before."

Soon, Ivan forgot his awkwardness and thrilled at the sound of the band while he held the pretty Miss Filmore in his arms. They made little conversation, as it was impossible to hear with the noise. His hand rested on her back, and they twirled and laughed and danced. She floated like magic in his arms.

When the music stopped, Ivan slowly slid his hand

down her rib cage. It seemed unnaturally long. He counted fourteen ribs as his fingers glided to the bottom. Can that be, when he'd learned that both men and women have twelve on each side? But then, what did he know? He'd only held Anna-Iza, and she was so small.

As they made their way to the food tables, several people eyed the couple with approving smiles. Aaron and Mary Hambuckle passed them by, so engrossed with each other, they didn't seem to notice Ivan standing next to Coreena with his hand tightened around her waist.

"Aye, Ivan," someone called. "Looks like you found the prettiest lassie here." The man waved. In a moment of self-consciousness, Ivan released his hold on Coreena. He nodded a friendly greeting at the man, thinking he worked at the Turlow Grain and Feed Mill but couldn't be sure.

"Danny told me you found Peter in the West Forest." Coreena frowned. "What will you do if he doesn't come home?"

Ivan lifted his head with surprise. "What makes you say that?"

"I-I just wondered." She relaxed her brow but stared hard at him. "The forest is a most dangerous place—or so I've heard."

"Well…yes, I guess it can be dangerous. If Peter doesn't return soon, I'll go searching for him again."

"I wish you wouldn't go back to that dreadful place." Coreena quietly drew away, turned to give him a forlorn glance, and walked in Emma's direction. Ivan stood there feeling abandoned. His mouth went slack. *Why does she feel this way?*

Regardless of her hostile opinion of the West Forest, Ivan would return, especially if Peter didn't come home soon. He wished to see his friends and Anna-Iza, too. Now his emotions were torn between the goddess and Coreena, having affection for both. *What am I to do?* He wished she hadn't mentioned the West Forest. It changed the tender mood they were both experiencing.

Ivan moved to the back of the room where Emma and Coreena busily cleared away the dishes, hoping to be helpful, but more interested in being in the girl's presence.

"It's getting late," Emma said. "We'd best be going."

"Thank you." Coreena turned and smiled at him, gently touching his forearm. "You were good company for me tonight."

"My pleasure." Ivan gave a graceful bow, happy she'd forgotten her remark about the West Forest. He had hoped to dance with Coreena again, to hold her in his arms, but the night went much too fast.

Emma called across one of the tables as she gathered up the utensils, "Ivan, could you go find Mule? Let him know we're ready to leave." She tucked in curls that had slipped from a fancy barrette.

"Of course." Turning to Coreena, he said, "Good night, Miss Filmore. I hope to see you again." He was tempted to kiss her on the cheek, but felt shy with so many people moving about.

"I hope so, too." She blinked those beautiful turquoise-blue eyes. "Thank you for attending our fundraiser."

Emma, Mule, and Ivan walked out into the crisp autumn air toward the carriage with Ivan's arm around Mule's waist, guiding him so he wouldn't stumble and fall.

Ivan grinned. "She's really quite lovely," he said, opening the carriage door for Emma to enter.

She gave a deep chuckle. "Told you so."

Chapter 5

Zephyrus
A dark-haired lad will come seeking and find maturity, wisdom, and friendship. He will risk his life for the Forest's survival. The oath of the Forest is to keep him alive.
The Black Book of Pearls. Chapter 77, Verse 7

"Do you believe Ivan Kimble will return to our Forest, sir?" Sebastian asked from inside the oak tree's huge trunk.

The wooden cavity served as the Sanctuary of Truth, where Sebastian's spirit resided in the Long Dark Cloak. Ten years ago, six additional relics once hung there, but they were stolen away and never returned.

"I'm certain of it," Zephyrus answered. "Ivan has developed a fondness for many of the people, along with a curiosity of our mystical ways. Not to mention our collection of odd creatures." He chortled.

"If Ivan hadn't arrived in our Forest when he did," Sebastian said and shuddered, "we might all be ruled by Tereus right now."

Looking past his twig-tangled eyebrows, Zephyrus gazed into the gray sky. He released a sigh. "You are right, my good friend. I've suffered greatly because of the poison that was delivered into my side by our own Silver Axe. If the antidote hadn't been applied when it was, in a few more days, I would've died a slow and most painful death."

"Once the other six relics are returned and safely inside the sanctuary, security and harmony will be restored to our forest," Sebastian said with a positive tone. "So much uncertainty makes me anxious."

"Ah, but where to find them?" Zephyrus had repeated this question many times during the past decade.

There was no doubt Lord Richard Graydon's brother, Henry, was the thief who had taken the precious relics. Why he'd done such a foolish thing was not clear. The only reason Zephyrus could think of was that Lord Henry Graydon desired more power than he already possessed. *How much is too much?* Zephyrus lowered his eyes, unable to understand the dark selfishness of men's hearts. Sebastian had been out on a rare assignment at the time, so he was not taken. The most vital relic, The Black Book of Pearls—the Forest's Bible, also disappeared with the others.

The pitter-patter of rain broke against Zephyrus's leaves, sliding down his limbs, wetting the earth that held his roots. It cleansed, purified, and revived the tree's spirit along with the center core. His far-reaching foliage felt as though it were being massaged and renewed by the rhythmic drops.

"How are you feeling?" Sebastian asked from inside the sanctuary.

"A bit improved," Zephyrus replied. "There is still poison lurking in my woody fibers. I sometimes feel the burn. Thanks to the recent rains, I'm getting better and better." He moaned. "Today, I do feel my age…over a thousand years old."

"I feel the same." Sebastian's voice croaked.

"Come out, now." Just as Zephyrus made the suggestion, the huge wooden door in his trunk opened with a loud creak. "There's no need for you to be cooped up inside the stuffy sanctuary."

Sebastian's purpose, as with the other six missing relics, was to aid Zephyrus—their master—by keeping the Forest safe. He had been Zephyrus's War Advisor long ago when Zephyrus was still a man and king of an ancient kingdom called Helvaka.

Within moments, Sebastian's spirit released from the Long Dark Cloak in a stream of wispy blue smoke. It collected in the shape of a person and at last, solidified. The old man stepped out from Zephyrus's wooden cavity and smoothed his disheveled white hair. Bushy eyebrows wiggled while he adjusted spectacles on his sharp nose. Sebastian stretched his arms above his head and yawned.

"Why are you tired?" Zephyrus teased. "Ivan did all the work."

"I would beg to differ, my old friend."

Spirits never sleep, the tree knew, and Sebastian had truly shouldered a heavy responsibility to protect Ivan during their recent travels.

His brother trees kept Zephyrus informed by sending updates about Ivan and Sebastian's progress. He learned about Ivan slaying the dangerous Swamp Dragons that inhabited Swamp Gorgon. Though the Great Tree was paralyzed with the poison in him, he sent an emergency message to Commander Simon and his troops at the South Castle to rush to Ivan's defense. The message, Zephyrus learned later, was never received because the electrical currents were frozen in the receiving tree's roots. Zephyrus's wicked brother, Tereus, had manipulated the communication. Somehow, Ivan and Sebastian bravely fought the dragons and won, but not without paying a high price.

Extending his palms, Sebastian declared, "It's raining harder than I thought." He stepped closer under the protection of Zephyrus's leafy branches and shook the wetness from his face.

"I always look forward to the early autumn rains." Zephyrus's thick wooden lips stretched into a broad smile. Gazing about, he said, "My brother trees also drink heartily to quench their thirst before the *Big Sleep* of cold winter."

The eyes of the surrounding trees opened with concern as they watched their master. Some whispered together, others fanned their leaves, and yet others kept still, watching their surroundings, alert to any danger. Zephyrus would live.

"I do miss my friends." Sebastian glanced up into Zephyrus's green eyes. "The six relics that once shared the sanctuary with me have been gone far too long. I miss them more and more every day."

"Ah, yes," Zephyrus groaned. "The Golden Lantern, The King's Scepter, The Bag o' Bones, The Scroll of Wisdom, and The Silver Axe—and you, Sebastian." He broke off, speaking softly, "The Black Book of Pearls. There are many fine points in the book that I can't seem to recall. The future of the Forest hinges on its return and foretold messages. We must find it."

Sebastian looked up at the Great Oak, arms crossed behind his back, rocking on his feet. His frown went deeper. "Where do you suppose the relics are, and how do we get them back?"

Zephyrus spoke with hope. "I do believe our young hero will return to us soon. He can't resist the many good friends he's made and the challenge to help us."

"A visit from Ivan will be most welcome." Sebastian nodded.

"He will return," Zephyrus said. "Ivan has much unfinished business in the Forest."

"Speaking of unfinished business, sir." Sebastian cleared his throat, averting his eyes. "Perhaps you are unaware because of your condition, but I'm worried about our dear Anna-Iza."

"Oh!" Zephyrus's twig and moss eyebrows rose. "What worries you? Is she in trouble?"

"Well, after Ivan and the White Knights killed the Black Knights, he took her into his arms and held her, soothing her fears—and he kissed her."

"Kissed her?"

"Here," Sebastian said, touching his forehead with his finger. "The goddesses are not to be touched, especially the High Goddess, Anna-Iza."

Zephyrus pursed his lips. "Must we be concerned about this now?"

"Well, we should address it as soon as possible," Sebastian said squirming under Zephyrus's stare. "Why they have such a foolish edict, I can't say. Ivan asked the same question. What are we to do about their obvious fondness for each other?"

"Do?" Zephyrus thought on the question, gazing into the distant meadow. "I had a discussion with the goddess a few days ago, and I say we do nothing. Let's see where their affection takes them. This is not truly our decision, but rather, her gods in a faraway land."

Sebastian jerked his head back. "But, Sir—what

if…something terrible comes from this? Will her gods demand that she and her goddess sisters return to their distant kingdom in the east? We would be devastated without them."

"Why don't you have a talk with Ivan when he returns? Find out what his intentions are, correct his path, if need be." Zephyrus gave what might have been a slight shrug. "Otherwise, allow the romance to take the course that's intended. Perhaps it will become something quite remarkable."

Sebastian's forehead lifted. "Remarkable, sir?"

Hoofbeats sounded from the west and interrupted their discussion.

"A half dozen men are headed this way." Zephyrus shifted his gaze in that direction.

Commander Simon rode proudly atop his large bay horse, with Sergeant Berkel following close behind, and four other soldiers. They halted under the wide spread of Zephyrus's canopy.

"The rain finally stopped," Simon called holding out his gloved hand. "It was sent just for you, Zephyrus, to help cleanse the toxins from your roots."

Zephyrus grinned. "I believe you are right. What brings you here so early in the day?" He wore a concerned look.

"Not to worry." Sergeant Berkel pushed off his horse and approached the tree. "We've come to ask about our lad, Ivan Kimble. It seems he couldn't stay out of trouble."

"We fought some hard battles." Sebastian strode forth, embracing first the sergeant and then Simon, after he dropped to the ground from his animal.

"There were some challenging victories to win."

Simon removed his gauntlets and tucked them into his wide belt. His parted brown hair, plastered against his head from the morning drizzle, continued to drip water. "You must know, Zephyrus, you have one tough and determined young man there, and we're all rooting for his acceptance into the Forest's special Council of Seven. What do you think?"

"I'd vote for inclusion" Sebastian shouted, making two fists and lifting his hands into the air. The other men, still seated on horseback, agreed and cheered.

Zephyrus laughed at their enthusiasm. "I never had any doubts, especially when he saved my life by bringing Fungoda's sap to heal me. We'll take a vote at our next Council of Seven meeting and see what the others have to say."

"It would be a big honor for him, sir." Simon gave a swift nod. "Perhaps we should ask Ivan if he cares to join."

"Of course." Zephyrus pursed his wooden lips together. "However, there are a few more tasks that he must accomplish before such an honor can be officially extended."

"Tasks?" Sergeant Berkel turned a questioning face toward Zephyrus.

"These are not for you to know just now. They will be presented as needed. Do tell me, commander, what was it you wished to share with me?"

"Well." A big grin spread his lips. "We came to announce that we've cleaned up Lake Gorgon as best we could. Burned all the Swamp Dragons' carcasses, and there were many. Now we'll have to wait for nature to purify the water, and the awful stink the dragons left."

"That is good news. Thank all of you for your hard

work. Soon we can call it Lake Emerald, once again.

One of the soldiers asked, "Have you heard when Ivan Kimble will return, sir?"

"Not yet." Sebastian took the question, while he wiped wetness from his spectacles. "But Zephyrus and I are sure he will be back soon."

"Let us know, then." Simon remounted his steed and indicated with a sweep of his hand that his men should do the same. "We have much to do at the castle before nightfall."

"Thank you for the good news," Zephyrus called as they turned their horses and trotted away.

The Master and the Peacekeeper raised his eyes to heaven. "Ah, High Intervener. Everything is as it should be. I am grateful."

Chapter 6

Return to the Forest

Two weeks passed, and still, Peter hadn't come home. The next morning, before Ivan went to the barn to milk the cows, he stood and stared down the long gravel driveway. He fretted like the many hens in the chicken yard. *Where is Peter? Has something happened to him?* Finally, unable to endure the doubt and the empty hole in his heart, he decided he must return to the forest.

After finishing his chores, he found an envelope that someone had slipped under the front door of his farmhouse. It was printed on fine linen paper with an official South Castle Royal Seal pressed into wax on the flap. Ivan's name was written in splendid calligraphy on the front. Perhaps it was an explanation about Peter.

Hands trembling, Ivan opened the envelope and found a folded fancy message. Written in the same calligraphy, it read: *Lord Graydon wishes for your presence at the South Castle. Please come when convenient. We will plan a grand feast in your honor. Yours Respectfully, Lord Richard Louis Graydon*

Ivan's grin turned into a burst of laughter. A personal invitation from *the* lord—such a privilege.

When school let out the next day, Ivan visited Dan Jacobs' home, telling him he'd made arrangements for his departure into the forest. He hoped to see Coreena again, to hear her lovely voice, and look into her bright blue eyes. Dan explained that his *sister* was at Graydon Hill School helping the teacher by preparing a test for the students. More disappointed than expected, Ivan realized he was quite fond of her.

A big smile spread on Dan's face. "I knew you'd like her. She feels the same about you. Matter of fact..." Dan raised an eyebrow, "that's all she's talked about since the fundraiser."

Ivan winked. They shared a secret.

"Since you're going away, I'll milk your cows and feed your chickens," he blurted. "Just tell me when."

"I'm leaving in the morning."

****

Canute and Alfred raced ahead, woofing as they neared the entrance of the West Forest. Bounty was not as enthusiastic, and being away from the comforts of his stable and ration of oats left him in a foul mood.

It troubled Ivan that Peter hadn't yet contacted him. He was irritated over his brother's lack of communication and continued thoughtlessness. Then, a rush of shame went through him. *There must be a reason. They'd just found each other, and he wouldn't let that opportunity slip into oblivion as before.*

He nudged Bounty toward the path that led into the Forest. His horse shook his head. *Does he remember?* The Forest War. The smell of sweating horses and excrement, the clash of swords, and cries of death from the Dark Army. Ivan would never forget. He shivered thinking about it.

He crossed a small wooden bridge over Blue-back Turtle Creek, where the turquoise-shadowed birch trees stood. There were no sentries posted at the guardhouse beyond the creek. *Where are they?* On his first trip, all the soldiers were celebrating at the South Castle's Annual Competition for the Shield of Honor. Everyone, that is, except the scoundrel who'd struck Zephyrus with the Silver Axe. Its lethal head, laced with an unknown poison, had nearly taken the Great Oak's life.

"Maybe by now they've discovered the axe-wielder," Ivan said to Bounty. "Hopefully, he'll be sentenced to Troll Transformation Prison for a very long time." He raised his head and called into the Forest, "Hello. Is anyone here?"

It looked like someone *had* been in the guardhouse. The broad window shutters were open, secured above by a wire. Inside the small structure was a teapot and two cups on a wooden desk with papers spread about. He was sure it would be okay to enter the Forest without official permission since he had Lord Graydon's personal invitation in his jacket pocket.

Laughter and friendly banter caught his attention. Farther down the creek, he spotted the two guards. One had just landed a fish. Leaning forward, he grabbed the line and held it. He heckled his partner, who dangled an empty hook. The scene tickled Ivan, reminding him of when he and Peter fished the streams on the Kimble farm. He recalled their joy and their parents' delight when their catch was enough for supper.

Ivan sighed with relief. It appeared the Forest had returned to normal. Woodlarks and tree pipits soared through the gray sky. A common redstart sang and welcomed him into their domain.

Just when he felt confident about his surroundings, a large flock of rooks gathered, circling overhead.

"What...?" Ivan ducked as several swooped toward him, turned at the last minute, and swept past in a flurry. They seemed to chorus, "Go home. Go home."

"Strange behavior," Ivan said. *Why are they so aggressive? Another Forest oddity.*

After the steady rains that week, the Forest was rich with the tangy smells of autumn, the foliage coaxing yellows, crimsons, and oranges into their leaves. "I'm anxious to see my friends," he said to his beagles as they followed along, sniffing their surroundings.

Soon, he reached the large circular clearing, standing at a distance, observing where Zephyrus stood. His branches and leaves, held high, shone like brilliant gold. Rough facial features had pushed through his bark. The magnificent tree lived.

Rocking on his feet before the tree, a thin man with his arms crossed behind him was having a lively, cheery discussion with the huge oak. White hair tousled, wire-rimmed spectacles hung on the end of his nose. Ivan recognized him at once. "Sebastian! Zephyrus!"

He urged Bounty into a trot.

Sebastian waved vigorously, and Zephyrus smiled. They called his name.

"Sirs," Ivan addressed from atop his horse and gave a bow. Alfred and Canute woofed a greeting. How different things were from his first visit to the Forest when he'd found Zephyrus moaning in pain.

Green eyes blinking, Zephyrus shouted, "It's a joy to see you and your companions again."

Sebastian stepped forward wearing the same loose-fitting tunic and sagging leggings he always wore. His wide grin broke into laughter. "I knew you'd be back. Thanks be to the High Intervener." He stooped to stroke the dogs. They wagged their tails and licked Sebastian's hands.

Ivan jumped from Bounty and hurried toward Sebastian. He wrapped his arms around the old man. "It's nice to see you, too." A sob caught in his throat while Sebastian was teary-eyed.

They discussed Zephyrus's health and whether the perpetrator who'd struck him with the Silver Axe had been found. Whoever the villain was, he had managed to dodge them.

"How are Commander Simon and his soldiers?" Ivan stroked Bounty's cheek, pleased his horse hadn't bolted off into the meadow, leaving him stranded.

"All your good friends are fine," Sebastian answered. "They are most anxious to see you again. In fact, they were here nearly an hour ago and asked about you."

Ivan smiled at the remark. Then, his eyebrows pulled down sharply, and he stared at the wood stump where Tereus had first appeared, spewing poisonous fumes that nearly cost Ivan his life. "Has Tereus returned to show his specter?"

"The demon has been silent and has not entered the above ground." Zephyrus blew air through his wooden lips.

"Is everything all right on the Kimble farm?" Zephyrus asked with sudden concern.

For a moment, Ivan stared at the pattern of damp leaves on the Forest floor. He didn't want to whine and complain, but he was worried.

"Something's wrong." Sebastian put his arm over Ivan's shoulders. "Tell us. Maybe we can help."

Ivan raised his eyes. His lips pressed together before

he spoke. "Peter hasn't come home. I'm afraid something has happened to him."

Genuinely surprised, Zephyrus and Sebastian chorused, "We didn't know he hadn't left our Forest with you."

The Great Oak's voice increased in volume as he asked the trees that surrounded him, "My brothers. Have you heard of Peter Kimble's whereabouts?"

Eyes pushed through their trunks. Their limbs lifted with doubt.

"Dorsett," Zephyrus yelled toward the three angled birch trees in the meadow. At once, six small brown eyes pushed through their white bark, followed by their open mouths and peaked noses.

"Sir?" Dorsett answered.

"Send a Root-Underground message to the South Castle. Question the whereabouts of Peter Kimble."

"Do you mean to say he's lost again?" Dorsett asked. Ivan detected light mocking.

"Maybe he doesn't want to be found," Winchester chimed with no malice, only a lack of good manners. Bristol, the third birch tree on the right, was about to speak, but Zephyrus cut him short. "Just send the message."

"At once, sir," Dorsett said.

"Thank you." A sad shadow passed over Ivan's eyes. It felt like a repeat of his first visit. Eventually, he'd found Peter, who promised to come home. Ivan shyly raised his head and inquired about Anna-Iza.

"She and her retinue are probably preparing for the Fall Season's Faery Festival," Sebastian replied. "The goddesses are always helpful and loving to these small creatures."

Ivan beamed. He would attend the festivities and see his dear Anna-Iza again. "Where is it being held?"

"In the wide meadow near the faeries' home. You'll recall"—Sebastian turned and gave a wave to the west— "I pointed out their ancient forest, off Sir Barkay and Faery Road. Not much more than a dusty trail, really."

"Would you like to go, Sebastian?" Ivan's heart beat faster.

"Sure." Sebastian nodded. "I haven't attended in years. It's a great deal of fun. Music, singing, and their traditional ceremonies. However, I must warn you, there's not much food. Faeries don't eat large portions like we do."

Though happy to attend, Ivan fussed. *What will I tell the goddess? Can I take her in my arms and hold her as I did on my first visit?* He was certain it wouldn't be possible. The goddesses, especially Anna-Iza, were untouchable.

"I see you've brought saddlebags," Sebastian said. "Provisions for a lengthy stay, I hope."

Ivan patted the bag draped over Bounty's rump.

"I can stay only a few days until I learn of Peter's whereabouts." He dragged his fingers through his hair, a gloomy look in his eyes.

"Ah, yes," Zephyrus said. "You are a farmer and must hire someone to do your chores."

"That's right." Ivan stepped closer to the gigantic tree. "Sir, I want to thank you for the bank draft you deposited into my account after my first visit. It was much too generous. I don't deserve it."

"Nonsense, my lad." Zephyrus's twig mustache stretched with joy. "You traveled to Fungoda to get the healing potion and then returned to save my life. I dare say, that was selfless on your part. And you protected the Forest from the vicious Dark Army by killing their commander. We owe you much more than we have given."

Ivan bowed and thanked him again. Then he remembered and turned toward Sebastian. "The acorn. Did you drop it into my saddlebags for me to find?" He reached into his shirt pocket and pulled the acorn out, rolling it between his fingers.

Chuckling, Sebastian wiggled his eyebrows. "Yes. I slipped it in so you'd remember us and return to the Forest. It worked, didn't it?"

"It did." Ivan laughed and squeezed Sebastian's upper arm with affection. "The truth is, I received a fancy invitation to visit Lord Graydon at his castle."

"Oh," they said in unison, surprised and delighted by the announcement.

"I know he wanted to meet you since your first visit." Zephyrus gazed at the young man admiringly.

"Is it possible Peter is still at the castle finishing his business?"

Sebastian's brow crinkled. "And what would that be?"

Shifting from foot to foot, Ivan realized he almost betrayed his brother's trust about the involvement with Tereus and the Dark Army. Peter confessed to him that he'd spied for Lord Graydon and tried to discover secrets for the Forest's survival. Apparently, not even Zephyrus realized how deeply entangled Peter was with the enemy.

"I-I'm not sure." Heat climbed up Ivan's neck. He didn't want to lie, yet he couldn't reveal more. "Maybe I assumed he had things to finish." His explanation seemed feeble, but to his relief, neither Zephyrus nor

Sebastian questioned him further.

"If he were at the castle, we would know," Zephyrus said. "He's either left the Forest, or—"

"Where else could he be?"

"Helvaka. There's no communication in the old kingdom."

"Why would he be staying in that dreadful place? It's in ruins, isn't it?"

Sebastian nodded a couple of times and stared into the distance. "It's dangerous to go there."

Silence lingered for some moments. A chill ran up Ivan's back. He lowered his head, biting his lip so as not to release a helpless cry.

"Perhaps later, we'll have an answer." Zephyrus's moss and twig eyebrows pulled into a frown. "My brother trees will send inquiries through their root systems and then inform me."

Ivan stroked Bounty's cheek. Now he had a new worry—Peter's safety in the ruined kingdom, if indeed he was staying there.

"If you need us," Sebastian addressed Zephyrus, "you'll most likely find us at the castle tonight. There are celebrations for the next couple of days. Royal visitors, you told me."

"Yes, I do remember Lord Graydon informed me of this in an earlier message. Now," Zephyrus said decisively, "take Ivan to the Fairies' Festival for a reunion and a *very light* lunch. You'll enjoy these precious beings. Then continue south to visit Lord Graydon. Nothing compares with his hospitality and good humor."

Sebastian moved toward the sanctuary. Zephyrus's trunk door slowly creaked open, scraping along the

Forest floor. They stepped into the Sanctuary of Truth. Familiar smells rose from the interior of the cavernous space, like decaying leaves and wet earth mixed with a faint cinnamon fragrance. The scent was both pleasant and comforting.

It saddened Ivan to see the empty pegs at the far end of the wall. They once held the other five Ancient Relics and a shelf where the Black Book of Pearls belonged. *One day, I will find them for the protection of the Forest. All will be well again.*

The ancient weapon, The Challenger, rested on two hooks on the left wall of the sanctuary. Its striking golden hilt bore images of oak leaves, vines, and acorns etched around a decorative cross. During his first visit, the sword had told Ivan that he was not part of the relic's collection but was deeply devoted to Zephyrus and the safety of the Forest.

"Hello, Ivan Kimble." The sonorous voice of the sword echoed off the walls.

"Good to see you, again." Ivan's throat and chest tightened as he caressed the long silver blade with affection. He remembered when he clutched the weapon while it penetrated flesh, killing two men. Shuddering, he pushed the gruesome memory from his mind.

"I feel the same," answered the great sword.

They talked for a while, catching up with both memories and regrets. Ivan said goodbye to The Challenger, inhaled deeply, and turned to Sebastian. "Should we be leaving now?"

"We can't forget who wears the Long Dark Cloak, can we?" Sebastian prompted and pulled it from the peg.

Ivan took the garment and swung it around his shoulders, tying the strings at his neck, feeling protected and safe. He recalled the many times Sebastian's spirit appeared and disappeared inside the garment, warming and healing Ivan's battered body. They walked out of the sanctuary waiting on the outside for Zephyrus to close his door, which he did.

"Come, Bounty," Ivan called.

Lifting his big head, the horse glanced at him but didn't move.

Sebastian snapped his fingers and twirled his hand. His gray horse emerged from the cloak that Ivan now wore. The animal was an apparition at first, hazy and without clear shape, but soon the image solidified, taking form before their very eyes.

"That's the way it's done." Sebastian slapped his hands together and grinned. "Hold still, Old Bones." Smirking, he climbed his obedient mount.

It's always a battle of wits with Bounty. Ivan walked toward his stubborn horse and swung into the saddle. They waved to Zephyrus and promised they'd return in a couple of days.

The feeling of frustration lingered in Ivan's heart.

What is Peter doing in Helvaka? Can I travel there and safely bring him home?

They rode side by side, west on Sir Barkay Road. Sebastian's face was tight.

"What's troubling you?" Ivan wondered if it involved Peter.

A deep scowl replaced Sebastian's expression. "Visitors."

Chapter 7

Wayland and the Wolflords

A shadow passed overhead. At first, Ivan figured it was the rooks he'd spotted earlier. Staring into the sky, he watched two of the largest bird-like creatures he'd ever seen. They weren't dragons—he knew their shape. Not kaleido-birds, which looked to be part ostrich and part rhea, and were too small. "These are huge and oddly proportioned," he said.

A quick jerk on the reins brought Old Bones to a standstill. "Just as I thought," Sebastian murmured, glowering skyward.

The giant beasts flapped wide, heavy wings, and rose higher to hide themselves behind the puffy clouds.

"Those are gryphons." Sebastian huffed, watching with disdain. "Mythical creatures, half lion, half vulture. Terrifying, aren't they?"

"What do they do?" Ivan tracked their flight until they disappeared.

"They hold up the front pediment at the South Castle. You may remember we talked about them during your first visit."

"Yes," Ivan said hesitantly. "You thought the gryphons snatched the kaleido-bird hens and fed them to the Dark Army. Such a crime is treason, isn't it?"

"It is a crime, no doubt. Strange looking, to be sure."

Sebastian tugged on his whiskers. "But why are they about in daylight?"

"You told me they were stone pillars until midnight and then set free to leave their posts at the castle."

"Right, again. Their job is to patrol the grounds searching for thieves or bandits." Sebastian's lips twisted with anger. "It's now clear, *they* are the thieves."

"What should we do?"

"Leave the whole mess to Lord Graydon. He will deal with them most harshly for this violation of Forest law." Sebastian's stern look remained.

Ivan gulped and hoped he'd never confront the deceiving gryphons with their lion-sharp claws. He imagined a quick snap of their hooked beaks could cut him in two.

"Seeing them now, with my own eyes in daylight," Sebastian said, "I'm sure they're responsible for stealing the female kaleido-birds."

Canute and Alfred barked in a frenzy. At first, Ivan thought it was because of the gryphons flying overhead, but then, he realized three riders were galloping toward them. "Watch out! They'll run us over." Ivan promptly tugged Bounty to the side of the road.

The first rider had a wild, wolf-like appearance. His roundish face bore a full beard, as black and heavy as his eyebrows. The man's forehead showed a pronounced widow's peak. His dark hair was gathered to the back, bound by leather into a ponytail.

"Hello, Sebastian," the wolfish man yelled, waving his hand vigorously. Their horses skidded to a jolting stop. Sebastian was about to introduce them when the rider who had yelled the greeting maneuvered his horse next to Bounty. "I'm Wayland the Wolflord. These are my Wolflord friends, Gan-let and Shayne."

The two of them looked much like Wayland, with pointed wolf-like ears that protruded through thick hair hanging loose. Although Shayne was somewhat older, thinner, and his hair had streaks of gray.

"I must say, before you judge me…" Wayland held up the flat of his glove. "I'm no longer a werewolf, and I don't consider myself a lord." He tipped back his head and laughed.

Ivan chuckled, though he wasn't sure what was so funny. Maybe he felt relieved that the newcomers were not threats. Leaning forward, he shook Wayland's hand. "I'm Ivan Kimble."

A thick silver medallion, bearing an amethyst stone in the center, clasped the front of Wayland's dark traveling cloak. Shayne and Gan-let had the same jewelry but were worn as necklaces.

Wayland glanced at Alfred and Canute and made a kissing sound. "After the stories I've heard about you and your beagles, I expected you'd be much older. Your reputation is well-known in our Forest. I'm happy to meet you."

"I pictured you looking like Hercules." Shayne's smile spread ear to ear.

Ivan squirmed in the saddle, being singled out, but he liked them right off.

Wayland nodded to Sebastian. They grasped each other's forearms and squeezed. This must be their method of greeting trusted friends, Ivan decided.

"I thought we'd see you at the Faeries' Festival today," Sebastian said. "This is an important celebration in their history."

"That was our plan earlier this morning." Wayland's

face turned grave. "There's trouble at the South Castle, and I feel we should go there directly to see if we can help."

Sebastian's eyebrows shot up, wrinkling his forehead. "What kind of trouble?"

Ivan jerked back. *Trouble?*

"We had a message that Zello torched the dragons' stable this morning," Gan-let explained with multiple hand gestures.

"Why in heaven's name would he do something barbaric as that?" Shock and anger flooded Sebastian's voice.

Gan-let shook his head. Shayne hunched his shoulders. Wayland thought for a moment and then said, "The tree-message we've received stated that Zello was livid because Fetters accused him of eating his hens. Isn't that foolish?"

"Zello doesn't even like chicken—their feathers cause him indigestion." Sebastian stroked his whiskers.

"His feelings get hurt easily these days," Gan-let said. "They say it's the nature of the brown-scaled dragons as they get older. I don't know if this is true or not."

Ivan was amused. On his first visit to the Forest, he'd heard one of Simon's soldiers make the same comment.

"Who knows anything about dragons, anyway?" Wayland threw up his hands.

"Something is not right here," Sebastian said. "Zello's a Forest hero, and one of Lord Graydon's favorites. I recall the dangerous missions he's been involved in—all for the safety and well-being of our great woodland."

"You may not know, Ivan"—Wayland leaned forward in his saddle—"that Zephyrus was once king of a long-ago kingdom called Helvaka. A mighty fine king at that."

"It's located northwest from here." Shayne threw his arm in that direction for Ivan's benefit. "Decaying ruins that no one would dare venture into," he added.

Gan-let lowered his open palms with fingers splayed. "We are well-acquainted with Helvaka because we used to live there with the rest of our pack. They still inhabit the place as werewolves."

"I do know about it," Ivan replied, "though I've never been there."

"Well, let's hope you never have the occasion to visit—it's horrible." Gan-let spread his arms wide. "Like there's the Fool's Pool—it will fool you every time—even take your life if you're not wise. And there's the tree of hissing snakes that can take power over you, and the wicked green banshees."

"Green. The worst kind." Sebastian chimed in.

"Enough!" Wayland raised his voice. "Ivan will never need to go there, so why scare him with all this?"

Ivan gulped, remembering Zephyrus had told him earlier that Peter may be hiding there.

Wayland's horse moved in close and tried to befriend Bounty by touching his nose with his own, but Bounty would have none of it. He snorted and turned away.

Ivan rolled his eyes. "You're so snooty," he said quietly.

"One more thing that might interest you," Sebastian said. "Not more than fifteen minutes ago, we saw the two gryphons from the South Castle flying overhead."

Gan-let looked up and scanned the clouds, trying to spot the gryphons. But they were long gone.

"Perhaps all this is somehow tied together, but I can't make sense of it." Sebastian faced the Wolflords. "You know the gryphons aren't allowed to leave their posts until midnight. They are frozen into the pillars that hold up the front pediment at the castle."

"Never gave it much thought." Wayland shifted uneasily. "We seldom go to the castle." He gave Gan-let a fleeting glance. "We always feel like freaks."

"You really shouldn't," Sebastian said. "Lord Graydon admires all of you who have endured the *transition*."

Fingering his wolfish ears, Wayland turned toward Ivan. "What this means is—in case no one has explained our savage history—we've made the choice to transform from werewolves into men."

"Sebastian mentioned it." Ivan hoped he hadn't spoken out of turn and the information wasn't too private.

"Someday, I'll tell you all about it in detail—if you think you can stomach it." Wayland scowled and snorted. "Now, we're on our way to the castle to see about the fire."

"We'll give your greetings to the faeries," Ivan called, knowing he was more interested in seeing Anna-Iza than meeting the little faery folks.

"You do that." Gan-let hesitated as he slid on his gloves. He threw a glance at Wayland.

Wayland's dark eyes penetrated Ivan's. "We've heard you had the Golden Lantern in your hands at one time."

"I did."

"What happened to it, then?" Wayland lifted his brow.

"We believe," Ivan said, "the Forest's shepherd, not knowing who the lantern belonged to, plucked it from Dorsett's lower branch and carried it away along with the Silver Axe."

Wayland's mouth dropped open. Apparently, he didn't know the axe had also been found and was again missing. He blew a puff of breath through his lips and made a spitting sound.

"I've heard the lantern is in the Witches' Village." Shayne leaned forward and patted his horse's shoulder.

"Yeah, that's right." Gan-let turned up his palms and wiggled his fingers. "I heard that rumor, too."

"More than a rumor." Sebastian snorted. "We figured the shepherd took the lantern to have the blacksmith fix the broken glass. The wick has also gone out. Can't relight it without a dragon's help."

Wayland cocked a thick eyebrow.

"It's true," Sebastian confirmed. "Only a dragon's fiery breath can relight the wick."

Nodding his head, Ivan confirmed the remark. Although, he wasn't sure Wayland believed it.

"Do you think the lantern is still at the Blacksmith's Shop in the Witches' Village?" Shayne drummed his fingers on the saddle's pummel, his heavy eyebrows bunched together.

"Yes." Sebastian scowled. "Don't you?"

"Nothing's ever that easy in the Forest." Shayne smirked and raked his fingers through wind-swept hair.

Ivan silently agreed.

"We'd better be going." Wayland nodded to his companions. "I hope to see you again, Ivan Kimble."

"Perhaps you'd like to meet us at the castle this evening." Ivan glanced at Sebastian to check if it was acceptable to invite the Wolflords. "I understand there's a huge feast honoring several of Lord Graydon's guests. It's sure to be filled with gaiety, music, and fine royalty."

Wayland hesitated and looked off into the distance.

"Lord Graydon would welcome you and the Wolflords," Sebastian said. "In fact, it's long overdue that you get to know the Lord of the Forest. There's much his kind heart would like to do for you. If you'd allow it."

"We'll see." Wayland appeared to think on the statement for a time. Then he waved and pressed his knees against his mount. The horses shot off along the road kicking up dust and stones.

"Good journey," Ivan called after them. He wondered and scratched the side of his head. *Can it get any stranger than this day?*

Sebastian must have read Ivan's thoughts. "It was good of you to invite the Wolflords to the festivities tonight. Being part of the Forest, they need to know what is available to them and how generous Lord Graydon is to the unusual creatures."

"Everyone wants to belong. Did Wayland and the Wolflords know my brother?" Ivan should have thought to ask.

"Oh, yes. They were famously close, that is, when Wayland could get away. Mostly, he was at his own village where he's their lord. Wise and fair-minded. He is much loved."

Alfred barked. Bounty shifted on his hooves.

"We'd better go." Sebastian turned Old Bones around and they headed down to the west.

Chapter 8

A Change of Plans

Far ahead, at the crossroads of Sir Barkay Road and Sheepherder's Path Road, Ivan recognized Commander Simon leading about twenty of his soldiers.

"They must be out on patrol." A frown creased Sebastian's forehead. "I suspect they're checking on the gryphons' absence from the castle. I'm glad they know about it and can inform Lord Graydon."

"If they weren't so far away, I'd yell at Simon to stop." Ivan stood in the stirrups staring ahead. He smiled with joy at seeing his friend.

"I'm thinking." Sebastian paused and stared into the distance.

"Thinking? What—?" Ivan got a queasy feeling in his stomach.

"We should forego the faeries' festivities and travel to the Witches' Village at once. I need to find out if the Golden Lantern is there. Would you mind terribly?"

"B-but...I thought I would see—" Ivan stopped. His disappointment at not seeing Anna-Iza raced through him. Sensing a sob rising in his throat, he swallowed hard.

"I am sorry, but finding the lantern takes priority over a faery celebration."

Ivan sighed and gave in. *Sebastian is right, of*

course.

The travelers turned off the main road and continued in a southwesterly direction. Ivan needed to ask again, now that they had more privacy. "Sebastian, how is Anna-Iza? Have you seen her and her sister goddesses lately?"

"Well, I am a bit concerned about your affection toward the High Goddess. Remember I warned you nothing can come of it?

Ivan's heart sank, and he stayed silent.

Slowing Old Bones, Sebastian answered, "Several days ago, the goddess had a conference with Zephyrus."

"Why? Is there a worry about her?" Ivan hands tightened on Bounty's reins. *Or is it because of me?*

Sebastian gazed at Ivan. His face hardened. "Best you ask Zephyrus," he said in a quiet voice.

Fear pierced Ivan's heart. He pushed. "Is she in trouble because of me? I…mean…you know I held her in my arms and kissed her. Did my carelessness cause her distress?"

"It's not for me to say." Sebastian shook his head, and his gray eyes flickered. "I shouldn't have said anything. It isn't my place."

Ivan bit on the inside of his cheek, trying to hold back his frustration. He'd asked a simple question and yet, for all they'd been through, Sebastian slighted him. *Has he stopped trusting me?*

As they rode on, not speaking, Ivan began to doubt himself and his place in the Forest. What had he done wrong that Sebastian, his good friend, had denied sharing?

Finally, Sebastian broke the silence. "I'm sorry, Ivan. It's truly out of my hands to disclose the nature of their discussion, but I'm sure Zephyrus will tell you in time."

"Forget it," Ivan said, choking back tears. "I don't need to know if it's such a big secret."

Sebastian sighed. "You don't understand. Some things are not mine to share."

"Then I'll wait until Zephyrus feels I'm worthy to be told." Ivan stuck out his bottom lip to be sure Sebastian knew his feelings were hurt. He decided he would be mad and withdrawn the entire day. In fact, he was nearly angry enough to return home.

But then...

"Ouch! Hey, ouch. That stings." Sebastian raised his arms and crossed them to protect his head. He glanced up into an old English walnut tree. "What are you troublemakers doing?"

Ivan ducked and just missed a small object that whizzed by, almost striking him on the bridge of his nose.

Several antopes—long-eared, squirrel-like critters with reddish fur, and long fluffy tails, threw walnuts at the travelers, and their aim was pretty good.

"We're trying to get your attention," one antope said, "but you're too busy being mad at each other."

"I'm not mad," Ivan insisted through clenched teeth.

"What is it, then?" Impatience filled Sebastian's response.

Eyes wide with fear, the walnut tree said, "Sir Zephyrus sent a message, saying there's trouble at the castle."

"Hey, up there! Will you please stop throwing those blasted nuts?" Sebastian shouted, pumping his fist.

"Don't bring those horses any closer." The other

antope covered his nose with his paw. "I'm allergic to horsehair."

"For heaven's sakes," Sebastian bellowed. "Be quiet." The critters scampered up the tree with their sharp claws for climbing, and they hid from sight.

"We've learned about Zello burning the dragons' stable," Ivan interjected.

"Wayland and a couple of his Wolflord companions informed us." Sebastian rubbed his head and examined his hand, apparently looking for blood. "They told us about the incident, but not why it happened."

"Sounds like I'm a bit tardy with my message," the walnut tree said. "Sir Zephyrus did say that Zello revolted and threatened to burn the stables to ashes if his demands weren't met."

Sebastian's mouth dropped open. "What demands? There's nothing he, or any of the dragons, could possibly want." He pulled on his mustache, while puzzlement etched his face. "The Wolflords have told us it's too late—the dragon stable was scorched to the ground."

"That's a real pity," the tree moaned.

"Somehow these conflicting reports don't make sense." Ivan pursed his lips and turned to face Sebastian.

"Contact Zephyrus," Sebastian gave a brief demand to the walnut tree. "Tell him to send Maynard with The Challenger, and meet us near Troll Transformation Prison. I need to check on Witch Merridyn Hempstead."

The tree promised to send the message at once.

Ivan's eyebrows came together. "Why are we traveling there? I thought we were going to the Witches' Village. And why do we need a weapon?" He'd killed two men with the magic sword and did not wish to repeat the deed. *Never again.*

"Earlier, Zephyrus asked me to stop and see Merridyn during our journey and inquire after her wellbeing." Sebastian's eyes narrowed with worry. "It's on our way to the village and shouldn't take too long."

Disappointed again, Ivan could hardly argue since Zephyrus asked them to check on some poor damsel in distress. They took off, glad to leave the walnut grove and the pesky antopes behind.

Ivan sniffed the air. "I smell smoke." He frowned. "Could it be from the smoldering stable at the castle?"

"No, it's too far south, and the wind is coming from the west. I suspect the smoke comes from the chimneys of the trolls' stone huts."

"Are we that close to the prison?" He cocked his head.

"You'll be able to smell the stench soon enough." Sebastian glanced around.

"I've only heard horrible things about it, and I know from my first visit that trolls are not good company."

Sebastian snorted and rolled his eyes, and then they continued down the road.

"Merridyn's story is a heartbreaker." Slowing his horse, Sebastian sat up straight, his thin shoulders pulled back. "The tragedy happened earlier this year, about springtime."

Ivan leaned in to hear every word. At least Sebastian trusted him enough to tell about Merridyn's plight, and he felt pleased about this.

"One of our most respected, well-loved witches has been accused of poisoning her husband and little boy."

"Oh, that's terrible," Ivan gasped. "How did such a thing happen?"

Before Sebastian could tell the story, Alfred barked

a warning. Canute dashed toward some shrubbery to their right.

"Stop, Canute!" Ivan yelled.

Several times in the past, his beagles had gotten into trouble chasing strange and dangerous critters—especially in the Forest. They heard a *kerplunk*, followed by an irate cry. If the beagles disturbed a troll, there was no telling what mischief they could cause.

Swinging off Bounty, Ivan rushed forward to the bushes. He parted the branches and couldn't believe what he saw.

****

A young lady, bent on her knees, head down, was sobbing. She didn't turn around or respond to Ivan's presence.

Sebastian dismounted and hobbled quickly to her side. "Merridyn, what happened?"

"What does it look like?" she shot back, tears streamed down her cheeks. Her basket of berries had spilled onto the ground. "That stupid dog knocked me over and scattered my whole morning's pickings. They are a nuisance and should be banned from our Forest."

Canute flopped onto his belly, front paws stretched out with his head buried between them. He whimpered along with the girl.

"I-I'm very sorry my beagle knocked over your berries," Ivan's voice quivered with remorse.

"They're ickleberries," Merridyn said through gritted teeth like Ivan was nearly as stupid as his dogs. "Now, I'll have nothing to trade for food from those miserable trolls." She covered her face with berry-stained hands, wept harder, and her thin shoulders shook.

Embarrassed and ashamed, Ivan didn't know what

to say. He had no experience with hysterical witches. He rubbed the bush's prickly green leaves between his fingers. "So, this is the ickleberry bush," saying it more to himself than the girl.

Merridyn's smudged face twisted with fury. "You idiot!" she screamed. "Your clumsy dog caused me to spill all these hellish berries, and you stand there, fingering the bush's leaves." It sounded like she wanted to spew angrier words at him, but a hiccup prevented it. Ivan shrank back and went mute.

"Merridyn, Merridyn. My sweet child." Sebastian kneeled next to the crying girl and wrapped his arms around her. "We are very sorry for the accident. Let us help."

Not waiting for her response, Ivan squatted beside Sebastian. They gathered the berries and placed them with care into the empty basket.

Sebastian cleared his throat. "This is Ivan Kimble. He's a friend from the outside."

"I could tell he was a foreigner," she said scowling. Merridyn pushed up a mound of wheat-colored hair and tried to pin it on top of her head. It looked as though it needed a good combing, washing, and removing the dried leaves.

Her pale complexion showed dark circles beneath her brown eyes. A tear in the waistline of her cotton dress was held together by a safety pin, and wet berry stains discolored the fabric. Ivan thought she was older than him, but he couldn't be sure. Her forehead looked swollen, distorting her eyebrows. Her fingers were short and stumpy—like a troll's.

Ivan bowed from his kneeling position. "M' lady," he said, hoping the act would ease her testy mood. "If there's anything we can do to make up for this unfortunate—"

"It's too late for that kind of falsity." She continued to throw berries into the basket, her lips pinched together. Waving rough, scabbed hands at them, she growled, "Leave me be."

"We're here to help you," Sebastian said.

"What are you doing in our Forest?" she abruptly turned and asked Ivan. "You must know people in high places to wander so free and unguarded. A spy, perhaps?"

"I accompany him," Sebastian replied.

"Well, then, you must know that I'm the infamous witch you were just discussing." She raised an eyebrow, her eyes opened wide. "I'm accused of poisoning my husband and little—" Her voice broke into a deep groan. "What's more, I'm banished from my village, kept here in this cesspool of trolls who harass me every day. Look at them, standing guard at the gate, timing my limited freedom. A bunch of drooling dimwits.

"Why Zephyrus permits them in his Forest, I'll never understand." She swiped at the tears that raced down her stained cheeks.

Sebastian took Merridyn's face between his hands and looked into her eyes. "Why did they put you here of all places? Why not the comforts of the castle where you'd be safe until your trial?"

She pushed Sebastian's hands away. Sarcasm oozed when she answered, "You don't know? Then you'll have to ask my dear, loving sister."

Sebastian's mouth dropped. "Lyla? Your own sister condemned you here?"

She scowled. "Lyla thinks I'm too dangerous to be

near anyone—especially children." Trembling with grief and betrayal, she lowered her head.

Ivan's heart wrenched. He moved closer, gently patting her on the back.

She jerked away. "I did not poison my husband and little boy. I would never do such a wicked thing. I loved them, deeply—forever. Sebastian, you must help me. I'll go mad if I have to live among the trolls and their filthiness much longer. They're thieves, quarrelsome, and dangerous. Please."

"You have our promise," Ivan said, not checking with Sebastian. "The least we can do is remove her from this awful place. The stench gags me."

"Yes, we'll help you." Sebastian jerked on his beard. "Be brave for a little while longer until we get clearance from Zephyrus and find soldiers to escort you to the South Castle."

"Can't we take her with us?" Ivan was alarmed, realizing Merridyn was *transforming. How long will it take before she shrinks in height and begins looking like the other trolls? It is a frightening thought.*

"We would be breaking the witches' laws by interfering right now. It's best to obtain authorization and then enlist our soldiers who can protect her." Sebastian's deep frown showed he wasn't happy with the delay, either.

In the distance, the tall rusty prison gate was closed, separating the troll prisoners from the freedom of the Forest. Several uniformed guards stood at the entrance holding spears, squinting with beady eyes. They sneered as they watched Merridyn and her visitors in the near meadow.

"Tell me," Sebastian said. "How did this all

happen?"

The witch looked down at her torn dress and dirty fingernails. She remained that way for some time until Ivan wondered if it were too terrible for her to tell.

"One beautiful spring day," she said in a soft tone, "I was preparing a mixture of dried herbs, roots, and special spices in a pot on my kitchen stove. My husband and little boy were suffering from nasty colds. Yes, even witches can catch colds when the rain and wind bring on chills. I know the ingredients so well I don't rely on a recipe. I remember..." She paused and glanced at Sebastian. "The kitchen window near the stove was open. A lovely breeze blew in and carried a broken oak leaf. I mention the leaf to assure you I recall every detail of that horrible day. I served the potion to my husband and son in fancy floral teacups, adding a little sugar and milk to cut the bitterness. They drank it from their beds, the poor darlings. Shortly after, my husband began to cough and groan. He spewed a fishy-smelling froth from his mouth. He yelled my name with an animal-like cry..."

Merridyn pressed her hands to her face and shook her head. "What went wrong? What happened? I've never made a mistake in measurements or ingredients. Never, never." She wept, wiping her nose on the sleeve of her dress. There she stayed, with her head cradled in her hands, and didn't move.

Sebastian cleared his throat. "Isn't your trial coming up next week?"

The girl nodded and pulled on her short fingers. Hands trembling, she stated, "I'm turning into a troll."

"No, that's not true," Sebastian fibbed. "It takes nine months to a year for the full transformation. We'll have you out of here within the day." He lifted her chin with his forefinger and gave her an encouraging smile.

For the first time, Merridyn smiled back, although unconvincingly.

"It's so barbaric. So brutal," Ivan said between gritted teeth. He studied the girl's enlarged forehead and wondered if Sebastian's comment was a bit optimistic. Ivan saw the distortion. She apparently knew it, too.

"My time is up," Merridyn whispered and stared ahead. "The guards are waiting for me."

Other trolls and prisoners stood behind the iron bars, snickering and clapping.

"Shut up, you bunch of vicious rats!" she screamed.

Ivan helped Merridyn to her feet and handed her the basket. She clutched it to her chest as though it was her last valuable possession on earth. When Ivan pulled Sebastian from the ground, he noticed his beige leggings had red berry stains on the knees.

"Please…" The girl looked into Sebastian's eyes. "You must keep your promise and help me out of this terrible place."

Nodding, Ivan rubbed his chin. He wondered how he could prove her innocence at the approaching trial. Her misery tugged at his heart.

She moved away, her head dropped to her chest.

Mounting, Ivan called after the girl, "I promise we will help you."

She turned briefly, her face a mask of despair.

Chapter 9

Troll Attack

"That poor, unfortunate girl." Ivan twisted Bounty's reins around his hands. "There must be something we can do for her right away."

Sebastian was quiet for some time. "This is what we'll do." He took a deep breath and said, "Not far from here, by the Ancient Oak Creek, Taline stands. She's very dependable and a discrete oak. We'll have her send a Root-Underground message to Zephyrus. He can issue a Release Decree for Merridyn's discharge. That should do it."

Yet, Merridyn's plight continued to gnaw on Ivan.

Did she carelessly poison her own family? If not, who did such a terrible thing?

Soon, they reached the clearing where Taline stood, large and imposing with a jumble of autumn leaves that fluttered in the breeze. The Ancient Oak Creek gurgled behind her.

"One of the finest Root-Underground communicators this side of the Forest," Sebastian boasted. "We'll send our message through her to Zephyrus right away."

"Are you celebrating Merridyn's release already, or happy we've reached Taline without incident?" Though Ivan's voice teased, he looked around him with unease, a feeling of being watched.

"Both." Sebastian grinned. "I see a basket hanging on one of her branches, covered with a fine linen cloth. I believe it's something to eat and not those awful sour ickleberries."

Ivan threw himself from his saddle. "Someone has thought to bring us lunch." He was sure it had been Anna-Iza.

Sebastian called to Taline, and he, too, slipped from his horse. "I assume the basket is for us?"

The oak opened her eyes. "A gift from the High Goddess, sir."

"She knows we're here?" Ivan squinted through the trees hoping to spot Anna-Iza on her brilliant white Andalusian—or even her winged silver steed.

"She had to return to the Faery Festival. However, she must've left the basket for a reason," Taline answered smugly.

Ivan approached the oak, blushing at his dumb remark. "Of course."

Taline gasped and stared at Sebastian's leggings. "What happened to your knees?"

He bent to examine the red stains. "Guess I crushed some ickleberries."

Chuckling lightly, Ivan hid his amusement behind the palm of his hand.

"This esteemed visitor is Ivan Kimble." Sebastian sidestepped and presented the young man with arms wide open. "Perhaps you've heard his name."

"Oh, Great High Intervener! You are the one who saved our Forest from a terrible destruction. You killed Tereus's War Commander, Kruse Hays. And Porcupine met his end, the dreadful Swamp Dragon that lived in

Lake Gorgon. We welcome and praise you for your courage, we—"

"Enough." Ivan threw up his hands, waving them vigorously. Shame washed over him. He wanted to forget these things and not be reminded.

"Send a message to Zephyrus at once." Sebastian stepped close to the tree. "Ask for a Release Decree for the witch, Merridyn Hempstead. Wait for Zephyrus's answer and then forward it to Troll Transformation Prison. Do you want me to spell her full name?"

"No need," Taline rushed her reply. "I've sent many messages on her behalf, but Zephyrus can do nothing for her. The witches are independent and very private, you know."

"Now, he will do something to help her." Sebastian's eyebrows angled.

"And then," Ivan said, "tell the soldiers to come and escort Merridyn to the South Castle where she'll be safe and comfortable."

"I can't imagine any mother poisoning her own husband and child. It's disgraceful." If a tree could lift her nose into the air, that's how it appeared.

"She's been wrongly accused, bound to the squalor of prison." Ivan clenched his fists and grated his teeth. "A poor decision by her sister, Lyla. She sent her to that terrible place."

Sebastian rested his hand on Ivan's arm. "Best we not say too much until after the trial."

Ivan nodded, embarrassed by his angry outburst.

The sound of galloping horses in the far distance, on a southerly road, caused Ivan to spin around. A splendid-looking carriage raced past them, a roll of dust in its wake.

"It's our royal guests on their way to the castle for tonight's big celebration." Sebastian stood on tiptoes, his hand pressed above his eyes. "Yep. That's one of them. A Russian carriage, judging from the colors and fancy royal emblem on the door."

"Russian?" Ivan stepped next to his companion as the four black horses disappeared from sight. "Lovely," he said, enthralled with the possibility of meeting some of his own countrymen.

"According to what Zephyrus has been told, there should be another carriage arriving about the same time." Sebastian stroked his forehead.

"Let's have lunch," Ivan said abruptly. He removed the basket from Taline's lower limb and walked to a fallen log where he sat. Canute put his paws on Ivan's knees, pushing his wet nose into the basket. Alfred gave a sharp cry and begged. "Be patient. I should let you both go hungry." He playfully pulled on Canute's ear. "Knocking that poor lady to the ground."

Sebastian laughed at the anxious dogs and sat next Ivan.

Unwrapping the sandwiches, Ivan gave one each to his beagles. He consumed his own meat sandwich with small bites, his usual method of eating. Gratitude lingered for his sweet and thoughtful Anna-Iza. *How did she know I'd be here and not on my way to the Faery Celebration? Someone must've told her.*

When he asked this question, Sebastian replied, "The trees are probably following our journey and reporting to Zephyrus."

"Then that means Anna-Iza has quizzed Zephyrus about our destination."

"Most likely through Root-Underground."

Sebastian molded the sandwich wrappers to form bowls and filled them with milk for the beagles. Canute licked Sebastian's fingers.

"Merridyn did not poison her family," Ivan said. "I can feel it. She wouldn't do such a terrible thing."

"I don't know much about the witches and their ways." Sebastian hesitated. "They prefer we stay out of their business. But I agree, Merridyn is not capable of murder. Neither is she careless about mixing potions. Her skills are legendary. I do remember hearing that Lyla is a jealous and vengeful witch. She resents Merridyn's abilities in all things witchcraft, as well as her expertise with herbs and healing."

Ivan nodded thoughtfully, polishing a big red apple on his jacket sleeve. "She must be removed from that horrid place at once. I saw the swelling of her forehead and the shortening of her fingers. You saw it, too. Troll transformation has begun."

"Indeed. Now we'd better go." Sebastian rose to his feet, straightening his back. He brushed at his knees and must have realized the stains would be permanent until the leggings could be washed.

"I'll leave the empty basket on this log." Ivan stood and neatly folded the linen cover over the top.

Sebastian froze. Then, he lifted his head, swinging it this way and that. His bushy eyebrows squeezed together. "Something's wrong."

They both reached for their horses' bridles, prepared to mount in an instant.

"What is it?" Ivan spun and searched through the thickness of trees. "I hear hard breathing, snorting. Are we in danger?"

"I think so," Sebastian whispered.

Ivan pulled the Long Dark Cloak closer to his chest. Canute barked with the same ferociousness as when confronted with the Swamp Dragons. Not to be left out, Alfred joined in, howling.

"Be still," Ivan hissed and hopped on Bounty.

"Hurry," Sebastian said in a low yet urgent tone. He mounted his gray horse.

Several rocks came hurtling from behind the trees. One struck Ivan on the forehead just above his left eye. He teetered for a moment grasping Bounty's mane for support. Pain gripped him, and then he slipped from his animal, hitting his head and shoulder hard on the ground. Darkness pushed in on him.

"Ivan, get to your feet."

Orange and yellow lights flashed through Ivan's brain. Red heat flamed in his skull.

Is that Sebastian's voice? So far away?

Frightened, Bounty whinnied loudly and crashed into Old Bones, who swung in a circle, stomping his hooves and nearly unseating Sebastian. Not known to stick around when trouble showed, Bounty shook his head and dashed away in the direction they'd just come.

"Ivan. Ivan, wake up."

He could hear Sebastian's voice, but it was faint. Within seconds, Sebastian turned ghostly in bluish-gray wisps of smoke and disappeared into the Long Dark Cloak.

Ivan groaned. He tried to roll to his side and get to his knees but collapsed.

"Pull the cloak to your forehead. I'll heal you." But Ivan didn't move.

The horde came running and pumped their spears into the air. Cecil, a fallen wizard, led the charge. Maloof followed, his short legs moving fast, attempting to keep pace. They shouted harsh troll words, excited to have their victim unmoving on the ground.

Maloof grinned and bared a mouth of dangerously sharp teeth. Drool ran down his chin.

Ivan opened one eye. The other remained closed, wet with blood. He felt the familiar tug on the cloak when Sebastian released himself with a swirl of smoke and then quickly solidified into a man.

Maloof gaped and scratched his hairless head at such a sight.

"Why didn't you heal me?" Ivan moaned, his fingers lightly touched his forehead.

"You must physically place the cloak on your wound when my spirit is inside."

"Of course." He groaned. "Now I remember."

Several trolls waddled toward Sebastian with their sharp-edged spears pointed at his heart, causing him to freeze where he stood. One of them stared at the red berry stains on Sebastian's knees. He pointed and laughed.

The trolls circled Ivan jumping up and down with enthusiasm. They grabbed him by his arms and legs and dragged him toward the nearest tree—Taline. Cecil smirked. He slapped Maloof's back in a congratulatory way, and when the dogs barked, Cecil disappeared into the bushes. Alfred chased after the runaway troll, but it managed to dodge him, weaving through the thick trees.

"Stop!" Taline screamed. "You fat, despicable creatures. Get your dirty hands off the lad." Her rage appeared to have no effect on the trolls. They were intoxicated with their own violent power.

Ivan moaned and tried to inch away. "Sebastian,

where are you? I'm dizzy and out of sorts."

"I'm sorry," Sebastian moaned. "These ravaging runts have me pinned with their spears. You must get to your feet. Now!"

Ivan reached for The Challenger at his side. His fingers touched—nothing. He groped for it again, and then he panicked. *I have no weapon.*

****

Alfred and Canute woofed and nipped at the trolls' ankles. Several trolls picked up rocks and whirled them at the canines. The dogs yelped and sped off to hide under bushes, panting and peering between the leaves.

More trolls ran into the scene from another direction and joined the horde. Together, they tried to prop Ivan up against Taline. Maloof pointed at a rope they'd brought. They were so short and Ivan so tall that it proved to be a difficult task to push, hold, and tie him standing against the tree's trunk. Why they insisted that he must be tied upright, Ivan couldn't figure but was too weak to protest.

"What are you doing?" Sebastian shouted. "Stop this at once."

"Sebastian. M-my head hurts." Blood ran down the side of Ivan's face. His hands were bound. He had no way to stop it.

"You must come to your senses," Sebastian screamed. "Get away from them, Ivan."

Noisy and quarrelsome, the trolls couldn't seem to decide which direction to wrap the rope around the boy. Maloof pointed and pulled one way while another troll tugged in the other direction, undoing what had already been done. Several braced themselves against Ivan, holding his limp body up against the tree. At last, they knotted the rope around him, tying it snugly to Taline. They stepped back, making pig-like snorting sounds, and rubbing their hands together.

"You're in big trouble, you useless lumps!" Taline shouted and swatted at them with her lower branches, but her limbs couldn't reach.

"Screaming isn't going to help," Sebastian said. "The more noise and chaos, the more agitated they become."

Ivan's head throbbed. "I s-see double trolls."

"Then-what-would-you-like-me-to-do?" Taline enunciated each word with emphasis. "Just stand here and allow the scourge of the Forest to mistreat our young hero?"

"Let's find out what they want," Sebastian suggested.

Ivan tried to lift his eyes and focus. He was too lightheaded to make sense of it. His skull pounded, and his breathing slow.

"Ivan, dear Ivan," Taline soothed. "These filthy runt-rats have tied you to me. Try not to struggle so much. It chafes me."

Suddenly Ivan thought he'd figured it out. The trolls must've felt that Ivan's humiliation would be a greater glory if they could bind him standing tall, yet helpless. *But then, what do I know about the twisted workings of a troll's mind?*

"The ropes are cutting off my circulation," Ivan whimpered. "What do they want of me?"

Unable to help, Sebastian called from where he stood a captive, guarded by four trolls. "I don't know, so I'll leave the negotiations up to you."

"What negotiations?" Ivan asked in a strangled

voice.

"Ask them what they want," Sebastian kicked at the closest troll but missed him.

Ivan hoped to scare the trolls by faking a command for help. He ordered Taline, "Contact Zephyrus immediately. T-tell him we need reinforcements."

"I don't think they understand that big word— reinforcements." Taline corrected, "Try soldiers."

They didn't appear to listen. Maloof stomped his foot on the ground, blubbering something unintelligible. He wore the same leather vest and breeches, stiff with filth that Ivan had seen on his first visit. Others had dirty, ragged shirts with buttons and cuffs missing, or they wore no tops at all. Only short pants covered with who knows what, but they reeked of urine and something rotten.

Stepping closer, Maloof's eyes pinched with fury. Spittle flew between his darkened teeth as he shouted, "Lan-ern, lan-ern. Mine. Warm an' bright."

A group of them pumped their fists into the air, calling for the lantern. Some gripped their bows with stumpy hands in a threatening manner. One reached behind his back for an arrow and notched his weapon.

They taunted, "Lan-ern. Lan-ern. Give lan-ern or— we eat you!" They giggled and turned to poke each other in their bare bellies.

Ivan eyed them, even more surprised. They could speak and almost made sense. Now he knew what the violent horde wanted.

Maloof moved toward his brother trolls and smacked several in the mouth. "Shud-dup!"

"Owww," the struck trolls hollered.

"You." Maloof jabbed his dirty finger at Ivan. "Lan-ern is Maloof's." He bent and picked up the same rock that had struck Ivan earlier. "You make Maloof fall." He pointed to a faded spot on his forehead.

It was true. On Ivan's first visit, he tried to grab the Golden Lantern from Maloof when Sebastian draped the cloak over and put him under a Stupor Spell. Maybe Maloof had fallen a bit harder than Ivan had intended. But it was too late to change that outcome.

"I don't know where the lantern is." Ivan blinked away the blood that impaired his eyesight. "It could be anywhere in the Forest."

"Uh?" Maloof's eyes opened wider, and his mouth sagged.

"Look. Do you see it here?"

Staring at Ivan's hands and arms bound to the tree, Maloof walked around Taline, checking Ivan's feet and between the ropes. He rubbed his head. "No lan-ern," he muttered. "Where?"

Shortly, Ivan's thoughts improved. "The lantern will not work for you."

"Uh?" Maloof grunted and looked up.

"It's broken. The fire gone." *Does he really understand my words?*

The befuddled troll snorted like a pig and brought up mucus. Spitting a huge wad, it just missed Ivan's boot. He shifted as much as possible, going weak in the knees.

"Fire gone?" Maloof's eyes seemed to lose hope. He lowered his hand and dropped the rock.

"The lantern must have the fiery breath of a dragon to relight it." Ivan struggled to keep his head upright, his thoughts in focus.

"Zello, to be precise," Sebastian yelled, from his

captured position.

Maloof let out an agonizing wail.

"Untie this lad," Sebastian ordered, "or I'll put you back into Troll Transformation Prison for the rest of your useless life."

Impatient with their prisoner, the other trolls raised their short swords and spears, stabbing their weapons into the air. Their intentions were clear—they intended to end Ivan's life—maybe Sebastian's, too.

"No!" Maloof thrust his palms forward in a halting gesture to his fellow trolls. It must have meant they wouldn't kill their prisoners—but not that they would gain their freedom.

Ivan looked deep into the troll's yellow-tinged eyes, and there he recognized a glint of awareness, of understanding—somewhere from long ago. A well of tears rode Maloof's lower lids.

"I'm sorry." Ivan strained against the rope and groaned. "I don't have the lantern, and it truly is broken."

Shoulders slumped in defeat, Maloof stared at the ground and kicked the rock he'd just dropped.

A decade ago, Maloof was a Forest wizard in high position—tall and elegant, wise and fair, greatly loved by his fellow wizards. And then, he fell from grace, though Ivan wasn't privileged to know the crime committed. After ten years in Troll Transformation Prison, Maloof was reduced to this pitiful creature.

"I believe he wants the lantern because it will help him feel big and important again." Ivan wiggled his fingers hoping for circulation. "Having warmth and light would give him the power and leadership he once knew. Does that make sense, Sebastian?"

Sebastian's eyebrows rose. "I'm sure I don't know

the workings of a troll's mind, but it seems logical."

"Reinforcements have arrived," Taline shouted.

Ivan didn't see or hear anyone, least of all, the clomping of horse hooves. He thought the oak was bluffing in an attempt to frighten the trolls away. "Get me out of these strangling ropes," he cried. "I have no feeling in my arms or legs."

Sebastian took a few steps toward him. "Let me release my friend."

The trolls snarled and shouted, "No." One poked him in his leg with his sword. Another hit him on his hip with the side of his spear.

"Ow!" Sebastian cried. "Stop that."

The trolls forced him to back away from their prisoner. "Are you all right?" Ivan cried.

"No, that hurt. I'll have you all hung, you low-life creatures."

The rope was too tight for Ivan to straighten his torso and twist free. He scanned the trees and across the meadow. "Where are the soldiers—Commander Simon and his two hundred men?"

It grew deadly still. The trolls abruptly stopped their incessant squabbling. They must have sensed, even with their limited instincts, that something was amiss.

Chapter 10

Elftens to the Rescue

Staring into a large grove of white birch trees, Ivan spotted tall, thin men in white tunics and black belts that held serious knives. Dark leggings hugged their legs while suede leather boots covered their feet. They stepped from behind the slender trees. Each new visitor was armed with an arrow.

So well camouflaged, Ivan hadn't seen them at first. The entire colony had the same oval, pale faces, with subtle variations in their features. Their delicately shaped, pointed ears protruded from their silvery hair.

"Elftens!" Sebastian exclaimed.

"Elves?" Ivan gasped. "They're real?"

"Descended from the Elven Family, as I told you on your first visit. They are shrewd and wise." Sebastian grinned in triumph. "Their archery skills are superior."

Attention-focused, the Elftens moved forward in perfect unison as they left the cover of the birches.

Ivan squirmed under the confining ropes and groaned in pain. Eyes tearing, he could scarcely endure another moment. *Are they friend or foe?*

Maloof babbled a warning to his horde. He shook his spear at the newcomers and taunted something raw. The trolls must've known better than to confront the Elftens, for they turned and deserted as fast as their short legs would carry them. They fell over each other when they tumbled down the embankment of Ancient Oak Creek, then scrambled, following the stream to the north. The last to go was Maloof, who snarled at the bound prisoner. "Lan-ern mine." He beat his chest with his clenched fists.

One of the Elftens, wearing a gold circlet around his head, pulled a crystal wand from a leather sheath strapped across his shoulders. He raised and aimed it at the tree.

Taline yelled, "Sytha! Don't aim that thing at our esteemed visitor."

Ivan shivered with fright. *Why is he targeting me?*

Sytha rolled the wand between his finger and thumb and pointed it at Ivan. A sly, mean scowl marred his beautiful face. "Why Taline, have you ever known me to miss my target?" He laughed and lifted his wand higher. Then he spun on his heel so fast, that Ivan saw only a flash of white light that left the tip. A dangerous crackle followed, along with the smell of burning rope. The bindings snapped and fell away. Unable to catch himself with his arms entangled, Ivan collapsed to the ground. He hit his head in the same spot the rock had struck him earlier, and the wound again began to bleed.

Sebastian gasped and ran to Ivan's side. He quickly dissolved and disappeared into the Long Dark Cloak. "Take the hem and place it on your wound," he instructed.

Ivan moaned.

"Bring the cloak's hem to your forehead," Sebastian repeated with a stronger voice. "I'll heal you."

Ivan sat up, dizzy and feeling sick to his stomach. He wiped the blood from his eye with the back of his hand trying to comprehend Sebastian's words. At last he understood and pressed the fabric to his head. After a few moments, he sighed with relief. Stretching his aching legs, he gritted his teeth as cramps burned through his thighs. "I-I've never been bound to a tree before. It's awful."

"You shouldn't be in this degrading position," Sebastian said.

Inching back, Ivan rested against Taline's trunk. His lids closed. "I'm still a bit dizzy," he mumbled.

"That wasn't nice of you, Sytha," the tree scolded. "Why would you do such a mean-spirited thing to our Forest's hero?"

The Elften stood facing Ivan with arms crossed, wearing a smug look. He shrugged. "I thought it was the quickest way to get him out of those tight ropes."

Sebastian pulled his spirit from the cloak and soon solidified into a man. "Are you all right?" He offered Ivan his outstretched hand.

"I'm okay. Thank you for healing me." Ivan accepted Sebastian's help. Shaking, he stood on his feet. His forehead was wet with blood, but gratefully, there was no pain.

Sytha turned to Sebastian and bowed. "It's an honor to see you again."

Stepping back, Sebastian frowned at the Elften and gestured with his hand with his arm outstretched. "This is Ivan Kimble."

When Sytha looked at Ivan, his glare returned.

What have I done to offend him? Ivan hesitated, reluctant to ask if the Elftens had seen his brother. Maybe Peter had visited them, made them angry, and now Ivan paid the price.

Closer in view, Ivan studied the gold circlet around Sytha's forehead and his long silvery hair that touched the top of his shoulders. Attached to the metal were three etched oak leaves, acorns, and vines, reminding Ivan of the same pattern on The Challenger.

"You are the hero from the outside?" Sytha's pale eyebrows came together. "Everyone's talking about you."

Ivan shrugged and turned his shoulder to him, pretending to look for Bounty, who was nowhere in sight. He wasn't sure if Sytha invited more discussion, a show of curiosity, or to further ridicule him. Stubbornly, Ivan wouldn't give him the satisfaction. He inched himself against Taline, breathing heavily. There, he found the support he needed to stay upright, thinking a helping hand would've been appreciated. Within moments, he decided he would go find Bounty and leave at once. *I don't need this kind of rude treatment.*

The other Elftens marched forward. Their faces showed no emotion, only a quick frown from time to time. They surrounded Ivan and Sebastian in a protective circle.

"Why were you tied to a tree?" Sytha's lips curled into a smirk. "That's hardly a place for a hero."

"It seems," Ivan turned around and stammered, "that Maloof thought I had the Golden Lantern, and he wanted it back." Ivan briefly told him what had happened.

Sytha jerked his head in surprise, and his eyes widened.

Ivan thought the Elften might burst out laughing at any moment.

"Why would Maloof think such a thing?" Sytha seemed to restrain his amusement.

Ivan brushed leaves and bits of bark from the cloak. A great deal of blood had dripped on his shoulder. "Well, I took the lantern from Maloof on my first visit to the Forest, and he thought I still had it."

"It doesn't belong to the trolls. Nor does it belong to you." Sytha's voice was sharp. "The lantern belongs in the Sanctuary of Truth."

"It's a long story." Sebastian sighed and shook his head. "We had it in our hands for a short time—then lost it."

"Lost it?" Sytha continued to push. The sneer never left his face.

Ivan retold the incident from several weeks ago. "The glass was broken. We believe a shepherd took it to the Witches' Village for repair. We have yet to learn about the Silver Axe that was near the lantern. It, too, disappeared."

"So, you had the lantern and the axe—both in your possession?" Sytha studied Ivan's face, one eyebrow cocked.

"No. I—I—you don't understand."

Sebastian huffed, sounding impatient with the whole thing. He turned to ask Sytha, "What do you know of this?"

"I know nothing." The Elften unfolded his arms and gazed into the distance. His sarcasm worsened, and he slowly faced Ivan. "Let me get this straight. The trolls ambushed you and bound you to a tree, wanting the lantern back that you no longer had."

"Something like that." Ivan felt more and more inept with Sytha's critical tone. He wished Sytha would leave and take his colony of pale faces with him.

Sweeping his hand toward his fellow Elftens, Sytha

said, "We're on our way to the South Castle. There's rumor of a fire."

"What's going on there, anyway?" Sebastian asked, suddenly furious. "Wayland told us Zello burned down the dragons' stable in a fit of rage."

Ivan suspected Sebastian's frustration was because of Sytha's rude behavior and not the report of a burned stable, which they already knew.

"I thought it had something to do with the Golden Lantern," Sytha said, "but now I'm not so sure."

"This is all very confusing." Ivan was relieved the subject had changed to the disastrous fire at the castle. "We're going to the Witches' Village to see if the blacksmith has the relic." He hoped that put an end to the interrogation and Ivan could leave.

A moment passed. Sytha didn't say anything. He frowned at Sebastian, his lips pressed into a thin line. When he turned to leave, he threw Ivan a resentful look.

"What's wrong?" Sebastian took quick steps and grabbed Sytha's forearm, staring at him with compassion. "I know a fuming Elften when I see one, and I know this is not your usual behavior."

Sytha jerked his arm away. "Wrong?" His nostrils flared, and his voice pitched. "*He* is what's wrong." His long index finger pointed. "*He* is an outsider and does not belong in our Forest. *He* fought our war, and the Elftens weren't invited—or even told about it. That's what's wrong."

Ivan shriveled, and his heart shattered.

"Now Sytha…" Sebastian's shoulders sagged.

"Don't try to pacify me. This has irked me—and the Wolflords, if I might say, since we learned of your war against the Dark Army. You know we're the best and most accurate bowmen in the Forest, and yet we were not told of the war until it was over. We could've saved many lives, but you bring this—this outsider—and give him priority. You even gave him The Challenger to fight with!" he sputtered. His light skin turned red with anger.

The other Elftens slowly nodded their heads but said nothing. One of them coughed into his hand and looked away.

"I know how you feel," Sebastian said. "You need to talk to Zephyrus. He has his reasons and will clear up all your questions. And, as far as *this outsider* goes, Ivan never asked to be part of our war but was forced to fight to save his own life. We were lucky to have him."

"Lucky, my foot!" Sytha turned his back to them, his arms again folded over his long, thin chest. His breathing intensified.

Embarrassed and humiliated, Ivan stepped away. His mouth went dry, and his throat burned. His hope of the Elftens—this Elften—being his friend was shattered.

At that moment, Taline interrupted. "Good news! Sir Barkay has approved Merridyn's release from Troll Transformation Prison. She will be escorted to the South Castle at once. You, Sytha, and your brothers were selected to guide Miss Hempstead to safety.

"Wouldn't Zephyrus rather have *him* escort her?" Sytha lifted and pointed his chin toward Ivan.

"No," Taline answered curtly. "You were chosen. Now get going."

"Wait," Sebastian called. "Sytha will need a Release Decree for Merridyn."

"I have received it," the tree said. "I'll send a Root-Underground message to an elm tree standing near the prison. Rustee is trustworthy and will pass on Zephyrus's instructions to the troll guards."

This seemed to satisfy Sebastian. "Let's go to the creek, Ivan, and wash the blood from your face and the cloak. Yet another washing for the Long Dark Cloak, uh, lad?"

Clenching his teeth, Ivan didn't smile. He couldn't speak, afraid his voice would crack, and he would break down and sob in front of everyone. Without lifting his eyes, he walked toward Bounty, who had returned and stood quietly in the shade. *I don't need this harassment. I'll leave the Forest and never return. No one really cares about me, anyway.*

Sebastian and Zephyrus kept secrets from him. Trolls threw rocks and tied him to a tree. An Elften mocked and ridiculed him. *Why should I stay?*

Alfred and Canute whined. They seemed to understand their master's broken heart.

"Your knees are bloody, Sebastian. Did the trolls throw rocks at you, too?" Sytha's voice seemed at a normal pitch now.

"Oh, that." Sebastian gave a strained laugh. "I squatted in some ickleberries. I hope the stains wash out."

The two of them mumbled in conversation. Sebastian spoke, then Sytha, and then Sebastian. The Elften's footsteps moved away, Ivan thought, back toward the birch trees where their horses must've been tethered. *Good riddance.* And then, someone's hand came to rest upon his shoulder. Ivan concluded it was Sebastian catching up with him, ready to explain, to make excuses for Sytha's bad behavior.

"I apologize. My temper got the best of me," the voice said.

Ivan didn't turn to face Sytha. He grabbed Bounty's reins, his mouth tightly closed. He wished the Elften would just go away, and he'd never see him again.

"Truly, I'm sorry. I was frustrated at Zephyrus for ignoring me—us—the Elftens, when war broke out. I felt he didn't trust us, and it hurt deeply. We've always been a part of everything in the Forest."

When Ivan didn't say anything, Sytha continued, his voice quivering, "Did Wayland mention this to you—about how mad we were for being excluded?"

Ivan slowly shook his head. If he showed the Elften how uninterested he was, then maybe he would leave and take his bad temper with him.

"I've asked Sebastian to explain it, but he's refused a number of times. Says it's up to Zephyrus to explain." Sytha added further, "I don't understand the secrecy." His voice was now softer, more regretful.

He understood what the Elften meant. When Ivan asked Sebastian about Anna-Iza and why she'd seen Zephyrus in private, Sebastian wouldn't say. It troubled him, even now.

"The bigger part of my rage is, well...I'm jealous of you and all you've done in the short time you've been here."

Sytha was so matter-of-fact, Ivan turned to meet the Elften's eyes to check his sincerity. He wasn't sneering, only a contrite tip of his head and a downward turn of his lips.

"Jealous?" Ivan repeated, puzzled.

"Yes. Everyone had something astonishing to say about you. Your bravery, your strength, your practicality, your pleasant demeanor. Even Anna-Iza said you were a person of honor and integrity." Sytha nodded. "The goddess would know this from her Kiss of Discernment."

Ivan remembered the kiss and how it made him feel. "Anna-Iza said that about me?" He replaced his frown with a cautious grin.

"She did. Now, Ivan Kimble, can we be friends?"

Alfred barked.

"There's your answer." Ivan laughed. A heavy load was lifted from his heart, and he felt happier than he had since he'd been attacked.

"Smart beagle." Sytha chuckled, too. He reached and gripped Ivan's forearm in an Elften greeting. Not unlike what Wayland had done when he greeted Sebastian earlier that morning.

Ivan squeezed back.

"Perhaps we'll see you at the South Castle late this afternoon." Sytha cocked his head, raised and wiggled his pale eyebrows. "For now, we must escort a lovely maiden in distress."

"I'll look forward to seeing you again," Ivan said, and he meant it.

How quickly things change. Only moments ago, I was ready to leave the Forest, feeling hurt and rejected.

Sytha walked toward a thick stand of birch trees. Blending in, he joined his brothers. Their horses snorted as the Elftens mounted and rode toward the Troll Transformation Prison to escort Merridyn to the castle.

Chapter 11

Ratlings at the Ancient Oak Creek

"His manners were deplorable, and I reprimanded him severely for his behavior," Sebastian groused. "What did Sytha say to you?"

"He apologized."

"Well, I should hope so." Sebastian's knitted brow loosened. "His father, Anton, king of the Elften Kingdom, has warned his son many times about his sharp tongue. If Sytha is to inherit the position, he must learn to curb his reckless remarks."

Ivan dipped his head in agreement. Although, he was pleased that Sytha told him of Anna-Iza's fine compliments.

"Do the Elftens know Peter?" he asked hopefully.

"I'm sure you would've asked that question if Sytha hadn't been so rude." Sebastian reached for Old Bones's reins and pulled himself into the saddle.

"You're right." Ivan mounted Bounty. "He didn't give me a chance before he pounced. It wasn't my fault I was forced to fight the Forest War."

"Of course not, and you heard me say as much."

Sebastian paused and then spoke, "To answer your question about Peter. The Elftens and the Wolflords knew, and I believe, loved your brother greatly. Sytha and Wayland were particularly close to him. They had many—let's just say—wild adventures together."

"It doesn't surprise me. Peter enjoys adventure and always made friends easily." A long smile spread across Ivan's face. "I'm missing him right now. I wish I could find him."

"We will, don't worry," Sebastian said. "The chasm in their friendship may also explain Sytha's harsh treatment of you."

"You mean Peter was the real reason Sytha was rude to me?"

"I believe Sytha was jealous of you, as he humbly admitted. And, while Sytha and Peter were good friends, I've heard they had what would be called, aah…a falling out. They don't mingle with one another anymore."

"Do you know why?" Ivan frowned, almost afraid to hear the answer.

"Sytha never told me, though I did ask a few times. I'm not sure he even told Zephyrus. So, you see, Sytha keeps secrets, too." Sebastian gave an uneasy chuckle.

"Everyone keeps secrets from someone." Ivan's tone was brusque.

"Only when necessary." Sebastian nodded and motioned toward the creek. "Let's go. We'll wash that blood off your head and travel to the Witches' Village. Maybe the baker's wife will make you a lovely supper."

"Why *were* the Elftens and the Wolflords left out of the war?" He didn't expect an answer since the subject seemed forbidden to him—like many topics in the Forest.

"It's a simple explanation. If Sytha would've calmed his temper and thought it through, it would've been obvious." Looking left and right, Sebastian leaned sideways from his horse toward Ivan. "I suppose I can tell you, but you mustn't say anything. It's Zephyrus's place to clear up this matter. Sytha is too proud and pigheaded to ask him."

Ivan turned to listen.

"Zephyrus was afraid he could die from the poison driven into him by the Silver Axe, and that would leave the Forest without leadership. No telling what chaos might erupt after that. So, he decided not to involve the Elftens or the Wolflords in our terrible war. It was his hope that peace would be restored if the people knew they had someone dependable to lead them. Sytha and Wayland were Zephyrus's choices."

Ivan admired the trust and honor Zephyrus placed on them. "You are right. That is simple and quite sensible."

Sebastian dipped his head in agreement, turned, and patted his horse's rump. They continued toward Ancient Oak Creek.

"Wait up! Mr. Ivan, sir. Sebastian, wait. It's Maynard, your Forest servant."

Ivan halted.

Reining in his horse, Sebastian rotated to the sound of Maynard's voice. "What are you doing here?"

"You asked him to bring the ancient sword, remember?" Ivan waved at the servant.

"So I did."

"Goodness!" Maynard exclaimed when he'd reached them. "What happened to your forehead, Mr. Ivan? There's blood in your hair and on your head. Perhaps, I'm a bit late delivering this weapon."

"I'll explain as we ride." Sebastian snorted. "There's always a long story attached to every dilemma."

"You are right." Maynard lifted an eyebrow.

Wearing his familiar attire of a black jacket and white shirt, he unbuckled the scabbard at his waist and handed it to Ivan. "A pleasure to see both of you." He bowed his head with respect.

"And you, too." Ivan's fingers tightened around the golden hilt as he remembered the battles they'd fought. If it hadn't been for The Challenger, he would've been counted as one of the many slaughtered during the Forest War.

"It's my honor to be with you again," the magical sword said.

"I hope I won't need this weapon." Ivan threw a worried glance at Sebastian.

"Just a *precaution*, my good lad," his companion said.

After tightening the scabbard's belt at his waist, Ivan adjusted it by his side. "Sorry you had to travel so far to deliver the sword, but it's just a *precaution*," Ivan mimicked Sebastian's words.

"I had to come this way just the same," Maynard said. "Zephyrus contacted me at the Faery Festival this morning. He asked me to help serve the special guests scheduled to arrive at the castle today."

"Earlier, we saw a Russian royal carriage traveling in that direction." Sebastian pointed south.

"Ah, then perhaps they've safely arrived." Maynard pulled out his pocket watch and studied it for a moment.

"Come to the creek where we'll drink, and I'll wash my face." Ivan touched his blood-matted hair.

"Then, you can continue on with us to the Witches' Village, if you'd like," Sebastian said.

The servant nodded, seeming a bit bewildered. "Why are you going there?"

"A short detour." Sebastian raised his eyebrows.

"Then we'll accompany you to the castle and find out about the stable fire." Ivan nodded. "We'll learn about the Golden Lantern and gather any evidence to protect Merridyn during her trial."

At the creek, the water crashed against the rocks as it pushed its way south, carrying fallen leaves and twigs with it.

"If you look into the shadows"—Sebastian pointed—"you'll see the Blue-back Turtles. They're fairly scarce now, but you'll not find them in any place in the world but here."

Ivan knew about the reptiles. When he and Peter were young, his brother had crushed one with a large rock just to watch it die. Ivan had wept. It was wrong to kill such a beautiful animal, but he hadn't been able to stop Peter. In the turtle's agonizing moments of death, Ivan recalled it said something like, "I'm passing my spirit into you. Use it wisely."

All these years later, Ivan wasn't sure about the memory. He had been a little boy, after all. Nor had he discovered what the turtle had meant by his comment.

"I don't think I've ever seen one," Maynard said, stretching his neck, though they were too far away to see it.

As the three approached the creek, Ivan buried his nose in the bend of his arm. "There's a terrible stench here. Is it the reek of gryphon scat?"

"I've never smelled such a thing." The servant wrinkled his nose.

"It's horrid." Ivan lowered his arm and shook his head. "What do you think it is, Sebastian?"

Holding up the palm of his hand, Sebastian said,

"Spirits don't have the gift of smell, you'll recall."

"Oh, I didn't know that, either." Maynard gave him a sad look.

"The stench is growing stronger." Ivan's forehead rippled as he scanned the area. Alfred and Canute held back, crouching near a gorse bush. *What are they afraid of?*

Bounty stepped close to the creek's bank. Tromping the tall grass, his shoulders quivered. At first, the other two horses snorted and hesitated. Then they joined Bounty, lowered their heads, and drank from the fast stream.

"Is there danger here?" Ivan asked.

"I'm not certain." Sebastian pivoted his head to look up the creek and down. "Something…"

Creeping from the gorse bush, Canute woofed toward the water and moved closer. Alfred held back, barking aggressively.

On the opposite side, several large boulders seemed to move—just a slight change in position. Ivan noticed. *Or am I imagining things?*

A pretty redstart flew down from a nearby tree and pecked at the bank where the dirt had shifted. She was intent on finding new worms or bugs for her family. Abruptly, she let out a sharp twitter, leaped from the slope, and returned to the canopy above.

More earth moved, tumbling over itself.

Ivan's gaze stayed fixed. "Sebastian, do you see…?"

In a quick moment, two, three, four rocks broke apart and rolled into the creek, splashing loudly as they hit the water. Huge amounts of dirt were suddenly shoved away by some kind of huge rodent.

A black animal poked his hairy head out from the

mound. It lifted its nose, sniffed, and let out a terrible squeal.

When Maynard's horse jumped and whinnied, Maynard leaned forward and gripped the steed's mane, trying to stay seated. "What is that awful thing?" he screamed.

Before Sebastian could caution them, Ivan yelled, "It's a rat! Big as a pony."

The dark rodent stopped and glared with beady red eyes. Heavy folds of leathery, dark flesh pulled down from the creature's cheeks, looking like jowls on a portly man. Its whiskers and nose twitched, and its nostrils expanded.

"Let's get out of here." Ivan stroked Bounty's neck, trying to keep him under control.

Throwing up a hand, Maynard yelled, "I-I have no weapon."

"Yes, leave us," Sebastian shouted.

The servant jerked on his horse's reins and turned him in the same direction they'd just come. "I'll get help," he hollered.

Ivan's eyes went wide. He waved briskly at Maynard. "Find someone, fast!"

Two more heads pushed through the surface, dislodging rocks and dirt that rolled into the water. The next creature was reddish-brown, the other silver-haired. Both had the same leathery-fleshed jowls and hungry eyes. Jumping from rock to rock, they crossed the creek until they reached the same side as Sebastian and Ivan.

"Ratlings," Sebastian shrieked. "Let's get out of here, *now*."

Concerned for his beagles, Ivan remembered their reckless actions when confronted with the dangerous

Swamp Dragons. "Canute, Alfred. Run!"

Frightened by the stench and barking dogs, Bounty reared, struck the air with his forelegs, and stumbled backward.

"Ho, Bounty." Ivan patted his horse's shoulder. He swung his arm down and jerked The Challenger from its scabbard. The sword came free the moment the black-haired Ratling leaped at Ivan—and he lurched back. The creature barely missed taking a bite out of Ivan's leg.

It all happened so fast. He couldn't raise the weapon quick enough and couldn't hold it tightly enough with only one quaking hand.

Sebastian shouted a warning.

The black Ratling came at him again, jumped higher, and aimed for Ivan's throat. Slipping to the side of his saddle to avoid sharp teeth, Ivan tried to right himself, but he'd moved too fast and too far. He plummeted to the ground and landed on his shoulder.

Pain shot through him. He was dazed and felt helpless. *What happened?*

Snarling, the black rodent crept closer. Its jaw worked up and down, and saliva dripped from its vicious mouth. Ivan blinked to clear his vision. He was horrified by the ravenous look in the creature's intense eyes. As it came within feet of him, ready to pounce, Ivan got a strong whiff of its foul odor. He coughed. In a flash, The Challenger tightened against his hand and shot upward on its own accord just as the Ratling dived at his prone victim.

The sword struck and split the creature from the base of its neck down to its groin. Mouth opened wide, the Ratling snapped back its head and screeched. A most terrible sound, like nothing Ivan had ever heard before.

Guts and blood spilled from the animal as it thrashed and scratched at the air with its badger-sharp claws.

"Ivan!" Sebastian shouted with raspy breath. "This miserable creature has me trapped. I can't escape."

It was an alarming sight. The reddish-brown Ratling's front feet held Sebastian's thin arms against the ground while his hind feet pinned Sebastian's frail legs. The creature didn't try to rip him apart as it could have. Instead, its attention stayed on Ivan and growled low and deep.

The silver Ratling, the largest of the pack, swept its long leathery tail so fast it snapped the air and then caught a rock that cracked in two. It sent pieces sailing into the trees.

"Ouchee," a tree shrieked.

The silver Ratling inched forward to where the black rodent lay on its side. Its legs kicked as it stiffened in death. Pausing, the silver Ratling licked the ooze of hot blood from his companion's slit belly, and then he drank greedily.

Ivan's chest tightened. He sat upright and strained to reach The Challenger. It had slipped from his blood-soaked hand after he'd slashed the belly of the black rodent. The silver creature seemed to study the situation. Its whiskers twitched as he moved from his feast and stepped closer to his next victim. When Ivan glanced away to grab the sword's hilt, the Ratling shot forward and knocked Ivan onto his back, putting distance between him and his weapon.

Sebastian hollered Ivan's name. "Grab The Challenger."

He couldn't reach it.

The Ratling pounced on Ivan's chest and weighed

him down. Dirt particles that clung to the rat's whiskers dropped onto Ivan's face. Long front teeth threatened, and the vile breath gagged him. A bare patch of leathery blue skin circled the animal's menacing eyes that glared at his victim.

"You deserve to die," said a voice that Ivan knew and would never forget. "My beasts will rip your throat out and drink your blood." Tereus's maniacal laugh smothered him.

Unable to pull air into his lungs, Ivan's heart beat fast like the rush of water in the creek. The silver Ratling jumped off and rolled his prey over with his claws. Just as Ivan struggled forward on his belly, trying to grab The Challenger, sharp teeth sank into his side. Powerful jaws snapped several ribs and then shifted its victim's body over to take another bite.

Ivan shrieked. Unbearable pain raced through him. Blood pumped out, saturating his skin and clothing. He struggled to escape, but the Ratling held him to the ground, its teeth going deeper. Its claws dug into Ivan's right arm and sent shocks of pain through his system. Something frothy bubbled from Ivan's lips and dribbled down his chin.

Darkness edged around him. He had to stay alert—his very life depended on it.

As if in slow motion, the silver creature opened his bloody mouth and took aim at Ivan's throat. It lunged. Ivan pulled his arm free and blocked the attack. With great effort, he pushed the beast away, beating at its head and snout. Ivan cried out for help.

The Ratling's saliva, hot and painful, shot through Ivan's veins. It felt like his insides were dissolving, along with his will to fight. His body burned with agony. With the last trickle of consciousness, he thought, *I'm dying. Melting from within.*

There was no way to measure how much time passed. It seemed like forever with forever layered on top of itself.

Distant sounds invaded his head. Galloping hooves. Maynard's voice, "This way. Hurry!"

A lady's shout rang, "Sytha, shoot the beasts before it's too late. Let your magic arrows fly."

The darkness turned to the blackest black that Ivan had ever experienced. He gave in to it. He had no choice.

Chapter 12

Revival

From another world, in the fiery deep caverns, harsh laughter vibrated against solid rock.

Tereus's voice, deep and cruel, had returned to torment him. "I warned you not to come back to my domain, Ivan Kimble. I told you to stay away. Releasing the Ratlings is only the beginning. Take heed and leave at once. Never return."

After what seemed like an eternity, Ivan crawled from the dark tunnel of his mind. He was aware his head lay cradled on someone's lap. A cool, damp cloth tenderly washed his face and neck.

"You poor thing," a voice cooed. "Poor, poor, dear man," Merridyn said.

Pain seared his entire body. He could scarcely breathe, and when he did, his lungs rattled.

His jacket and shirt had been removed. The Long Dark Cloak lay over him for warmth, covering the fresh wounds on his side.

"I'm here, inside the cloak," Sebastian said. "Close your eyes, and I'll heal you."

Ivan groaned, tipped back his head, and gurgled with anguish. Soothing warmth flooded through him. He felt the soft tapping of Sebastian's healing fingers against his side. His ribs came together, locked into place, and mended. He smelled his own flesh as it joined and fused with a soft sizzle. Though it stung, he could endure it.

And then, the pain was gone. His wounds felt cool, but tight.

He wanted to thank them. Sebastian, Maynard, the Elftens, and Merridyn, but his swollen lips were unable to form words. Confusing images swam through his head. Gray rocks melted like jelly, mounds of Ratling hair swirled away in the wind, ribbons of blood—his blood—flowed into the creek.

"Thank goodness." Merridyn placed a cool cloth over Ivan's forehead. "Bounty found us—nearly ran us over—like he was chased by the demon himself. We knew something was terribly wrong."

"I met up with Sytha and the Elftens, Merridyn, too." Maynard squatted and placed his hand on Ivan's shoulder. "I'm so sorry I left you. I-I…"

"It wasn't wise for you to be here with no weapon." Sebastian gave the servant a forgiving nod. "You found the help we needed."

"Maynard raced toward us after we left the Troll Transformation Prison with Merridyn." Sytha wiped his brow. "I hate to think what could've happened if the paperwork had taken longer than it did."

"I'm sure our hero will survive this horrible attack." Sebastian's voice trembled with regret inside the cloak.

Erikk, an Elften, came forward. "What do you want done with the carcasses?"

"Drag them into a pile and burn them." Sytha looked at each dead creature and shook his head with disgust. "Do it quickly, and don't let a single hair remain."

Another Elften moved next to the bodies, rubbing the frown lines on his forehead. "Will burning them stop other Ratlings from surfacing?"

Shrugging, Sytha answered, "There's no way to know. I thought these hideous creatures were exterminated from the Forest fifty years ago."

"Is that so, Sebastian?" Erikk addressed the spirit inside the cloak. "At one time, were they all eliminated?"

"Sebastian is trying to mend Ivan's wounds," Merridyn scolded. "Don't bother him."

"My father told us stories about annihilating these creatures from hell," Sytha said. "It's written about in the Black Book of Pearls."

Several Elftens agreed.

Minutes passed. Ivan blinked, looking up at Merridyn's delicate chin, her eyes sad and worried. He tried to close his mind from reliving the terror of the silver Ratling that attacked him. The wretched smell, its penetrating red eyes, teeth that sunk into his ribs, snapping several. If this was the kind of torture Tereus warned him about, then he truly did not belong here—ever.

Ivan's throat was so dry he could scarcely speak. "Th-those horrible creatures…"

"Dead and being burned," Merridyn answered with a forced smile.

"You washed your face," Ivan mumbled. "You look younger."

"Ha!" Sytha slapped his thigh. "You're almost clawed to death, eaten alive, and you compliment Merridyn's clean face."

The witch blushed.

"He's definitely on the mend." Erikk grinned, looking relieved.

"I believe you are healed now," Sebastian's weary

voice spoke from the cloak. "Ratling saliva has some peculiar properties that I don't recognize, and I'm not sure if I neutralized it." The spirit released himself along with wispy gray smoke from the garment, and shortly, his form solidified. "How are you feeling?"

Ivan slowly sat up and looked away. A swirl of verbal threats, mixed with maniacal laughter and dark clouds, rushed through his brain.

Merridyn gazed into Ivan's eyes. "Something's not quite right with him."

Ivan tried to suck air into his lungs but could scarcely continue. "A voice spoke to me…"

Going to his knees next to him, Sebastian took Ivan's face into his hands. "Who? Tell me what the voice said."

Ivan didn't respond.

"They're gone, now. The Ratlings have been destroyed." Sytha bent and rested both palms on Ivan's shoulders.

"Burned to ashes." Erikk coughed and held his hand over his nose, waving the smoke away. "And a most vile stink it is."

"I'm cold." Ivan pulled the Dark Cloak around his bare chest and shuddered.

Sebastian turned to ask the Elften standing nearby, "What's your name?"

"Tanner," he answered.

"Would you bring Ivan's clothes from where they're drying?" Sebastian pointed to nearby bushes. "And Erikk, try to find that darn horse of his." He indicated the animal's general whereabouts with a tip of his head. The Elften moved hurriedly in that direction.

The beagles left their hiding place and crept closer.

Alfred licked Ivan's face. Canute nudged his master's hand with his cool nose wanting his ears rubbed. The dog's affectionate gestures failed to bring Ivan to full awareness. In a daze, he lifted his hand and petted Alfred.

"He spoke to me," Ivan finally said, looking at no one.

"Who?"

"Tereus. He warned me to leave the Forest, or worse would happen."

"Bah." Sebastian squatted, put his arms around Ivan, and rocked him gently like a loving grandfather. "It's only an idle threat. He's bound to the underworld and can do nothing."

Sytha's brow crinkled.

I've heard the voice, his words. And this isn't the first time.

"He...Tereus, told me Peter doesn't want to come home. My brother doesn't care about me. He wants me dead." Ivan wrapped his arms around his head, lowered it to his bent knees, and sobbed.

"That's absolutely untrue," Sebastian said with a sharp voice. "Tereus always lies."

Merridyn dropped to her knees and pushed Sebastian away. She tightened her arms around Ivan and bawled as though her very heart were broken. Her stumpy troll fingers stroked his back. "I'm so sorry I was mean to you. I couldn't help it. Troll Prison made me a hateful person."

Sytha touched the top of Merridyn's head. "I said spiteful things to him, too. I was angry and jealous."

Tanner returned with Ivan's damp shirt and jacket draped over his arm. "What's going on here? Are we having a cleansing of the souls?"

Sebastian shrugged and sighed.

"I'm feeling a bit better," Ivan said after a while. "Thank you—all of you for your help—and friendship." He sniffed, wiping tears from his eyes.

"You are very important to us and a blessing to our Forest," Sebastian said.

Merridyn took Ivan's hand and held it. "You are a very fine friend."

"Here are your shirt and jacket." Tanner handed them to the lad. "I'll go to the creek and wash the cloak. The stench is terrible." He took the blood-soaked garment and strode in that direction, cautiously looking for any signs of more Ratlings.

Standing, Merridyn brushed the grass from her shabby dress. She let out a little cry and pointed. "Oh, my High Intervener. Those raw red marks on Ivan's side."

"The rodent bit him twice, leaving its poisonous venom in him." Sebastian straightened, clasping his hands together. "I thought I'd removed it all but can't be sure. The scars will disappear in time."

Erikk returned with Bounty in tow. For the first time, Ivan noticed the Elften's horses were soft blue with darker manes and tails. Fine-looking animals. Another oddity.

"You should've been halfway to the castle by now," Sebastian said to Sytha. "What detained you?"

"Paperwork." Sytha repeated the reason and rolled his eyes. "Never figured I'd be grateful for the stupidity of trolls, but it took some time to convince the main guard that we had clearance for Merridyn's release."

"I didn't know they could even read." Erikk

grimaced.

"Most of them can't." Sytha's forehead wrinkled. "That's what took so long."

"In this case, we, too, are grateful for the delay. If you hadn't come around when you did..." Sebastian blew out a puff of breath.

Standing clumsily, even with Merridyn and Sytha holding him, Ivan's legs quivered. He ran his fingertips down the full length of scars along his side, and terror revisited him. *I must leave the Forest, and it must be soon.*

Merridyn helped him with his damp, ragged shirt that still retained a whiff of Ratling saliva. She held the jacket and tenderly eased him into it.

The tears in his clothing and the lingering smell were the least of his problems. He was grateful to be alive.

Gesturing for Erikk to bring his horse closer, Ivan abruptly announced, "I'm going home." He avoided their eyes. "I don't belong here, and I don't wish to stay any longer."

Sebastian's frail body jerked. "I know how you must feel, but this couldn't be foreseen. You have many friends who love you. They—we—rushed to help."

"I know, and I'm thankful to all of you. But I'm leaving."

"Wait." Sebastian walked after him. "Please reconsider and make the journey to the Witches' Village with me."

Ivan chewed on his inner cheek, considering Sebastian's plea. Right then, he wanted to go home to the farm, his chores, and the Graydon Village School. Comfort and dependability awaited him there.

But, if I leave, how will I find Peter and learn if Tereus is lying?

Merridyn stood on her toes, wrapped her arms around him, and hugged him gently. Stepping back, she removed a chain from around her neck that held an ornate key. "This is to my cottage in the Witches' Village, number 13. She draped it over his head. "Help yourself to anything you need. If you knock on Arnie and Season's door, number 11, they'll be happy to make you supper." As further enticement, she added, "Season makes the best stew you've ever tasted. She uses dried herbs and spices from her garden. Arnie is the village baker. His fresh bread is renowned."

"It sounds good." Ivan licked his lips as he reconsidered.

"Oh, and Season will wash and mend your clothes, too."

Tanner brought the wet cloak from the creek and shook away the excess water. He held it out and waited for someone to claim it. Ivan hesitated, even pulled back a little.

"I'll wear it until it dries." Sebastian reached for the garment, draped it over his shoulders, and tied the strings. His bushy white eyebrows rose as he searched Ivan's face for a change of mind. None came.

"I have no need for it." Eyes downcast, Ivan turned away.

Nearly somersaulting onto his horse, Sytha said, "You're greatly appreciated, Ivan Kimble. I admire your courage and selflessness." He chuckled and added, "You'd make a fine Elften."

"Th-thank you, I-I…" Ivan tilted his head, trying to find the right words.

Waving, Sytha's gaze fixed on him. "Hurry to the castle. We'll feast and dance with the pretty ladies there."

Ivan was more secure now that his friendship had been mended with Sytha, but he still wanted to leave. The message about Peter wishing him dead coursed through his veins. Despair tried to pull him back into the dark tunnel.

The Elftens gave Ivan a pat on the back and uttered a farewell.

"Don't worry about the fire." Erikk covered his nose. "It'll go out by itself and will burn the beasts—nothing else."

Tanner helped Merridyn mount the blue stallion she'd ridden. He took her hand and squeezed. Then he leaped on behind her, encircling the witch's waist. Ivan noticed the tenderness, the glazed look in the Elften's eyes, and he was pleased about Merridyn's new friend.

She turned to smile and wave at them. "I'll see you at the castle."

"I'm traveling with Sebastian and Ivan," Maynard stated. "Someone has to look after these two vagabonds."

One of the Elftens called back at them, "You should be safe with Maynard protecting you." They laughed good-naturedly. Hooves pounded against the ground as a collection of blue horses left Ancient Oak Creek. Merridyn happily followed.

As soon as they were out of sight, Ivan walked in Bounty's direction. "I can find my way out of the Forest," he said over his shoulder.

"Hold up. I have an idea." Sebastian dashed after him.

Ivan kept going until his companion grabbed his

arm.

"Wait!" Sebastian called.

"You're not going to talk me out of it this time. I'm going home."

They faced each other. "It's late in the day, and there's not enough time to leave the Forest. It will be dangerous to ride by yourself in the dark. Let's stop at the abandoned Harvesters' Cottages—it's not far from here. We'll travel to the Witches' Village tomorrow at daybreak." He took a hurried breath and added, "And…you are still in shock and need to rest after what you've been through."

"It will do you good." Maynard nodded. "I'll lodge the horses and find something to eat in the cupboards.

"If you still want to leave in the morning, I'll ride back with you." Sebastian released Ivan's arm.

Rubbing his forehead, Ivan's fingers got tangled in his blood-dried hair. They hadn't made it to the creek to drink or wash before those terrible creatures had attacked. He'd never go back to that horrible place for any reason. Never!

Canute cried, circling Ivan's legs. He must have heard Maynard's comment about eating.

"All right, but tomorrow I'm going home. It's safer with my cows."

Chapter 13

The Night Scream

True to Sebastian's words, the Harvesters' Cottages were not far. It was impossible to count the number of small structures, unkempt and weather-beaten, scattered behind the wattle fences and clusters of gnarled oaks. The front lawns showed neglected gardens with tall weeds and dried vines.

"Seasonal workers leave after the crops are in." Sebastian swept his hand in an arc. "Next spring, they'll be back to plant, harvest the fields, and tend their gardens."

"Which ones are empty, Maynard?" Ivan halted, trying to spot a suitable place to stay for the night. Feeling dizzy from the toxins that must still circulate in his body, he was anxious to settle in and lie down.

"I believe all are, sir. Even the caretaker leaves."

"Are you all right?" Sebastian's cheeks tightened with concern.

"I'm not feeling real well," he answered, holding his forehead.

"We'll find a place to rest soon." Maynard's brow wrinkled with worry.

After they selected a cottage, Ivan pulled his saddlebags from Bounty. He pushed against the arched wooden door. It creaked and groaned as though the hinges denied them entrance, warning of danger. Old cooking odors, combined with the stale smell of unwashed linens, assaulted Ivan and Maynard upon stepping inside.

"Charming," Ivan mumbled and held his nose.

Ivan managed to find the strength to help Maynard stable their horses and scrounge up what hay they could find to feed the animals, and then they pumped fresh water into a trough. Behind a shed, Ivan found an old battered milk pail and filled it from a well near the front entrance. He hauled it into the cottage and set it on a rickety wooden stand covered with oilcloth.

Tottering, Ivan reached out a hand to steady himself. Maynard caught him with a firm grip around his waist. "You must drink and rest. It will help you feel better."

"I'll take care of him." Sebastian indicated that Ivan should sit on one of the three slender beds in the room while he washed dried blood from the boy's scalp. He motioned to Maynard. "Find us some food. Check every cottage if need be."

"Sir." The servant bowed and moved toward the door.

"No need for protocol. We're in the wilderness, not the castle."

"I understand your meaning." Maynard chuckled and walked out into the cold, late afternoon air.

Plopping onto one of the beds, Ivan closed his eyes and hoped to ease the throb in his head. "The room is spinning, and my stomach feels awful."

Sebastian removed the now-dried Long Dark Cloak that he'd been wearing and threw it over Ivan. "I must've missed some trace of the Ratling's venom." His image turned to gray smoke, entered the garment, and dissolved the last of the toxins trapped in Ivan's veins.

When Maynard returned, he had two cans of soup and one can of beans in his arms. "It isn't much, but it should feed us tonight." He moved to the small kitchen area and prepared their supper.

Ivan sat up on the bed and spooned the hot soup into his mouth, reluctant to eat too much since his stomach was queasy. His beagles showed no hesitation and gobbled down as much as the servant would give them.

"Those Ratlings are the most horrible creatures I've ever seen in the Forest." Maynard's brow wrinkled.

"Tereus brought them back for the purpose of killing me," Ivan said. "You noticed the creature didn't claw Sebastian to death, as it easily could have."

"You're right. It could've killed me anytime it pleased." Sebastian placed his hand over his heart. "They were definitely more interested in you. I prayed the High Intervener would save you from a horrendous death."

"Your prayers must've worked," Ivan said dimly. "Tereus told me he had worse—much worse waiting for me—unless I left the Forest."

"So, that's why you wanted to leave?" Sebastian raised his voice with surprise.

"No. It was because Tereus said Peter didn't care about me."

"You believe his lies?" Sebastian gave Ivan a long, hard stare. "I told you Peter loves you greatly."

"Then where is he?"

"We'll find him. Maybe the witches can tell us something useful." Sebastian's lips spread a hopeful smile.

Ivan forced a nod, not feeling satisfied.

"You need to sleep now," Sebastian said and

stepped away.

During the night, Ivan awoke in the darkness with a strange feeling of helplessness.

He wondered where he was until he remembered they'd settled into a dust-and-mud-occupied cottage, northwest of Ancient Oak Creek. The cans of soup Maynard had prepared were just passable. Ivan wondered how long they'd been on the shelf. He burped, and a foul taste coated the roof of his mouth,

Alfred and Canute snored beside his bed. All was quiet, and then…

A terrifying scream suddenly penetrated the limestone walls of the cottage.

Ivan shot to his feet and stood on the cold floor beside his bed. A bewildered Sebastian pushed himself from his chair and stood shakily.

"What in the world was that?" Maynard's voice trembled. He propped himself up on his elbow and looked around in the darkness.

They waited for Sebastian to explain, but he had no answers.

Another blood-curdling wail before it receded into the distance. It sounded like a woman's cry for help.

Ivan reached for his trousers, and his bare legs shivered.

"No." Sebastian grabbed Ivan's upper arm. "We mustn't go out there until the light of morning. Whatever it is, the damage has been done." He lowered his head, shaking it slowly.

"But someone is in danger." Ivan glanced at him, eyes beseeching. "Maybe we can help."

"It could be a ploy to lure us out into the open and harm us." Sebastian moved to a window where he spread the sun-faded, dirty curtains aside.

"What do you see?" Maynard asked, frozen in place.

"Nothing. It's too dark."

Ivan pulled on his shirt, ignoring the gaping tear where the Ratling had bitten him, buttoned it, and turned his face away from the odor that lingered.

"I forbid you to leave this cottage," Sebastian said with a strong voice and scowled.

"But…someone is hurt, she—"

"You've got to get over feeling like you need to save everyone." Sebastian pointed at the bed. "Now get some sleep. Daylight is only a couple hours away."

Reluctantly, Ivan crawled into bed and worried about the poor lady. *Could it be someone like pretty Merridyn who screamed for help, and no one came to her aid?* He slept fitfully, turning his pillow trying to find a spot that didn't smell like old dandruff and drool.

The next morning, Ivan whirled the cloak around his shoulders and glanced at Sebastian who seemed satisfied that Ivan would now wear the garment. Donning the scabbard, he shoved The Challenger into its hold. "I'm happy to have you by my side," he said to the sword. "I think we are going to need your protection."

"Anything I can do to help you," The Challenger replied.

"How are you feeling?" Sebastian glanced up from a rickety wooden chair with no cushion for comfort where he'd spent the night.

"Much better, but for lack of a solid night's sleep."

Maynard yawned. "I'm about the same. I keep thinking about that desperate lady that hollered in the dark."

"I'm stepping out to relieve myself." Ivan opened

the door for his beagles to follow. They raced in front of their master examining several suitable bushes.

"I'll accompany you." Maynard hurriedly tied his shoes and stood to make his bed as neatly as any trained chambermaid.

The crisp morning air greeted them as the sun hugged the horizon. Maynard wrapped his arms around his chest and blew out a puff of air. "I should've grabbed my jacket."

Ivan gazed at row after row of shabby cottages with deep remorse, searching for any evidence of the lady who'd screamed in the night. Maybe Sebastian was right, there was nothing he could have done. He would never know.

"I think we should look around to find the cause of the screams." Ivan threw a questioning glance at the servant.

"If you wish." Maynard visibly gulped and licked his lips. "But let's do our sleuthing on horseback. Then we'll have a chance to escape, if need be."

"That sounds sensible."

They did their business and returned to the cottage. Determined to convince Sebastian they needed to investigate the strange cries they'd all heard.

Now, if only Sebastian will agree.

"We want to scout about and discover who made those terrible noises last night." Ivan looked down at his boots, hoping to avoid Sebastian's disapproving eyes.

At last, the ripples left Sebastian's forehead and he sighed. "Okay. We'll follow a couple of paths around the cottages and see what caused the disturbance. If we can't find any reason, we'll agree to leave at once and make way to the Witches' Village."

After retrieving their horses from the stable, they moved slowly between two dilapidated structures where one of the roofs had collapsed. Suddenly, Maynard threw his arm forward. "Look there, ahead."

Ivan gawked at a small lamb trapped in a wattle fence. Its head and forelegs were stuck in the tangle of misshaped wooden limbs. Tongue hanging out, it didn't move.

"Is it...d-dead?" Maynard whispered.

"Stop here," Ivan said as he slipped from his saddle to see if it was still alive. "Keep the beagles quiet so they don't startle her." He tried to be silent as he drew closer, afraid she would become terrified and struggle to release herself.

When Ivan was three feet away from the animal, it raised its head and bleated. Not the human sound they'd heard the night before. "Please, little lamb, be still now. I'm going to help remove you from the fence." He kept his arms and hands to his sides, with no unnecessary movement under the cloak.

The lamb cried out once more, its eyes wide with fear. She pulled and tugged and rammed against the wooden structure trying to break free. But it only made her imprisonment worse.

Ivan squatted before her, lifted and gently pushed her head out, and then guided the injured leg from its entanglement.

At once, she stood to her feet, stumbled, took a few more unsteady steps, stumbling again. She turned and gave Ivan a large-eyed curious stare, then limped into the brush where her mother called with loud bleats.

"Well done." Sebastian released his hold on Canute and clapped his hands. Maynard did the same with

Albert.

"I don't think she was badly hurt," Ivan said, wiping the lamb's blood on his trousers.

"That's a relief." Sebastian grinned.

Now that the major trauma was over, the beagles were noticeably put out that they didn't get breakfast that morning except cold soup from the night before. Canute whimpered and jumped at Ivan begging for more food.

"Sorry, ol' mate. I'm sure we'll be well-fed once we reach the Witches' Village." Ivan glanced at Sebastian, who confirmed this with a nod.

Mounting their horses, they left the Harvesters' Cottages, riding side by side,

They made several stops to wait for Canute who heaved his breakfast on the grass. Ivan dismounted and selected a log to sit on. He pulled his beagle onto his lap and rubbed his belly, speaking soft, encouraging words. Canute whimpered and squirmed. Then his beagle leaped from Ivan's arms and retched again. Alfred stayed close, pawing at Ivan's leg, or touching his brother's nose with his own. The scene played out several times. Apparently, that morning, he'd eaten some bad soup—or something. Sebastian and Maynard fussed over the sick dog. Their sympathy and patience never wavered. When Canute seemed recovered, well enough to travel, they continued their journey.

Chapter 14

Witches' Village

It was mid-afternoon before the three weary travelers reached their destination. "There's the entrance to the Witches' Village." Sebastian pointed.

Ivan read the sign as they rode down the gravel covered pathway. *You are Entering Witches' Village. Do you have Permission to Step on Hallowed Ground? No trolls or Ghouls Allowed.*

"Dogs are always welcome." Sebastian mollified Ivan's worried look.

"This is where I turn off." Maynard shifted in the saddle and stretched his legs.

"Are you safe on the road alone?" Ivan frowned.

"Several soldiers in Simon's garrison will be waiting for me on Sheepherder's Path Road, a little farther south from here.

"How did this come about?" Ivan turned to Maynard with a surprised look on his face.

"We arranged it yesterday, while you were being cared for by Sebastian. Having them meet me seemed like the safest thing to do."

"Safe journey then," Ivan and Sebastian called, waving.

An arching, rusted-metal structure stretched over the entry of the Witches' Village. It featured cut-outs of flying witches on broomsticks wearing big pointed hats, cats with their backs bowed in fright, stars and moons scattered at random.

"Is this a joke?" Ivan was quite amused.

"It certainly is," Sebastian replied. "The blacksmith has a great sense of humor. There isn't anything he can't fashion out of metal."

A mass of weathered, twisted tree limbs were woven together to form a wattle fence, looking like thick snakes that formed a barrier around the entire village. Ivan liked the unusual look. Propped against the fence were straw bales, bundled corn stalks, and various size pumpkins.

Ivan grinned. "Charming."

Canute jumped sideways when he faced the display of pumpkins. He spun around and barked at one of the big orange things that showed a frightened carved face. Joining his brother, Alfred woofed at the straw scarecrow after a mouse poked out its nose and sped across the field.

"That's a good dog." Sebastian laughed.

As they entered, Ivan studied the odd construction of the village homes. Unsettling, yet fascinating from an engineering viewpoint. Built on a series of rolling hills, the cottages were half-timbered with shingled roofs and small turrets. Some were two, three, and four narrow stories high with multiple balconies protruding on every side. The chimneys puffed white smoke, while the afternoon breeze carried it away.

Inside the entrance, they tied the horses' reins over a hitching rail. Ahead lay open fields where Ivan smelled the rich plowed earth and saw farmers working the land. On foot, Sebastian led the way walking a winding stone path that seemed to stretch haphazardly through the hills.

"I'm not real sure how to find my way in this maze of cottages," Sebastian mumbled, squinting. "It's been ages since I've been here."

Some of the houses were so tall and close together that only two people, shoulder to shoulder, could squeeze between them. The labyrinth of structures repeated itself in different color combinations and directions. Several privileged large trees and gardens were allowed space to grow on the hills.

"Why is it so crowded?" Ivan followed Sebastian. Stepping aside, he avoided a low picket fence.

"It began with a colony of thirteen witches in the mid-fifteenth century," Sebastian replied. "More came, banding together to avoid the persecution that happened over the years. This area was declared hallowed ground by the elder witches."

"They've been here since then—in this place?"

"No. Long ago, the witches settled near the Windermere Mountains in the far north." Sebastian looked up from house to house, twisting his head. "They were routinely invaded by the ghouls who lived too close for comfort. Those ghastly beasts stole and destroyed the witches' property countless times. The small coven finally moved to this sacred location. They felt safe here and started families, planted gardens, and farmed their crops. We skirted their community fields that located near the entrance."

Ivan had noticed.

"Well, the witches prospered and grew. Maybe grew too much and too fast. There's barely room for any new homes on these sanctified hills. That's why they build narrow and high."

"What makes the hills so sacred?" Ivan swiveled to

study the layout, but his view was blocked by thick clusters of houses with jutting chimneys and balconies.

Sebastian pushed his spectacles higher on his nose. "If I remember right, it's written in the Black Book of Pearls that these hills would be awarded to the witches. I believe it has something to do with the burial of their great witch rulers from long ago."

Ivan gazed at his feet, wondering how many past elders lay buried under his boots.

"There's also a Protection Spell on the village," Sebastian said. "Placed here a century ago."

"Do the witches know Peter?"

"Oh, yes," Sebastian answered at once. "There are few people in the Forest who don't know Peter. He had a lot of time to wander, make friends, and get into mischief. You'll have to ask if anyone has seen him, lately."

"I'll do that. But for now, how do we find Merridyn's cottage?" Ivan scanned the area trying to make sense of the numbering system. "The key she gave me says number 13. Where would that be?"

"Well…" Sebastian looked up, shielding his eyes from the afternoon sun.

A man with a head of thick, rusty brown hair opened the shutters above their heads on the fourth floor. He stepped out on a small balcony, staring down quizzically. Just when Ivan believed his beagles were too tired to react to their strange surroundings, Canute yipped and growled. "What are you doing in our village?" the man asked in a gruff voice.

Sebastian called back. "We're looking for Merridyn Hampstead's cottage, number 13."

"What do you want of her?"

Ivan folded his arms around his chest in an attempt to cover his torn shirt and cloak. He must look like a lowly beggar, or a vagabond, as Maynard had called them earlier. Taking a deep breath Ivan said, "We have Merridyn's permission to stay at her cottage for the night."

"Oh. And where's your proof?"

"A key." Ivan pulled it from beneath his shirt, showing it to the doubtful man.

"Well, then." He scratched his head. "Why didn't you say so in the first place?"

"Friendly chap, isn't he?" Ivan whispered.

Sebastian chuckled under his breath. "People here are leery of strangers. They still fear the possibility of ghouls returning to pillage their homes and fields. It may also explain why they don't want a tight connection with Zephyrus, his rules and regulations."

"They don't trust him?"

"Just cautious." Sebastian shifted his feet.

"Hold on. I'll come down and lead the way," the man called. His footsteps sounded on the flights of stairs. One, two, three, four.

Sniffing the air, Ivan smelled stew simmering and the yeasty aroma of baked bread. He licked his lips. His stomach rumbled. *Coming to the Witches' Village is the right decision.*

Faint conversations came through the open shutters and half-doors of the closely packed cottages. "I believe everyone knows we're here," Ivan said quietly.

"Probably." Sebastian glanced this way and that, his manner cautious. "It's their way of protecting the village. They listen to everyone's business."

Canute raised his head and barked.

There was a loud hiss. Above them, on the balcony railing, hunched a charcoal-colored cat with white paws, staring at Ivan with narrowed yellow eyes. He hissed again.

"Well, look who's here to greet us," Sebastian said. "It's Pousses."

Ivan remembered Pousses as a nasty tempered, persnickety cat that could fly. He usually lived at the castle—spoiled as they come.

"Why aren't you at the castle?" Sebastian asked the cat.

"Lord Graydon is expecting company," Pousses replied in a meowing voice. "He has no time for me when those snooty lords and ladies show up in their fancy carriages. I hate all that pretend-stuff."

Head tilted upward, Ivan said, "Yesterday we saw one of the royal carriages traveling south on Sheepherder's Path Road. That must mean they've arrived safely."

Pousses huffed. He tucked his paws under his chin and yawned.

"Brat," Sebastian said under his breath.

The man who'd stepped out from the Dutch-door wore an apron that smelled of flour and yeast. The thickness of his sideburns made his face appear broad and mysterious. Right then he frowned, but the lines around his mouth showed he knew about smiling and laughter. He glanced at the beagles that sniffed his trouser legs. They must've caught the delicious smell of baked bread.

The sky turned blue-gray as the sun moved closer to the horizon. Ivan wondered if they'd disturbed the man's supper.

"My name's Arnie." He offered a hand, his eyebrows knitted. "The village baker."

"Oh. We were told about you." Ivan bowed and introduced himself and Sebastian.

"And who mentioned me?"

"Merridyn Hempstead suggested we knock on your door." Sebastian pulled on his whiskers. "She told us you were good friends and close neighbors." He allowed his sentence to fade away when Arnie's attention was diverted.

"You must be Peter's younger brother." Arnie cocked his head, eyeing Ivan. "You look a lot alike. Tall. Same shape face. He talked about you all the time."

"Did he?" Excitement pounded in Ivan's chest. A quick and warning look from Sebastian caused Ivan to wait before asking further questions.

"I'm Sebastian of the Cloak." He extended a hand, and the man shook it in a friendly manner.

Arnie smiled at him. "I've heard a lot about you."

"I don't leave the Sanctuary of Truth very often. Mostly for my own protection and safety. Though I did visit your village years ago and was fascinated by your goodwill and unity."

Arnie nodded and looked pleased. "We've all heard the tragic news about the attack on Zephyrus and the Forest War."

"He's recovering nicely." Sebastian placed his hand on Ivan's forearm. "Thanks to this lad beside me."

Arnie leaned in closer to examine the young man. "I'd be interested to know the details."

"We'll tell you later, after we've rested and had some supper." Sebastian glimpsed at Alfred and Canute, indicating they'd need to be included.

"Follow me, then. I'll show you Merridyn's cottage." He turned to Sebastian. "I realize you have no need for luggage. How about you, young fellow?"

"I left saddlebags on my horse. He is tied at the entrance."

The baker scratched at his sideburns. "I'll have someone stable the horses and bring your bags, then."

Thanking him, Ivan asked, "Shouldn't Merridyn's home be near yours since you are number 11?"

"You'd think so, wouldn't you?" We intentionally keep them out of sequence for protection from undesirable visitors."

They trailed the baker up and down stone pathways, over and around small hills and gardens, and crisscrossed through several witches' lawns until Arnie halted in front of number 13. The door was painted purple with swirling gold designs of half-moons, planets, and stars. Thrusting his arms forward with a comical gesture, lifting his chin, he presented the cottage. "Here you are!

"Merridyn is extremely important in the community," Arnie said. "Her skills with herbs and spices, mixing potions, healing and the like, are legendary. This unique gift gives her the honor of having the most sacred number on the hill. A privilege, by the way, that makes some folks unhappy."

Ivan wondered if Arnie meant Lyla, Merridyn's sister. That would, in part, explain Lyla's jealousy. But he didn't think it polite to ask right then.

A pot of geraniums had withered and died on the top stoop. To the right, a small herb garden was fashioned in a semi-circle. Mints and tarragon grew in the middle while patches of yarrow, chervil, and chives surrounded it. It was well cared for, weeded and healthy. Ivan recognized some of the plants from his mother's own garden.

Arnie grunted and stooped to examine the pot of dead geraniums. "Looks like Benny forgot to water these flowers."

Clearing his throat, Ivan said, "This keyhole isn't real, only painted on the door." He removed the key chain from around his neck.

The man chuckled under his breath. "No need for it." Arnie pushed the door open. "See—not locked. The key simply indicates the number of the house. Actually, it's a useless formality. If you aren't meant to enter, the door won't open. Part of the Protection Spell."

"Yes, I see," Ivan mumbled, wondering how a door would know such a thing.

They entered the cottage where Arnie lit two kerosene lanterns, but Ivan hesitated. "These are my beagles, King Alfred and King Canute."

"It's fine to bring them inside. Merridyn would approve. She loves animals."

Ivan peeked at Sebastian and remembered the girl's hysteria when his dogs had knocked her over in an ickleberry patch. It was true—prison had changed her basically kind nature.

The guests stepped into the kitchen. "The bedrooms are always on the third and fourth floors. The privies are on the first—down that hall. Bathtub, too. Kitchen may seem a bit cramped, but it serves Merridyn's needs—that is, it has in the past. Everything else probably explains itself."

All sorts of herbs, gathered in small tied bundles, hung from the ceiling. They added a pleasant fragrance to the room.

"You must be hungry after your journey." Arnie brushed flour from his apron and then pulled a clean tablecloth from a cupboard. "I'll get your supper in a minute."

Ivan licked his lower lip remembering what Merridyn said about the delicious stew that Season, Arnie's wife, was known to make. Sebastian helped spread the tablecloth while Ivan went through several drawers until he found cutlery.

A well-used recipe card was propped on the counter next to a mortar and pestle marked: Colds, Coughs, and Chest Complaints. The card read: *Add bergamot or red mushroom powder for a good sleep.* Ivan supposed the ingredients looked harmless enough but couldn't be sure. The names of herbs, garlic, yarrow, and horehound written on labels, were wrapped around various bottles resting on the counter.

He recalled what Arnie had said, "Everyone listens to everyone else's business." *Did Merridyn's close neighbors see or hear an intruder who had poisoned the potion?*

"We try to keep the cottage tidy in case Merridyn comes home." Arnie removed dust from the countertop with the flat of his hand. "There, that's better. You should have time to rest and become acquainted with the place while I'm gone." He moved to the door where it opened on its own accord.

Alfred dashed past Arnie's legs.

"Is it okay to let them wander about and do their business?" Ivan asked.

"Perfectly safe." Arnie stooped and picked up Canute, pressing him to his chest. "You are a beautiful beagle. Maybe you want to stay with me and not go home

with Ivan, huh? I'll feed you good bread every day."
Canute squirmed to get down. Arnie set the beagle to his
feet and the three of them left cottage number 13.

After he removed the cloak and unbuckled the
scabbard that held The Challenger, Ivan plopped down
on a short couch near the kitchen. He laid his head back,
intending to rest for only a moment, but he quickly fell
asleep.

Chapter 15

The Baker and His Wife

A soft rap on the door awakened Ivan with a start.

Sebastian raised himself from a comfortable rocker in a corner and answered the knock. A pretty lady, her curly brown hair covered with a paisley kerchief, entered, carrying a lumpy flour sack with what smelled like freshly baked bread. Behind her, a young lad held a hot cauldron's handle with a quilted mitten. It appeared almost too heavy for such a slight fellow. He placed it on the table and stepped back, not lifting his gaze to greet the strangers.

Ivan shot off the couch, embarrassed that he'd fallen asleep. The intoxicating aroma of food drew him to the stew pot. He lifted the lid where he spotted big chunks of lamb, potatoes, and several root vegetables steeping in thick gravy. Taking a deep breath, he inhaled the delicious aroma that made him weak in the knees from hunger.

The door swung open. Arnie entered the kitchen, allowing Alfred and Canute to race ahead of him. "This is Season, my wife." Arnie took the bag of bread from her. "And, this is Benny, the blacksmith's son." He placed his hand on the boy's head, ruffling his hair. "Doesn't say much." The boy flushed and turned his face to the floor, again.

Season gave a curtsey and smiled at her guests.

"I love your dogs," Arnie said. "Are they brothers?"

"They are."

Not known to be shy when they got a whiff of food, Canute nudged Arnie's ankle, jumped up, and pawed at him. Since Canute had emptied his stomach during their journey to the Witches' Village, Ivan knew his beagle was ravenous.

"Ha!" the baker laughed. "You little rascals smell my rosemary bread and honey-nut scones, don't you?"

Alfred and Canute wiggled their hind ends rapidly as their tails whipped the air.

"Our guests' horses are tied at the entrance," Arnie said to the boy. "Would you please stable them and bring Ivan's saddlebags?" Benny bowed and hurried out the door.

"Goodness. What happened to your clothes, young man?" Season's eyes expanded twice their size. "You have a fight with banshees?" She shoved her hand through the large tear in Ivan's jacket and shirt. "They give off a foul odor. Let me have those later, and I'll wash and mend them tonight."

"Thank you, ma'am." Ivan bowed and gave her a big grin. The Long Dark Cloak, now draped over the couch where he had fallen asleep, would need the same attention. He indicated with a sweep of his hand. *What good luck! We are in the company of two fine witches who are willing to help us.*

"Same goes for your leggings." She tipped her head toward Sebastian. "Looks like you skinned your knees trying to escape the same battle as Ivan."

Sebastian seemed tickled over the comment, but he didn't explain their unfortunate meeting with Merridyn.

Placing a small crock of butter on the table, Season turned to the counter and sliced various kinds of bread with shiny brown crusts. "This is what Arnie bakes in his ovens for the villagers," she said, giving her husband an admiring look. She put the tray on the table next to the butter, straightening the cutlery and napkins for their guests.

Arnie filled the bowls with stew and fed the beagles who lost no time gobbling it up.

Season addressed their guests with some skepticism lacing her tone, "You must know Merridyn very well to have gotten the key to her cottage."

They sat at the table with Sebastian at the end, where he fiddled with his cutlery. Though their hosts must've known that Sebastian, as a spirit, didn't eat, they seemed to think on it for several moments.

"Yes, we arranged for her removal from Troll Transformation Prison." Ivan reached for a slice of bread and slathered a generous measure of butter.

"The Elftens escorted her to the South Castle yesterday afternoon," Sebastian said. "She's probably being treated like royalty by Lord Graydon right now."

Season's face brightened. "Thank you both." She teared. "It must've been simply dreadful for her being confined in prison with those heathen trolls. Bad enough she lost her husband and little boy, but to suffer without trial in that beastly dump. Well, it's simply shameful."

Sebastian and Ivan agreed.

Ladling the stew into the bowls on the table, Season said, "Sorry you don't partake, Sebastian. You have no idea how satisfying my stew is." She chuckled at her lack of humility.

"So, I've gathered by the compliments of your

friend, Merridyn." He grinned.

"Most residents don't believe Merridyn was to blame." Arnie changed the subject and shook his head. "But we are at a loss to figure how such a thing could happen without anyone seeing a stranger in our village."

Recalling the details Merridyn had told them, Ivan studied the distance from the kitchen window to the small stove near it. *Short enough for the length of a man's arm if he stretched a bit. She said a broken oak leaf had blown into the open window. Yes. It was entirely possible for someone outside to drop in the poison. But what proof was a broken leaf? And who did such a terrible thing?*

Resting his arms on the table, Sebastian leaned forward and told them the reason for their visit to the village. "We thought you had the Golden Lantern and that Bartholomew was going to replace the broken glass."

"That's true." Arnie ran his fingers over his whiskered chin. "Bart fixed it, and then he personally took it to the South Castle yesterday, along with four or five strong men from our village. They carried spears and bows over their shoulders with quivers full of arrows, not about to take any chances of losing the lantern again."

"Richard Graydon must've been well-pleased." Ivan blew over the hot stew to cool it and took his first bite. He wanted to moan with pleasure at the taste, but good manners ruled his silence.

"That he was." A return smile played at Arnie's lips. "We plan to use Lord Graydon's generous contribution to help pay for Merridyn's trial—next week, I believe it is."

"Zello's fiery breath must light the wick, you see."

Season explained further, "He's the castle dragon. The lantern is of no use until that's done. And now, that short-tempered dragon has burned down his own stable. Have you ever heard of such nonsense? What has gotten into this Forest, anyway?" Shaking her head, she rose from her chair and put a fire under the tea kettle.

"The Ancient Relics are too precious to be careless with." Arnie leaned to his side and checked if the beagles wanted more stew. They did, and with a nod to Season, she refilled their bowls.

Ivan took advantage of a short lull in the conversation. "Tell me, have you seen my brother, Peter?"

Arnie raised his eyebrows and pursed his lips. "Haven't seen him for a long time, have we?" He turned to his wife. "Peter used to visit quite often, sometimes helping in my bakery and staying for supper. We enjoyed his company—and he loved Season's cooking."

"My brother promised to come home, but he hasn't." Ivan blinked moisture away, hoping Arnie hadn't seen it. "Now I'm worried something has happened. No one knows where to find him."

"I'm sorry." Arnie sat up straight in his chair with a determined look. "If we hear any news, we'll let Zephyrus know at once."

"You might ask Bartholomew," Season suggested. "Peter was good friends with him and his family. He was very fond of little Benny, too."

"Can Benny speak, or is he just timid?" Ivan remembered his own shyness and tendency to stutter when he was younger.

Arnie pulled in his shoulders. "About the time Merridyn was accused of poisoning her family, Benny stopped speaking."

"No one knows why he suddenly went mute," Season said. "Not even his parents, and that makes them very sad."

"Curious." Sebastian swept his fingers through his unruly hair.

"How did you get that bump on your forehead?" Arnie stared at Ivan. "And those long tears in your clothes? Looks like you've taken quite a beating."

Ivan nodded and told how the trolls bound him to a tree and stoned him. "They thought I had the Golden Lantern, you see."

"I tell you…" Arnie's brow wrinkled. "Those trolls can be a real nuisance. I wish I could train them to help in my bakery. Make them productive citizens."

"I wouldn't put much hope in that possibility." Season lifted an eyebrow. "Goals and ambition aren't traits that trolls inherit after Transformation Prison." Arnie nodded.

Sebastian related the story about the return of the Ratlings. "Those creatures were resurrected by Tereus. He wants to see Ivan dead for his interference."

Season's mouth dropped open. "You poor soul." She placed milk and sugar on the table and, with a shaky hand, filled their cups with tea.

Ivan thought her emotions were overwhelming her.

"I've always wondered if the stories about those Ratling creatures were a myth to keep people away from Ancient Oak Creek." Arnie wiped his mouth with a napkin and leaned back into his chair. "You know, the red mushrooms grow where the creek curves to the southwest. Maybe someone was trying to protect the new fall crop."

Ivan remembered the mushroom powder that had put his beagles under a deep slumber during his first visit. He recognized how they would be valuable to the owner.

"I don't think the mushrooms have anything to do with it," Sebastian said.

"Wait." Ivan leaned forward, suddenly excited. "Could that be the ingredient that poisoned Merridyn's potion?"

"We've investigated the possibility." Arnie gave a dismissive wave with his hand. "In small or medium dosages, it would bring on sleep, but it's not harmful."

"And big dosages?"

"It would make someone mighty ill, but it's doubtful it would take their life."

"Even if it were the mushrooms…" Season hesitated and sipped her tea. "Who would do such a dreadful thing?"

They all looked at each other. Sympathy covered their faces.

"Tell us more about the reappearance of those hideous Ratlings." Arnie clenched his hands together. "We often go to that creek to do some fishing."

Sebastian skimmed over the major events of Ivan's first journey into the Forest in order to tell them why Tereus threatened Ivan's life. "He killed the Dark Army's major commander during the Forest War, and Tereus is not about to forgive that."

It was like experiencing the horror all over again. Ivan pushed his empty bowl away and stared at the tabletop. He wished they'd drop the subject.

Arnie's jaw slackened. "You *are* a hero."

"Not by choice." Ivan turned his head.

"Then the silver rodent jumped him and sank his teeth into Ivan's side." Sebastian scrunched his eyebrows and glanced at Season. "Broke skin and ribs. That explains the long tears in his clothing—and the stench."

Season shot from her chair, hands covering her ears. "I can't hear any more of this. It shouldn't happen to one so young." She jerked off her paisley kerchief and threw it to the floor. "You must protect this lad, Sebastian. How can you be so careless?"

"Season…" Arnie cautioned with a hard look.

She pumped her fist into the air. "You are a poor guardian for this boy. Maybe Zephyrus should have sent Sytha or Wayland to protect him." Her eyes filled with tears. She swiped them with an angry stroke of her fingers.

Arnie made a move to stand. "That's enough. You don't understand what Sebastian has been through. Be still now."

"And how would you know so much?" Season scowled deeply at her husband.

"I listen to messages from Root-Underground when I'm able. Customers come by and gossip," Arnie blasted back.

Her face red with anger, Season sniffed, rose, and left the kitchen. Calling over her shoulder, her voice cracked. "I'll make a nice fire in your room and run a bath for you, Ivan."

"T-thank you, ma'am."

"B-but—he's fully healed now," Sebastian said in his own defense, as though trying to hide his humiliation.

Chapter 16

The Dream

"Sorry about the outburst." Arnie drank his tea, looking miserable. "Things haven't been the same since the unfortunate poisoning earlier this year. My wife cries and yells at the slightest thing."

Sebastian slumped in his chair, gaze fixed on the pattern in the linoleum floor. "Season is right. I've been a terrible guide and protector."

"It's not true." Ivan moved his chair closer and draped his arm around Sebastian's shoulders. "I don't blame you for anything. It was my decision to enter the Forest. I wanted to find Peter—to see you and Zephyrus again—all my good friends."

Blinking several times, Sebastian studied his hands, not meeting Ivan's eyes.

"Please, don't be hard on yourself." Ivan squeezed a bit harder. "You didn't bring the Ratlings. Tereus did. He told me so." Wiping moisture from his forehead, Ivan swallowed. *No one is safe with me.*

They discussed Merridyn's fate. It was clear she and her family were highly thought of in the village. "This should speak well of her during her upcoming trial," Arnie said. "How quickly everyone forgets the nice things she's done for them. Saved lives, cured their ailments, listened to their complaints."

Ivan's eyes drooped, feeling heavy.

Peeking out from the hallway, Season said, "Your bath is ready, Ivan. Hand over your clothing."

Ivan did as she ordered. He grabbed the towel she'd tossed to him and wrapped it around his bare shoulders. Knowing she would ask Sebastian to strip, Ivan hesitated for a moment just to watch Sebastian squirm.

"Might as well give me your leggings." She wagged a finger at Sebastian.

He raised his head in alarm and turned sideways in his chair. Crossing his hands over his legs, he blushed. "You mean I must remove them?"

"How else would you expect me to wash them? Now, let's have 'em."

Sebastian reluctantly went into the privy. When he returned, he was wearing a too-long bathrobe that must've belonged to Merridyn's dead husband. He handed his leggings over, acting contrite from the severe tongue-lashing she'd given him.

Ivan hid a grin behind his hand because of Sebastian's shyness, and then he left the room.

"Don't worry, we'll take good care of the cloak," Season turned in the opposite direction and yelled down the hall after them. "No one will steal it while it's in our cottage."

"You'll see us early morning, and we'll bring your breakfast before you leave for the castle." Arnie rose from his chair, massaging his bum. "Not used to so much sitting." He groaned. Ivan knew how that felt.

Alfred and Canute jumped up from where they were sleeping and received several pats on their heads from their new friend. The door closed by itself when Arnie and Season left.

"You'd better check on me in half an hour." Ivan turned to be sure Sebastian had heard him.

"Yes, I know. You have a habit of falling to sleep while in the bathtub."

Ivan stepped into the narrow tub, relishing the hot water and bubbles that engulfed him. He reached for a bar of lavender soap, a face flannel, and started by washing his feet. The lovely fragrance of lavender took his thoughts away to Coreena. He remembered it was a scent she wore. The bath was relaxing and peaceful as anything he'd done that day, except eating a delicious dinner. His thoughts faded like the bubbles surrounding him. His eyes slowly closed.

What seemed only a moment when someone called to him and shook his shoulder.

"Thanks for waking me." Ivan climbed from the tub and donned a green nightshirt folded over a wicker chair for his use, he supposed. He patted Sebastian on his back as they climbed the narrow, uneven staircase to the top floor where their bedroom awaited.

Sebastian chuckled. "Didn't want you to drown. It would be another unfortunate mark against Merridyn's reputation and her cottage."

They stepped into the guest room. Like the entire house, it was small. A bed, an insignificant dresser, a nightstand with a bowl and pitcher for washing, filled the space.

"The nightshirt fits pretty well," he said. "Merridyn's husband must've been about my size, maybe a little shorter."

Adjusting his wire-rimmed glasses, Sebastian scrutinized Ivan's attire. "Looks all right. My robe is too big, but I'm happy to have it."

Ivan sat on the bed and wiggled his toes. "It's been quite a day." He sighed, tracing the long scar through his nightshirt, remembering the terrible attack.

"The first time I came to the Forest, I went looking for Peter. I'm beginning to believe Winchester, the birch tree's remark about Peter not wanting to be found."

Sebastian snorted. "Something is amiss, and we're going to find out what happened to him."

"Thanks, my friend. I'm grateful."

"There's no cloak to wear tonight to keep you warm." Sebastian plopped onto the wicker chair while shifting several pillows to cushion his form. He leaned his head back, and in spite of a spirit never sleeping, he yawned.

"I know," Ivan said.

The soft bed and thick comforter of down feathers felt cozy and protective. Ivan pulled it to his chin. His eyes fluttered and closed. Alfred and Canute curled on a rag rug near the small fireplace.

"Good night and sweet dreams," Sebastian whispered gently.

Ivan mumbled something in return, just before he gave into sleep.

****

In the night, a strange and unwelcomed dream visited him. Near Ancient Oak Creek stood a very large, dark-trunked tree with crimson-blood leaves. Thousands of red mushrooms growing nearby broke into a familiar Russian folk song. Their voices were raw and unpleasant. When the singing stopped, the tree addressed a crowd of faceless people wearing hooded cloaks or heavy coats with the collars drawn up against their necks. Ivan somehow knew they were all waiting for a hanging.

"Oh, no!" Ivan shouted in his dream. His chest tightened until he could scarcely inhale. *"It's Merridyn."*

Her pretty face was made up in gaudy colors with two big spots of red rouge on her cheeks, bright orange lipstick, blue eyelids, and heavy black lashes. Her hair was woven with small limbs of oak leaves, beech masts, and tangled with a string of ickleberries.

Ivan gasped. He tried to make his legs move toward her, to save her, but he felt paralyzed.

She stood on a rickety chair, hands bound tightly in front. A rope, tied around her thin white neck was knotted over a strong branch. The tree's face wore a smug, righteous look. The sign pinned to Merridyn's chest read, *Murdering Witch—Condemned to Die.*

"Do you have anything to say for yourself, murderer?" a man asked in a loud, harsh voice.

"Hang her. Hang her. Hang her high!" the merciless crowd chanted.

From a distance, Ivan could only see the backs of their covered heads. Who are they that call for her death?

"No," Ivan shouted. "She didn't do it. Please…" No one heard. No one cared.

"I'm innocent," she screamed. "I didn't chop down the Golden Tree. Do hear me. I'm innocent!"

What? Chop down the Golden Tree? Ivan rolled over in his sleep, confused by his own dream. He thought her punishment was for the unfortunate death of her husband and son.

"She's a liar," the angry crowd yelled in his nightmare. "Kick the chair! Let her swing."

Maloof wound in and around the people with a huge grin on his face. He clapped his stumpy hands and muttered, "Dat good. Dat good."

Someone in a sleeveless gray cloak, the hood masking his face, stepped forward. He gave the wooden chair a swift kick. Falling over, one of its legs broke. The rope jerked so hard it squeaked, followed by a strangled cry from Merridyn.

Ivan shrieked. He jolted and sat up. Sweat trickled down his forehead, wetting the collar of his nightshirt. Breathing rapidly, he tried to recall where he was.

"Can't you spend your limited sleeping hours in a better dream?" Sebastian lifted his bushy eyebrows and shifted in the wicker chair. "You've been moaning for ten minutes."

"I thought they'd hung Merridyn." Ivan coughed from the dryness of his throat. "What a horrible nightmare."

"The dream doesn't mean anything."

Ivan shook his head and threw his legs over the side of the bed. "I might as well get up." He realized with a start, he had no shirt or trousers, and so the nightshirt he wore must do. "As soon as Season brings my clothes, I'll dress and we can leave."

****

Shortly, they heard a knock at the door. Sebastian leaned forward in the wicker chair, cocking his head. Alfred and Canute shot up and raced down the three flights of steps, barking as they descended.

When Ivan and Sebastian entered the cold kitchen, a large-framed man wearing a long leather apron, said in a deep voice, "I didn't mean to wake you. Season asked me to feed your beagles. Said there were guests here. Arnie's at the bakery getting bread for breakfast, and Season is finishing some sewing."

Ivan liked how that sounded.

"Bartholomew, how are you? It's Sebastian."

"Oh, and so it is. It's nice to see you after such a long time. Where's the Long Dark Cloak? Can't recognize you without it." He chuckled.

"Being washed and mended," he said. "This is Ivan Kimble. His farm borders our Forest to the northeast. Ivan, this is the village blacksmith, Bartholomew."

"Call me Bart. Sure, I know your name and most everything you've done since you've entered our Forest. The way the story is told, I thought you'd be as big as Sampson, pulling down pillars and crushing people. You're a mere lad." He laughed in a friendly way. "How old are you, anyway?"

Ivan liked Bart—the rough look of his hands, the strands of silver in his short beard. "I'm fifteen," he answered. The huge scar on his left side wouldn't say much about his stealth or bravery, however. Unless Sebastian brought it up, he wouldn't mention yesterday's ordeal.

"That's darn young." Bart stepped back and looked Ivan up and down.

Seemingly ashamed, Sebastian turned away and didn't speak. He must've considered the bawling-out Season had given him the day before. Standing near, Ivan patted his companion's back. "I don't hold it against you."

Sebastian took Ivan's hand and squeezed.

Bart handed the saddlebags draped over his shoulder to Ivan. "Benny was supposed to bring these, but he complained it was too heavy, so here I am."

A delicious smell of smoked meat came from under a cloth-covered basket that Bart held in his other hand. "This here's for the dogs. I'll feed them while you get

153

dressed." He made a gesture with his fingers like a sweeping broom for Ivan and Sebastian to leave.

"Season is washing and mending our clothes." Ivan wrinkled his forehead, feeling a bit awkward.

The blacksmith now appeared to understand the situation and nodded. He pulled two bowls from the dish drainer.

"I'll take care of that." Ivan reached for the meat, divided it, and placed the bowls on the floor. Alfred and Canute dove in with gusto.

"I heard you wanted to talk to me." Bart glanced at Sebastian and took a seat at the table.

"It's about the Golden Lantern," Sebastian said and sat next to Ivan. "I believe we've worked out the details."

"Yeah." The blacksmith raised his dark eyebrows. "One of the Forest shepherds brought it to me so I could replace the glass. Apparently, he didn't know he held a valuable Ancient Relic in his hands. I told him I could replace the glass, but the lantern would never work without dragon fire to relight the wick. At least we witches know that much."

"Did he believe you?"

"Didn't seem to." Bart brought his broad shoulders together. "Thought I was pulling his leg."

"The shepherds don't know about the dragon population at the castle." Sebastian pursed his lips. "No reason to tell them. They'd be afraid the dragons would swoop down and snatch their prize sheep."

"I gave him one of my working lanterns in exchange for the broken one. He seemed happy with the arrangement."

"Was the Golden Lantern the only relic he brought to you?" Sebastian tugged at his robe to cover his bare legs. His cheeks turned pink.

"Well, I guess so. He didn't mention another item that needed fixing."

"It didn't need repairs," Ivan filled in. "When the shepherd took the lantern, the Silver Axe might've gone with it. Both were placed near the three birch trees before they disappeared."

Bart considered the question. "He didn't say anything to me." The blacksmith moved to the fireplace, went to his knees and crumpled paper, then placed several sticks of kindling on top. Alfred and Canute pushed at his hands, trying to help. They were more of a nuisance, but Bart stroked their heads and kissed their noses. When the fire caught, he added a few logs and seemed pleased with his efforts. He stood and brushed his hands on the sides of his worn trousers.

"Season told us that the lantern was taken to the castle," Sebastian said.

"Delivered it personally." The blacksmith lifted his chin with pride. "Me and a few other trusted witches from the village. Well-armed, we were."

Ivan looked at Sebastian. "That seems to solve the mystery of the Golden Lantern. It's safely at the castle."

"Be sure Zephyrus knows this right away." Sebastian rubbed his hands together, warming them by the fire.

"I believe Lord Graydon sent a message thanking us," Bart said.

"Ah. Then all is as it should be." Ivan cracked a grin.

That castle's some impressive collection of stones, isn't it?" Bart stretched his arms wide. "I'd forgotten how huge it is. We got lost a number of times when we attempted to tour the buildings and grounds by ourselves."

"I've never been there," Ivan said. "We're headed there from here. Lord Graydon sent a personal invitation."

Lifting his eyebrows, Bart bobbed his head with approval.

"What's the story about Zello's revolt at the South Castle? What kind of stupidity is that?" Bart asked in a loud voice.

Sebastian tugged the collar of his robe as though chilled. "No one seems to know."

Ivan rose and put the kettle on for tea. He was uneasy wearing another man's nightshirt and hoped Season would arrive soon with his clothes.

"We'd better see about breakfast and be on our way." Sebastian pointed to the sliced raisin-jitnut cakes and other bread items left over from dinner.

Just as Bart was about to take his leave, Season swung through the front door carrying a basket of fresh eggs, sausages, tomatoes, and a small round of cheese. Ivan and Sebastian's clothes were draped neatly over her other arm.

"Sorry," she exclaimed. "I just finished the mending. Benny agreed to bring your horses to the entrance in about an hour."

Grateful, Ivan reached for his shirt and jacket and examined the long tears. They were perfectly mended. He bowed and thanked her.

"My pleasure. Now, you both get dressed. I'll have a big breakfast for you quick as a witch's smile. Arnie won't be joining us. He already has the oven filled with dough."

"Here's your leggings, Sebastian. I'm sure you

wanted them as fast as possible." Ivan handed them to his companion.

They walked down the hall toward the privy and dressed as they were told.

As he re-entered the kitchen, Ivan adjusted The Challenger's scabbard around his waist and twirled the Long Dark Cloak over his shoulders. Season had done an excellent job sewing the cloak's long tear. Now he felt complete, relieved to have all the items he needed for their journey.

Sebastian straightened his tunic and pointed. "Look, she got the stains out of my leggings. Good thing, since I only have one set of clothes to my name."

"You are a great cook, Season. Just as Merridyn told us." Ivan ate several portions of eggs, sausages, and fried vegetables at his own pace. When she asked about his unusual slow eating method, he looked up, and his mouth parted to speak.

With a careless wave of his hand, Sebastian said, "Don't mind him. He always eats like he has all the time in the world."

"I was going to say on my own behalf," Ivan replied, a bit terse, "I'm enjoying this delicious breakfast. Thank you."

Bart gave Season a gentle punch on her arm and then cackled. "That's what you get for asking questions when you shouldn't."

Ivan shifted uncomfortably in his chair. He hadn't meant to embarrass her.

Season's face reddened, followed by a guilty look. "Sebastian, I'm dreadfully sorry for the terrible things I said to you. I had no right to interfere. Please forgive me." Her head lowered as she blinked.

"Not to worry." Sebastian smiled. "After a thousand years, I've had worse said to me." He laughed as he must've recalled a few stabbing comments from his past.

Ivan shot from his seat, almost knocking over his teacup. "I just had a thought. What if the poison someone put into Merridyn's concoction was meant for her—not her family?" He gestured from the open window to the small kitchen stove. "It would be easy for a passerby to slip something into a boiling pot."

Sebastian followed Ivan's pointing finger. His bushy brows rose and twitched. "Could be. But who'd want to see Merridyn dead?"

"Who'd want to see her husband and child dead?" Ivan scowled, feeling more and more helpless to find an answer.

"It's worth considering." Season nodded and paused. "I'm reluctant to mention this, but I think Lyla is a likely candidate." Before anyone could accuse her of placing blame without proof, she stood quickly and collected the dishes from the table, tossing scraps to the beagles.

Bart looked down at Canute and Alfred before answering. "It just doesn't seem likely that Lyla would kill her own sister because she's jealous."

"Unless…" Ivan said, "Lyla didn't realize the potency of the poison, but only wanted to make Merridyn very sick."

"It won't be easy to make a case." Sebastian exhaled deeply.

"Now, I'd better go to my shop. There's much to do today." Bart waved at his guests.

Sebastian and Ivan stepped out the cottage door and thanked them for their hospitality as they departed. The entire village was up and moving about. Voices hummed, animals snorted, fowl clucked, and neighborhood dogs barked.

"The community starts early here." Ivan slung the saddlebags over his shoulder and trailed Sebastian, who seemed to have a grasp on where they were going.

Alfred and Canute followed their master while Sebastian trudged through the maze of houses, gardens, and meticulously planted herbs and vegetables. There was even a small lily pond they hadn't noticed when they'd first arrived. Perhaps they'd taken a different path. Ivan couldn't be sure.

Retracing their steps to the entrance of the Witches' Village, they wound their way down the hills. Ivan fingered the number 13 key at his neck. Since he was going to the castle where Merridyn was staying, he would return it personally. He thought on his theory about the intended victim—or victims of the poisonous brew. Even if it had been Lyla, was her jealousy enough reason to kill her own sister—and family? He shook his head. The motive for the crime still eluded him.

Some distance from the entry, several witches, dressed in suspendered clothes or bib overalls, were working in the fields they'd passed by on their arrival. Some of the workers stopped their labor and leaned on shovels. They stared suspiciously. Finally recognizing Sebastian, they waved and shouted greetings.

One witch yelled from far away, "There's some kind of revolt at the castle, you know? Something should be done about it."

"We're going there now," Sebastian hollered back.

Little Benny, Bart's son, met them at the front entrance, straddling Bounty. He held the reins of Old

159

Bones along with an unfamiliar, saddled horse. The boy slipped off with a long drop to the ground and handed Sebastian a note.

As Ivan reached for his horse's bridle, Benny's face twisted with fear. He backed away and ran as if a band of banshees were after him.

"What do you suppose has gotten into him?" Sebastian asked and scratched the side of his head. He read the note from Arnie, "Please take *Standby* with you to the castle. It will make Merridyn very happy."

"Of course," Ivan mumbled and watched Benny disappear through the fields. *Is he afraid of me?*

Chapter 17

Vaguers

"The witches are good people." Holding Standby's reins, Ivan guided Bounty around the bend, and they headed south toward the castle. "I thought they'd be casting spells, mixing weird potions, and chanting to their witch-gods."

"None of that nonsense." Sebastian snorted. "Just common folks raising their families and caring for one another." Ivan wondered about the second part of Sebastian's statement. The exception being Lyla who'd confined her sister to live with the trolls.

"Then again…they do possess some special skills, or magic, that we're not privileged to know." Sebastian glanced at his riding companion and wiggled his eyebrows, leaving Ivan to wonder what he meant.

The flat landscape showed ancient stone walls in ruin, broken wattle fences, and sparse vegetation. Gorse bushes held onto their special plots of soil. The hardy birds that stayed year-round, like the nuthatches, chaffinches, and robins, sang their melodic songs. Crested lizards shot off through short grasses to hide from curious dogs.

Wild ponies meandered near a small knoll where they grazed, minding their own business. Canute and Alfred ignored them. They'd probably learned their lesson during their first visit when they chased the ponies at Lake Gorgon. Their disobedience caused a lot of trouble, and Canute suffered greatly for his lack of discretion.

Ivan breathed in the scent of damp earth and realized they'd left much of the forested area behind. "Where are all the trees?"

"Only half of the Forest is tree-covered. Nearly an equal amount is farmland and villages."

This surprised Ivan, as he hadn't thought about the ratio of forest versus farmland. He watched the beagles crouch along as they skirted bushes and then ran to catch up. "They've been acting strangely since we crossed the wooden bridge a ways back."

"Listen, I think I should warn you..." Sebastian swiveled his head from side to side.

Ivan knew that tone of voice. He'd heard it before and didn't like it.

"Bart told me while you were getting dressed this morning that Vaguers were sighted somewhere between the Harvesters' Cottages and the castle. I thought you should know so we can be on the lookout. Keep The Challenger at the ready."

Ivan's heart zigzagged through his chest. "What's a Vaguer?"

Sebastian slowed his horse and met Ivan's eyes. "It doesn't compare to anything you've ever seen."

"Tell me what to expect." Ivan gulped, thinking about the Ratlings.

"We know Tereus created them over a thousand years ago when he vied for the throne with Zephyrus. But we haven't seen them for nearly fifty years now. "They do the most horrible things to people, all in an effort to steal a man's Essence."

"What's that...like your spirit?"

"Not exactly. Only the High Intervener—God, can take your spirit. It's your soul they are wanting—everything about you. Your memories, fears, happiness, love. The things that develop and define your personality, who you are—like your identity." His mouth turned down in a grimace. "That's what I've always believed, anyway."

"For what reason?"

"So they might live again. They're like the half-dead, wanting to restore the other half of their life."

Ivan shivered. "What do they look like?"

"Man-like, I've heard, of different heights, wearing tattered gray-green military uniforms that hang on their skeletons like death camp victims." Sebastian took a breath, gazing into the distance. "Long thin hair, as you'd expect on a near-corpse—wandering, searching for suitable prey."

Ivan pushed away the cloak's fabric and rested his hand on the golden hilt of The Challenger. Tereus warned him he had worse waiting for him. *Did he mean the Vaguers?*

"You've seen them?"

"No. Commander Tom Shiffert killed three of them about forty years ago. Tom was a young man at the time, full of purpose and courage. He described the creatures to me. Said they were gruesome to look at—sent by the demon himself."

Ivan remembered Tom—the old commander who lived in the Hurst-on-the-Vert.

"Why do they call them Vaguers?"

Sebastian paused. Ripples of worry marked his

brow. "Well, because of how their victims react once the creature sets a spell on them. It's as if their big yellow eyes, sunk deep into their sockets, render their victims into a hypnotic state. Tom said it's like being a marble statue having no awareness of the danger that awaits you."

Ivan shivered. "H-how do they do that?"

"The Vaguers leap on you and suck your Essence out—through your mouth. Their long black tongues probe up into your brain. I don't know much more than that. It's enough to scare the wits out of a person."

"You're right." Ivan wiped the wetness from his forehead. "Have the Vaguers returned to the Forest because of me? I mean, did Tereus send them to steal my soul?"

"I don't know." Sebastian stared at Ivan, considering. "But I'm anxious for your safety."

Now Ivan really needed to leave the Forest—and never return. *What am I doing here? If Peter wanted to come home, he would've by now.*

"This is very hard on you, I realize," Sebastian said. "Please, don't give up on your mission yet."

"How did you know what I was thinking?"

"Because it's what I would be thinking," Sebastian defended.

They rode on until they came to a shallow, gravelly stream. A cluster of fuzzy, brown cattails swayed on the banks. Ivan analyzed the movement with apprehension and worry.

"Let's drink and water the horses while we can." Sebastian urged Old Bones to the creek's edge. Bounty and Standby followed while the beagles came up beside them and lapped thirstily. Ivan slipped off his horse and massaged his rear end. He scanned the stream's opposite bank looking for movement of rock or soil.

If the Ratlings returned, he wanted to be ready to leave at once. There was no sign of disturbance. He sighed with relief, lowered to his knees, and cupped water into his hands.

Canute shot off howling. Alfred held back, his chest shivering. He looked up at his master with pleading eyes and whimpered.

"What set him to running?" Sebastian searched for the cause.

"I see a fine carriage ahead, sideways and blocking the road." Ivan pointed. "They must be in trouble."

Sebastian jerked on his mustache, considering their next move. "It might be some kind of ambush. Or maybe it's a broken wheel," he added hopefully.

Mounting, they rode closer. Ivan grabbed Standby's reins once more, afraid the horse might bolt away. The carriage was richly adorned with decorative gold trim that outlined the form of the coach. Bright tassels hung from the four corners next to fancy side lamps.

"There!" Ivan stood in the stirrups. "A girl in red, sitting on the side of the road."

Four black steeds pulled at their harnesses and whinnied, terrified at the arrival of other horses and the sound of the newcomers' voices.

They approached with caution. The carriage travelers, two men and an older lady, and the young girl dressed in red, separated from the others, sat on the moist grass staring through the breaks in the trees. The ladies elegantly dressed, wore precious gems glistening on their fingers. Their traveling cloaks, now soiled, hung loosely around their shoulders.

Sebastian called near the carriage, "Are you all right? What happened?"

No one moved.

That's when Ivan saw the skeleton-like form in a filthy, threadbare uniform that hung loosely on his frame, moving toward the girl in red. He kneeled in front of her. The shadowy figure pulled the strings of her satin cloak with long, bony fingers and then grasped the sides of her head with the heel of his wiry hands.

Ivan screamed, "Hold there!" The creature turned, showing darkened teeth to the advancing riders. It was like nothing Ivan had ever seen. The most grisly-looking expression glared back at him. He knew at once it was what Sebastian had called a *Vaguer*.

Its gaunt skull was covered with dried, wrinkled skin. A thick brow hung over, shadowing huge eyes, just as Sebastian had described them. Even from a distance, Ivan saw the penetrating black slit in the center of yellow—like a reptile's eye. A long dark tongue waggled from its mouth, mimicking a poisonous snake sensing a meal. The creature ignored Ivan's call and returned its attention to its victim.

The pretty girl stared vacantly and made no move to save her life.

Leaning into her, the Vaguer's eyes appeared bright with anticipation. Wire-like fingers curled inside her lower jaw while his other hand gripped her upper jaw, prying, pulling. He pushed her to the ground and fell on top of her. His mouth opened over hers.

She doesn't seem to know she's in grave danger.

"Stop! In the name of the High Intervener, you must not do this." Sebastian nudged his horse, and Old Bones jolted toward the ill-fated scene.

"Canute, Alfred. Get him." Ivan jerked The Challenger from its scabbard. Tightening his grip on the hilt, he galloped forward.

The Vaguer raised his head, licked his lips, and looked furious to be interrupted.

The beagles rushed the vile creature. They leaped at him, knocking him over onto his back. Canute jumped at the Vaguer and tore a piece of cloth from the faded uniform. Determined to do his part, Alfred bounded onto the half-dead man's chest and chewed at his throat.

Ivan flew off Bounty and ran toward the melee, where the beagles had the creature pinned to the ground. "Canute—Alfred, move." They reluctantly backed away, growling.

The Challenger rose in Ivan's hands, sweeping downward. The blade swept full force and sliced bone, removing the Vaguer's head. Ivan kicked it, and it rolled next to a stump. The Vaguer's ragged clothing released a puff of foul air and deflated against the earth, showing an outline of his yellowed bones.

Ivan trembled with fear. His mouth went dry.

Three more of the beasts crept from behind the dark trunks of surrounding trees. Large evil eyes stared at the four passengers who sat paralyzed on the ground. For a brief moment, it seemed they would throw themselves upon the victims and consume them. When they saw Ivan, they hissed menacingly, wavering in their indecision. They glanced at each other and growled.

"They sense you are wearing the Long Dark Cloak—and hold The Challenger," Sebastian said. "Things of powerful magic frighten them."

Ivan took a gulp of air. Sebastian's words offered little comfort.

The beagles would have none of it. They turned their fierceness on the dark beings. Alfred barked and nipped at the heels of the nearest creature. Canute bit into the scrawny leg of another. Its high-pitched scream echoed through the woods. Several Vaguers turned and whisked away through the thickness of the Forest.

The last creature stopped and threw a vengeful look at Ivan and burrowed blazing eyes into him. Slowly it raised its hand and pointed a bony finger. "You are next." He snarled. "With your Essence, I, Kagutt, will live forever. My screams at the Harvesters' Cottages nearly drew you to me, didn't they? What a fine treat that would've been to have you then." Maniacal laughter hung in the still air as he turned and disappeared into the darkness of the trees.

Alfred and Canute took on the chase until Ivan called them back. "Stop!" Ivan yelled, "They may grab and swallow you."

The dogs returned and whimpered, unsatisfied.

Sebastian checked the other three victims, separated from the girl in red. He stumbled toward the stylish woman with gray hair, swept up in Grecian curls. She sat in a trance, hands limp in her lap. Her regal, satin blue traveling cloak was badly soiled with dirt and grass stains as though she'd fallen several times trying to escape. The cloak's ribbon had been ripped away. Smeared makeup circled her eyes.

Squatting, Sebastian took the lady's shoulders and squeezed. "Are you all right, Ma'am? Can you hear me?" He turned and mumbled toward Ivan, "She's in a trance, but the Vaguer didn't get her."

Ivan burned with fear, but he couldn't stop now. The travelers needed their help.

"Let's check the men." Sebastian walked toward them. They sat unmoving and did not blink. Examining the smartly dressed men, he saw no signs of invasion. With a deep sigh of relief, he announced, "I believe they'll recover, too." He picked up a shoe with a fancy gold buckle that belonged to the older of the two, he discerned.

Canute and Alfred sniffed at the luggage on the ground. The leather straps that held them in place on the coach platform were broken. An open case had spilled richly decorated female clothing onto the dirt. When the beagles smelled nothing to eat, they returned to the front of the carriage, whining and clawing at the wheels.

"Quiet now." Ivan leaned down and petted Alfred and Canute, lavishing affection on them for their bravery. "Without you, it could've been a terrible outcome."

The four skittish horses flattened their ears and pulled at the harnesses. Their large frightened eyes glanced toward the trees beyond where the passengers sat in a daze.

"We saw a carriage race by yesterday," Ivan remembered. "They must have made an overnight stop before continuing on to the castle today. Or are there two carriages?"

A scowl deepened on Sebastian's forehead. "I think this is the second one." He walked to the front. "Our first victim."

The driver lay slumped on the seat, his arms hanging lifeless.

Ivan leaped up from the right side, leaned over the man, and stared into his face. His eyelids were bloody and sunken. His jaw broken, ripped to distortion. Ivan cried out, jerking back in horror.

From the opposite side, Sebastian let out a painful groan. The Vaguer had sucked out the driver's eyes along with his Essence. "This barbaric act will give the life-sucker additional years of life," Sebastian said and sighed ruefully. "These Vaguers are a nightmare from the darkest place imaginable—the very depths of hell."

Ivan agreed with a slow tip of his head. His stomach threatened to heave its breakfast.

"The driver's Essence is gone." Sebastian stood frozen. "Everything about him now belongs to one of those vultures. Zephyrus will be devastated over the return of these wretched things."

Legs weak, Ivan nearly collapsed. He looked away, unable to focus on the man with the distorted jaw. "I've caused these awful monsters to come back. Tereus is trying to get me. I have to leave the Forest as quickly as possible. I can't have more people die because of me."

Quiet for a long moment, Sebastian exhaled a hefty breath while his body shook as though an arrow had struck his heart. "Tereus is getting stronger," he whispered.

Chapter 18

Royal Passengers

Sebastian shook his head, squinting with worry. "Someone above ground has joined the demon. It would give him more power—God help whoever that person may be."

For a moment, Ivan was anxious that Peter was still involved and Tereus had taken control of him. He shuddered at the thought. Though Ivan had warned his brother about the danger, Peter became angry and rebuffed Ivan's words of caution.

Ivan clutched the carriage support bar and leaned his forehead against his arm. Tears collected, and he allowed them to pierce his deep sadness.

"There's nothing we could've done," Sebastian murmured. "Fortunately, we were here in time to stop them from doing more damage than they did."

"This innocent man nearly had his jaw ripped from his face...n-no eyes." Needing a moment of privacy, Ivan sniffed and pulled the hood of the Long Dark Cloak over his head, shutting out the revulsion before him.

Sebastian's face scrunched with grief. "Have a good cry, my friend. It will help release the terror. I'll try to encourage the guests to return to their seats. Maybe the horses will stop shivering and can be guided back to the road."

Ivan did sob as though his heart were breaking. If only they'd gotten here earlier, they could've saved the driver. If only part of Sytha's retinue had accompanied them on the journey. *I never should've returned to the Forest. If I hadn't killed Tereus's Commander in battle, none of this would be happening.*

Stepping down from the carriage, Sebastian moved toward the passengers sitting on the lawn. "Put this canteen to your lips," he urged the younger man. "You'll feel better if you drink." The boy didn't respond. Sebastian then offered it to the older man who'd lost his shoe. "How about you? Would you like water?"

Finally, Ivan eased himself from the carriage step and wiped his nose on the sleeve of the cloak. Canute rushed to him, stood, and put paws on Ivan's legs. Alfred whimpered in a sympathetic way, dragging on his belly toward his master.

Frustrated, Sebastian glanced at the passengers. "They're still in a trance."

Fingers trembling, Ivan untied the Long Dark Cloak's strings and moved to Sebastian's side. "Throw this around their shoulders. You can heal them at once."

He shook his head. "I'm afraid the cloak's healing powers can't penetrate their stupor. The cloak can only work with physical injuries. I suspect they'll need a few days to sleep it off." He dragged his fingers through his jumbled hair. "That was the case decades ago when Vaguers paralyzed several of Tom Shiffert's soldiers—put under this same spell. In that way, the creatures could extract their Essence at their convenience. Like a fly trapped in a spider's web, yet their victims are unaware of the danger."

"We'd better check on the girl," Ivan said. *She's not*

moving. Her shoulders are slumped, hands trembling from the cold. "Then, we should leave right away." He strode back to where the luggage had broken loose from the carriage. The largest trunk containing petticoats and delicately embroidered dresses with matching capes had to be repacked. He hefted it onto the platform, positioned the smaller pieces on top, and strapped them into place.

Someone groaned. Ivan rushed to the girl. Her ashen face lifted to gape at him and slowly turned toward Sebastian. She glanced behind her at the other passengers but didn't seem to recognize her family.

"How do you feel?" Ivan cupped her face in his hands and looked into her eyes. She was about his age, perhaps a bit younger. The girl blinked. Her fists suddenly went up and beat at his chest, screaming. She tried to get away by scooting backward, shouting violently.

Ivan realized his blunder by holding her face. It was what the Vaguer had done. Dropping his hands to his sides, Ivan drew back to protect himself. "You're speaking Russian," he said and answered in the same language.

The girl's eyes went wide.

"We're friends of Lord Graydon's. We will take you to the South Castle."

She cried hysterically, and her body shook. Ivan carefully gathered her into his arms and held her while he rocked her gently. "It's all right. We'll protect you." He hoped it was the reassuring words and gesture she needed. "You and your family are safe now."

Sebastian tried to revive the older lady, but nothing seemed to work. "Her mother, perhaps? The bearded man must be her father, and the young one could be her brother—or even her betrothed. A royal young lady would never travel without her family or a trusted guardian."

Ivan gave a nod, indicating he'd heard and understood. "What's your name?" he asked the girl.

"Tatyana," she whispered low, not offering a last name.

She held onto him as though she might never let go. While he was grateful to have earned her trust, he was anxious to leave this dangerous place.

"The girl should stand for better circulation," Ivan said to Sebastian, "but I don't believe she'll release me."

"Hold her for a few more moments. The spell seems to be wearing off a bit." Sebastian gave him a sympathetic look.

"All right." In the grass lay a golden cross that must've broken from its dainty chain. Picking it up, Ivan put the jewelry in his jacket pocket to keep it safe. It didn't belong to a Vaguer that was certain.

"Tell me about them—these terrible creatures." Ivan motioned his head toward Sebastian.

"They were once warriors who fought with Tereus against Zephyrus in the ruined kingdom."

"Helvaka?"

"Yes. At some point, they must've realized their chosen leader was a tyrant and deceiver. They rebelled against him and sided with Zephyrus to help destroy Tereus and his wicked army. As punishment for their rebellion, Tereus seized and destroyed their Essence, condemning them to the pit of darkness. Now they've been recalled, roaming the Forest to reclaim life—any life—so they might live again."

"A real pity," Ivan's voice croaked.

Sebastian handed the canteen to Ivan, who drank deeply. "I noticed there is more water in the carriage."

Stroking his white beard, Sebastian continued, "When Tom Shiffert was a young commander of this region, Maloof and Cecil helped drive the Vaguers into the fiery underground with their wizardry. So you see, at one time, the two fallen wizards did contribute to the wellbeing of the Forest."

"That's good to know," Ivan said thoughtfully.

"The Vaguer's life force is controlled by Tereus, condemned to serve him forever. I don't know how this is accomplished, but Zephyrus told me it's recorded in the Black Book of Pearls."

"They made a poor choice. And then, wanting to do the right thing"—Ivan lowered his voice—"it was too late to change sides."

"That's how I understand it."

The young girl released her grip on Ivan and moaned. She leaned back and looked at him as though trying to remember who he was and why he'd held her in his embrace.

"My name is Ivan Kimble." Speaking in Russian, he said, "This is Sebastian. We will help you."

"What happened?" Her eyes opened wide. "My dress. My cloak." She smoothed her clothing with a bejeweled hand, shock frozen in her pretty young face. Then, understanding must've flooded her memory. She struggled to raise herself from the damp ground. "My parents. My brother."

Ivan helped her stand and guided her to her family.

"Mother. Father. Why are we here? What have they done to you?"

Her Russian was elegant, like Ivan's own mother

and father's. They too, had been royalty in faraway Russia.

Sebastian moved next to the girl. "They will be fine. We need to get them back into the carriage. The sun is lowering—we must leave at once."

Tatyana went to her knees and draped her arms around her mother's neck, whimpering like a child. "Mama, Mama. See me. Talk to me. Papa, why do you stare? What do you look at through the trees?"

"You were attacked," Sebastian said with no further explanation.

Soon, the young lady looked up at Ivan with violet eyes, her smooth forehead wrinkled. "Thank you," she spoke in English.

Ivan tipped his head and answered in the same language.

Tears welled, catching her lids. "You are Russian?"

"Yes." He offered water from the canteen.

She drank, and some calm seemed to settle over her. The girl moved to her father, passing her hand in front of his face. Turning to her brother, she called, "Sergei. Do you hear me? What has taken your thoughts so far away?" She searched Ivan's eyes. "Will my family recover?"

"I-I don't know, ma'am. I've never experienced such horrible creatures in my life."

"Most people haven't," Sebastian replied.

"You just killed one," Tatyana said in a quiet voice. They gazed at the deflated uniform where the skin-rotted bones lay eschewed, the head wedged against a stump. The smell was worse than a Ratling. Terrible yellow eyes stared up at them.

"It isn't human," Ivan whispered.

"You saved my—our lives. I am deeply grateful," she whispered.

He glanced away, ashamed. *How can I accept her gratitude? They are in this situation because of me, because I've defied Tereus. The Vaguers returned to steal my identity, my dreams—to kill me.*

Shortly, they led each passenger to the carriage. They didn't resist, only followed blindly. Ivan helped Tatyana take a seat between her mother and father. She smoothed her long skirt, flinching at the dirt and stains in the fabric. "You and your companion are most kind. Is he your grandfather?"

"No. I'm visiting. Sebastian is a dear friend." Ivan paused, then said, "Please excuse me while I see to the horses."

She bowed her head, acknowledging his request to take leave.

Sebastian climbed onto the driver's seat and gathered the reins into his thin hands.

Ivan came up beside him. "Sebastian?"

"What?"

"Will the Vaguers be waiting for us up ahead?"

Staring at some point in the distance, Sebastian slowly pulled in his shoulders. "I don't know, but stay alert. Keep your hand close to The Challenger."

And then, a strange woody voice spoke, that Ivan didn't recognize. "Would you like to send an emergency message to the castle?"

Sebastian and Ivan swung around, startled by the easy tone of the question.

"You can send a message?" Sebastian inquired of a nearby alder tree.

"Root-Underground opened this very moment.

Please tell me, in case the lines of communication freeze within our roots again."

"We weren't aware communication stopped between the trees," Ivan murmured.

With hands cupped to his mouth, Sebastian dictated, "We've been attacked by four Vaguers. The passengers will need medical attention at once. Ivan and I will lead the royal carriage to the castle. Please dispatch an escort to meet us on South Castle Road. Be sure to tell them our location and names," Sebastian directed at the alder.

"Yes, sir. *Preparing to send*."

****

Ivan moved with soft, quiet steps as he approached the four black horses. "Whoa, boys. Easy now." With a gentle hand, he led the team, easing the carriage back onto the gravel road.

Spooked, one flared his lips, nervously swishing his tail. Reins jingled when they tugged at their harnesses. Ivan grasped one of their bridles and spoke in a calm voice, "It's okay. We're going to the castle now. There's alfalfa and oats waiting for you."

"How are they?" Sebastian called from his seat above.

"They're frightened."

"Who isn't?" Sebastian stared to his right and searched the trees. His lips pressed closed.

"Come on, Alfred, Canute. Leave the ghastly creature to rot." Canute jerked his nose from under the Vaguer's dirty uniform and woofed. When they trotted toward Ivan, he reached for the beagles and lifted them up, placing them in front with Sebastian.

"Can you handle the carriage horses?" Sebastian asked as Ivan approached.

"Yes."

"Prop the driver next to you. Pretend he's alive." Sebastian climbed down, motioning to Standby, Merridyn's horse. "No need to explain the dead man to our passengers. It would only upset them. I suspect they'll sleep, except that pretty little lass in red. Oh, and wipe the blood from the driver's face. Let's not advertise this loss of life in case we meet someone on the road."

"You're riding Merridyn's horse, then?"

"Yes, she's an obedient animal."

Ivan observed Bounty giving Standby a playful nudge to her neck, and it surprised him. Maybe his horse was capable of making friends, after all, but Ivan didn't see this trait very often.

"I'll tie Bounty and Old Bones to the back of the carriage." Sebastian walked toward the animals and gathered their reins.

Pulling himself into the front seat, Ivan adjusted The Challenger at his side. He took a deep breath, straightened the deceased driver, and avoided looking at his distorted face.

A canteen, attached by a leather strap, was draped over the carriage brake. Ivan grabbed it and was about to take a long drink when he realized it was ickleberry wine. He wrinkled his nose. "It may be useful just the same." Wetting the hem of the Long Dark Cloak, he washed the blood from the driver's face.

"Let's go, Ivan," Sebastian yelled through cupped hands. "We need to reach the safety of the castle. Fast!"

Standby was a fine lead horse and seemed to understand her responsibility of calming the four frightened carriage stallions. Sebastian held tight to the slim saddle with one hand, the bridle with the other, his scrawny knees pressed the animal's ribs.

Silver reins jangled when Ivan gave a gentle slap against the black horses' rumps. He exhaled a breath of gratitude to be alive and on the move. *How will this be explained to the passengers when they come out of their stupor? Will they blame Lord Graydon for this—his lack of protection to visitors?*

Something caught his attention on the floorboards of the carriage. When he gave it a shove with his boot, he noticed it was a couple of knapsacks. *Had there been two drivers?* He shivered, and his heart beat faster.

There was no hint of Vaguers hiding behind trees. Ivan wanted to believe they'd been scared away and wouldn't ambush them. Since the beagles didn't bark or cause a raucous, Ivan figured they were safe—for now.

He hoped the garrisons would come in full force to search the lands from one end to the other until they removed the heads of every last creature.

A herd of fallow deer, with wild ponies mixed in, dashed through an open field, startling Ivan from his worries. *What has set them off?* He looked to Sebastian, hoping he would slow his horse and explain, but he, too, stared at the stampede of animals.

Then, he saw the reason.

Leading the troops of rescuers was an Elften. The thin, glinting circlet around his head showed it was Sytha in the front. He stood in the stirrups of his pale blue horse, appearing perfectly balanced. His bow rose in a fisted hand. Racing behind the Elftens was a clan of Wolflords. Ivan realized the Wolflords all had a similar look, including long, wolf-shaped ears. Several of Commander Simon's soldiers carried colorful castle flags and banners. Ivan cheered with relief.

At last, he and Sebastian were not alone and vulnerable to the hideous creatures that roamed the Forest. Sebastian pumped his hand into the air and yelled, "Hallelujah!"

Ivan brought the four horses to a stop.

Reaching the carriage first, Sytha swept off his horse and hopped onto the front seat with ease. "Move over," he commanded the dead man who had slumped to the side. Discovering his error, he gasped. His eyes flew open. "Oh, God in heaven—a Vaguer got him."

"Yes," Ivan said. "Four of them in the woods, about a half-hour back. We managed to kill one."

"Are…are you all right?" Tanner, the Elften, poked his head inside the carriage.

"I-I am able to speak," Tatyana said in a low, shaky voice. "My family still sleeps."

"What happened?" Sytha leaned past the corpse, met Ivan's eyes, and shifted his feet to accommodate the beagles.

Ivan blurted the details of the encounter, telling him about surprising the Vaguers.

"Did they attack the passengers?" Sytha asked.

"They were put under a spell of some kind, leaving them in a deep trance. Tatyana seems to be recovering. She's the lass in red."

"I know about the Vaguers." Sytha's hand clutched the bow hanging over his shoulder. "But I haven't had the privilege to kill any of them with my golden-tipped arrows." His teeth ground together in disgust. "This must be one of the carriages Lord Graydon is waiting for. Who are they?"

"Russian royalty. Tatyana and her family. She didn't give me a last name. I believe they will recover."

Sytha stood up, waving his hand in the air. "That's Commander Simon coming toward us, and he looks furious. Do you know him?"

"I met him on my first visit." Ivan recalled the friendship they'd formed after a rough beginning.

"He's a good leader. Simon and his men will scour the countryside looking for signs of those Essence-suckers." He paused before he spoke again. "By the way, it looks like there was another driver. I see two knapsacks on the floor."

"I noticed that," Ivan said.

The Elften snorted and stepped from the carriage. "I'm going hunting for Vaguers. I'll see you later at the castle."

"Sytha," Ivan called.

He turned.

"The fire—Zello—the Golden Lantern?"

"You have enough on your hands right now." Sytha swung onto his horse that just happened to pass by at that very moment—on purpose.

Ivan rolled his eyes at the horse's discipline and timing. *If only...*

Simon came along the left side of the carriage riding his big bay animal. "You'd better get this rig off the road. You're blocking traffic." Though his words were teasing, his scowl showed he understood the seriousness of the situation. He reached his hand up and placed it on Ivan's arm. "Glad to have you visiting again."

"It isn't what I expected." Ivan lifted an eyebrow. "I've never experienced anything quite so horrible."

"Don't worry, we'll hunt the vampires down and rid the Forest of them."

Someone called his name. Simon's officers,

Sergeant Berkel and Lieutenant Pezzuline, whom Ivan also met on his first visit, raced toward the carriage.

"Can't you stay out of trouble?" Pezzuline called in a stern manner, though Ivan knew he was joking. "We're always saving your bum!"

Ivan grinned in spite of himself. "By the way," he said to Simon, "you might search the area where we've just come from." He indicated the two knapsacks at his feet. "Check if there's another victim."

Simon gave a slow nod. His brow crinkled. "Tonight's feast won't be very cheerful for our foreign visitors, but we'll try to make it back in time to give them a warm welcome. Our mission now is to find the Vaguers and kill them—every last one." He saluted and rode off, his shoulders pulled back in a determined way.

The royal horses stomped their hooves and shook their heads. "Easy boys," Ivan said, gently pulling back on their bridles. "We'll be on our way in a moment." Just as he was about to give the reins a shake, Sebastian rode next to him.

"Is there room for another passenger?"

"I'd appreciate the company." Ivan motioned him to climb aboard.

Sebastian slid off Standby and hefted himself onto the seat. He scooped up Alfred, who turned and licked Sebastian's cheek and beard.

Wayland trotted along Ivan's side and pointed at Shayne and Gan-let. "We'll ride behind and guard you." One of the Wolflords grabbed Standby's bridle, encouraging her along.

"We're happy for your protection."

Canute growled, sniffing the man's lifeless body. Alfred and Canute dove into the open knapsack and consumed the sandwiches but ignored the pickle.

Leaning from the front seat, Sebastian waved to them as Simon and his soldiers rode off for the big hunt. "Godspeed and good luck," he hollered.

They were on their way once more as fear rose and circulated through Ivan's bloodstream.

A portion of the Elftens and soldiers led the carriage, while the Wolflords followed watching for any dangerous skeletal creatures camouflaged behind the trees.

Now well protected, Ivan turned and gave Sebastian a profound sigh.

Chapter 19

Lord Richard Louis Graydon

Ivan was not prepared for the extravagant scene of the Romanesque structure that came into view. With rolling green hills and streams, meadows bordered by forests and fields, the South Castle laid out before them in its magnificent splendor.

"Bart is right." Ivan drew a breath and swallowed. "This is an impressive collection of stones."

"It's expanded a great deal since I saw it nearly a decade ago." Sebastian sounded as startled as his companion. "It boasts no less than seven round towers, with countless turrets of various sizes."

"I can scarcely count the many pinnacles that adorn the structure." Ivan tipped his head trying to take it all in. His critical eye with interest in architecture and engineering pushed to the forefront. "I'm trying to imagine the force of workmen who made this castle possible."

"The original was built as a Roman fortress more than fifteen hundred years ago." Sebastian pointed, twirling his finger. "There ahead, near the entrance, is a watch tower complete with arrow and gun loops. Still used today for practice, I understand. Those high battlements define the third story of the main structure with thick stone walls."

"Impressive." Ivan stared, his mouth parted.

Sebastian agreed. "The thickness helps keep out the cold, but not entirely. Even with the two giant fireplaces in the great room, there's often a winter chill."

"I'm anxious to see it."

"The castle is constantly being built. Did you know?" Sebastian's eyebrows came together in disapproval.

"You told me Richard Graydon continues to expand as atonement for his brother, Lord Henry. A decade ago, he betrayed the people of the Forest."

"Well, I guess I did tell you. He never ceases to build and build." It seemed Sebastian was about to say more, but instead, he straightened the corpse by taking hold of his shoulders and pushed.

"I feel pity for the poor fellow," Ivan said. "He'll never drive a carriage again."

"A real shame." Sebastian shook his head, biting his lower lip.

They were silent for a time.

"Have you noticed how the old stone walls glow almost golden?" Sebastian swept his hands in a proud arc toward the castle before them.

"Magnificent." Ivan studied the huge construction in the distance, where there was an abundance of windows and stone balconies.

"They've been cleaning the outside for months in anticipation of Lord Graydon's royal guests, Zephyrus has told me."

Ivan and Sebastian spotted the Elftens and soldiers galloping behind them as they led the carriage across a long, covered bridge with four double arches. The river beneath curved around the castle and rushed to the south, spilling into the waterway of the Solent, Ivan supposed.

Gardens were profuse with blooming red roses. Immaculate lawns, bordered with lush trees and flowering bushes that reached as far as Ivan could see. Carved gargoyles scowled menacingly at them from the top of castle walls.

"They are protectors." Sebastian lifted his head and stared at the stone protrusions. "Though, it's difficult to appreciate them with their threatening features."

"They *are* scary," Ivan said.

As they drew close, Ivan was disappointed there was no drawbridge leading to the entrance. He'd seen pictures of them in his history books, imagining it as part of the South Castle. Perhaps there had been one but it proved to be impractical over time.

Red squirrels chased each other on the grass. A small herd of the less common sika deer grazed at the edge of a woody area. Fortunately, Alfred and Canute were resting at Sebastian's feet and didn't see the animals.

Ahead, the troop veered to the left onto a gravel road.

"They're going to the stables." Sebastian made a sweep of his hand. You can circle this long drive around the tall fountain in the center of the lily pond and stop in front. The staff will greet you as you pull the carriage. Matter of fact, I see the doors opening now."

Ivan wasn't concerned with the servants. His attention was drawn to the giant marble gryphons on either side of the arched front doors. Facing out from the wide portico, their vulture-like heads glared with defiance. Their muscled-lion bodies sat on their haunches, feet anchored to a four-foot pedestal, looking ready to leap at them at any moment. Long wings with highly carved detail protruded from their shoulders to the ground. Their lion tails curved and became part of the stone wall behind them.

"They are overwhelming," Ivan said, mesmerized by their immense size and fierce look.

"Splendid, aren't they?" Sebastian twisted his face. "I don't relish the thought of telling Lord Graydon that his favorite beasts have betrayed him and left their posts during daylight."

"What's the story carved on the pediment?" Ivan pointed to the triangular stone shape above and between the gryphons.

Sebastian cocked his head with a curious look. "How did you know that word?"

"I've read books on Grecian style architecture," Ivan said and shrugged.

"Oh, I see. It's the history of gifting the gryphons to Lord Graydon when they were just youngsters. He'll tell you all about it if you ask."

The castle staff of about a dozen men and women burst through the door, forming in a semi-circle. Spreading out, they tugged on their aprons, adjusted their caps, and drew their waistcoats closed. "They make a welcoming presentation," Sebastian said.

"Ivan, sir," someone called.

He searched for the owner of the familiar voice. "Maynard!"

The servant bowed and reached for Ivan's hand to help him down from his seat. "Ah, it's good to see your pets, too." Alfred and Canute barked with joy, restless to jump from their cramped spaces.

Moving to the other side of the carriage Maynard

guided Sebastian's old legs to the top step of a narrow stool he'd placed for him. "I've heard there was trouble on the road." A scowl formed on his forehead.

"That's right." Sebastian clipped his response.

"Will you be joining us?" Maynard asked the slumped driver in front.

"No," Ivan said. "He's quite dead."

"Oh my!" Maynard jumped back, horrified. His head scrunched into his shoulders.

"Let's see to the passengers." Sebastian leaned in through the open door to examine them. "Take them to the infirmary at once," he ordered the two footmen near him. They appeared annoyed that Sebastian gave the orders.

"How are they?" Ivan moved toward them. The parents and brother were still in a trance, their eyes half-closed. "Lady Tatyana. Are you all right?"

A bit dazed, she looked as though she'd just awakened. "I'm thirsty," she said. "Our water is gone."

"We'll take care of that. You and your family will be driven to the infirmary to be examined. Then you can rest," Ivan told her. "I-I'm so sorry this has happened."

"Thank you for your kindness." Her eyes were sad. "There is a feast planned this evening. Will you be there?"

"Perhaps." Just remembering, Ivan reached into the cloak's pocket. He pulled out the golden cross on its delicate chain and placed it into her hand.

She stared at it for a moment. "Please. You mustn't tell anyone about this cross."

"No, of course not—that is, I found it on the ground near you." For a moment, he worried that she thought he'd stolen it while she was in a stupor.

Tatyana nodded and said in a whisper, "We will not return to our country."

"Oh. Then I hope we meet again." Ivan wondered if it was the right response to her secret confession. He didn't know.

A servant in an ultramarine-colored waistcoat with matching breeches stepped forward. "Lord Graydon is waiting," he said in a stiff voice. "We will see to the passengers."

Sebastian and Ivan made their way up the castle steps, knowing their guests were well-cared for.

Ivan placed his hand on the mythical creature's cold-stone flank and gawked. He pulled in his breath, scarcely believing what he saw. Canute stood on his hind legs, barked, and scratched at the pedestal that supported one of them.

"Don't." Ivan pulled his beagle away. "He may snatch you in his sharp beak and eat you when he's freed."

"There to the west is the South Castle University and several chapels." Sebastian indicated with a tilt his head. "You'll probably get a tour of the grounds when things get straightened away."

For now, Ivan wasn't much interested in the grounds or the university. He took a deep breath and tried to relax his clenched hands, prepared to meet the esteemed Lord Richard Graydon.

****

The servants held open the large arched doors, bowed, and welcomed the travelers.

"I'm afraid there's much chaos here," a voice came from behind.

Ivan hadn't realized Maynard followed them. He

turned to clap the servant on his shoulder. "It's good to see you."

"Zello's gone quite mad and burned his stable." Maynard pulled his fingers through rust-colored hair, shaking his head at the same time. "And now, those blasted Essence-suckers have distressed our guests. I don't know what's happening in this Forest, but it's not like it used to be."

Ivan *knew* what was going on. *It's because of me. I've caused these terrible things to happen by defying Tereus. Tomorrow, right after breakfast, I'll leave and never return. There's no reason to put everyone in danger.*

An arm went around him.

"Don't take it so hard." Sebastian looked into Ivan's eyes and gave a sympathetic smile.

How did he know I feel so gloomy?

They entered the foyer. Ivan was at once aware of the vastness—of everything. High vaulted ceilings with double windows in the back of the room that reflected a sunlit sky. Heavy polished furniture lined the wall, and a plush oriental carpet covered the center of the long corridor.

Suddenly feeling uneasy, Ivan asked, "My beagles? Can they…?"

"Of course," Maynard said. "Your dogs are revered both here and in the Forest."

Alfred and Canute pressed their bellies to the floor, looking out of place and forlorn, and shot off to hide under a brocade-cushioned chair. They must've thought they were being scolded.

"They'll follow when they feel more at home," Ivan said, brushing away Maynard's concerns.

Splendid swords were crossed and displayed on the walls. Suits of armor held lances and ancient spears lined the corridor. One held a great shield with an image of Zello blowing orange and red flames. Ivan had seen the same icon on the banners the soldiers carried and on Commander Simon's breastplate.

A thin, average-height man with striking white hair, mustache and neatly trimmed goatee approached. "I apologize," he said with a genuine smile. "I meant to meet your carriage, but a few lingering details had to be dealt with. Welcome. Welcome to the South Castle." He went to Sebastian, and they embraced. "It's a pleasure to see you again, my dear friend."

"Ah, Richard. It's an honor to visit." Sebastian's face beamed. "It's been almost a decade."

"Has it now?"

Ivan waited to be introduced. It was protocol in the Russian court, and he suspected it was the same in an English castle.

Putting on a serious face, Sebastian smoothed his frazzled hair. "Lord Richard Graydon, it's my privilege to present Ivan Kimble, your neighbor to the northeast."

Although Lord Graydon grinned, his eyebrows curved with silent knowing and empathy. Ivan was about to bow when, to his surprise, the lord threw his arms around him and squeezed. "An honor to have you here," he said laughing.

"T-thank you, sir. I've been looking forward to meeting you—for some time."

"Such fine manners, but you don't need them here. Not with me. I enjoy things a bit more…casual. Isn't that right, Sebastian?"

"Indeed." Sebastian chuckled.

Dressed in what appeared to be clothing fashioned from the late fourteenth century, the lord wore a rich velvet jacket in turquoise, a lace jabot at his throat. The matching breeches were decorated with gold braid and button trim, just as the jacket. His white leggings, a bit wrinkled at the ankles, covered his thin legs. Shiny coat of arms buckles adorned his black polished shoes.

Sebastian asked, "Are you dressed in this extravagant manner for your Russian visitors?"

"You noticed?" He looked pleased. "Actually…" He made a show of brushing his jacket with the side of his hand. "We scheduled a Shakespearean performance this evening, held in The Zephyrus Auditorium. I was to be King Lear. But alas, there's so much strife right now, I felt it was best to cancel."

"That's too bad," Sebastian said with no trace of remorse. "The costume does look good on you, however."

"Thank you. I'd rather hoped the day would turn out better for your first visit." Lord Graydon's brow lifted.

Ivan had hoped so, too, though he didn't voice this.

Stepping back, Lord Graydon examined his visitor. "You do look a great deal like your brother. Tall, it would seem—for your age. Same shape face and straight nose." He nodded as he added, "Yes, a most striking figure."

Ivan's eyes shot open, feeling a blush on his cheeks. "H-have you seen Peter lately?"

The lord pulled on his goatee. "I'd heard he went home with you, and I was pleased. Several weeks ago, wasn't it?"

"Peter…" Sebastian paused. "Was to follow later, but then he didn't. Ivan has returned to find what has detained him."

"I was hoping you'd heard from my brother," Ivan said. "You were famously close, I understand."

"Yes. A smart lad. Full of fun and jest. I love him very much and always hoped for a son like him, but the blessing of a new wife and children hasn't happened."

Ivan smiled and filled his lungs with air.

"Then," the lord continued, "I realized it was best for him to go home where he could make something of himself. Find a direction in life. Marry…have a family."

Ivan felt a rush of gratitude for Lord Graydon's high opinion of his brother. He desperately wanted to ask if Peter had been released from his duties as a spy, but no one was to learn of Peter's secret—it might still endanger many lives. Perhaps later, Ivan could have a private conversation with the lord. Then he could speak freely.

"The staff has prepared refreshments for you in the library. Maynard will show you the way. I'll meet you there in a few minutes. I have many questions."

"And we have a lot to say, too." Sebastian glanced knowingly at Ivan.

Leaning into Ivan as they walked, Sebastian whispered, "Do you suppose anyone has told him about the Vaguers or his distraught Russian guests?"

Ivan shrugged and pressed his lips together.

They hurried down the long corridor. The floor, covered with thick rugs, muffled the sound of their steps. Large paintings in gilded frames were hung on the walls with measured spacing between them. Ivan glanced hurriedly, noticing they were portraits of past lords and ladies, as well as English Royalty. He was sure there were no paintings of Lord Henry Graydon anywhere in the castle. Henry had betrayed his people by stealing the

Ancient Relics from the Sanctuary of Truth…an unforgivable and treasonous crime.

"This is the main dining room." Maynard motioned to his right. Going a little farther, the servant stopped and pointed left. "And this is the Great Room."

Ivan veered in that direction, wanting to see inside. It was huge, with a fourteenth-century fan vaulted ceiling, dark paneled walls, tables, and chairs assembled for serious gatherings and meetings.

"Quite the sight, isn't it?" asked Lord Graydon as he came up behind them.

"Striking." Ivan breathed. "Simply striking."

A short distance away, Maynard opened the library's double doors. A pretty young girl, wearing a servant's cap and apron, hurried inside. She carried a silver tray holding a teapot, cups, and saucers, with a selection of appetizers and small cakes.

"My Lord." She curtsied, after setting the tray on a side table, turned, and took her leave.

"Get used to her face," the lord said with a chuckle. "You'll see three of them—triplets—serving our supper this evening. I think she is called Christiana, but it's difficult to tell them apart."

Maynard waited for them to sit. "Anything else, sir?" he asked, with a serious lift of his chin.

Lord Graydon glanced at the servant as though he'd just noticed him. "I—no, Maynard. I think we are well taken care of. Thank you."

The door ajar, the beagles rushed through the entrance. They dashed around the large room, sniffing everything. Canute went under the piano, circling its legs. The wide fireplace seemed to fascinate Alfred, where he stared and woofed at the blazing fire. It was not unusual behavior for the beagle.

Maynard coughed behind his hand. "May I take your beagles for a brief walk?"

"I would be grateful," Ivan said.

The lord turned to the servant. "Do let me know when there is news of the second carriage. It should've arrived by now. You may close the doors, and don't let anyone disturb us."

Does the lord know about the first carriage? Had no one told him the awful news? Ivan glanced at Sebastian, who lifted his shoulders.

"Yes, sir." Maynard backed away, called to the dogs, and they scampered after him.

Rich mahogany bookshelves filled with leather-bound books of various sizes lined the walls. Ivan had never seen so many, not even in the Graydon Village Library. He breathed in the scent of leather and lavender-scented furniture polish.

"Please, take a seat and be comfortable." Lord Graydon indicated the matching wingback chairs to his guests.

Ivan removed The Challenger and laid it on the floor next to him. He turned to Sebastian, signaling whether he might remove the cloak. The two fireplaces on opposite sides filled the room with warmth.

Sebastian approved with a nod.

Before taking his seat, Ivan reached for the teapot on the large tray. "May I pour?"

Their host nodded, seemingly impressed with Ivan's good manners. "And try a honey oatcake. They really are delicious. I believe our baker put chopped dates in them instead of currants."

Ivan shook his head and returned to his chair. He

took his cup and saucer in hand. "Anything sweet makes my teeth hurt." His laugh was light so as not to offend his host.

"I scarcely know where to begin." Lord Graydon sat and took a trembling breath. Any trace of laughter or joy had left him. He paused for a long minute and stared at the ceiling.

Ivan realized the grief and problems that must overwhelm the owner of the castle.

When the lord faced them, moisture glistened in his eyes. "I was told by one of the footmen that a driver was killed. A second one is missing."

Sebastian nodded slowly.

So, the lord did know of the tragedy. He had held himself in check until they could talk privately. Ivan breathed relief. He didn't want to be the one to break the awful news to his gracious host.

"How are the passengers?"

Fidgeting in his seat, Sebastian answered, "They'll recover." He went on to tell the horror of their encounter with the Vaguers.

The Lord leaned forward and patted Ivan's hand. "You are a blessing to our Forest."

Ivan's ears turned warm, finding it impossible to accept the lord's compliment. "The Elftens, Wolflords, and Simon's entire garrison went hunting the Vaguers. They'll search for the missing driver, too."

"Are there more than four of those horrible creatures hiding in the Forest?" The lord laced his fingers together, twisting them back and forth.

"At least three remaining. No way to know for sure," Sebastian said.

The smell of cheese and sausage got the best of Ivan.

He helped himself to both, stacking them on small squares of jitnut crackers. The lord took a piece of cheese and nibbled, though he didn't seem much interested in eating.

Ivan swiveled to view the entire grandeur at once. The arched mullioned windows gave the room a sense of long-ago elegance and grace. Some shelves held treasures from faraway countries like delicate vases, strange masks, huge shells, and colorful coral.

"There's another item we should address." Sebastian sighed, breaking Ivan's thoughts.

"I know," the lord said. "Sytha and Wayland gave me a full report of the Ratling's attack."

"I declare, it was as frightening as anything I've ever encountered." Sebastian's bushy eyebrows lifted. "Ivan was within seconds of death."

"I'm dreadfully sorry." Lord Graydon closed his eyes and frowned deeply. He was quiet for some moments. "You should have that bruise on your forehead looked after. Was it from the Vaguer's attack?"

"It's fine." Ivan gently rubbed the spot. "Thanks to the healing cloak." Since Sebastian hadn't mentioned the bruise was from a rock thrown by an angry troll, Ivan let it go. *The lord has enough worries to deal with.*

"What's causing these wicked things to happen?" Lord Graydon scowled and reached for his cup of tea with unsteady hands. "We rid the Forest of those vile Vaguers over fifty years ago. Now they're back. Why?" He made a face after a sip of tea and set the cup down with a clink. "It's already cold."

Ivan tightened his jaw. *I'm responsible for the creatures returning.* Sebastian laid his hand on Ivan's arm, cautioning him to stay silent.

"I've speculated that Tereus has found a new thrall," Sebastian said. "Someone above ground who is willing…and capable of carrying out his scheme to rule the Forest."

"Who in heaven's name would be so shortsighted?" Lord Graydon's voice rose.

Sebastian lifted his spectacles and rubbed them with the hem of his tunic. He pressed his lips together until they nearly turned white.

Changing the subject, Ivan asked about Merridyn's recovery.

"She's in the Sleeping Room of the infirmary, where it must remain dark with no visitors. Only the doctor and one nurse are allowed to check on her. Poor child."

"But will she recover from th-the troll symptoms?" Ivan asked.

"The doctor is quite certain it will wear off, thanks to Merridyn's own remedy."

"Everyone speaks well of her potions." Ivan smiled and made a mental note to visit her if they would allow him.

Sebastian pulled himself to the edge of his chair.

"We must call for the arrest of Cecil. Could you issue a notice to the garrisons to capture him for trial?"

"Cecil? Isn't he a fallen wizard?" Lord Graydon's white eyebrows rose. "What's his crime?"

Sebastian threw Ivan a glance. "Yes, he spent a year in Troll Transformation Prison, and now he's free. But he's held onto some of his powers and caused a great deal of chaos."

After a few moments, Sebastian continued, "Cecil also threw fireballs at the two young orphan boys when they were going for help. It knocked them out cold.

You'll recall, since the wizards were banished, fireballs are illegal in our Forest."

"Yes. I remember when Pousses returned with singed patches on his fine coat. My dear pet was angry for weeks." Lord Graydon frowned. "He wouldn't even talk to me."

"Just yesterday, Cecil and Maloof caused trouble at Ancient Oak Creek," Sebastian chimed.

"I'll issue an order for the commanders to capture and hold them both." The lord pulled his fingers through his hair. "This is more complex than I'd realized."

Clearing his throat, Sebastian continued. "Joseph, the spirit in the Golden Lantern, told us that Cecil and Maloof initially got the Lantern from Hoxx, the leading ghoul who lives in the Mountain of Smoke and Fire. Some sort of deal was struck with him, but Joseph didn't know what it was."

"I suppose none of that really matters, now," Ivan chimed in. "The Golden Lantern was returned to the castle by the blacksmith. In fact, Zello was put to the task of relighting the wick, and then…"

There was a soft rap on the door. Lord Graydon turned around, his eyes narrowed with irritation. "Yes. Enter."

Maynard opened the library door. Canute and Alfred raced inside and explored the room all over again. The servant bowed and left.

Ivan ruffled their ears. They licked his fingers. Alfred yawned and curled up on the rug in front of the fireplace. Canute lay by Ivan's side.

Leaning forward, forearms pressed against his knees, Lord Graydon said, "Our Animal and Gamekeeper told me Zello was so angry for being accused of burning the stable out of spite, he went to hide in the Azurite Mountains. He took the Golden Lantern with him."

"What?" Sebastian pulled back in the chair so fast that his spectacles nearly fell from his nose. Ivan's teacup clattered.

"I'm afraid it's true." The lord nodded. Sadness showed in his eyes. "Zello took the lantern from the castle early this morning. Just who helped him steal it is yet unknown. It was the news that detained me from meeting your carriage."

"That's illegal, isn't it?" Ivan said, shocked at the announcement.

Sebastian groaned. "It just keeps getting worse."

"Where are these mountains?" Ivan tipped his head, trying to recall. He wondered if he and Sebastian should go there and have a talk with the dragon. Maybe it was just a matter of soothing his hurt feelings.

"They are located southeast, off the South Road entrance." The lord indicated with a slight wave of his hand. "Many people know nothing of them, blocked from their memory."

"Odd behavior for our friendly dragon, isn't it?" Sebastian shifted in his seat.

"It is." The lord's white eyebrows lifted. "Although, I believe he was trying to garner attention for his innocence and would've appreciated some gratitude for his part in the Forest War. Zello snatched up a couple of soldiers in Kruse Hays's army. Some say his actions brought the war to a quick end."

"I agree. We both saw it happen." Sebastian bobbed his head. "It was quite a sight. Our soldiers whooped and cheered for Zello's help."

Ivan pursed his lips, remembering the two men cradled in Zello's arms while in flight. He was sure the dragon would intentionally drop them to their death as punishment, but he took them to safety, where they were imprisoned in the castle.

The lord stood, and a muscle twitched in his thin face. "You'll excuse me for a few moments. If you need the lavatory," he addressed Ivan, "it's through the door at the end of this room." He walked in that direction, looking sad and beaten.

After he'd gone, Ivan turned to Sebastian. "It's a lot to absorb in a short time. I feel sorry for him."

Sebastian must've felt the same frustration because he squeezed his forehead with the span of his fingers and thumb. "It's all so unexpected. The rise of the Vaguers is his greatest concern, I'm sure. And now, all this about Zello leaving with the lantern." He moaned.

Ivan poured more tea, adding a little milk to cut the strength. "I'm to blame."

"How's that?" Sebastian turned to meet Ivan's eyes.

"I told you. Tereus warned me not to return to the Forest, and I stubbornly ignored him. You can't deny he summoned the Vaguers' return. And, he created those awful Ratlings to kill me." Ivan slumped into his chair, breath caught in his throat.

"Now, Ivan, you must reconsider…"

"I'm leaving after breakfast tomorrow," he announced firmly. "I don't want to endanger other people—or you."

"Let's see what a new day brings." Sebastian clasped his fingers together.

Ivan reached for more cheese and sausage. "Are you going to tell the lord about the gryphons?"

"No. It can keep for now. I don't believe they are snatching kaleido-birds at this time. We saw them in daylight, and that alone will carry a severe punishment. However, I think the reporting should be Simon's job."

Shortly, Lord Graydon returned and sat. He must've doused his face with cold water, as his mustache and goatee were damp.

Sebastian lifted his head and sighed. "Tell us about Zello burning the dragons' stable."

Chapter 20

Dragons' Stable Fire

"We have six dragons here at the castle," Lord
Graydon said. "Two adult females, two young males, an
infant born just last week—and Zello, the alpha male. A
couple of weeks ago, our Animal and Gamekeeper
reported that our favorite dragon was fuming after being
accused of eating those strange birds that squawk too
loudly and too often. You know about this, I believe?"

"Kaleido-birds." Ivan informed. "Zello's feelings
were hurt because he was no longer trusted."

"Can't say I blame him." The lord absently traced
the carved decorative pattern in the arm of his chair. "A
pity. A real pity. I've known Zello since he was as small
as a crested newt. He'd never burn his own stable out of
anger or spite. I believe it may've been an accident."

"Oh?" Sebastian's brow shot up with new interest.

"According to one of the stable hands, Zello was
trying to light the Golden Lantern's wick. As you know,
it takes a dragon's breath to relight it." Lord Graydon
looked at his guests, raising one white eyebrow.

Ivan nodded, having heard this several times.

"I was told," the lord continued, "a spark flew when
Zello coughed. It caught and smoldered in the stable
straw. Before long, the building was ablaze. Dragons are
deathly afraid of fire—except their own. Zello caused

more chaos by panicking, and he charged through the stable walls to save the others. Fortunately, all escaped. The structure where the winged horses are stabled didn't suffer any damage."

"Were you here when it happened?" Ivan asked.

"In the library… right over there." He pointed behind a bookcase to a large drafting table and boxes of files. "I was working on some architectural drawings. By the time I was notified, the fire was beyond stopping."

"At least it sounds like Zello's innocent of spiteful destruction." Sebastian tightened his hands together.

The lord's face wrinkled with despair. "I also believe he was angry, and so he grabbed the lantern and fled to the Azurite Mountains." He reached for a cluster of grapes, popping one into his mouth. "First, he's accused of eating those kaleido-birds, which is absurd. And then, people at the castle blamed him for intentionally setting the stable fire, endangering the entire kingdom. Because of that, I'm sure his feelings were devastated."

Sebastian shrugged, though his frown stayed. "I think you got it right."

The heat in the room made Ivan drowsy. He caught himself just as his head dipped.

"I'm afraid our heroic guest has had quite a dizzying day." Sebastian pushed up from the chair. "Perhaps a short nap before the festivities this evening?"

"Of course!" The lord showed embarrassment for not considering this earlier. He rose to his feet, retrieved the Long Dark Cloak, and placed it over Ivan's shoulders.

Thanking his host, Ivan donned the sheath that housed The Challenger, buckled it at his waist, and adjusted it at his side.

"Please follow me." The lord turned and walked toward the door. "I'll show you to your bedchamber. Tomorrow, right after breakfast, I'll give you and our Russian guests, if they are up to the task, a tour of the castle and grounds."

Ivan would enjoy sightseeing, but then, he must leave the Forest. Surely, the lord *would* understand his reluctance to stay.

When Sebastian opened the doors to the library, Maynard jumped up from a cushioned chair, straightened his waistcoat, and hurried to the guests.

"I'm taking them to their room," Lord Graydon explained. "Could you walk the dogs once more and then return them to the Blue Room on the second floor?"

"I'd be happy to." Maynard whistled to Alfred and Canute. Their nails made a delicate clipping sound on the marble tiles in the hallway as they followed eagerly.

Ivan and Sebastian climbed the stone stairway behind their host. It curved around until it reached the next level.

"This way." The lord turned to the right. He unlocked a thick arched door with decorative solid brass fittings. They stepped in. "I think you'll find everything you need, even a change of clothes. Something fancy for this evening's festivities, if you wish."

"I'm sure we'll be fine." Sebastian stalked the room and searched behind the heavy curtains. He even peeked into an armoire and closed the door gently.

Ivan looked into a large closet at the end of the room. "Empty."

"Not to worry." Lord Graydon chuckled at their concerns. "There's only one way in and out. That's why

I selected it." He dropped an ornate key into Ivan's open palm. "We are the only ones with access. You'll be perfectly safe."

"We're grateful." Ivan stifled a yawn.

The huge four-poster bed, with a multi-layered canopy and blue patterned comforter, commanded a great deal of space in the room. The walls were the same pale blue as the Elftens' horses, while darker shades were used as accents. Ivan was delighted to see his saddlebags hanging from a hook on the door. Someone had thought to bring them. There he found his toothbrush, hair comb, and a change of clothing. It wasn't likely he'd dress in the fancy clothes that were laid out for him—too fussy.

"There's fresh water in the pitcher." Lord Graydon pointed. "Anything you need, ask Maynard. He requested to be posted outside your chamber. We wouldn't want anything to happen to either of you."

Before Ivan could thank his host, Lord Graydon wrapped his arms around him and patted his back. "You don't know how I've looked forward to meeting you after all the fine things Peter has told me." He blinked rapidly. "That's why I sent you a personal invitation to visit. And now, seeing you, the young man who saved our Forest, brings me such joy."

"I-I...my honor to be here," Ivan stammered, surprised a second time by the lord's unabashed show of affection.

"Enjoy your much-needed nap, my good lad."

Sebastian closed the door behind their host, exhaling a long stream of breath.

Ivan wasted no time removing The Challenger, his boots, and socks. He collapsed on the bed, spreading his arms wide. "Aah, this feels good."

Sebastian sat down on a tufted parlor sofa. "This doesn't look very comfortable," he grumbled, shifting on the hard seat. An open window near him ushered a lovely breeze of fresh air that seemed to carry the scent of moisture.

"Are you asleep?" Sebastian asked a few moments later.

"Nearly." Ivan opened one eye.

"I think it went as well as it could, under the circumstances." He paused, glancing out the window. "It looks like rain."

"Poor Lord Graydon." Ivan's voice grew weak. "His troubles are many and heavy."

"That they are. That they are…and will probably get worse."

Ivan slept.

****

Hours later, someone tapped on their chamber door. "What?" Ivan groaned and turned over on the bed.

Sebastian rose from the sofa. "I'll see who it is." One of his hands held his back, and he groaned. "This *is* a hard seat. It should be hauled off and dumped at the dragons' stable once it's rebuilt."

Ivan opened his eyes, but he didn't move to leave his comfortable position.

One of the triplets entered, holding a wide tray by its handles. "Supper for our fine guests." She set it upon the table and removed the silver dome while pushing the elaborate floral display aside.

Delicious smells wafted through the steam, evident by Alfred and Canute when they leaped from their resting places near the fireplace. Sniffing the air, Canute barked and raced toward the food.

"Why do we need this delivered when there's a feast tonight?" Sebastian stuttered. "I was just about to awaken him, and we'd get dressed."

"Oooh." The girl drew out a sad moan. "The celebration has been canceled. The feast was served, however, and is now past. All those people had to be fed, you understand?" She straightened her cap over a mass of curly red hair. "My lord wishes to move the festivities to another evening when his guests are feeling recovered. And…"

"And what?" Ivan propped himself on one elbow.

"Oh. Excuse me, sir. I thought you were asleep." She blushed. "The second driver of the carriage." She removed the large vase of fresh flowers from the table and set it on a clean desktop.

"Yes…" Ivan held his breath.

"They found the man in a most awful way." She lowered her voice and planted her hand next to her mouth. "His eyes were sucked out of their sockets. It was one of those dreadful Vaguers. You know about them?"

"Sadly, we do." Ivan fell back onto his pillow, throwing an arm over his eyes.

"Yes, sir. A terrible thing. When my lord learned of this, he decided to cancel the celebration—musicians, jugglers, and storytellers. It wouldn't seem right to celebrate when two men have died today."

Sebastian stared at the ceiling. "It was the right decision, of course."

"Thank you for the food, Christiana," Ivan said.

"My name is Rowena. We're triplets, you know? But Christiana did tell me you are a visitor from the outside."

"Yes, well…" Sebastian cleared his throat

209

impatiently.

"When you didn't appear for supper, my lord thought you would both enjoy food in your chamber. It's nearly nine o'clock."

Sebastian's mouth dropped. "How did it get so late?"

"The usual way, I suppose," the girl said in a casual voice. "My lord mentioned you both had a dreadful day and to let you sleep as long as you needed. If you wish to join him in the dining room with his other guests for fruit and a glass of port, you are most welcome."

"No. It's already late." Ivan swung his legs over the side of the bed, going weak from the delicious smells coming from the tray. He stretched his neck around the girl to see what awaited on the platter for him and the beagles.

"Did everyone attend the supper?" Sebastian asked.

"It was very solemn, I must say. Commander Simon and his men were there. The Elftens and Wolflords asked after you. Our Russian guests didn't appear, which is reasonable." She fingered the ruffle on her apron and paused. "Three of them are still confined to the Sleeping Room, not to be disturbed. Lady Tatyana asked for tea to be brought to her bedchamber. She's most upset and weeps for her family." Rowena unrolled napkins holding fancy cutlery and moved another chair to the table.

She probably didn't realize Sebastian was a spirit and wouldn't be eating.

"I've heard Lady Merridyn is still in the infirmary," she said, "but she seems to be improving quickly."

Ivan thought Rowena was well informed for a servant. "That's good news. Hopefully, we'll see her tomorrow."

Sebastian walked the girl to the door and opened it.

"I am hungry." Ivan sat as soon as the servant left.

Alfred and Canute stood next to Ivan with begging eyes. Their tails swung hard and fast.

"I'll fill the wash bowl." Sebastian moved toward the pitcher and poured water for the beagles.

Ivan's stomach rumbled when he smelled the roasted meats and vegetables. Several small dishes had various kinds of preserves and jellies accompanying the delicious array of sweets.

Selecting two china plates, Ivan filled them for his pets. "Canute, if you don't like the smoked turnips, please don't push them onto the floor. Do you hear me?" The dog glanced up from where he lapped water, looking hurt from the reprimand. Ivan set heaping portions down for them.

Tying a bib around his neck, Ivan forked a piece of lamb. Then he took a slice of pork and placed half a pheasant on an extra plate next to him. The bird's skin smelled of a mixture of herbs and was cooked to a golden brown. A basket of fresh bread with a linen cover sat on the table. The aroma of yeast wafted under his nose. "It reminds me of Arnie and Season's hospitality." Ivan grinned. "Care to join me, Sebastian?"

"I believe I will take a seat and have a spot of tea." He chuckled lightly.

As Ivan ate, he reflected on the events that afternoon. He was secretly glad the festivities were canceled, too fatigued to face a crowd of people. He was struck with remorse to learn the second driver had been killed, though both he and Sebastian suspected it.

Early tomorrow, Ivan hoped he could have a private word with Lord Graydon. This would be the most reliable way to learn if Peter lied about being a spy. He shivered, considering the possible answer. *What if Peter wasn't honest about his duties to the lord?*

After eating his fill, leaving a portion on his plate, Ivan drank more tea, ignoring the selection of desserts. Sweet biscuits, oatcakes, and scones sprinkled with sugar looked appetizing, but he wouldn't indulge. He thought of Coreena and how she loved sweets. Suddenly wishing she were here next to him to enjoy the delicious treats. Odd. He hadn't thought about her much at all since he entered the Forest.

Somewhere in the hallway, a clock struck eleven.

Ivan crawled into bed, turned onto his side, and drew the cloak close to his chest. He wondered where Peter's room had been. *Do I occupy it now? What did my brother do all those years while he lived at the castle?* Another question washed over him. *What did he do to repay Lord Graydon for his kindness and generosity?*

Well, he defended. *Peter is a spy, watching for the Forest's safety. Yes, that's it. My brother is a hero. His reports are invaluable.*

In the night, rain pounded the castle rooftops, turrets, and grounds. Moist, cold air rushed through the open window. Sebastian soon closed it, then stacked and relit the logs in the fireplace. Ivan guessed his curious beagles helped but more likely got in the way. He smiled, pulling the comforter under his chin.

Ivan's mind slipped into a quiet place where his dreams emerged in bright rainbow colors with a vision of Anna-Iza and Coreena. He frowned. *Why do I care so deeply for them both?*

Chapter 21

The Morning Feast

Alfred and Canute squabbled over a bone left from Ivan's dinner. They chased each other around the Blue Room until Ivan told them to stop and behave.

Ivan sat up in the big bed, stretching his arms wide, and yawned.

"Good morning." Sebastian placed a bookmark in the novel he'd been reading. "Your beagles are feisty." He smiled at them, reaching over and patting Canute's head.

"They are," Ivan replied. "I slept deeply and didn't have any ugly dreams from the horrors we experienced yesterday."

Sebastian's bushy eyebrows lifted. "You needed your rest."

A soft knock sounded at the door.

Pushing up from the parlor chair, Sebastian again grumbled about his back. He went to the door and opened it.

"Sir, I've come for the supper tray." One of the triplets, they weren't sure which, moved toward the table. "And Maynard is here to fill the tub for your bath."

The servant bowed, grinned at Sebastian and Ivan, tipped his head, and disappeared behind a decorative curtain where the water sounded in a rush. Ivan followed, pulling off his nightshirt.

"Thank you, Rowena," Sebastian said after a brief time of making small talk with the girl.

"Oh no, sir." She stopped. "I'm Fiona. My sister brought your meal last night. You enjoyed it, I see."

Sometime later, Ivan emerged from behind the curtain and into the room, fully dressed and drying his hair on a thick towel with the words *South Castle* embroidered on the hem. "It was delicious," he said, remembering how much he had eaten.

Fiona reached for the tray and curtsied. "If there's anything you need, please let me know."

"We'll do that." Sebastian was anxious for the pesky servant girl to leave. Ivan could sense it.

Maynard gave a little chuckle. He opened the door for the girl, where she placed the plates and platters on a trolley. "We will see you shortly for a lovely breakfast," she called over her shoulder.

Ivan raised his eyebrows. "How can anyone tell them apart? And they're all so pretty."

"They are, but a little old for you." Sebastian replaced the vase of flowers in the center of the table. "Besides, you have bigger worries."

"I know." Ivan splayed his palms. Sebastian must have misunderstood. He only meant to be polite and make thoughtful comments about the girls. He wondered about Anna-Iza. *Did she attend the feast last night? If so, I'm sorry I missed my chance to see her.*

"I'll leave The Challenger under the pillows until after breakfast. It's too cumbersome to wear around many people."

"Suit yourself." Sebastian locked the door after Ivan stepped out and tied the strings of the Long Dark Cloak around Ivan's neck.

"Come on, Alfred. Canute. It's time for breakfast."

****

Maynard led Ivan and Sebastian into the large dining room, opening the double doors with a grand gesture. The aroma of fried sausages and mushrooms met him when he drew in a deep breath. Ivan hoped it might be a small, cozy affair with only a handful of people at this early hour. In spite of the large meal he'd eaten the evening before, the aromas caused his stomach to rumble. His beagles wagged their tails happily.

"Lord Graydon has a place for you at his table." Maynard turned and said, "Follow me."

Voices quieted. The chairs were pushed back, and people stood, clapped, and cheered. Frightened by the noise and stomping feet, Alfred and Canute scooted under the table.

Ivan didn't know what to make of it.

"They cheer for you." Sebastian took Ivan by the elbow and guided him.

Lord Graydon rose from his seat. With his chin lifted and eyes bright, he clapped more vigorously than any of the guests.

Jumping in front, Sytha grabbed Ivan by his hand, while Wayland reached for Ivan's forearm and pulled him toward the Lord's Table.

Ivan's cheeks turned warm. "Why are they clapping?"

The lord put his arms around Ivan and embraced him. "We are grateful for your visit and help, of course."

"But…what have I done?"

"Sit here." Sytha patted the seat next to him and Richard Graydon. "We have much to talk about."

"Where *am I* supposed to sit?" Sebastian griped. There was no open chair for him.

Wayland grinned and pointed. "On the opposite side of our table with Simon and his men." Sebastian grumbled, crossed his arms, but sat where he was told.

The applause faded, and the people went back to eating the sumptuous spread.

One of the triplets, extending her full attention, held a platter and served their special guest.

Sitting to Ivan's right, Sytha said and pointed with discretion, "There's Tatyana with a castle entourage beside her. Her father, mother, and brother are doing better, but they didn't come to breakfast this morning. I'd like to get to know the lady better while she visits. Could you teach me Russian in a few minutes?"

Ivan laughed.

Tatyana smiled and gave a polite wave. Ivan waved back.

"Maybe I'm too late to win her fancy." Sytha pouted.

"Not to worry." Ivan cut a sausage into small rounds and ate one. "It's because we are both Russian, and she feels comfortable around one of her own countrymen."

Lord Graydon stood and tapped his spoon on his crystal water glass. "My good ladies and gentlemen. It is my honor to introduce this fine lad. Ivan Kimble has done much for our kingdom." He leaned toward him and put his hand on Ivan's shoulder, listing his achievements.

The accounts made him sound daring and brave. Ivan knew better and shriveled. He cast a long look on the opposite wall, wishing the lord would stop. Besides, he had the help of Sebastian, who healed him countless times. The Elftens, Simon, and his men—so many were there to help him out of trouble.

The lord mentioned Ivan's courageous beagles during the Vaguers' attack.

When the name Vaguers was mentioned, the audience gasped. They turned to one another, their eyes round with fear.

"Yes," the lord said. "I'm also appalled these horrible Essence-suckers have returned to our Forest. New restrictions are set to limit your travels. Until further notice, an Elften or Wolflord must be your escort at all times."

A rush of worried voices swept the dining area. At once, questions and growls changed the cheerful atmosphere.

"We hope these limitations are temporary. Until then…" the lord raised both arms high, "let's all be cautious." He hesitated for a time and continued. "I was informed this morning by Commander Simon, that of the *four* Vaguers that threatened the lives of our Russian visitors, three have been killed."

"What about the fourth?" a guest asked with a quivering voice. "Are there more of these hideous creatures in our Forest?"

No answers came.

Ivan couldn't tell who had asked the question, but by the tone of his voice, he was frightened.

Sytha rose from his chair and gestured for silence. "We will find them and remove their heads. I promise you."

"Yeah! There's no escaping the Wolflords' hunting skills." Wayland shot to his feet and pumped his fists into the air. "Until then, please obey and don't venture beyond the safety of the castle unless we accompany you."

Ivan swallowed hard. He remembered Kagutt's awful threat. *Is he still out there waiting for me?*

Lowering the palms of his hands, Lord Graydon paused until the room went quiet. No one spoke. "Let's not think on this now, but enjoy breakfast and our lovely Russian guest."

With that, he introduced Tatyana, making an apology to her family, who were recovering in the infirmary.

The people politely applauded.

"We are expecting another carriage of Russian guests very soon." The Lord's gaze swept the crowd. "They are renowned and most anxious to meet you."

Tatyana stood gracefully, looking comfortable as she addressed the people. She thanked everyone, especially Lord Graydon, for his concern and kindness toward her parents and brother. She praised Ivan and Sebastian for their bravery in saving her from a terrible fate. "I shall never forget what you have done."

Ivan shifted in his seat, looking down at his plate.

"Don't be concerned." Sebastian leaned forward from the opposite side of the table. "These things are not your fault. You did what needed to be done to help others. No one could ask for more."

Simon looked puzzled. "What's that supposed to mean?"

I'm a fraud, and no one knows except Sebastian. "How did you know what I'm thinking?" Ivan glanced at the old man. His fork stopped short of his mouth.

"I'd be thinking the same," Sebastian said, slowly nodding.

Maynard shoved two large bowls of food under the

table for Alfred and Canute. He patted Ivan's shoulder and congratulated him. "I'm proud of you. I wasn't aware what a big part you and your dogs played in saving our guests."

"I didn't plan any of it." Ivan cut a broiled tomato and took a bite.

"It was not my intention to insult you, Ivan, sir." Maynard took a step back and bowed.

"No, wait, I'm sorry. I didn't mean to be curt." Ivan blinked rapidly. "I just…well, it's all a bit overwhelming."

"Of course. I understand." Maynard moved farther down the table to serve the many guests.

Motioning toward Ivan, Wayland said, "I need to have a word with you—soon as the morning feast is over."

Ivan's cheek muscles jerked. He knew by Wayland's tone it was serious. *Does he have information about the other carriage?*

"Toast?" One of the triplets presented a tray heaped with buttered toast and a variety of preserves.

Ivan removed several slices when Wayland waved her away with some annoyance.

"What do you want to speak to me about?" Ivan was too impatient to wait.

Wayland whispered behind his palm. "I-I know where Peter is."

Ivan stared at his Wolflord friend. "Where?"

"Helvaka. Hiding, just as we suspected."

It was true then. Ivan froze, a toast wedge stopped mid-way to his mouth. His hand shook.

"I can't say much here." Wayland looked around, checking their privacy. "Sytha knows, too."

"How did you find out?"

"My brother, Davaan told me—he lives there. He's still a werewolf, you know?" Shame flushed over him.

"When did he tell you this?"

"We met at the edge of South Castle Road just past dawn this morning, and he gave me the message. Peter wants to see you."

"Let's go at once." Ivan pushed back his chair and tossed his napkin on the table.

"No!" Wayland grabbed Ivan's hand and shushed him. "He wants to meet you at the end of next week."

"Why not now?"

He shook his head. "Davaan was unbending about the meeting time and date. I don't know why. Didn't say."

A soft cry left Ivan's throat. "Something's wrong. I need to talk to Lord Graydon about this. I'll leave as soon as possible."

"Don't discuss it with anyone." Wayland's teeth clenched, his thick brows angled. "Davaan will get into trouble for snitching. He knows it's dangerous to enter Helvaka without protection."

Sytha bobbed his head. "Better listen to him."

"But I came here to find Peter—and *now* I have to wait until next week. He must be in great danger. Will you and Sytha go with me?"

"Yes, but not now." The Wolflord's mouth tightened, a cheek muscle pulled taut. "Please, you must agree to these terms."

Turning in his seat, Sytha said, "We will lead you in and out of the old kingdom, werewolves and all. For Davaan's safety we must go when invited. He will secure our passage."

"Why? What can't we overcome? I have the cloak. I'll take The Challenger, I'll—"

"Everything despicable lives in Helvaka." Wayland cut the eggs on his plate. The yolks broke and met with the fried potatoes, saturating them in yellow. He sopped it up with a broken piece of toast. "I was one of them—a werewolf. I know what it's like and what must be done."

"It's a hell-hole," Gan-let said, waving his hands. He sat next to Wayland and must've overheard.

"Besides…" Sytha glanced at the people at his table. "You'll be back for Merridyn's trial about that same time."

"I wish I knew if Peter was all right." Ivan steadied his arms on the edge of the table.

"Fiona." Sytha motioned to the servant. "Pass the fruit and vegetable plate this way. You know Elftens don't eat this kind of—food." He indicated the heap on Ivan's plate and made a disagreeable face.

No one seemed offended by the remark. The girl delivered the tray while she flashed a big grin at them. Did she overhear? *I don't think so.*

"What did Davaan say about Peter? Is he in good health?" Ivan's face contorted with worry, imagining Peter with a clan of werewolves. They could tear him apart, bury his bones, and no one would ever find him.

"I guess so." Wayland shrugged and glanced around. "Try not to look so shocked. People will ask what we are talking about. No one must know."

Ivan sat back in the cushioned chair, having lost his appetite. He fiddled with his fork. *I must talk to Lord Graydon—alone. Is Peter all right, and is he still in the lord's employment?*

Chapter 22

Zello's Return

Quick footsteps sounded on the breakfast room's wooden floor. Everyone looked up to see who walked with such haste and determination.

The surly footman Ivan saw when he'd first arrived at the castle marched directly toward Lord Graydon. The man's face was grave, his gaze riveted. He nearly tripped over the beagles as he hurried past and looked annoyed because of it.

Alert, Lord Graydon squared his shoulders and watched the man approach.

Bending from the waist, the footman whispered into his ear. The message was quick.

"Excuse me." The lord rose to his feet, dabbed his mouth with a napkin, and moved to where Ivan, Sytha, and Wayland sat. "Zello has returned," he said in a low voice.

Motioning Commander Simon and his soldiers with a sharp nod, the lord left. The men pushed their chairs away and abruptly followed. The room emptied in only moments. Everyone wanted to see what called Lord Graydon away with urgency. Several servants put down their trays and hurried after them. Alfred and Canute got lost amid shuffling feet, but Ivan was sure they'd find their way. They were hunting dogs, after all.

Outside the castle, horses were tethered or held by the stablemen.

When the lord looked behind him, aware of the exodus, he stopped with a jolt. Holding up his hands, he cried, "Please, too many people will upset our dragon. Do return to the dining room and continue your breakfast."

Zello has returned. Ivan inhaled deeply and then smiled.

"Have another helping of rice-apricot pudding," one of the triplets yelled, but she didn't turn back either.

Bounty stood outside the castle entrance, where he sidled and whinnied. The rushing crowd and other horses made him jumpy.

"There! There's Zello." All heads tilted to study the flying image in the backdrop of a gray sky.

"Where? I don't see anything," several people remarked.

Sytha pointed, breathless. "He has the Golden Lantern."

Impossible to miss, the lantern glowed and swung in Zello's front claws, spreading wavering spokes of light far and wide.

"It's magnificent, isn't it?" Lord Graydon whispered.

"The lantern or Zello?" Ivan gasped.

"Both, really." The lord chuckled.

"Why do you suppose he's returned?" Wayland swiveled as he tracked the dragon's flight.

"Who knows?" Lord Graydon shrugged. "I've never known Zello to be so rebellious."

"Let's ride to the stable." Sytha swung his arm to the south for Ivan and Wayland's benefit. "Maybe he'll land there." The Elften's pale-blue horse made his way through the crowd and found his master with no provocation.

Sebastian and Wayland mounted quickly, anxious to see where the dragon was going to land. In a rush, they rode forward, coming to Sytha's side. There they waited for Ivan.

Bounty was the last to find his master, showing no urgency or enthusiasm. Ivan leaped on and gave his horse a harder than usual nudge in his ribs. Turning in circles, the animal snorted, raised his head, and tried to nip his master's knee. "Stop that, Bounty."

"Go on. I'll meet you there." The lord waved them away and climbed into the royal carriage that awaited him. A well-dressed man and two elegant ladies joined him and took their seats inside. The passengers poked their heads out the windows to gawk.

Who are they? Ivan wondered.

"The stables are around the castle on the southeast side." Sytha pointed in that direction. He took off, and all trailed after him.

Ivan smelled the aftermath of smoke and ashes as they approached the destruction of the building. It must've been an elaborate two-story structure before it burnt to the ground.

As Sytha's horse came to a halt, he slid off with a graceful twist, hitting the ground on steady feet. He adjusted the sheath of arrows and a bow that rested over his shoulder while he waited for the others. When Wayland and Ivan rode next to him, they dismounted quickly but not nearly as graceful as their Elften friend.

Huffing and complaining, the stable keeper leaned against his shovel and looked up at Wayland. When introduced to Ivan, they nodded to each other.

"What happened here?" The Wolflord clapped the man on his back. They seemed like fair friends.

"I'd like to know who's ta clean up this mess," the stable keeper said in a loud voice. He wiped his calloused hands over his sooty face. "We've been at it since yesterday. This is as far as we got. Good for nuttin', lazy bones. Those dang dragons don't do a thing all day."

"Nice to see you, too, Mr. Harowitz," Sytha teased when he joined them.

The man looked embarrassed for a moment. "Well, it's us that's gotta make the stable right again, ain't it?"

Ivan felt sorry for Mr. Harowitz. Scarcely a board was left standing. Piles of smoldering hay and straw had been raked to the center of the charred structure. Watering troughs were destroyed, pipes broken, and the area blackened with soot.

The crowd was large and growing larger. Several people raced into the area on horseback, covered their noses, and sneezed. *Too many people, horses, and commotion might upset the dragon even more.* This worried Ivan.

He could scarcely take his eyes off the huge beast circling in the sky. Ivan remembered Zello's powerful wings pumping with effort when he carried two of the Dark Army's men away, one under each arm. It was quite a sight.

A column of smoke and fire shot from the beast's mouth. The crowd oohed and aahed, stepping back, shocked and frightened.

The dragon spiraled downward. It appeared he would land near the smoldering stable. When he was close, Zello bellowed, "You want the lantern—come and get it. Come and get it! Come and get it."

His message is certainly clear. Ivan thought.

Then with a sudden upswing, the dragon rose, pumping his wide wings to reach new heights.

Shortly, Lord Graydon and his guests arrived. Pausing on the carriage step, the lord exclaimed, "What on earth?" He stepped to the ground and held the door open for the fine lady to exit.

"Mr. Harowitz," the lord called.

"Sir?" The man gave a swift bow to his master.

"Explain Zello's outlandish behavior."

"Well…" The stable keeper rubbed the back of his neck. "He's come back with the lantern. Wants someone to go fetch it from him."

"I know that much!" the lord snapped impatiently. "Why's he behaving in this way?"

"Can't say for sure." Mr. Harowitz stared at the ground. "He's mad for being accused of eating those kaleido-birds, I'd guess."

Lord Graydon blinked and sighed deeply.

One of the stable hands spoke, "The workmen were hard on Zello, blamed him without mercy about the fire. I told 'em not to be so mean-spirited about it."

Sytha came beside the lord. "Richard, let's ask one of the female dragons to go meet Zello and take the lantern from him."

Mr. Harowitz shook his head. "I doubt any of them would go after their alpha. They tend to be loyal, and that would be what ya' call, in-sib-ordation."

"Insubordination," Sytha corrected.

"How will we get it back if he decides to return to the cave in the Azurite Mountains?" Ivan joined the discussion, waiting for a sensible response.

A bewildered look creased the lord's forehead. Abruptly, his eyes opened wide. "I have an idea. Perhaps an excellent one."

"Let's hear it." Wayland moved forward.

"Mr. Harowitz, would you be so good as to bring Bellion from his stable? Number three, I believe." Lord Graydon gave an elegant sweep of his hand in that direction.

"Yes, sir. I knows where ta find him."

"Who will ride the winged stallion?" Wayland backed a few steps.

"Can you?" the lord asked with pleading eyes.

Wayland shook his head frantically. "No! Bellion would never allow a freak like me—or any former werewolf—on his back. We were once his enemy, and he can still smell the wolf in us." He turned his face away. Redness crept up his neck to his round cheeks.

"There's nothing freakish about you or your clan," the lord replied sternly. "You are no longer werewolves. And—I happen to think the world of all of you." He smiled sincerely, grabbing Wayland, pulling him into an embrace. "I'm proud to have you as part of our kingdom."

A joyful look flashed across Wayland's face. He blinked away moisture. His grin showed a row of gleaming white teeth. "Thank you, Lord Graydon, for your kind words."

Ivan smiled, too. He knew Wayland had long felt inferior in the lord's presence. Now, he could put those unfounded feelings away forever.

"Sytha?" Lord Graydon's hazel eyes stared. Hope edged his tone.

"Sorry, my lord. I would, but Bellion and I had a

recent spat, and he has yet to forgive me."

The lord grunted. Apparently, remembering the incident, he agreed.

"What did you argue about with the snooty flying steed?" Wayland's brow lifted high.

A mischievous grin pulled at Sytha's lips. "I called him a self-centered, self-indulgent, pile of horse-poop. Worthless as yesterday's garbage."

"That would probably turn me against you, too." Wayland could scarcely stifle his laughter.

They turned to gape at Ivan.

"Ride a winged stallion?" he hesitated. "I-I don't know—I've never been off the ground before."

"You're best suited for the job." Sebastian studied him with renewed interest.

"Why do you say that?" Ivan crossed his arms over his chest and his jaw tightened in a panic.

"Bellion may allow it." Sytha nodded. "You haven't done anything to make him mad—yet."

"B-but I…" Ivan turned, hoping for support from the Wolflords—or other Elftens—but they agreed wholeheartedly with Sytha and bobbed their heads in unison.

Ivan was about to protest by taking steps back and throwing up his arms. Then he spotted her in the crowd. Anna-Iza rode toward him on her stunning Andalusian, her face serious.

When the hood from her purple riding cloak fell away, her hair spilled around her shoulders. At last, Anna-Iza was near. Ivan's heart thumped in his chest.

The world stopped. He opened his mouth and breathed deeply, his nervous hands cold and shaky.

She slipped from her horse—*Rainier, Ivan*

remembered. Her twelve sister goddesses dismounted and pulled their riding cloaks closer to their necks to cut the morning chill. They watched the dragon's amazing flight with awe.

Smoothing her auburn curls, the goddess strode toward him.

"Anna-Iza," Ivan gasped. "It-it's wonderful to see you again."

"It *is* my pleasure." She smiled—just at him. Sweet and sincere.

Sytha drew next to her and put his arms around her slight form in an affectionate embrace. Elftens were privileged that way, but mortals were not. Wayland bowed.

"Little goddess." Lord Graydon approached her. "What brings you here?"

"We planned to visit Merridyn at the castle's infirmary. But one of the triplets said Zello had returned, and everyone was gathering at the dragons' stable to witness this." She put her gloved hand over her nose to indicate the unpleasant smell of lingering smoke and dung.

Ivan stared at her, hoping he didn't appear too love-struck.

She spotted Sebastian coming toward her and opened her arms to him. "We praise you and Ivan for removing Merridyn from that awful prison. I am deeply grateful."

"It was only fair." Sebastian pointed at Ivan. "He gets much of the credit."

Anna-Iza nodded. "I've heard some of the details." She smiled knowingly.

Ivan felt a blush coming on. Changing the subject,

he pointed to the sky. "Zello has returned with the Golden Lantern."

"Oh, yes!" She tipped her face skyward. "Why does he have it in his claws? It belongs in the Sanctuary of Truth."

Lord Graydon rolled his eyes. "Well, I'm not sure we have the complete story." As he was speaking, one of the ladies from his carriage appeared at his side and rested her gloved hand on his arm.

"Pardon me. Allow me to introduce—this is Lady Jenna." The lord's eyes brightened and stayed on her. "She's my special guest for a few days."

Anna-Iza and her sister goddesses curtsied. Their eyebrows lifted at the mention of Lady Jenna's name. They smiled perceptively and welcomed her, as well as the other guests from the carriage who exited with care.

"Do tell *us* about the Golden Lantern." The elegant Jenna motioned toward the other couple to draw closer, and they did so.

The lord briefly related what happened to the stolen lantern.

When the story ended, Anna-Iza slowly shook her head, her eyes large with surprise, even astonishment. She turned to Ivan. "How have you fared after such brave and daring adventures?"

"I-I'm fine," Ivan stammered and gazed at her. For a moment, he worried about her cool behavior. *Have I been fooling myself? Why would she care about a mere intruder from the outside?*

The crowd clapped and cheered. "A good lad. A bold and generous young man," they chorused with all eyes on Ivan. Now he felt the heat cover his face and neck. Perhaps Zello planned to return the lantern, and all would be forgiven. He searched the sky and saw the dragon circling wider and wider.

"Come get it, or I'll drop it," the beast roared. A stream of fire shot from his mouth.

The people gasped and talked loudly amongst themselves. "He seems uncommonly angry," a man in the crowd said.

Mr. Harowitz shuffled toward them, holding the bridle of a magnificent black horse. The animal's great wings spread wide and made a commanding entrance. He gave his shiny mane a toss, his nose held high, as he pranced through the mass of people.

"Move aside. Move aside." Mr. Harowitz swept his free hand in front of him with obvious meaning.

Lord Graydon stroked the horse's dark forehead, acknowledging his presence with a slight tip of his head.

"How may I serve you, my lord?" Bellion tucked his front leg back and made a short bow.

"I would like Ivan Kimble to ride on your back so he can grab the Golden Lantern from our stubborn dragon."

The winged horse raised and swung his head, nearly hitting Ivan in the chest. Jumping back, Ivan wondered if it was carelessness or a hostile gesture.

"I'm honored to meet you." Ivan bowed. Though he wasn't sure he meant those words. Not yet, anyway.

The stallion backed up. He rolled his upper lip and showed yellowed teeth. "I will not allow this outsider to ride me. He is a deceiver, a liar, and a manipulator. You would do well to throw him into the smoldering fire."

Everyone gulped. Especially Ivan, whose mouth fell opened, his eyes stung with tears.

Embarrassed, Lord Graydon jammed his fists into

his sides. "What is the reason for these insults? Where are your manners?"

Bellion snorted and shook his head.

"Ivan Kimble is a castle guest." The lord was so angry, his fine goatee quivered. "The lad is responsible for saving Zephyrus's life."

"I don't care whose life he saved. I will not tolerate another boy-man from the outside on my back. You can't trust them." Ivan wondered who the horse had referred to.

"That's enough!" Sytha's pale face turned bright crimson. "Get away, you horse-poop, garbage heap. Don't expect any considerations from the Elftens—ever!"

"Or the Wolflords." Wayland's jaw crunched, and he waved his fist above his head.

With that, the angry horse turned from the stunned crowd and jeered, "He's a liar and a fraud. That boy wants you to trust him, and then he'll turn on you, take possession of the Forest and everything in it. Wait and see."

Ivan couldn't speak. He gawked after the spiteful stallion, wishing he were on Zello's back—anyplace, but the ground. All the joy he'd felt seeing Anna-Iza drained away. *Did Lord Graydon believe the accusations? My friends?*

"I am most ashamed for this display of rudeness." The lord put his arms around Ivan and patted his shoulder blades. "Please. Don't believe that disagreeable horse. He's clearly offended about something."

"This behavior is most uncalled for," Lady Jenna said, fanning herself with her handkerchief.

"You mustn't take Bellion's remarks personally,"

Anna-Iza said. "He's been hurt deeply, but no one knows why." She rubbed her horse's sleek neck. "Perhaps my Rainier can speak with him sometime soon."

"I would be happy to talk with him, mistress," the Andalusian replied, bowing his head.

The goddess turned to her sisters. "Let's go to the infirmary and visit Merridyn."

"Must you go?" Ivan felt a burning behind his eyes. She'd seen his humiliation, and that stung even more.

"I do regret it." She gazed at him. "I had hoped to see you at the feast last night, but they said you were exhausted from the horrors of your journey. It's understandable."

As he stood there, he realized he hadn't moved an inch. Paralyzed with pain, his heart shattered into pieces.

"They told me what you did. The trolls, the Ratlings, the Vaguers." Anna-Iza's brows came together in a delicate frown, and then she smiled brightly. "You have done so much, Ivan Kimble, and here you are, preparing to mount a flying horse and retrieve the Golden Lantern." Her thick lashes fluttered. "You are the most generous and courageous person I've ever known. I'm so proud of you."

In that moment, his spirits lifted, and the pain disappeared. "Thank you. I-I…"

Ivan thought his chest would explode with joy. Anna-Iza's opinion meant everything to him. Yes, he would ride a flying horse to save the relic. He would even ride the dragon to prove his bravery. For her. Only her.

The High Goddess mounted. "We have to hurry if we want to see Merridyn. Her hours are limited to visitors." She looked back, gave a tender smile, and waved. Her retinue galloped after her.

Sytha gave Ivan a push with his shoulder. "Your girl? I only wish she were available. I would've had her first." He grinned, poked Ivan in the chest with his index finger, and walked away.

Chapter 23

Fluorescence

Mr. Harowitz's mouth hung open. "Guess it's not Bellion's day," he muttered. "I'll go git Fluorescence. She's more accommodatin'." He strolled back to the stable. No one objected.

"A better choice." Lord Graydon nodded first at Lady Jenna and then winked at Ivan.

Zello showed his impatience and roared, "Come and get it. Now!" A long column of orange and red flames shot from his mouth. His head swung back and forth, looking for a taker to his challenge.

"Goodness, he is mad," someone said in the crowd.

Fluorescence followed Mr. Harowitz's lead. The people backed away, allowing plenty of space for them. Her brilliant white coat gleamed, surrounding her graceful body with sparkles in rainbow colors.

A small boy who stood in front of the crowd struggled to escape his mother's hold. "I want to touch her," he cried.

The flying mare was smaller than Bellion but sturdy, solidly built through her flanks and shoulders. She opened her feathered wings. Calm and steady, her large brown eyes swept through the gathering and came to rest momentarily on Ivan.

Ivan had never seen such a striking animal. Her coat

glimmered in the sunlight, reflecting tints of soft pink, lavender, and gold. He stepped forward, anxious to greet the magnificent horse. *Will she like me or humiliate me in front of everyone?*

Frowning, the lord asked the winged horse, "Do you have a problem with a young man from the outside riding on your back?"

"We don't have much affection for outsiders," she said, now scrutinizing Ivan from head to foot.

"This is no ordinary outsider." Lord Graydon introduced him and rested his hand on Ivan's shoulder. "He's been a great help to us and the Forest."

She raised her head, nickering softly.

Ivan stroked Fluorescence's soft muzzle. She sniffed at him and folded her great wings next to her body. "He seems agreeable enough. What do you want of me?"

"It's like I told you." Mr. Harowitz pointed above. "That dang dragon has the Golden Lantern and is threatnin' to drop it."

Fluorescence struck the ground with her hoof. "Zello does have his unpredictable moments. Just look at the destruction of the dragons' stable."

"We believe the fire was an accident," Lord Graydon said in a firm voice.

"That's what I want to believe, too." Fluorescence shook her head up and down.

Stepping next to him, Sytha draped a casual arm over Ivan's shoulders. "This good soul has agreed to go after the lantern if you'd allow it."

She swished her long white tail and tossed her silky mane, eyeing him once more.

"I-I've never flown before," Ivan admitted. "If there

are any tricks you can tell me, I'd like to hear them."

The outsider's humble statement seemed to sway the horse's final decision. She nodded her approval and said, "Just hold on. We'll plan our strategy as we go."

Ivan wiped the sweat from his forehead and neck, wondering what he was getting himself into.

Giving Ivan a nudge, Sytha said, "You'll do fine. What's so hard about reaching out and grabbing the ring of a simple lantern?"

"If it's so easy, why didn't you volunteer for the job?" Ivan threw Sytha a surly look.

"I'm not in good standing with the flying horses like I said." Sytha raised his nose in the air. A small smile cornered his lips.

"You'll do great." Wayland gave him a soft punch on his arm.

Ivan clutched a fistful of Fluorescence's mane and swung onto the animal's back. He shifted his weight until he found what he hoped was solid seating.

"Perhaps I should join you." Sebastian chuckled. "Or did you plan to leave me behind?"

Teeth chattering, Ivan waved him aboard. "Sorry. I'm so nervous, I almost forgot about you."

At once, Sebastian turned into wispy blue smoke and disappeared into the fabric of the Long Dark Cloak. Ivan felt a gentle push to his back as Sebastian's spirit entered.

There were gasps and curious whispers from the crowd over such a trick. An old man had dissolved and suddenly vanished into a cloak. It must've seemed quite a phenomenon to them. By now, Ivan was accustomed to it.

The people backed up and made a wide path for the

winged mare and her brave passenger.

Fluorescence took several steps forward, moving into a trot. She picked up speed and pushed hard off the ground. They rose higher and higher. The great spread of her wings beat against what now had become an overcast sky.

The animal's muscles contracted and expanded under Ivan's rear as her wings rose and fell, catching the wind that lifted them. He held on tightly and realized how difficult it was to stay seated even with her broad back.

"A-a saddle. Couldn't I have a saddle?" Ivan's voice trembled.

"Easy," Sebastian said. "Press your knees firmly against her and try to relax. You'll need your agility to catch the lantern."

When Ivan studied the tiny figures below, he fully realized what it meant to leave the safety of the ground. A ripple of terror streaked through his chest. He swallowed hard and wished he hadn't agreed to such a foolish plan. *Why did I? It was to impress her, the goddess. I've done foolish things, but this is the most dangerous of all.* He recalled his sword fight with Burtack, the mighty Black Knight. *My head nearly got separated from my neck with that dumb decision.*

He looked for Anna-Iza below and hoped she would be watching, astonished at his courage. But he didn't see her. *If she can ride a flying horse, certainly I can, too.* His jaw locked with determination.

Seen from above, the castle layout was immense. Farther to the west, South Castle University spread out like a small city. Huge lawns, pools, buildings, and trees looked like toys.

"Stay focused on Zello," Sebastian said. "Try to determine a pattern to his movements so you can anticipate your best position."

Fluorescence angled and caught a thermal updraft. They rose higher as her outstretched wings glided closer to Zello. Ivan felt himself shift to the left. Gripping the horse's mane, he quickly righted his position. Already his thighs were strained from the attempt to hold firm.

The winged horse turned her head to say, "Bellion is watching. He must be envious. This flight would've given him everlasting fame." She snorted. "Haughty, stupid, and obstinate creature if there ever was one."

Ivan silently agreed, but now he had bigger worries. He felt Zello's eyes on them.

"We'll get a little closer," Sebastian said from the Long Dark Cloak, "and then you must tell our dragon to give you the lantern."

The huge beast flew directly at them. His great dark wings pumped, gaining speed. At the last moment, he banked right and soared above their heads. The lantern swung crazily in his claws.

"Ivan, don't let him drop me!" It was Joseph's spirit inside the Golden Lantern.

"What are you doing, Zello?" Fluorescence yelled and whinnied. "Stop this childish behavior."

"Give us the lantern," Sebastian shouted from the cloak. "We can make amends for your grievances."

"We know you didn't eat the kaleido-birds," Ivan said as convincingly as he could. "We know the stable fire was an accident." He reached a hand above his head, opening his palm. "Please give me the lantern."

At this point, when Fluorescence jerked under him, Ivan wisely decided he should hold on with both hands.

Zello hesitated, appearing to study Ivan as he circled and coasted lower. "Who are you?"

"I-I'm Ivan Kimble. I've come to get the lantern."

"He saved Zephyrus's life," Sebastian shouted so his voice could be heard.

Zello snorted smoke. "Save! My dragon's arse. You are the outsider who axed our master, and now he's dying."

"No, that's not so," Ivan said. "Zephyrus is nearly recovered from the blows of the poisonous axe."

Circling, the beast seemed to consider the new information.

"What's he doing?" Ivan watched intently.

"Weighing the truth, I suspect." Fluorescence raised her head, analyzing the situation. "I think someone's been feeding him a bunch of lies, and our poor dragon doesn't know what or whom to believe."

In a flash, Zello turned sharply, coming back at them with greater speed. Ivan sucked in his breath.

"Hold on!" Stretching her powerful wings, the horse pumped hard and swerved. Ivan crouched against her neck, anticipating a collision from the dark shape that hurtled toward them.

Zello's long webbed wings just missed Fluorescence's head when she banked hard to the left. Ivan's weight shifted so fast, he couldn't regain his balance. He slipped—and slipped further still.

"Ivan! Ivan," Sebastian yelled. "Right yourself."

It was too late.

Unable to hold on, his sweaty hands slid through Fluorescence's shiny mane. He screamed as he tumbled into the vast sky while the fabric of the cloak billowed in the updraft.

"Don't panic," Sebastian yelled. "Fall naturally, so Fluorescence can gauge your position. She'll know what to—"

Fall naturally? What did that mean? Ivan somersaulted, arms flailing wildly. He shrieked. The winged mare turned, flying with such speed she was a blur of iridescent white.

She dove under him, but he knew he was too far right and with one leg bent. Ivan held out his arms, hoping it would slow him down so he could better tell where the horse was situated. It scarcely helped, if at all. She corrected her position several times until at last, he felt she was rightly in place. He ker-plunked onto Fluorescence's broad back, and he let out another scream. Quivering, he clung to her neck, paralyzed with pain and fear. The abrupt landing crushed him and left him without breath.

"Nicely done, Flo," Sebastian said. "Your outstanding flying ability has saved your passenger."

"What about how I feel?" Ivan croaked, experiencing red-hot pain in his groin.

The crowd cheered and roared. *It must have been quite a spectacle.*

Zello spun around. The lantern's light now beaming even more brightly.

"Joseph is speaking to his captor from the Golden Lantern." Sebastian's voice rang clear. "I hope he's telling our dragon there's no harm done. If only he'd release the relic."

Ivan grabbed Fluorescence's mane with both hands and held on tightly as the giant beast above flew toward them a second time, slower, more deliberate. His huge wings beat against the sky, sending gusts of wind in their direction.

As Zello drew closer, Ivan smelled the dry, musty odor of the dragon's dark scales, just as he remembered on his first visit to the Forest. Zello's thigh muscles contracted and relaxed with each uplift of its wings. It seemed his reptile eyes bored through them, his nostrils flared and closed, flared and closed. *What is he so mad about?* Ivan wondered.

Now Ivan saw the curved horns on the dragon's head, the spikes on the sides of its face, and his small maw. The dragon's spines nearly tapered to his tail, except for several missing where his neck met his shoulders. For a rider, Ivan guessed.

"Catch it. I'm leaving." The beast sounded beaten.

Sure enough, Zello released the lantern. It spiraled through the air and made a whistling sound as it plummeted. *Is it Joseph, the spirit within, crying out to be rescued?* Ivan trembled. A muscle jumped in his jaw. If he caught the heavy lantern in his bare palms, it would rip them apart.

Unexplainably, the golden object slowed its descent, although how it did this was a puzzle. Ivan reached up, arms spread, and the lantern gently settled into his open hands. "Nice to see you again, Ivan." Joseph's shaky voice floated from inside the lantern.

At last, the Ancient Relic was safe. Ivan let out a whoop and hollered, "I've got it! I've got the lantern."

Fluorescence nickered softly.

Spectators had multiplied by the hundreds. They went wild with relief and happiness. Their thunderous shouts rose upward. Ivan grinned in spite of the throbbing pain. He was alive.

Zello flew nearer to Fluorescence, a look of shame

illuminated in his eyes. "I'm s-sorry. Sorry for the trouble I've caused. I was wrong about many things. Thank you, Joseph, for the truth." Zello raised his head and roared. A long fiery streak of yellow, orange, and red cut across the sky. With that, the legendary dragon did a spectacular roll against the gray of late morning. He twisted his huge body a second time and turned south toward his cave home in the Azurite Mountains. The dark, undulating shape grew smaller and smaller until it disappeared.

Ivan clutched the winged horse's mane with one hand and hugged the cooled lantern to his chest with the other.

"It's good to be back," Joseph said with a sigh.

"We agree." Ivan was happy that Fluorescence gradually spiraled downward. Her long wings outstretched silently, gliding on the wind.

"Why didn't you speak the truth to Zello while he held you captive in his cave?" Ivan asked.

"I tried," Joseph said. "He wouldn't listen. Someone filled him full of lies, and that's what he believed."

"Do you know what caused him to behave in such a hot-headed manner?" Sebastian asked from the cloak.

"Pretty much what Ivan said about the missing kaleido-birds, and the stable fire accident," Joseph replied. "Your sympathetic words eased his anger, and he seemed to lose interest in destroying the lantern. I tried to reassure our dragon that we all loved and admired him."

"And that's why he finally let go of you?" Ivan asked.

"Partly. But I almost believe…"

"What?"

"I almost believe," Joseph repeated, "it was when he looked into your eyes. I thought I heard him say, 'You have finally come to save our Forest.' "

"Was he talking about me?" Ivan lifted his dark eyebrows.

"I would say so," Joseph said. "You'll have to ask Zello when he has a cool head again, if you get a chance to see him."

"He will need our affection and comfort in the days ahead," Sebastian said. "Even tough old, brown-scaled dragons need to be loved."

The mare's wings flapped while she circled lower through the cool sky.

She's magnificent, Ivan thought as he tried to find a position that didn't send shooting pains through his thighs.

"Wrap the Long Dark Cloak's fabric around your legs," Sebastian said. "I'll take the burn away. It won't do to have your admirers see their hero holding his crotch and limping in agony."

Ivan gave a little laugh of embarrassment and did as Sebastian suggested. When the pain disappeared, he sighed with relief.

Wondering why he didn't consider the easy solution earlier. Then he remembered that one of his arms held the lantern while the other gripped Fluorescence's mane for dear life.

The horse settled smoothly near the burned-out stable. Her luminous wings opened wide enough to allow Ivan to slide off with the lantern pressed against his chest.

"You're safe now." Ivan tapped the glass panels with his forefinger, nodding with satisfaction.

"I'm just as happy to be on the ground as you are," Joseph replied.

"The bravest thing I've ever seen," someone in the crowd yelled—and then Ivan realized Wayland had uttered the words. The two embraced.

"You're quaking," Wayland said. "It's okay, you are safe, now."

Ivan handed the lantern to Wayland and exhaled loudly.

Joseph spoke, "Thank you for saving me. I thought I'd end up as a pile of metal and glass somewhere on the ground." He chuckled nervously.

Several soldiers approached. They saluted, or slapped Ivan's back, and complimented him on his unique flying skills.

"You stupid, brave fool." Simon's eyebrows knotted with anger. "You could've gotten killed."

"I-I couldn't think about that." Ivan's hands still trembled while feeling every bit like the fool Simon accused him of being.

Fluorescence didn't seem to place much importance in her role. Instead, she remained at Ivan's side and nudged him with her soft nose. "You are a good student. Anytime you wish a ride just for fun, let me know."

"Sure." Ivan stroked her smooth cheek. A ride *just for fun* didn't sound like much fun to him. He managed a grin and thanked her.

Mr. Harowitz led Fluorescence back to her stable. She swished her tail, seemingly unconcerned, and trailed along with her keeper.

Sebastian's spirit left the cloak in swirls of white and purple smoke. With all the excitement, no one seemed to notice the phenomenon this time. "I thought I'd lost you when you tumbled off. I knew it would be tricky when Fluorescence moved too fast for you to adjust to her speed. But you survived. Thank the High Intervener."

"I'm very grateful to the High Intervener as well." Ivan coughed into his hand, hoping to calm his shaky nerves.

Bystanders applauded and cheered as they pushed their way toward their hero. They all wanted to congratulate and praise him. He didn't deserve it and wished it would stop.

Raking his fingers through wind-whipped hair, Ivan clutched the lantern. He frowned, realizing how close he'd come to death.

Chapter 24

Merridyn's Recovery

A horse galloped fast from the west side of the castle. Long honey-blonde hair blew in the wind. The soldiers, preparing to leave the destruction of the burned dragons' stable, halted and stared. A fast rider usually meant trouble.

When they discovered who it was, the men chorused, "Hello," and they waved.

Merridyn brought Standby to a stop and dismounted. She rushed to Ivan and threw her arms around his neck. "Anna-Iza said you were riding Fluorescence. We watched you from the hospital balcony for some time until I couldn't endure the drama any longer." Frowning, she cuffed him on the shoulder. "Don't ever do something like that again."

Ivan tipped his head to avoid further scolding and changed the subject. "You're better?"

Giggling, she twirled around. "Look." She tapped her forehead. "No distortion. And my fingers have all returned to the right length."

"That's great news." Ivan cheered. His fear that Merridyn would turn into a troll dissolved right then, and he couldn't be happier.

Sytha came beside them and patted the girl on her back. "Good to see you recovered."

Thanking him, she wrung her hands and pulled on her fingers, out of habit, Ivan guessed.

"I didn't have much hope when you decided to nose-dive off Fluorescence," Merridyn rolled her eyes. "It scared me to death."

Ivan tightened his lips. "I felt the same."

"How did you learn to ride a winged horse?" She stepped back and stared at him. "I wouldn't try such a thing until I was well trained."

"I-I—"

"He volunteered," Sytha interjected with a big smile.

Ivan gave his Elften friend a smoldering look, recalling *who* had volunteered him.

"Did you enjoy flying?" she asked, her voice a bit shaky.

Thinking on it, Ivan pursed his lips. "I did. Next time, I'll demand a saddle."

"You were simply wonderful, Ivan Kimble. I'm so proud of you." Merridyn grinned, clapping her hands like a delighted child.

Wayland, along with several soldiers and castle staff approached and congratulated the girl on her recovery. Squeezing his way forward, Tanner leaned into Merridyn and took her hand. "I'm so happy you were released from your hospital bed. Now you can join the excitement."

She lowered her eyes and looked at the Elften through her lashes. A little blush circled her cheeks.

Ivan saw Tanner gaze at her affectionately.

"Well…" she said, looking shy, "I haven't exactly been *released* yet. When Anna-Iza and her sister goddesses came to see me, they said Ivan had jumped on Fluorescence's back and demanded that Zello return the

Golden Lantern. I felt I had to witness this great event. Anna-Iza was impressed with your courage and willingness to help."

A big smile stretched across Ivan's lips. *Anna-Iza had watched the whole thing!* He wondered if he should be elated or mortified.

"She had to leave but was positively glowing." Merridyn wiggled her eyebrows.

"It takes a lot to impress a High Goddess." Wayland gave Ivan a soft punch to his arm.

Thrilled by the message, Ivan's neck grew warm, and he was certain it crept to his face. His happiness expanded.

"How long will you stay?" she asked Ivan.

"I should be leaving for home soon," he stated regretfully.

She fussed with her wind-blown hair, trying to sweep it on top of her head, pinning the curls with pearl clips. She looked so different compared to when he'd first met her—untidy and angry, with stained fingers from picking ickleberries.

"You won't forget your promise to come to my trial?" She looked up at him with pleading eyes. "I depend on you to support me through this difficult time."

"I…well. I hope to come and help in any way." Ivan shifted his feet, questioning what he could offer to prove her innocence. Perhaps Sebastian and Zephyrus would guide him in the matter.

She gave a serious nod.

"Oh, here." He reached into his jacket pocket and pulled out a key. This belongs to you. We are most grateful. Thank you for the use of your lovely cottage. It had everything we needed."

"Don't you think Season is a great cook? And Arnie bakes the best breads?" She wore the biggest grin.

"Yes," Sebastian and Ivan chorused.

"This day calls for a celebration," Lord Graydon's voice rang out. "You are all welcome to attend The Feast of the Golden Lantern's Return. We are most pleased that Joseph is in fine condition and happy to be home.

"That's right, my lord," Joseph's crackling voice emanated from the lantern.

The crowd clapped, raised their hands in the air, and praised their host for his generosity. Lady Jenna tucked her arm through Lord Graydon's and smiled sweetly.

A few moments later, a uniformed man from Simon's army rode in, leaned down, and whispered something in Sytha's ear.

When the Elften swung his head, his pale blue horse came to him at once. He grabbed the reins and mounted hurriedly, as did his brother Elftens. They left at once without turning to explain or saying a word. All faces were suddenly tense and somber.

Ivan turned to Sebastian. "Why didn't they tell us?"

"It's a curiosity to me." Sebastian stared after them.

"Excuse me, Merridyn. I must find out what this is all about." Ivan handed the lantern to Lord Graydon. "Keep it safe."

"Please be careful," the lord called.

A stable hand brought Bounty and Old Bones forward, and their masters quickly mounted. Ivan worried that something may have happened to Anna-Iza and her sister goddesses. His throat tightened, and he couldn't swallow.

Alfred and Canute barked.

"Come on," Ivan said to his beagles. "Let's go!"

They raced up the gravel driveway, rounding the bend. Ahead, congregated on an open lawn, were about fifty of Commander Simon's soldiers. He was having a serious discussion with Sergeant Berkel and Lieutenant Pezzuline.

"What's going on?" Ivan asked Sebastian.

"I don't know. Let's move closer."

Lieutenant Pezzuline rubbed his eyes with the heel of his hand. "Those Vaguers are skilled at disappearing—and reappearing. You wouldn't think a rack of bones could move so fast. We spotted a number of them near the Harvesters' Cottages."

Ivan gulped, trying to still his pounding heart. He and Sebastian had stayed at one of the cottages the night before. There was a terrible scream in the night that he later learned was indeed a Vaguer.

Simon's frown stayed fixed. He dismounted and slapped his gauntlets against the palm of his hand, deep in thought. When he saw Ivan's beagles racing his way, Simon bent to his knees, embraced them, and scratched their ears. "Alfred. Canute. Such good dogs you are."

"What happened?" Ivan asked the men. The soldiers had circles under their eyes from lack of sleep, hair and clothing scruffy. Several had cuts on their cheeks and foreheads from going through the brush, he surmised.

The commander shot Ivan a blazing look. "You mean *after* you fell off a flying horse and about broke your fool neck?" Simon wasn't smiling. He must've waited to give Ivan a lecture and save him the humiliation in front of Lord Graydon. Now Ivan was embarrassed with a new audience.

"Oh that, well…"

Finally, Simon's scowl softened, but he didn't

smile. "I'm glad you lived through it and fetched the lantern from Zello." He saluted. "Good job, Kimble."

He blinked, bewildered at the sudden change. The last time Simon made that very statement, Ivan thought he'd be imprisoned for killing Kruse Hays. Now he was being praised. Sometimes, he couldn't figure Simon's shifting moods.

"You and your men ran into some trouble?" Sebastian's old face tightened.

"That's right," Sergeant Berkel replied. "We came across a number of Vaguers over by the Harvesters' Cottages. We believe they've been there for some time. Waiting."

"And you killed them all?" Ivan was hopeful.

"We managed to bring down about a half-dozen," one of the soldiers answered. "They're not easy to kill since they are nothing but a rack of bones." He stroked a clotted cut on his cheek. "We chased the others but lost them in the trees and bushes.

"How many in total?" Sebastian asked.

"We counted about a dozen," the same soldier answered. "Since they all look alike, it was difficult to get an accurate count. There may have been more, but we didn't see them."

Ivan edged closer, addressing Lieutenant Pezzuline, "Then, we must go after them at once." His hand reached to his side to grasp The Challenger's hilt but suddenly remembered it was in his room.

"No," Simon said. "The men haven't slept or eaten. They've been on the hunt most of the night."

"You're right, of course." Ivan cooled his enthusiasm, feeling pushy.

"Lieutenant, dismiss the men." Commander Simon

dismounted and watched his weary men. "We'll head out searching in three hours."

The soldiers slid off their horses, rubbed their weary eyes, and stretched their legs. Then they entered the castle to satisfy their rumbling stomachs while stable hands led the horses away where they would water and feed them.

Sytha, Wayland, Ivan, and Sebastian, stood under the castle's broad portico, discussing the situation with Commander Simon and several of his remaining soldiers.

A Wolflord poked his head out the front double doors. "Hey! A huge lunch is being served. Come get it while it's hot."

Sytha held up his index finger. "In a minute."

"Where do you think the Vaguers went?" Ivan inched closer to Simon.

"We were just discussing that," the commander replied. "My men say they've scattered in different directions throughout the Harvesters' Cottages and, we believe, into the Forest, as well."

Ivan felt they should hunt the horrible creatures before they killed more innocent people. He remembered Kagutt, and his threat to steal Ivan's Essence. He couldn't stop his hands from quivering.

Touching Ivan's arm, Sebastian shook his head. "Don't be so impatient. The men need to eat and rest. We'll wait on them for a bit."

Sensible advice.

Sytha and Wayland started toward the castle's open door. "You want to ride with us when we go hunting?" Sytha asked over his shoulder.

"Yes, but I-I really need to return the relics and then

be on my way home."

"I understand." Sytha hesitated and turned. "Well then, I insist we escort you safely to Zephyrus. I'm sure the commander has things well in hand."

"Thank you. I'd be grateful for your protection."

Lord Graydon's carriage arrived, stopping in front of the castle. A footman helped him out along with his guests. Ivan suddenly saw his chance to ask about Peter. He dashed down the steps leaving Sebastian behind, who wore a sudden baffled look on his face. Confronting the lord, Ivan asked, "Sir, I was w-wondering if I might…ah, have a word with you."

"But of course." The lord reached for Lady Jenna's hand as she stepped from the carriage, and he introduced her to Ivan. The other guests, a man and woman, impeccably dressed, also climbed out. They thanked the lord for a most entertaining day, complimenting Ivan on his extravagant acrobatic performance.

The lord grinned at Ivan's bashfulness, patting him on his shoulder. He addressed his guests, "Why don't you have lunch in the dining room and then retire—take a nap before this evening's festivities? I'll be along shortly." They agreed it was a splendid idea.

"Join me in the library, Ivan. It's more private." The lord walked briskly, swinging the Golden Lantern by its ring. They climbed the steps where servants held the doors wide. "Please tell Maynard to bring a glass of ickleberry wine to the library—and lemonade for Ivan."

"At once." The servant bowed.

Sebastian caught up with them as they continued down the long corridor.

Lord Graydon turned his head and asked, "What part of the castle and grounds would you most like to see?"

"I-I'd like to see it all, but I must leave shortly."

"Oh!" The lord's white eyebrows shot high. "You didn't want to talk about a tour?"

"No. It...it's about a-a more delicate subject, if you don't mind."

Sebastian stared at Ivan with surprise and curiosity. "You aren't staying for the Feast of the Golden Lantern tonight? It's in your honor, you know."

The lord seemed just as puzzled as Sebastian, and perhaps a bit hurt.

"I'm sorry. We don't know what awaits us on the road back to Zephyrus." Ivan looked away for a moment to hide his embarrassment.

"I understand," the lord said, though it was obvious he was disappointed.

When they were seated in the wingback chairs, Sebastian let out a long sigh. "This has been a most unusual and extraordinary day."

Maynard rushed in and set the drinks and refreshments on a small table between the lord and Ivan. He glanced at Alfred and Canute, but they seemed comfortable on the rug in front of the fireplace.

Reaching for the glass of wine, Lord Graydon took a sip. Likewise, Ivan picked up his lemonade and drank half. It refreshed and satisfied his dry mouth. He leaned forward and was prepared to ask about Peter, but Sebastian interrupted.

"What's worrying you, sir?" Sebastian faced the lord.

Lord Graydon twisted the stem of the wineglass in his hands. "I'd be obliged if you'd take the Golden Lantern to Zephyrus." He picked it off the floor and handed it to Ivan. "It'll be safe in your hands. You'll have an escort, of course. I'll ask Simon, several Elftens, and Wolflords to ride with you."

"We'd be happy to deliver it. I've already discussed it with Sytha, and he's willing." Ivan smiled proudly as he imagined Zephyrus's joy when he saw the lantern and Joseph.

Lord Graydon coughed lightly into his hand. "Once again, I apologize for Bellion's rude behavior. I don't know what's gotten into that cantankerous horse."

Staring ahead, Ivan stifled the stinging feelings caused by the stallion's harsh rejection. He wished the subject would be forgotten but felt it would be rude if he didn't answer. "Fluorescence served our needs. The lantern is safe, and we'll be pleased to return it to the Sanctuary of Truth."

The lord cocked his head, taking a long, quiet look at his guest. "You forgive easily and graciously. I'd like to learn your secret."

"My lord, if I may be so bold." Sebastian raised an eyebrow. "Is it because you haven't forgiven your own brother for stealing the relics from the Sanctuary of Truth?"

"Indeed," the lord answered. "I will despise Henry and his betrayal to our people for as long as I live."

Ivan lowered his eyes. He was uneasy to hear about the lord's resentment toward his brother, when Ivan would give anything to find Peter.

"Please excuse my anger and bitterness. This is something I must manage for myself. But you had something to ask me, and here I go on with my hardened heart."

"I'm wondering if…well." He gave Sebastian a quick glance. "I was curious whether Peter has reported to you and is now released from his *spying* duties. It seems the only reason he hasn't come home."

"Released?" Lord Graydon lifted a surprised face, and that's when Ivan's heart pounded against his chest.

"What's this? Peter is in your employment?" Sebastian sat upright, a deep scowl forming over his eyes. "I know nothing of this."

"I didn't exactly give him the assignment," the lord slowly answered. "I felt it would be too dangerous for him to penetrate the Dark Army. He could've gotten hurt—or killed."

"But he told me…"

"Peter asked for my approval to infiltrate our enemy and learn their secrets. I didn't disapprove, but I was very cautious about my instructions for allowing him to spy on them."

The lord's answer was the best Ivan could hope for. *My brother has told the truth. He took on the duty to gather information for Lord Graydon—for the safety of the Forest.*

"How did you learn this?" Sebastian stammered, reaching across to grab Ivan's forearm. "Did Zephyrus know anything about it?"

Heat rose to Ivan's neck, ashamed for letting Peter's secret out. But he had to learn the truth before he left for home.

"Who told you this?" Sebastian questioned again, sputtering.

"Peter explained this before I left the Forest on my first visit. He told me he needed to give a full report to Lord Graydon before he could return home."

"Why didn't you tell me?" Sebastian's mouth turned downward.

257

"I have my secrets, too." Ivan lifted his chin. "And it wasn't mine to share."

Lord Graydon chuckled. "Now, now, Sebastian. No point getting out of sorts over this. Surely, Ivan has his reasons for not divulging the information."

"I-I promised Peter," Ivan said.

Crossing his arms over his chest, Sebastian grunted and pouted.

"Don't worry about it." Lord Graydon reached for Ivan's hand and gave it a squeeze. "No harm done."

"Then Peter gave you the full report he'd promised?" Ivan stared into the lord's eyes, imploring him to agree.

The lord blinked. "No. I haven't seen him for some time. As I've said, I'd heard he returned to Graydon Village with you."

"Well," Sebastian sulked. "It's done now, isn't it? The war is over."

Ivan bit his lip and paused. "Did Peter say what information he planned to get for you?"

"We had a brief conversation about it." The lord stroked his goatee. "He said he'd try to find out how many men Kruse Hays commanded and how well equipped they were. Also, if indeed, they planned an attack, what route, or routes, they'd take."

"Mart-Mart could have told you all that." Sebastian sank deeper into his chair, tightening his arms even more.

A little huff of laughter left Ivan's lips. He remembered the small, bronze-tipped owl from his first visit. *Maybe Mart-Mart could've answered some of the more important questions.*

The lord's frown reappeared. "Do you know where

Peter is now?"

"We've only heard rumors," Sebastian answered quickly, "but we plan to search on Ivan's next visit. It will allow us more time to track him down."

The lord laced his elegant fingers together and seemed satisfied. Ivan was glad not to explain further. He'd already said too much in front of Sebastian.

"Did I answer all your questions?" The lord nodded with empathy.

"Yes," Ivan said. "It means Peter wanted to be helpful and risked his life to gather information that would benefit the Forest."

"I suppose it does," Lord Graydon replied.

Chapter 25

The Medallion

Ivan reached down and stroked Alfred's ears, wondering if Sebastian would stay angry with him for the rest of the day.

Lord Graydon suddenly raised his head. "I have something I want to give you."

A gift? Ivan opened his eyes wide.

Jumping up from his chair, Lord Graydon strode to the library's east wall and pressed his thumb against a small button on the bookshelf. A hidden panel slid open with scarcely a sound.

Stretching his neck, Ivan wondered what was kept there.

The lord brought out a fancy box lined with purple silk. "I'd like you to have this medallion." The jewelry had a sixpence-sized amethyst in the center of a thick silver disc.

"The stone will ward off evil curses, trances, and some basic spells. You'll notice all the Wolflords wear them. This was their gift to thank me for accepting them into our kingdom. It's for my protection, they told me."

"If it was meant for you"—Ivan clasped his hands together—"I couldn't take it."

"Nonsense, my boy." The lord lifted the piece from its case and placed the chain around Ivan's neck. His intense gaze held Ivan's for some seconds. "Promise you'll wear it when you visit the Forest. It will bring me comfort to know you are safe—just in case."

Ivan's cheek muscle flexed, and he nodded in agreement. Canute gave a sharp bark.

"Even your beagle senses its powerful magic," Lord Graydon said. Tipping back his head, he laughed.

"What is the writing around the disc?" Ivan fingered the piece turning it round and round.

The lord thought on the question for a moment. "It's written in the Ancient Legend Script of the druids. It reads, The Love of the Forest Protects You."

Ivan thanked him and drank down the last of his lemonade. He clutched the medallion and hesitated taking it. *Maybe if the lord wasn't looking, I could slip it back into its fancy box, but that would be rude and ungrateful. I'd better wear it to please him.*

"There are many forces that would like to see you leave the Forest and never return." Lord Graydon pursed his lips, his frown deepened. "I'm sure they consider you more than a nuisance. This is especially true because you killed Kruse Hays's chief commander and saved Zephyrus's life with the healing sap."

Ivan was surprised Lord Graydon knew of the past conflicts and details. *But then, why shouldn't he? After all, he is lord of the castle and the Forest.*

"Now," Sebastian added, "you've rescued the Golden Lantern. That's sure to ruffle some feathers."

The lord gestured for Ivan to help himself to fruits and nuts on the tray. Ivan picked up a handful and chewed them. "I'm most worried about the Vaguers." Lord Graydon heaved a sigh. "They may come near the castle. Just how we'll exterminate them, I'm not certain."

"Sir, I think the solution is The Challenger." Sebastian nodded as he said this. "Ivan used the weapon to kill one of them."

"I believe you may be right. Good call, Sebastian." The lord looked pleased. "By the way, where is the sword? I noticed earlier you weren't wearing it."

"It's safe in our bedchamber, under the pillows," Ivan said. "You promised the room was one of the safest in the castle."

"And so, it is." Lord Graydon slowly nodded.

A soft knock on the door startled them and the conversation stopped.

The lord groaned. "I sent Fiona to bring tea and breakfast scones.

Alfred jumped up from his favorite spot near the fireplace and raced to the door. Fiona pushed a silver cart that held a large tray of hot scones and jam, as well as biscuits drizzled with chocolate and crushed jitnuts. She filled a cup of tea for Ivan.

Lord Graydon cleared his throat. "As your lord, am I not served first, Fiona?"

The servant girl spun around, a deep blush meeting her hairline. "Oh, my Lord. I'm so sorry. I-I…" At a loss for words, she closed her mouth and lowered her eyes.

He chuckled and patted her hand with affection. "You girls must know I'm not much for protocol. Only when entertaining dignitaries. Go on now, serve the tea, and leave with a smile."

"Oh, thank you, sir." She curtsied and hurried away, the beagles following. She hesitated at the door, bent, and stroked the animals. "I wish you could go with me."

"That's a good idea." The lord held up his hand in a halting manner. "Would you mind taking Alfred and

Canute for a walk to do their business?"

"I'd be happy to, my Lord." The girl ushered the two beagles out the door.

Ivan sipped his tea, reached for a scone, and took a bite. "Lovely butter flavor."

"Sir. What will happen to Zello?" Sebastian scratched his whiskers. "Will he stay isolated in the Azurite Mountains or return to his females?"

The lord leaned back into his chair and looked worried. His cup and saucer rested on his lap. "He will be summoned to stand trial and be judged at open court. Late next week, isn't it?"

Ivan and Sebastian confirmed this with a nod.

"Could we have a private trial for Zello without half the Forest people showing up to watch his humiliation?" Sebastian sat up straighter. "I mean, if Zephyrus could hear Zello's personal testimony, I'm sure he would be cleared from any malicious accusations."

The lord considered the suggestion. He smoothed his mustache with his index finger. After a time, he answered, "I believe that's a solid idea. I'll send a message to Zephyrus. If you happen to mention it, tell him I wholeheartedly agree."

Ivan and Sebastian let out a long exhale, turned, and grinned at each other.

There was a sharp rap on the door.

"Enter," the lord yelled with some impatience in his voice.

Commander Simon raced in, his hair wet and flat, uniform dripping.

"What happened to you?" Sebastian asked.

"Raining hard." Simon saluted and wiped his face with the palm of his hand.

Turning in their chairs, they looked out the windows.

"And so it is," Sebastian said.

"You'd better come with me." Simon's jaw tightened.

The lord grabbed the lantern. Puzzled and worried, all three rose and followed.

A rough farm wagon was parked at the front entrance of the castle. Two of Simon's soldiers climbed down from the wooden front seat. One rushed to the back and pulled away a tarp, spilling puddled rain onto the ground. There lay a corpse of a man in bloodied overalls.

Ivan gasped. The contents of his stomach rose, and something sour threatened to spew out.

"Oh, God." The lord uttered a soft cry. The farmer's eye sockets were sunken—empty. There was no mistaking the slack, distorted jaw, and dried blood. "This is the work of a Vaguer." He averted his head from the dead man.

The stern set of Simon's brow said it all. Several of his soldiers had just walked out the castle door and gaped at the body. The dead man's skin was soft and gray. Arms and legs limp at his side as though his very bones had been dissolved. One soldier turned aside and threw up his breakfast. No one blamed him since they all felt the same revulsion.

"That's Samuel Carringer. Has a small farm outside the castle's border," the soldier said. "A wife and three young children."

The lord groaned a most painful sound.

A cold shiver rushed through Ivan. The yellow-eyed devil had stolen the man's precious Essence, the total sum of Samuel Carringer. Ivan wished he could burn all the vile creatures, and they'd never be allowed to rise again.

A piercing scream broke the solemn mood. Nearby stood Fiona, eyes wide, her hands pressed hard against her gaping mouth. "Oh, my heavens, my heavens. What happened to Sam?" Fiona cried as rain wetted her curly red hair.

Canute and Alfred shot off across the castle lawn, whimpering, not looking back.

Everyone waited for Lord Graydon to speak. "You're soaked, Fiona. Go inside."

She shook her head, and her bottom lip trembled. "This is the work of a-a..." her voice cracked to where she could hardly speak.

Ivan rushed to the servant girl's side. Sensing her legs giving out, he grabbed and held her upright. "I'm so sorry, Fiona," he said. "Did you know Mr. Carringer?"

"M-my—our neighbor."

"We'll get them. We'll get them all," Simon said with such force that blue veins protruded from his neck.

"I'll call the men together," a soldier said. Taking Fiona from Ivan's arms, he led the hysterical girl back inside the castle.

"Simon," Lord Graydon called. "Ivan must return the relics to Zephyrus and travel to his farm home. Can you spare a few men for an escort?"

"Of course." Simon saluted. "I've already arranged a mix of Elftens, Wolflords—some of my best men."

"Excellent," the lord said. "I know Ivan must leave at once in order to arrive home before evening.

"It's a long ride." Simon twisted his leather gauntlets in his hands, his look uncertain.

"Well, then." The lord hesitated. "Perhaps plan on

traveling halfway by staying in the Harvesters' Cottages until daybreak. Then continue your journey the next morning."

Ivan wanted to speak up and argue the suggestion. He needed no part of the place where the hideous Vaguers dwelt. He and Sebastian had heard strange noises and painful screams when they stayed there the night before and didn't wish to repeat the horror of the Essence-suckers.

"Come on." Sebastian motioned with an impatient wave of his hand. "Let's get these men moving. Maybe we can make it as far as Zephyrus and stay in the soldiers' barracks tonight."

"That sounds sensible," Ivan uttered, hoping that would be the case.

"Since The Challenger is in your room," Lord Graydon said, "and I'm the only one besides you with a key, I'll go get it." He handed Ivan the Golden Lantern. Climbing the castle steps to the entrance, the lord turned, paused, and stared at the corpse. "Take the wagon to the stable until arrangements can be made. Post a couple of guards, and don't allow anyone near it." His shaky hand rubbed the back of his neck.

The two men, who'd brought the wagon, climbed to their seats and drove away. The wheels crunched menacingly against the wet gravel. Slow and grave.

Ivan's gaze met Wayland's stricken face.

"This is gruesome," Wayland muttered. "And I thought werewolves were bloodthirsty—but they kill to eat and protect themselves—these creatures are from the very depths of hell, created by the devil Tereus himself."

Silently, Ivan agreed. *I know who conjured them— and I know why.*

"Do you plan to ride with us?" Sebastian asked Sytha.

The Elften paused, his brow furrowed with the tough decision. It seemed he struggled with his answer after he'd seen the mangled face of Sam Carringer. "Yes." He finally nodded. "My main duty is to see Ivan safely through the Forest."

"Men," Simon shouted and raised his sword for emphasis. "We'll split the ranks. Part of you will hunt the Vaguers. Show no mercy. A small division will escort Ivan to Zephyrus. Sytha and Wayland will distribute their men as they see fit. Understood?" The commander swept his gaze over the nervous men.

Soldiers glanced at one another with worried looks. But none protested.

The rain came down in pounding sheets. Some, who hadn't yet mounted, found refuge under the portico's overhang.

Ivan's concern turned to Sebastian. "Your powers are weak when wet. Will you be okay?"

"Not to worry about me. I'll dissolve inside the Long Dark Cloak to protect you. Perhaps the sun will come soon and dry the garment." They stood on the lawn, waiting for the troops to divide. With that, Sebastian's spirit swirled smoky blue-gray and entered the cloak resting over Ivan's shoulders. Old Bones dissolved into a puff of smoke and disappeared along with Sebastian.

Rain or not, the servants brought bundled supplies from the castle and helped pack them into a small wagon with high sides. They threw a new tarp over the top, tying it down with rope.

With no humor, Lord Graydon returned and handed

Ivan his saddlebags and The Challenger. He rested his hand on Ivan's shoulder and said, "Thank you for returning the lantern. We are most grateful."

Ivan nodded, taking both items in his grip. He approached Simon, and there he offered him the magnificent sword. When the commander hesitated, Ivan raised the hilt higher and waited for him to take it. "This should help you on your mission."

"Keep it until you reach Zephyrus," Simon said. "You've formed a solid bond with The Challenger. You were meant to wear it."

"But Simon," Sebastian protested from inside the cloak. "The Challenger will aid you in bringing down the Vaguers."

Commander Simon wiped a raindrop from the side of his nose. "We now know to remove their heads in one swift move. Not an easy maneuver to make unless you can get close to them."

Buckling the scabbard around his waist, Ivan adjusted the weapon at his side.

Soon the rain tapered to an annoying drizzle.

"We're getting a very late start," Ivan said, his patience waning. "I don't wish to stay at the Harvesters' Cottages, and—it's a long trek to Zephyrus."

"What's the matter?" Sebastian questioned from the cloak. "I sense you're feeling some hesitation—even regret."

"I feel it's my duty to be part of the hunt. Yet, I'm anxious to return the relics and be on my way."

"It's time you headed home," Sebastian said firmly. "Your farm duties await you."

Lord Graydon's eyes glistened. "Please be careful—and wear the medallion on the outside of your shirt. It will protect you."

Ivan pulled the piece by its chain and laid it against the cloak. He thanked the lord for his concern and generous hospitality.

"I thoroughly enjoyed meeting you and your visit to the castle." Lord Graydon embraced him and patted his back with affection. "Come again. You are most welcome anytime."

Lowering his head, Ivan said, "The Carringer family, sir. I can contribute."

"I'll take care of them, but thank you for your offer." A sad smile tugged at the lord's lips. "Godspeed, son. May your journey home be safe and without incident."

"Thank you." Ivan mounted his chestnut horse and pulled the hood of the cloak over his wet head.

"We'd best be going," Sebastian's voice edged impatience from inside the garment. "The longer the delay, the darker it will become."

Ivan wondered if there was a hidden meaning in Sebastian's words.

Chapter 26

Dangerous Ride Home

"Come on, Ivan," Simon yelled. "We must leave at once."

"Look after our hero," the lord called to the group and waved. He stepped back, his eyes shadowed with fear.

"He'll be safe with us." Sytha saluted.

The rain finally stopped. Fog rolled in and covered the ground. Some of the men grumbled that visibility was poor.

"This won't be an easy ride," a Wolflord said, and Ivan silently agreed.

Hooking the lantern on the back of Bounty's saddle, Ivan said, "I hope it won't be too bumpy for you, Joseph. I must have both my hands free—in case I need The Challenger."

"Not to worry. I've survived this position before."

The troops rode north on the long driveway that led to South Castle Road.

Subtle signs of fall were nudging at the Forest. Leaves drifted from the trees, acorns fell from oaks and rolled out of their caps, and the holly tree put forth shiny red berries in abundant clusters. Even the cool air was a reminder of autumn's approach.

"Shouldn't we take the northeastern trail? It would

take us more directly to Zephyrus?" Ivan pointed at a rough split in the road to the right that he hadn't noticed before.

"Simon knows what he's doing," Sebastian answered from the cloak. "That road isn't much more than a footpath filled with ruts, tree roots, and overgrown brush. I suspect he wants a more traveled route, having the protection of other Forest inhabitants if need be."

"And besides," Sytha said, "we want to investigate the Harvesters' Cottages. It's only a short distance out of our way. I hope you don't mind."

Ivan sighed and braced himself for what he hoped would be a brief stop and nothing more. The detour would surely delay them from reaching Zephyrus. Daylight hours would disappear quickly. He wondered if Joseph's beaming light could guide them without alerting their enemies.

Near the junction of South Castle Road and Sheepherders Road, Commander Simon halted and issued orders. Some of his soldiers divided from the troops and turned toward the South Castle University near where Sam Carringer's farm was located. They said their goodbyes. Others followed north, watching their surroundings with sharp eyes.

Sam Carringer's face haunted Ivan. *What if Kagutt sucked out my Essence? What would happen to my farm? My beagles? Peter?*

They rode on. Few spoke, but rather rested their hands on the hilt of their swords. *Will their weapons be enough to kill the Vaguers—removing their heads in one swift move?* Ivan stroked The Challenger. "I'm grateful you are with me." As Ivan said this, Tanner's horse slipped on the rocky road and nearly threw his rider.

Righting himself skillfully, he held his hand high in the air and shouted, "I'm okay—a careless step by my mount. Not to worry."

Ivan exhaled with relief, and all the riders exercised more care on the slippery rocks.

As the procession approached the entrance to the Harvesters' Cottages, Ivan squirmed in his saddle, and his blood raced. He searched from side to side for any disturbance but didn't see anything peculiar or dangerous.

The sky continued overcast and threatening. Trees appeared as ghostly shapes in the fog, spooking horses and men alike. Bounty shook his head and whinnied. Alfred and Canute barked until Ivan told them to shush.

"It's turned colder." Ivan clutched the cloak tighter.

"There's something foul in the air." Wayland guided his horse next to Ivan. "We werewolves know smells." He sniffed again.

Suddenly, a skeletal figure wearing tattered army garb appeared from behind a stand of elms. Grayish flesh pulled tightly over his skull while his bony fingers gripped the tree on both sides. Like playing hide-and-go-seek, he glared from one edge of the tree and then the other.

The frightening face stared at them with piercing eyes. Sytha and Gan-let were beside Ivan in an instant, buffering him from danger.

Wayland grabbed Bounty's reins, jerking him to a halt. In one smooth motion, a soldier pulled an arrow from his quiver, ready to loosen it into the Vaguer's heart—if he had one.

"Your common arrows cannot harm me, soldier," the creature hissed. "You should've realized this by now."

Sytha whipped his wand from its sheath and pointed it at the Essence-sucker.

"But *that stick* could do some damage," the Vaguer said, his yellow eyes widened.

"I will scorch you and all your kind from the earth." Sytha's jaw tightened.

The Vaguer seemed to ignore the threat. "There are many of us hiding in the woodland. Waiting."

"Waiting for what?" Wayland glanced around.

"For this one. Only this one." The Vaguer's arm lifted and pointed at Ivan. "Give me the boy and we will leave your Forest forever. It is our promise."

Sytha snorted at the bold Vaguer. "Who'd believe your lies?"

Ivan jerked his head back and gasped. His heart thumped against his chest. "No!" He hollered, "I won't be left for dead."

"Don't fear me this time," the creature growled. "It's not me hell-bent on the boy, but my master."

Sytha and Wayland stared at each other, their eyes narrowed. "Tereus?"

"That's right, the demon of the fiery caverns." The Vaguer's stained and crooked teeth showed behind a venomous grin.

"You destroyed the farmer." A soldier shook his fist angrily. "Sam was my neighbor and friend."

"No, not me." The Vaguer held up a halting hand. "Another like me now has a new life. I've made myself known to you to tell you about another man—a human. He rode in a royal carriage with his entourage that never reached the castle to join his Russian friends. We attacked and took what we needed to survive."

Ivan inhaled, imagining such a horror. His own countrymen. Royalty. Their Essence stolen in a most awful way.

"Where are the bodies and the carriage you speak of?" Sytha raised his brow.

"You will find them behind the cottage with a collapsed roof."

"I remember that cottage," Sebastian spoke from the cloak.

"Why are you telling us this?" Ivan managed to ask.

"Yeah, what do you care?" Wayland's nostrils flared.

"Care? I don't care—only to tell you, there was an older, bearded man, his mistress, and several others in the carriage. His name was Boris Tackyevich, Minister of Defense. We know this because he screamed his royal importance more than once. I consumed his Essence and ended his life. Yet I have not changed to have a whole life because he was so foul."

"You killed him," Wayland shouted, about to throw himself off his horse. "You monster!"

"No!" Sytha's hand shot out to grasp Wayland's arm. "It may be a trick."

"You are right." Simon nudged his bay closer. "Stay alert."

"I only ask that you hear me." The Vaguer showed himself fully from behind the tree, his arms spread from his sides.

"Then make it quick," Sytha shouted. "We have things to do."

"I did you a favor. Boris didn't deserve to live," the Vaguer jeered. "After I took his Essence, it made me violently ill. I didn't know we could consume repulsive beings." His gray skin wrinkled on his forehead. "He was even more revolting than I am." He gave a croak of laughter.

"That's confessing a mouthful," a soldier snarled.

"What of it?" Ivan felt more emboldened as his fingers came to rest upon the hilt of The Challenger.

"I puked up his Essence, but lay in the wet leaves writhing in misery, trying to recover from the experience. I had the worst gut ache."

"Are we supposed to feel sorry for you?" Sytha mocked, motioning for his men to quietly surround the Vaguer.

"Don't you see? Boris was responsible for ordering thousands of his own people to be tortured and slaughtered. If anyone opposed him—they died."

Ivan felt chilled to the bone listening to the account of his country's dark history. But he knew it was true.

"Why bother telling us this?" Wayland spoke. "You and your kind consume the souls of living men."

"Like calling the kettle black, isn't it?" another soldier taunted.

The creature's eyes smoldered with hatred. He glanced into the surrounding trees. His wire fingers folded, making a fist. "Do you not understand?" The Vaguer lifted his bony arms. "Boris. This deplorable excuse for a man, this mass murderer of men, women, and children, is the same kind of master I'm forced to serve. Since the time Tereus revived us from our graves, we have been in his bondage. Living a half-human life."

For a brief moment, Ivan felt sympathy for the wretch. Deceived, his fate was torn from him forever.

"Tereus, the dark lord." Wayland spat as though the words were filthy.

"Yes." The Vaguer's wide mouth sneered. "He is to be feared above all else."

Sytha held his wand upright, prepared to release its power and destroy the vile creature.

"Wait. Wait," the Vaguer cried. "We can still make a deal for the boy. I promise. You'll never see our kind again in your Forest."

"We don't sacrifice human life," Sytha said through clenched teeth. He lifted his arm and—the power of his wand cut the air with bright sparks that flew from the tip, hitting its target with deadly accuracy.

Horrified, Ivan squeezed his shaky knees to stay seated on Bounty. The horse snorted, and his nostrils flared. Ivan wondered if Bounty's heart raced as fast as his own. The Vaguer slumped against the elm he was standing near and slid to the ground. "Thank you," he whispered. "It is better I die than to live this empty life." His body dissolved and turned into a putrid mass of what smelled and looked like pus. Only his yellowed bones remained.

Before Ivan could stop them, Alfred and Canute ran to the puddle and sniffed.

"Don't go near him," Ivan bellowed.

Alfred shook his head and sneezed. He turned from the rot and scampered away. Canute hurried after him.

"We'll bury him." Wayland dismounted. "The corpse could poison the Forest animals."

They stared at the slimy patch and covered their noses.

Ivan slid from Bounty while his beagles barked and ran in circles. He went to his knees, gathering them to him. Stroking their backs, he calmed them. "I know, boys. The Vaguer is disgusting, dead or alive."

It was impossible to get the scene out of his mind. The creature had pointed at him, bargaining for his life—his Essence. Ivan rubbed his face with his hands and tried to erase the memory of the Vaguer's starving look.

A soldier approached with a shovel and began to dig beside the Vaguer's remains.

"How did you know to bring a shovel?" Ivan asked.

The soldier appeared puzzled for a moment. "Why, to bury the corpses, of course. We plan ahead."

Embarrassed by his dumb question, Ivan nodded.

The other men spread out, searching the area for other Vaguers. Weapons were drawn, held in steady grips. Spears and bows clutched in hands, a mace or sword rested at their sides. Ivan heard these items would not kill the skeletal creatures, but what about swinging the maces and removing their heads? Surely this would also end the Vaguers' existence.

Sytha, Simon, and a few of his men returned. "What did you find?" Wayland asked.

The Elften shook his head. "Not a sign of them on the perimeter."

"Maybe they're all hiding near Sam Carringer's farm in the south," Gan-let suggested.

"Could be. Or they're hiding in the cottages." Simon straightened his back and took a deep breath. "Will you help look for the second carriage?" he asked Ivan. "The Vaguer mentioned the cottage with the fallen roof."

Remembering Sam Carringer's face, his eyes, his broken jaw, Ivan agreed.

"After that, we'll take you to Zephyrus," Simon promised.

"This may not be a good idea," Sebastian spoke. "We really must—"

"I want to help, if only for a short time. It's my d-duty, somehow." Ivan looked at the road north that would lead him to Zephyrus—to safety. Maybe agreeing to the search was a grave mistake, but responsibility pulled at him. *After all, it is my fault the Vaguers are here.*

With a shout and a sweep of his hand, Sytha waved forward. "Now, let's find the royal carriage. The bodies are most likely near."

Wayland whistled for his horse. When it came, he threw himself into the saddle. "It's getting late. We can't waste any more time."

"Bounty," Ivan called. The chestnut gelding swung his head in Ivan's direction, his eyes large with terror. He wouldn't move. Having no choice, Ivan went to the animal and stroked his quivering neck. "I know how you feel, but we need to help."

At last, his horse and beagles joined the procession and turned onto the well-traveled road that led to the main entrance of the Harvesters' Cottages.

"Spread out!" Simon swept his arm around. "Search everywhere for a sign of the carriage and its team. There should be a couple of harnessed horses, maybe as many as four. They can't have gone far tethered with hardware around their necks."

Ivan's jaw twitched. "I think we should stay together, don't you, Sebastian? If we get separated, it will be easier for the creatures to attack."

"Just keep your eyes on the soldiers, and don't let them out of your sight." Sebastian's statement held shaky caution. "I must say, this creeping fog has me quite anxious."

As they moved between the whitewashed cottages,

abandoned gardens, and a small brook, the troops separated and took their own paths. Some dismounted to search the rickety stables and houses. One soldier walked through a neglected plot where he pulled up a withered turnip.

"Over here," someone shouted. "A couple of horses—and—there's a carriage up ahead."

"This way." Wayland pointed. "That's the cottage to the west with the collapsed roof. A portion of the soldiers moved in that direction while the remainder surrounded the grounds searching for any signs of the dreadful creatures. Ivan, Wayland, and his men followed, eager to catch the horses and find the passengers who occupied the royal carriage.

Two of the horses stood shivering under a canopy of the thick trees, their harnesses absent.

"Who released them from the carriage?" Ivan asked.

Sebastian seemed to think on the question for a moment. "Maybe it was Sam Carringer.

Ivan bowed his head and shook it slowly. "If so, his thoughtfulness cost him his life."

A nearby soldier stood in his stirrups, searching in the distance. "With the size of that carriage, I'm sure there would've been four horses. But where are they?"

Leaning forward on his pale blue mount, Sytha's torso stiffened, and his jaw tightened. In one swift move, he jerked his bow from his shoulder, reached and notched a golden-tipped arrow.

Alfred hesitated. Canute howled.

"S-something isn't right here." Wayland turned his head to and fro.

No sooner had the words left his mouth, than a horde of shadowy, skeletal figures rushed from behind trees, cottages, and stables.

Chapter 27

Vaguer Attack

A horde of Vaguers stampeded toward the group, waving their long bony arms, a loud yodeling sound emitted deep within their throats. They continued their fierce race, weaving in and out between the trees and cottages. Their large yellow eyes targeted the men who had positioned themselves for the onslaught.

Petrified, the horses screamed, reared, and pawed at the air. Men tried to calm their mounts, or they'd be thrown to the ground as Vaguer bait.

"Draw your weapons," Commander Simon yelled.

Ivan pulled The Challenger from its sheath. He gripped the hilt with shaky hands. "They're coming," he shouted to Sebastian.

"There are many," The Challenger hollered to Ivan through the sudden melee. "You do remember how you fought Burtack, the Black Knight? Allow me the freedom to bring the Vaguers down."

"Y-yes," Ivan choked. His heart pounded at the memory.

"Hold on and follow my lead as you've done in the past." The great sword swept in a powerful downward motion and removed the skull of the first victim.

"Let's do it again," the sword sang.

Bounty pushed through jittery horses where soldiers

tried to shove blades into the creature's hearts. They soon discovered their weapons were futile unless they severed the Vaguers' heads. It was difficult to get a fair swing when their steeds bunched and sidled into each other, snorting and panting.

The scent of decaying flesh soon permeated the air. Bounty shook his long mane and blew mucus. He pulled at the reins attempting to escape the noise and confusion.

"It's okay, boy." Ivan stroked his horse's shoulder. "We'll slaughter every last one, and the Forest will be free of them." He checked the hook that held the lantern to his saddle. It seemed to hold.

"I'm glad to be a spirit," Joseph said in a squeaky voice from the Golden Lantern.

A Vaguer rushed forward, where he gripped Wayland's leg and wrapped his thin fingers around his calf, trying to jerk him from his mount. Wayland yowled like an injured wolf. He clutched his sword and horse's neck at the same time. Ivan maneuvered Bounty next to his friend, breathing in gasps, and raised The Challenger. It slashed through the air with one swift stroke, meeting the Vaguer's throat. His head went flying, twirling in the air several times. The attacker crumpled and dissolved into a slimy mass. His cranium rolled down into a shallow ravine.

"Got another one," The Challenger called with enthusiasm in his sonorous voice.

"Thanks," Wayland stuttered through white lips. "I thought my Essence would be sucked out in an instant." His hands trembled as he stroked his wet face with his palm.

"Don't let them escape or hide in the cottages," Simon hollered when the Vaguers turned to run.

"Lieutenant Pezzuline, take your men and head southeast. Sergeant Berkel, ride southwest and watch for any escape routes."

"Yes, sir." They saluted and took off with soldiers following.

"If we separate, it will be easier for them to attack us," Ivan protested once more. For a moment, he wondered if he was acting cowardly. He pushed the thought from his mind, straightened his shoulders, and raced after Sytha and the Elftens.

They rode between the cottages, forged a shallow creek, and skirted ickleberry bushes that had been picked clean.

"This fog has thickened rather quickly," Joseph said from the lantern. "It will hinder the men from finding and destroying these terrible creatures."

Ivan agreed. Just then, a brown horse in front of him slipped on the wet grass. The animal went down and lost his rider. Quickly, Ivan reached the soldier, extended his hand, and pulled the man to his feet. He was clearly hurt, Ivan observed. A sprained ankle, at the least. The man stumbled to his steed and struggled to swing his leg over the saddle. Breathing heavily, he turned to Ivan. "Thanks for your hand, young man." The soldier saluted.

"Here! Over here," someone shouted.

"I hear the voice," Ivan said, "but I'm not sure where it's coming from."

"This way," Wayland yelled as he skidded toward Ivan. "Behind those decrepit cottages to the west." He jerked on the reins, turned his horse, and sped off in that direction.

"Alfred, Canute, come," Ivan hollered at his beagles that were investigating on their own. "This is no place to be left behind."

A portion of Simon's soldiers galloped in the direction of the shouting. They must've believed someone had found the other two horses. The Elftens circled around the other way. Ivan understood their plan to trap the Vaguers and annihilate them once and for all.

To make matters worse, the gray sky became darker, and it began to sprinkle.

"Drat!" Sebastian growled. "I'll get wet again. That's not good for my healing powers."

Sytha and his golden-tipped arrows were bringing the Vaguers down in rapid succession. His fellow Elftens cheered, shooting golden-tipped arrows of their own. This wasn't the first time Ivan marveled at the speed and accuracy of the Elften's archery skills. Without them, Ivan shuddered to think what the outcome would be.

"Keep them running!" Simon shouted. "Don't let them take refuge in the cottages."

Flattened uniforms and detached grayish skulls littered the meadow, reminding them what had invaded the Forest, endangering and taking the lives of the inhabitants.

Ivan's breakfast rose from his churning stomach. He leaned over and heaved on a Vaguer. The creature looked up at Ivan and gave him a toothless grin. His laugh was like a creaky door opening. *How could they be so heartless?* Jaw clenched, Ivan swung Bounty around, swept The Challenger in a powerful arc, and separated the Vaguer's head.

Another Vaguer rushed from behind a tree, grabbed and tore at a soldier's trousers. The man shrieked, falling from his horse, and rolled away to avoid the hard hooves of the other stallions. Several Wolflords moved close to rescue the soldier who wailed and clutched his bleeding leg. Wayland swung off his mount, pulled the man into his powerful arms, and positioned him behind Gan-let on his horse.

"I'll take you to get help." Gan-let, the Elften, rotated his stallion and headed in the direction of the supply wagon where medical help stood by for the wounded.

Furious, Ivan kicked Bounty in the ribs and raced through the trees where he removed Vaguer heads right and left. He was determined to kill them all, especially Kagutt, before the dreadful creature found him. Then, the Forest folks would be safe, and his fear of losing his Essence would vanish.

"Hold on, Ivan," The Challenger warned. "You are putting yourself in unnecessary danger."

Sebastian cautioned the same, his voice impatient and scolding. "Soldiers and Elftens are trained for this—you're not. Slow down—don't be so hotheaded."

Anger and fear drove him just as it had when the Dark Army attacked the Forest. Ivan acted foolishly then, and he was acting just as bull-headed now. But he couldn't help himself. These creatures had no place in Lord Graydon's great kingdom. *It's because of me they are here. They threatened every life—including mine. The responsibility rests with me to annihilate them.*

At that moment, two black horses raced through the woodland, screaming like they were chased by a demon from hell.

"They must be the other two horses that pulled the royal carriage," Ivan said, "but their harnesses are missing, too."

Their abrupt appearance and panic caused Bounty to

shoot off and follow the runaway stallions. His ears pulled back, and his nostrils flared. He dashed through the trees and brush with no thought of his passenger.

"Wait! Bounty, slow down," Ivan cried.

The Golden Lantern pounded against the horse's flank, driving the animal even harder. Though Ivan jerked back on the reins, his stubborn horse was too terrified to stop.

"Halt, Bounty!" Sebastian shouted from the cloak.

Ivan nearly toppled off when his horse took several quick turns. "Hold on, Joseph," he said to the spirit in the lantern. "Bounty's on the run."

Finally, his mount slowed to a trot, lungs heaving, and sweat soaking his neck. He looked back, shook his head and showed some remorse.

Ivan calmed his own heartbeat, took a shuddering breath, and tried to steady his shaky hands.

"Where did they go?" he asked, rotating to search the area. "And Alfred and Canute—where are they?" Ivan called his beagles through cupped hands, but they didn't answer.

"We shouldn't have separated from the soldiers," Sebastian grumbled. You are lost, with no one to come to your rescue. Turn back now and find the troops."

"Ivan didn't have much choice," The Challenger defended.

"That dang horse of yours…" Sebastian's sentence faded.

"I think the soldiers are this way." Ivan pointed. "Or maybe that way." He moved his finger to the right. "It's difficult to tell with the fog. It muffles my senses as well as my sight."

Shivering with the damp chill, Ivan drew his jacket

closed and buttoned it to his neck, concealing the medallion that rested against his bare chest. "I don't remember this pile of rocks or this bent tree." He pulled his fingers through his damp hair as he searched for a return path and evidence of his beagles.

"Blast it all," Sebastian yelled.

"What's the matter?"

"I feel so useless right now. This wetness denies me my powers. I can't help you find your way, I can't heal you, and I'm unable to protect you."

"Don't worry," Ivan said. "We've been in worse fixes." The truth was, he was quivering with cold and fear.

They came to a small, fast stream where Bounty stopped, lowered his head, and drank. Ivan considered doing the same. His head felt woozy from lack of food and water, especially since he'd thrown up his breakfast on the Vaguer.

He was about to swing off his horse when... "What was that noise?" Sebastian asked.

Ivan's pulse raced faster than the stream in front of him.

A terrible voice. Coarse and hollow. "Imagine my good fortune finding you here—right where I want you." The tall, skeletal figure moved from behind a stand of elm trees.

"K-Kagutt," Ivan stammered. He reached for The Challenger. Before he could pull his weapon, Kagutt dashed at Bounty. Yellow eyes wide, he thrust his bony arms into the air, yodeling a bloodthirsty cry.

The frightened horse reared. He pawed the air, twisting his torso.

"Don't Bounty. Stop—please." A scene flashed

before him when he fell at Lake Gorgon as Bounty's saddle slipped over his rump. It had nearly cost Ivan his life. Once more, his horse stood on hind legs, front hoofs struck at the air.

"Hold on, Ivan," Sebastian said. "Pull The Challenger."

It was impossible to stay seated. Ivan flew off his horse and landed on his back. Breath left his lungs that he struggled to reclaim. His head hit the edge of a stump. Lights exploded before his eyes—red, yellow, and white. He sank into a misty gray fog, fighting to find his way out.

The Vaguer was on him. Bony hands gripped Ivan's face in an iron hold.

"I've been waiting for you," the creature rasped. "You were promised to me by the Great One beneath the earth."

"Help me, Sebastian," Ivan moaned. His lips trembled.

"My-my powers are weak, they…I…" Sebastian mumbled on. Panic froze his voice.

Ivan whimpered a cry of help, gasping for air.

"You are mine." The Vaguer laughed. "All mine."

Groaning, Ivan tried to twist his body to dislodge the horrible monster who would steal everything about him. He was paralyzed, unable to move more than a few inches.

"I'll live forever with your Essence— pure…moral…honorable." His face came near. Rotten breath gagged Ivan.

The creature gripped Ivan's head with his icy hands. Unable to move, he struggled to pull The Challenger, but his strength was gone.

"Open. Open your mouth, now!" Kagutt breathed fast and deep. His thumbs pressed hard into Ivan's eyelids.

Ivan screamed. He tried to find the strength to throw off his attacker, but the Vaguer was too strong, and Ivan lay dazed from the fall onto his back.

"This is what I need." Kagutt lowered his head, his lips locked onto Ivan's. A long, hot tongue entered Ivan's throat, moving upward, where it probed and teased. Kagutt moaned with pleasure, his reward of a new life awaited.

No! Ivan fought to turn his head and remove the awful intrusion. The terrible creature held him in a vise grip. *What will happen to my beagles? Peter? I will dissolve right here, like Samuel Carringer. My Essence gone, my eyes sucked out. Oh, God. Help me.*

Darkness surrounded him, threatening to whisk him away.

Sebastian squeaked, his voice tight. "Ivan, show the medallion."

It was covered under his clothing. And now he was powerless in the Vaguer's tight hold.

"The medallion. Pull the medallion—it will save you," Sebastian finally yelled.

His thoughts were dimming, his will to live, melting. Ivan swirled off into another world, dark and evil where selfishness and all-encompassing power resided.

Clopping sounds from a horse approached from somewhere. The thump of a man's boots hit the ground—hurried steps moved toward him.

Kagutt raised his head. Its invading tongue jerked from Ivan's mouth. "Go away," he snarled to the newcomer. "He's mine."

A swooshing noise, like something was propelled through the air. An abrupt lurch was followed by a guttural scream.

It sounded like...

Weight suddenly fell from Ivan's body. Sharp thumbs released his eye sockets. The Vaguer's harsh breath escaped with a hiss. Kagutt slumped off and struck the ground next to him.

For long moments, Ivan lay frozen on the wet grass. *"Whaa-hap— Sebassh? Do I sh-till hab my Esssensss?"*

"Oh, Ivan. I'm so dreadfully sorry," Sebastian cried. "I-I'm supposed to protect you, and I've failed. I can't even heal you."

Raising himself on one elbow, blinking rapidly, Ivan turned his throbbing head. Kagutt lay near him, a golden arrow through his heart. The skeleton lay flat where flesh dissolved into a puddle of pus, his wild eyes frozen open.

"Dat's Schysha's arro," Ivan whimpered. Swift feet approached. *Oh, no. More Vaguers to finish me.* "S-Sebaash," he whimpered, "hell-p me."

Someone spoke. A phrase he knew so well.

"Little brother of mine."

"Peeeter! H-how dit oou find meee?" Ivan's throat burned while he tried to focus through stinging eyes.

"Are you all right?" Peter fell to his knees. He took Ivan by the shoulders and pulled him onto his lap, cradling his head against his chest. "My dear brother. My dear, dear brother." He rocked him gently. "I told you not to come back. I warned you it wasn't safe."

"You must help him," Sebastian moaned. "I'm quite useless now."

Stroking the rain from the cloak, Peter said with a nod, "I remember your powers are limited when wet.

This is a real pickle."

"Yes," Sebastian replied with shame.

Tenderly Peter wiped Ivan's face. "Your head is bleeding."

"Oow b-bad iss it?" Ivan faltered. He wanted to talk, to ask questions, to be reassured, but his thinking was fuzzy, his throat on fire.

"It's fairly deep and bleeding heavily." Peter pulled a handkerchief from his pocket and pressed it against Ivan's scalp. "Pressure on the wound should help."

Peter unbuttoned Ivan's jacket and spread the fabric to help his brother breathe. He gasped. "A-a Forest Medallion." He fingered the disc, rubbing the ancient writing and sixpence-sized stone. "Where did you get this?"

"Lord Graydon thought it would protect him from those creatures," Sebastian answered.

"Useful, if it's visible," Peter's tone was tight. He adjusted the medallion, placed it on Ivan's chest, and blew out a puff of breath.

"He didn't have time to pull it from under his jacket," Sebastian said. "Kagutt came at Bounty in a mad frenzy."

"I didn't mean to scold, honest. I just wondered why it was buried under his clothing."

"P-Peter." Ivan swallowed with difficulty and grabbed his brother's forearm. "Where have you b-been? I returned to *za* Forest to find you and to—"

"I can't explain now. So much to tell you." He caressed Ivan's face with tenderness. "I tried to fix things, to undo what I've done, but I've made a real mess."

Ivan groaned and strained to move his stiff, bruised

body. He dropped his hold on Peter's arm. "Where did you get one of Sytha's golden-tipped arrows?"

"That doesn't matter right now. I'm sorry, Ivan, but I can't stay. I'll be in trouble for killing a Vaguer."

"T-trouble?"

"Tereus resurrected them to kill you. When I learned of it, I worked every angle to slip away and warn you without letting him know I was your brother." Peter moaned. "I was almost too late."

"Peter, listen to m-me…" Ivan's words were drowned by his brother's fearful words.

"Thank God, Kagutt didn't steal your Essence." He took Ivan's hand and squeezed. "Did you know he's been waiting for you?"

"Wh-who told you?"

Peter hesitated before he answered. "I hear things. Rumors. I wanted to warn you before something like this happened."

"I have m-my friends to protect me." Ivan's head throbbed. He was exhausted.

"Well, they're not here now, are they?" He sniffed.

Ivan groaned and tried to move.

"Little brother of mine," Peter managed to speak through his tears. "How do you get yourself in so much trouble?" He bent to kiss Ivan on his forehead. "I love you with all my heart. I hate to see you hurt like this. Did no one tell you what Kagutt—any Vaguer could do to you?" His voice trembled. "Please, I beg you. Leave the Forest and never come back. You must avoid Zephyrus's lofty schemes."

"S-schemes? I-I don't know what you're talking about." Ivan scowled with closed eyes, too painful and swollen to open.

"Try to bypass Zephyrus when you return in a week. Take Foothill Road to Helvaka. Your safe entrance will be arranged. Please come. I need your help."

"How can I help you?"

"I can't speak now. I hear the soldiers and Elftens coming. If they see me, they'll be enraged, believing I'm responsible for calling the Vaguers to attack. But it's not true—I didn't."

"What about Sebastian? He must accompany me when I return. He's my guide, my healer, m-my friend."

Peter exhaled loudly. "Yes. Well, I suppose there's no way to dodge Zephyrus." His fingers caressed Ivan's cheek. "My dear brother. I'll look for you in a week. Someone will contact you when you return to the Forest. They will give you instructions. There will be time to explain my misfit behavior." He leaned down and whispered, "Does Sebastian know why I hide like a thief?"

"I've learned some things," Sebastian's tone was gruff. "But Ivan is reluctant to tell me more."

"I wish you hadn't mentioned anything at all," Peter said. "It's always been between you and me, hasn't it?"

Ivan released a little cry and swallowed hard. "You promised to come home. I was so worried about you. I thought something must've happened."

"I must go." Peter laid his brother carefully on the ground. "I'm dreadfully sorry to leave you this way, but Simon, the Elftens, and the Wolflords are not far behind. You must be very important for them to send an army after you." Peter stood and brushed his hand against his trousers, where wet leaves and dirt fell away. As he moved toward his horse, he said over his shoulder, "Alfred and Canute are racing toward you, too." Then his beloved brother mounted and left swiftly.

Single hoof beats pounded the earth, and Ivan knew Peter was gone.

"He saved my life. He loves me—he said it." Ivan put his hands over his face, his body wracked with sobs. The tears stung his fiery eyes.

Darkness surrounded him.

Chapter 28

Recovery

"Should I get the supply wagon to load Ivan into?" A nearby soldier asked.

"No." Wayland reached for Bounty's reins. "This will be faster." Together Wayland, Simon, and the soldier hefted Ivan onto his horse. Ivan was too weak to be of much help. His head bobbed from side to side, and he groaned about his sore mouth and eyes.

"Be careful." Simon stabilized Ivan while Wayland pulled himself up and settled behind his passenger. There he encircled him with his arms, holding him tightly. The Wolflord's frown went deep. "Can Ivan make it to the cottage we've picked for him? He's pale and doesn't look so good."

"He's tough," Simon said. "Now lead Bounty and be careful about it. We'll follow close."

After the men transported Ivan into the cottage and laid him gently on the single bed, they left the soldier to care for him. "Don't allow anyone in unless you know them," Simon instructed. "We'll have the wagon brought around with food and medical supplies."

"Yes, sir." The man saluted.

****

"Ivan, can you hear me?" Squeeze my hand," said an unknown voice. He tightened his grip.

Moaning, Ivan tried to speak, but his mouth was raw with painful sores. "What's that dirty smell?"

"That would be the moldy straw mattress and pillow you are lying on, I'd guess," said the same man. "Your head and eyes are bandaged from a bad fall and the attack from one of those horrible Vaguers."

"Who are you?"

I'm a soldier in Simon's regiment. I was told to stay and look after you. There are about a dozen guards outside with sharp swords protecting this place."

"Wh-where am I?"

"You're in one of the better Harvesters' Cottages," Wayland answered with a huff. "The best we could find with such late reservations, you understand." He chuckled at his own weak attempt at humor.

A different man approached and sat in a squeaky chair. By the sound of his footsteps, Ivan determined he was heavyset. "He's awake?"

"I believe he's thinking straight," Wayland replied.

"My name is Dr. Sinclair. I'm from the castle's infirmary."

"How long have I been asleep?"

"About a day. A couple bad nightmares." The doctor placed his hand on Ivan's forehead. "Fever's gone. You've had a nasty fall, but the injury seems to be healing quite well."

Ivan's hand flew to the bandages that covered his head and eyes. "My-my eyes, are they okay?"

Dr. Sinclair sighed. "I don't know yet. The Vaguer did some damage. Broke blood vessels. Put a lot of pressure on them." He hesitated. "I want to take you to the infirmary where I can examine you with better equipment. Up to now, I didn't want to move you."

Ivan touched the bandages wrapped around his head and eyes. "I'd like to take these off. I can't see anything."

"Don't worry. You *will* see again." Wayland moved closer and put his hand on Ivan's shoulder. "Sebastian is sure to heal you."

"Wh-where is he?"

"The Long Dark Cloak is with Simon and his men where they need its healing powers," the Wolflord said.

"Eventually, The Long Dark Cloak was dry enough to help others, but not for you just yet. I'm sorry to say." Dr. Sinclair patted Ivan's arm in a fatherly way.

"They've been searching for the last of the Vaguers in this area," Wayland said. "I believe we got most—if not all of them when we raided the cottages and then moved farther southwest. It was just after you shot off into the woods. What were you chasing, anyway? Were you trying to get out of shovel-duty—that is, to bury the Vaguers?" Deep concern edged his voice.

Ivan was ashamed. He turned his face away. "I-I-wanted to kill them all for what they did to Sam Carringer—for what Kagutt wanted to do to me."

"Can't say I blame you," Wayland murmured.

The cottage door opened slowly as it creaked on rusty hinges. "How's our hero?" someone whispered and tiptoed into the room.

"Sytha?" Ivan turned his head, though he couldn't see the Elften's face.

"That's me. Making a quick stop to check on you before I return."

"Peter saved my life. He killed K-Kagutt just before…"

"I figured that when I pulled my arrow from the creature."

"Where did Peter get one of your golden-tipped arrows?"

"We practiced a lot of archery when he lived at the castle. Several times I gave him one as a gift. I shiver to think what would've happened if he didn't have it and wasn't a decent shot."

"Kagutt was moments from taking everything from me." Ivan couldn't control the trembling in his voice. "Including my life. Thank the High Intervener Peter found me."

"I agree." Sytha's light footsteps moved closer. "If I ever see Peter again, I'll be sure to let him know how grateful we are. How's our patient, Dr. Sinclair?"

"Better today. I'd like to take him to the hospital to examine him more closely. He's now in an acceptable shape to be moved."

Before Ivan could disagree, Sytha responded, "No need for that. Simon will return soon with the Long Dark Cloak. I believe we've rid the Forest of Vaguers. All that's left to do is dig holes. Hole and more holes."

"Holes?" The doctor's voice sounded surprised.

"Graves for the Vaguers," Wayland called from the small kitchen area. "They need to be buried to prevent their poisonous pus from infecting the animals if they chance to eat it."

"Have you found the carriage—th-the passengers?" Fear laced Ivan's questions.

Sytha lowered his tone out of reverence. "Behind the cottage with the fallen roof, just like the Vaguer said. Too late to do anything for them. Several of Simon's men took their bodies and carriage back to the castle. Picked up more provisions and brought Dr. Sinclair to attend you."

"Naturally, Lord Graydon was horrified his royal Russian guests had been mutilated," Dr. Sinclair said and rose from his chair. "How about a nice cup of tea, young Ivan?"

"I'm making broth and tea for him right now." Wayland lifted the kettle from the fire and poured the liquid into two cups. Ivan heard him approach the bed he was lying on.

"Yes, I'd like that very much." Ivan attempted to sit up but found he didn't have enough strength. Sytha and Dr. Sinclair reached under his arms and propped him against the bed's headboard.

"It's very hot." Wayland carefully passed the cup and saucer into Ivan's open hands. "Sip it slowly."

Thanking him, Ivan breathed in the herb-flavored aroma. He hesitated to drink until it cooled. His mouth was still tender from Kagutt's probing tongue. Then he remembered with a start. "Where are Alfred and Canute?"

Wayland answered, "Not to worry. We put them in the cottage next to yours along with some tired soldiers, so they wouldn't disturb you. They don't appreciate being separated."

"Tell me what happened." Sytha turned his chair around and straddled it with his long legs. "How did Kagutt catch you? What did he do to you? Few have lived to tell the tale."

Ivan told what he could remember, but his head hurt, and his lips were dry and cracked. "It was a nightmare I'll never forget."

Reaching his hand out, Sytha squeezed Ivan's shoulder. "I'm so very sorry. We should've kept you in our sight. We all should've considered your safety first."

"Not your fault. I was hard-headed and wanted to slay every Vaguer I could find."

"Admirable goal," Sytha said. "In the future, stay together so we can protect each other."

It was exactly as Ivan had said—more than once—while trying to keep up with Simon and the Elftens, but his suggestion was lost in the fury of the chase. He sipped tea. Though aromatic and flavorful, it stung the inside of his mouth.

"Ah, by the way, you should make a special effort to console Sebastian when he returns." Sytha leaned forward and rested his arms on the top of the chair. "He's miserable about letting you down when you needed him most."

"I don't blame him. The cloak was rain-soaked, and Sebastian's powers were limited." Feeling sleepy, Ivan held out the cup and saucer.

Wayland took it. "That's true. But he feels dreadful about it and hopes to make amends."

Ivan nodded. "It was my doing. I took off like I was possessed, slashing Vaguers right and left. The Challenger enjoyed the quest as much as I did." If his lips weren't cracked, he'd smile about his own comment.

"Sebastian told me you had the Wolflord's medallion tucked beneath your jacket." Sytha cleared his throat. "It was for your protection."

"I know," Ivan admitted sheepishly. He didn't explain further. Peter had already reprimanded him, and nothing could change the outcome. Gratefully, Sytha let it go.

"Here's a bowl of broth," the doctor said. "You really need to eat something."

Ivan panicked. "Where are the lantern and The

Challenger?"

"I'm just above you," Joseph, the spirit in the Golden Lantern, said. "Though you can't see it, my light is warm and glowing for your comfort inside this dim cottage."

"The Challenger is with Simon and his men," Wayland answered. "It's the perfect weapon to remove the Vaguers' heads. The troops should be back soon." He glanced out the window, sounding a bit worried.

Since Wayland was close by, he took the bowl and carefully spooned broth into Ivan's mouth. He winced from the pain.

"The soldiers will be roasting venison a little later," Sytha said. "If the cloak heals you like it usually does, you should be able to enjoy a sumptuous feast with us to be served shortly."

"I'll look forward to it." Stomach growling, Ivan sipped several more spoonfuls of broth that Wayland offered him.

Soon, he could hold up his head no longer, and he drifted off to sleep.

In his dream, Anna-Iza emerged from a deep forest and walked toward him. Though the trees' canopies shaded the ground, he knew it was her by the way she moved and the hooded, velvet cloak she wore. As she drew closer, he saw her sweet smile. *Now, I will ask if she cares about me.* She turned her head and gazed at another girl who'd left the cover of trees and stood a short distance away.

Coreena! He'd scarcely thought about her since he entered the Forest. The two girls observed each other, their faces emotionless.

"He is meant to be mine," Coreena said, her voice

soft with compassion.

"I know." Anna-Iza bent her head and then repeated, "I know."

****

"Can you sit up, Ivan?" the doctor asked. "I'll remove your bandages."

"Is it morning?" He pulled himself up with weak arms and yawned. His strange dream rushed at him. *What did it mean?*

"Late morning," answered a familiar and kind voice.

"Sebastian!" Ivan laughed. When he reached out, the old man stooped over and embraced him, placing a gentle kiss on his forehead.

"Yes, we just got back. Our mission lasted longer than I would've guessed. Of course, I demanded to see you at once."

"Who else is in the room?" There were shuffling feet. A chair scraped against the floor.

"I'm here," Simon called.

"And I've returned, too." Sytha clapped his hands so Ivan could locate him. "Wayland is finishing his breakfast in the next cottage and calming your beagles. They'll be here soon."

"One more bandage. Hold still." Dr. Sinclair carefully unwrapped the cloth.

Coolness swept over Ivan's face. He squinted and then blinked rapidly.

Simon gasped. "You look like a monster."

"Only a little red and swollen," the doctor said to placate his patient. "I can't determine how much damage the Vaguer has done to your eyes just yet."

"Not to worry." Sytha chuckled and stepped back. "Now, Sebastian can work his magic."

There was a rush of wind and a gentle swishing sound. Ivan knew from the many times he'd heard it that Sebastian had turned to smoke and entered the Long Dark Cloak.

Within moments after Sytha draped the fabric over Ivan's head, the soreness and burning disappeared from his mouth. Ivan took a deep breath of relief.

"I've heard about the Long Dark Cloak and Sebastian's healing abilities for many years." The doctor gave a short laugh. "But I've never seen it happen before. Too bad you're confined inside Zephyrus's sanctuary—that stuffy old tree. If you could be in-residence at the infirmary, you'd make my job seem like a vacation."

"Mine, too." Simon raised his hand.

Sytha removed the cloak and draped it over the back of a chair. "Good job! You look almost normal."

"I feel much better." Ivan extended his hand to the doctor. "Thank you for taking care of me until Sebastian could return."

"You're an important young man." The doctor smiled. His head was nearly bald, though plenty of strands of hair grew out of his ears and nose. "Simon has informed me of your heroic deeds. Just how you got tangled in the Forest's calamities, I can't figure."

Ivan questioned this, too, as well as during his previous visit. He wondered how he got caught up in fighting Burtack and Kruse Hays. *There are certainly better-qualified fighting men—and more courageous than me.* He scratched his head and squinted.

"Tut-tut. Let's not be touching that wound, young man." The doctor thumbed away Ivan's thick hair. "Yes. Nice. Very nice recovery. Though I believe it's healed, we shouldn't risk infection."

With a puff of colorful smoke, the spirit left the cloak, materializing into his solid self. "I'm happy to help." Sebastian glanced at Ivan's eyes and head wound. "Yes, much better."

"Then, I'm released to see Alfred and Canute?"

"You are." Dr. Sinclair gathered up his scissors and discarded bandages.

"We're fixing to have lunch in a short while," Simon said. "I'm sure you'll want to join us."

Ivan's stomach growled. He swung his legs over the edge of the bed, anxious to see his beagles and eat.

"Isn't that the sweetest nightdress you've ever seen?" Sytha rolled his eyes, dipped his head, and fluttered his eyelids.

"W-what?" Noticing his clothing, Ivan fingered the delicate ribbon on the scooped neckline with pearl buttons going down the center placket. "A lady's nightgown," he exclaimed. "I'm dressed like a-a woman."

"It's the only apparel we could find." Simon chuckled. "I think you look just lovely."

"Adorable." Sebastian joined the teasing.

Ivan laughed good-naturedly. "Pink is a good color for me, I believe."

"Your clothes have been washed. All Vaguer stench is gone." Simon pointed behind a dusty curtain, indicating the place where his clothes hung, and Ivan could change into something more suitable.

Soon the group left and strode toward the open lawn near the next cottage.

Alfred and Canute raced to Ivan, barking and turning in circles. The men were instantly alert. Soldier's hands went to their swords while their attention darted about.

"I believe it's safe." Simon called to them.

Dropping to his knees, Ivan pulled the beagles into his arms. He kissed their noses and stroked their heads. Spotting The Challenger, held in one of the soldier's hands, Ivan reached for the weapon and strapped it on.

"How's the venison coming?" Simon asked. "We're starving here."

Roasting on a spit over an open pit, the chunk of meat smelled delicious. Ivan breathed in the aroma wishing he could eat at least half of it. The other side dishes were covered with cloths to keep the flies and bugs away.

"It's about done," said one of the Wolflords, turning the crank.

"Men," Simon said, "bring tables and chairs from the cottages into the open area here and set up for a feast. After all, it's not every day we can claim victory by slaughtering the very creatures Tereus summoned to kill us."

Ivan placed his hand on his now healed head wound, remembering the horror of the attack. He couldn't forget. He couldn't forgive himself. *What would the men think of me if they learned the truth*?

His appetite returned, and feeling better, Ivan consumed a big lunch in his usual slow manner. He cut fried mushrooms into even smaller pieces, placed a thick slice of venison to the right, positioned the baked potatoes on his plate to the left, and made room for three pieces of thickly buttered bread.

Simon, Sytha, and Wayland, along with a number of soldiers, talked about the hunt. The longer they sat waiting for Ivan to finish, the more stories they told, each becoming more intense and daring. Ivan raised his eyebrows as though questioning the accuracy of the soldiers' tall tales. Just the same, he knew the chase and killing of the invading creatures would be tales to tell for a long time in the future.

"Get used to waiting on him when he eats." Simon pointed at Ivan and rolled his eyes. "He thinks he's some kind of prince and has all the time in the world." The men chuckled, and Simon smiled. He patted Ivan's knee and winked. "We're glad you've recovered."

"I didn't think there would be so many Vaguers." Wayland groaned. "Let's hope they never rise again."

Ivan quickly nodded in high agreement. Then he wondered, *What kinds of monsters will Tereus conjure to do away with me in the future?*

Chapter 29

Journey to Zephyrus

Soldiers saddled their horses while supplies were loaded into a wagon. Sergeant Pezzuline came beside a couple of the soldiers and checked the various food items, medical supplies, and a few useful tools being carefully packed.

Commander Simon addressed them. "I'd like you to stay and clean up these cottages. I want ten men to follow me." He pointed and called their names. "Elftens and Wolflords, divide your men as you wish. We're escorting Ivan and the Golden Lantern to Zephyrus."

The soldiers who would follow their commander raised their hands and cheered. Obviously pleased about leaving the cleanup job to others.

Simon mounted and stroked his animal's thick neck, "You have all performed admirably during this unexpected calamity, and I salute you." He swiveled his head right and left until he'd included all who served him so courageously.

The compliment brought smiles, while pride glowed on their faces.

"Sergeant Pezzuline, check the injured. Give me a report when I return."

"Sir," the sergeant answered with a lift of his head and a salute.

"Now that I think on it." Simon looked around at their surroundings. "I realize how valuable these cottages are to the workers who come and help harvest our fields."

"Convenient for travelers like us, too," Wayland added.

"I don't believe Lord Graydon knows of their shabby condition." Simon rubbed his forehead. "I'm going to address this problem with Zephyrus and ask that he furnish building supplies for the soldiers. They can do the repair work while the weather is still agreeable."

Several men hunched their shoulders and puckered their faces. Clearly, they didn't believe this was a job for a soldier. Ivan thought it was a solid idea, and he would've been happy to lend a hand, but he didn't think it was his place to say so.

Mounting Bounty, Ivan positioned The Challenger comfortably at his side. His horse turned his head toward his master. "You dumped me again, and it nearly cost me my life. I should be angry with you, but I know Kagutt scared the wits out of you, too."

"We'll have to teach that horse of yours better manners." Sebastian stroked his own mare. "Now hold still, Old Bones, until I get seated.

Cradling the Golden Lantern in the crook of his arm, Ivan addressed Joseph, "Soon you'll return to the Sanctuary of Truth."

"A glorious day in my life," Joseph's voice was almost giddy.

Ivan turned and hooked the lantern on the back of his saddle, as he had done many times.

"It wouldn't take too long to get those thatched roofs fixed." Simon paused, apparently unwilling to let the subject drop. "Repair the windows and remove some moldy boards." He made a pulling motion with his hands. "A number of my men love to work in gardens. They could till the soil and replant. Rebuild some of those wattle fences, too." He bobbed his head as he spoke, affirming his grand idea.

Sytha rode next to Ivan and said in a quiet voice, "I'm not *one of those* who love to plant gardens or fix fences. But I'm in favor of anyone who wishes to improve this decrepit place."

Ivan grinned. Sytha rode ahead and joined his own kind while Wayland dropped behind to where the other Wolflords rode to protect their flank.

The day turned warm and sunny as they traveled north on the Sheepherders Path Road. Fallow deer and black-faced sheep grazed in the meadow. The fresh smell of wet grasses and leaves was fragrant and comforting. Wrens and robins, with their red breasts and gray heads, darted after insects, now plentiful after the rain. Blackbirds, swept in and out, joined the eating frenzy.

"How are you feeling?" Sebastian's bushy eyebrows came together when he glanced at Ivan. "Would you like to stop for a bit and rest?"

"No. I'm feeling well enough." Ivan scratched the side of his head, careful not to touch the tender scar. His lips twisted. "If only…"

"You wanted more time with your brother, didn't you? And to learn what's holding him, and, if indeed, he's hiding in Helvaka?"

"That's right." Ivan slowed so Old Bones could draw up beside Bounty.

"What was it Peter didn't want you to tell me?"

"What?" Ivan wavered. Hoping if he stalled long

enough, he could avoid answering the question.

"Peter asked you if I knew why he hides himself like a thief. Are you going to tell me the full story? How much trouble is he in?"

Ivan looked skyward and chewed on his bottom lip. "I've already told you too much."

"Perhaps I could be of help. Explain the situation to Zephyrus and…"

"No. Peter wouldn't want that, and it's not my place to snitch." He dared not reveal to what extent Peter had joined Tereus and his dark forces—only as a spy to help Lord Graydon. Now, Ivan feared that Peter had gotten himself in deeper than he'd expected, and the consequences could be disastrous.

"If he needs help of any kind, I'm sure Zephyrus could solve the problem."

Ivan shook his head.

His companion sighed.

"I do have a question for you, though." Ivan focused his attention on Sebastian and Sebastian encouraged him with a nod.

"You heard Peter's curious statement about Zephyrus's *lofty schemes*. Do you know what he meant by it?"

The old spirit appeared to think on the question. Finally, his face wrinkled with frustration, and he answered, "I don't think it meant anything, though he may resent Zephyrus's control over the Forest. If there's anything to it, he will surely tell us."

"Peter doesn't seem to trust Zephyrus. I heard it in his voice, and I don't understand."

"Ah." Sebastian sighed. "Who can understand another person's feelings?"

310

Ivan thought about the statement. *How well do I understand my own brother after all this time? I want to believe the best in him, but things are not as they used to be.*

The troops picked up speed. Ivan and Sebastian were forced to ride faster and stay closer together. Old Bones was clearly having difficulty alongside Bounty.

Alfred and Canute's tongues hung out as they ran to keep the pace. Though Ivan felt safe in the company of the soldiers, Wolflords, and Elftens, he scanned the hills and trees for any disturbances. *Who knows what strange creatures might leap out from the brush and attack us?*

Turning east on Sir Barkay Road, they slowed their horses.

"You are safe with all these men." Sebastian suddenly glanced at Ivan. "Dr. Sinclair told me you woke up this morning moaning and calling out. What interrupted your peaceful sleep?"

"I had two dreams, and both haunt me, even now. I dreamt about Kagutt. My mouth was frozen open. Kagutt was over me as though he were—" Ivan choked. He shook his head, trying to rid himself of the hideous nightmare.

"I'm dreadfully sorry." Sebastian released his guilt with a rush of apologies. "You were left in my care, and I couldn't help you. I've failed."

"Please, don't blame yourself. It couldn't be helped."

The old man plucked at his eyebrows and pushed his spectacles higher on his nose. "It was almost too late." He groaned. "If it hadn't been for Peter rushing to help you…"

"My dear brother came through for me. I hope you'll

tell Zephyrus this. All the Forest should know that Peter saved me from a terrible fate."

"I will personally tell Zephyrus of the heroic act." Sebastian wiped away a tear.

"I didn't bring the subject up to make you feel sad and guilty." Ivan twisted the reins around his hand. "I wanted to share my fears, hoping to lessen its weight on me." He bowed his head.

"You are our dearest friend." Sebastian's tone was soft. "It's an honor to have you in our Forest."

Absorbing the compliment, Ivan thanked him and embraced the feeling of being loved, appreciated, and needed.

"And the other dream?"

Taking a deep breath, Ivan said, "It…it was about Anna-Iza. She walked toward me from the Forest. She looked unhappy and puzzled at the same time. Another girl approached her."

"Did you know this girl?

"Yes. Her name is Coreena."

"What! Who's Coreena?" Sebastian's brow crumpled, and his mouth fell open. "D-did you meet her in the Forest? Where is she?"

"Stop asking questions, and I'll tell you." Ivan couldn't imagine why her name had set Sebastian to sputtering. "I met her in my village, a very lovely young lady. Her brother is caring for my farm while I'm gone." Ivan thought to correct the statement that Dan was not Coreena's brother, but he figured it was more complicated than Sebastian needed to know.

Noticeably upset, Sebastian pressed his lips together. He raked his disheveled hair with his fingers. "A girl from your village? Yes, well, that's bound to happen. You're a handsome young man, and the ladies would be attracted to you." He breathed deeply, and his frown lingered.

"Well…" Ivan hesitated, unsure whether he should continue.

"What happened? In your dream, I mean." Sebastian encouraged him to tell him more.

Ivan repeated what the girls said to each other, though he didn't understand it himself.

He gasped. "Oh, dear me."

"It was only a dream. Nothing to worry about." But Ivan wondered why Sebastian was nearly beside himself with alarm.

"Yes, yes. Nothing to be upset about." Sebastian's elevated eyebrows relaxed, his mouth closed, yet he kept glancing at Ivan.

"Please, tell me. Why does her name distress you? Do you know Coreena? Has she visited the Forest?"

Sebastian seemed to force a smile. "Oh, it's nothing. An old man who worries too much. Let's catch up with Simon and his soldiers."

Ivan released a long exhale. He was frustrated that his friend was sometimes so mysterious and unwilling to share his inner thoughts.

****

Simon slowed as they approached Zephyrus.

"You're almost home, Joseph." Ivan smiled widely. He unhooked the Golden lantern and held it in front of him. "Can you see what's ahead?"

The spirit let out a whoop of pleasure and released his image. His smoky apparition rose, with his arms outstretched, and descended slowly to the ground. Joseph stumbled and tried to find his footing. Ivan swung from Bounty, rushed toward him, and grabbed his arm. It was as Ivan remembered when he first steadied Joseph after his initial release from the lantern. Arm in arm, swinging the lantern, they walked toward Zephyrus.

"This is indeed a happy day in my long life." Joseph's voice cracked. "I've often wondered if I'd ever experience my return to the sanctuary." Ivan grinned, feeling a deep satisfaction in his role to recapture the ancient relic.

"Zephyrus, wake up. Your friend in the lantern has returned," Wayland yelled, pumping both fists into the air, his white teeth showing through a wide grin.

"It's not time for the Big Sleep, yet," one of the soldiers teased the old oak. "Were you napping?"

The Master of the Forest, Zephyrus's eyes fluttered. "As the days become cooler, I find myself weary, yearning for a long winter's slumber."

The troops surrounded the tree, hailing their success. Truly, they had a lot to cheer about.

Alfred and Canute barked, wagging their tails as they ran and tried to avoid the horses' sharp hooves.

Ivan jingled Bounty's reins, encouraging his steed to hurry and follow him on foot. When Sebastian slipped from the back of Old Bones, Ivan hurried to steady yet another pair of strained legs.

"Too much riding," Sebastian complained. "My back is stiff."

"You're home, Joseph, my good friend." Zephyrus's mass of twig and moss eyebrows shot up. "Thanks be to the High Intervener."

"It's been a very long time, sir." Joseph's eyes watered.

"I've been told you were kept prisoner in the

Mountain of Smoke and Fire, Joseph. A most frightening place." Zephyrus's heavy wooden lips grimaced.

"Yes, such was my fate." Joseph nodded. It was Hoxx, the ghouls' leader, who struck a deal with Maloof to take me away. From there, I changed hands several times until Zello carried me off to the Azurite Mountains."

"Ah, yes. I know of this," Zephyrus said and sighed.

Ivan was glad Joseph told no more of the story, like Ivan's chase through the sky on Fluorescence's back.

"I'm thankful to these men." Joseph's hand swept toward Simon and his soldiers, the Elftens, and the Wolflords. "Mostly, I have this young lad to thank for his courage and dedication to my safety." His eyes settled with affection on Ivan.

"We are ever grateful, Ivan Kimble," Zephyrus said.

"I'm glad I-I could help, sir." Ivan bowed, sensing warmth that spread to his neck.

"Tell me what happened while you were gone." Zephyrus seemed anxious to hear Ivan's story. "I've heard the most bizarre but spotty reports from the birch trees. There was an outrageous story about Vaguers rising from their graves. Is this true?"

"Yes." Simon dismounted and spoke in Ivan's stead. "Another evil deed by Tereus, your wicked brother."

Zephyrus groaned, his green eyes locked onto Ivan. "I'm sorry. How can I—we—ever repay you for your sacrifice and bravery? It seems you have helped the Forest once again."

"I-I…" He didn't expect such a show of appreciation in front of everyone. Now the warmth invaded his cheeks as his hands slipped into the pockets of the Long Dark Cloak.

"We love and appreciate you." Sebastian raised his voice over the murmurs. "With the Golden Lantern's return, there's new hope the Forest will be restored to its original harmony."

"Only if the other relics are recovered." Ivan shifted his feet and hoped the attention would soon be focused elsewhere.

"Quite right," Simon said. "I believe there's a good chance that will happen in the seasons ahead."

"Come forward, my good lad." Zephyrus's tone was kind. "I thank you for returning the Golden Lantern to the Sanctuary of Truth. Having Joseph back in his place brings me great joy."

Ivan lowered his head and stared at the layers of wet oak leaves on the ground. "I'm glad I could help." Though he wasn't sure his statement was entirely true, it seemed the polite thing to say.

"I've learned you flew on Fluorescence's back and retrieved the lantern from Zello." Zephyrus frowned. "It was a dangerous thing to do."

"Foolhardy," Simon groused.

"Downright careless." Sytha fisted his hands on his waist and pursed his lips. "You could've been killed."

Ivan's mouth dropped. "It was Sytha's idea!"

When Zephyrus winked, Ivan had the feeling the tree already knew the full story.

"Now, we must conclude our business." The Great Oak turned serious.

"Business?" Ivan looked up into the tree's green eyes.

"You'll find a draft in your account at the Graydon Village Bank, just as before," Zephyrus said. "It should help cover any expenses you may have incurred while in the Forest."

Odd. Those were the same words Zephyrus spoke to him the first time he visited. He was as embarrassed now as he'd been then. "Sir, there's no need—"

"You deserve it. So I—we, the Forest—give it freely with deep appreciation. Now, let's hear no more of it."

Glancing away, Ivan wished the announcement could've been more private.

"Not to worry." Simon tapped Ivan on his shoulder. "Zephyrus is very generous to all his subjects. He fully understands the risks you took."

"Remember," Sytha injected, "Though Zephyrus was king long, long ago, he hasn't forgotten people's monetary needs."

"Will you return when the Forest Court Trials commence in about a week's time?" The tree looked hopeful. "A young girl's life is at stake."

"I promised Merridyn I'd be here for her support," Ivan answered.

Hearing the news, Simon clapped. The others followed suit. They whistled and loudly called their approval.

"We know she's innocent!" Wayland shouted, arms out, showing open palms.

Sytha nodded, grinding his teeth. "We need to find the culprit who poisoned Merridyn's potion."

"What about Zello's trial?" Sebastian pulled on his whiskers.

"I've received a request from Lord Graydon for a private hearing for our confused dragon. I readily agreed." Zephyrus looked pleased. "We'll work out the reasons for Zello's misbehavior. For all he has done in the service of the Forest, I believe we can be lenient."

Satisfied, Sebastian and Ivan turned and grinned at each other.

"I'll be leaving the Forest, then. Thank you for your kindness and friendship," Ivan blurted, throwing his arms around his good friend, Sebastian. "Be sure to tell Zephyrus about Peter saving my life," he whispered.

"I plan to when I can get his attention." Sebastian rested his free hand on Ivan's shoulder and squeezed. "Zephyrus will be overjoyed to hear it."

"I'll see you in a week, then," Ivan said quietly, "and we'll go find Peter."

Sebastian's brow lifted, and then he frowned. "I'm wondering if Peter was free to find you, why did he return to Helvaka, that abysmal place? That is, if indeed, where he came from. Why didn't he go hide or go home to you as he'd promised?"

Ivan shrugged and lowered his voice. "Tereus seems to have a strong hold on him, and he's being held against his will. I suspect Peter's also worried about my safety while in the Forest."

"Imagine that," Sebastian simply mumbled.

Sauntering toward Ivan, Sytha wrapped his arms around him. "We'll look forward to your return."

Wayland hugged him with a strong, intense grip. "Great having you visit." His eyes brimmed with tears. One slid down his cheek and lodged in his dark beard. "Remember—" he lowered his voice—"after the trial, Sytha and I will lead you into Helvaka. We will find Peter and bring him home safely."

"I'm counting on it." Ivan swallowed, hoping it would stop a cry from his throat. He handed the lantern to Sytha and untied the cloak, draping it over Sebastian's arms. Lastly, he unbuckled the belt that held the scabbard where The Challenger was housed. His loss was immense, and it cut through his heart.

"You'd make a grand soldier." The commander embraced Ivan and patted his back. "Consider joining my regiment." It was the second time Simon had suggested such a thing. With an uncomfortable laugh, Ivan pulled away. Nothing would change his mind about being in Simon's or anyone's army. *Never happen.*

Bounty snorted, impatiently pawing at the ground, reminding his master it was time to depart. After Ivan mounted, he felt the loss of the cloak warming his shoulders, the light of the Golden Lantern, and the protection of The Challenger. He unbuttoned his jacket and removed the Wolflord Medallion from around his neck and handed it to Wayland. "Keep it safe until we meet again."

"I'll look forward to your visit." Wayland pocketed the treasure.

"Would you like us to escort you to the border?" Sytha made a move to remount his horse. "You never know where those nasty trolls might be waiting to throw a rock or two."

"Thank you. It's not that far, and I feel safe enough with my beagles protecting me."

"Very well, then." Sytha gave a short bow. He suddenly turned toward Zephyrus when his name was called. "Sir?"

"I said, will you and Wayland come see me in a few minutes and talk privately? I believe we must clear up the matter of you being left out of our Forest War."

A grin spread on Sytha's face, and his turquoise-blue eyes became brighter. "Yes. I would like that." Wayland winked at his Elften friend.

Ivan nodded with joy. Now Sytha and Wayland would stop resenting Zephyrus's decision to leave them out of the Forest war. All would be set right again, as it should be.

The men waved at Ivan, yelling their goodbyes and good wishes.

Ivan threw a glance over his shoulder. He was sorry he hadn't had the chance to talk further with Zephyrus. Good manners prevented him from interrupting to ask questions. Now he must return home to do his chores. Besides which, Simon had hijacked Zephyrus's attention, making a case for major repairs to the Harvesters' Cottages. Zephyrus listened intently.

"Come Alfred, Canute. We're going home."

Chapter 30

Pousses' Surprise

"We have to hurry," Ivan said to his rambunctious dogs, "or we won't be home before dark. I wonder if Dan will milk the cows this evening. I didn't give him a specific time when I'd return."

Canute woofed and raced ahead, while Alfred trotted next to Bounty.

Something niggled at Ivan. He needed answers to many questions. *How does Anna-Iza truly feel about me? If Zephyrus has a lofty scheme, does it include me? Who poisoned Merridyn's cold remedy potion?* Those were questions for another time. He sighed. Right now, he was near the border of the Forest, prepared to cross over to his farm home.

"Spsst. Spsst."

What could it be? A snake? Another strange Forest animal ready to attack and claw me to bits?

He jerked Bounty's reins, bringing him to a halt, and glanced around. Canute crouched and trembled.

A Vaguer? Ivan shivered. His hands turned icy.

Another hiss sounded.

Alfred raised his head and barked up an elder tree. "Who is it?" Ivan called.

"Humph-foe. I'm in the tree—where you'd expect a flying cat."

"Pousses! What are you doing here?"

"I'm waiting for someone."

Ivan searched for a rider, but there was no sign of a visitor or another advancing horse.

Lying lazily on a thick branch, furry wings folded against his charcoal fur, the cat eyed Ivan suspiciously. "When are you coming back to the Forest?"

"Next week," Ivan stammered, wondering why it would matter to the surly feline.

"Why are you returning, and who invited you?"

"I promised Zephyrus and Merridyn that I'd be here to give my support during the Forest Court Trials."

"What do you know about it?" Pousses raised his brow.

"Not as much as I'd like to. Do you know who dropped the poison in Merridyn's potion?" He wasn't sure why he asked the question. The cat scarcely said anything to him unless it was nasty. If Pousses knew something, he'd probably not share his answer—especially with Ivan.

The feline glanced to his right, then to his left, and deep into the meadow toward the south. "It was one of those shrunken wizards."

"A troll? Which one?"

"Cecil." The cat snarled. "No good for anything except causing trouble. You know that ugly creature threw a fireball at me and singed my fur? It burned and took a long time to heal."

"I heard about it. Why would Cecil poison the cold remedy?" Ivan forced patience, and curiosity caused him to delay.

"You'd have to ask him. Trolls don't talk to cats—they eat them."

Ivan tapped his finger on his upper lip. Cecil was deceitful, but Ivan couldn't believe he'd intentionally end a man and child's life. "He's too short to reach the window."

"Not if someone provided him with a ladder."

"How could I prove this?"

"You ask a lot of questions for an outsider."

"I want to help Merridyn."

Pousses seemed to think on Ivan's answer for a time. He brushed his whiskers with his paw and then licked his toes. "In that case, you'd have to make a connection between Cecil and Lyla."

"Merridyn's sister? Did Lyla put the poison in the potion?" He'd been told Lyla was a jealous and vengeful witch, and that seemed a good reason to suspect her. *But surely, she would never poison her sister's family. Would she?*

The spoiled cat looked down at Ivan with a snarl. "How do I know you aren't trying to get answers from me so you can destroy our dear Merridyn?"

Ivan ignored the stupid remark and asked, "If it were Lyla and Cecil, someone would've seen them. She's a familiar face in the village, but Cecil—trolls—are not allowed in the Witches' Village. Tell me, please."

"You must think deeper and—perhaps more devious to learn the answer." Pousses sounded impatient.

"I-I don't know what you mean."

"Get the blacksmith's boy to speak."

Ivan was more confused than ever. "Benny?"

"He saw it happen, but he's terrified to tell."

Well, that makes sense. "Benny's afraid, and he doesn't like me."

"Appears a lot of people don't like you." Pousses

glared at him. Ears twitched.

"Wh-what?" Ivan lifted his eyebrows.

"I don't much like you, either. I trust your brother even less."

Ivan winced, genuinely puzzled. "Why? What have we done?"

"You both plan to kill Zephyrus and take over the kingdom." The cat jeered with disdain. "I'm not fooled—many of us aren't fooled. Peter wants to sit upon the throne and rule the entire Forest. He has given his loyalty to the wicked one."

"That's not true." *Peter would never give his allegiance to Tereus, though he may be in deeper than he'd planned.*

"You believe only what you want to believe." Pousses hissed again.

"Is Peter connected to Cecil?" Ivan rubbed the back of his neck, stiff from looking up.

"Not deeply, but they serve the same master."

Ivan's heart was heavy. "Surely, you are wrong."

"Suit yourself."

"When I return next week, I'll ask Peter about his loyalty to the Forest."

Pousses stood on his paws that looked like fancy white boots. "I'm talking to you now because you said you'd help Merridyn. I don't care a whisker about you or your brother." He turned and eyed Ivan with a cynical glare. "There's much for you to learn before the trial."

How does the cat know so much? Ivan blinked.

"One last thing."

"What would that be?" Ivan asked.

"Helvaka is a very dangerous place. I would think again before venturing there."

How did Pousses know about my trip to Helvaka next week? Ivan's mouth dropped open. He felt resentment rising over Pousses' cryptic answers.

The charcoal-gray cat stretched its feathery wings and leaped from the tree's branch, taking flight.

"Wait. Please." Ivan raised his hand, reaching toward him. "Tell me. Why—"

Flapping wings abruptly stopped. Pousses swerved back toward Ivan. "Inform my visitor I couldn't wait any longer, and so I must leave. Lord Graydon will have my dinner ready—I need to hurry."

Ivan frowned, knowing Pousses thought only of himself. He shifted in the saddle, mulling over the cat's comments.

"Who am I waiting for?" Ivan yelled skyward, unsure if the cat could hear.

"The High Goddess."

Ivan gasped.

"Anna-Iza is coming? Here? Now?" Ivan was at once shaken. His knees weakened. With unsteady hands, he tried to make himself presentable. He raked his fingers through his hair and licked his tongue over his teeth. "My saddlebags! Where are they?" He turned and knew at once they weren't on Bounty's back.

With so much confusion, he'd forgotten them at the Harvesters' Cottage. "Drat. My comb and toothbrush are inside."

A swoosh of huge wings beat from above. Ivan looked up. His heart thumped against his chest. A winged silver stallion circled. On its back was the lovely goddess, Anna Iza. Her purple cloak billowed out behind her. She saw him, grinned, and waved.

"Ivan, wait for me." Her words carried on a soft

breeze.

Of course, I'll wait. Forever, I'll wait for you. He slid off Bounty and whispered, "Alfred, Canute, she's coming to see me."

****

Forever I'll Wait For You

The flying horse spread its powerful wings and glided to the ground, soundless and gentle.

Anna-Iza's hood fell away from her auburn-colored curls, bouncing, as the animal pranced toward him. The silver stallion bent one leg behind him and bowed.

"Moonbeam, this is Ivan Kimble, a visitor to our Forest." Breathless, her pink cheeks glowed from the ride—and her excitement from seeing Ivan.

"I'm most pleased to meet you, Mr. Kimble." The horse lowered his long, glossy wings and folded them against his sides. "I've heard a great deal about you."

"What have you heard?" Ivan approached the animal and stroked its shiny neck, grinning, hoping to learn Anna-Iza's deepest thoughts.

The goddess gave her mount a playful nudge with her knees. "Don't tell him all my secrets, now." She laughed.

Moonbeam shook his head and pawed the ground, nickering softly.

"Why are you here?" Ivan stared at the loveliest girl in all the Forest.

"Well." Anna-Iza blinked and swept her tumbled curls away from her forehead. "Pousses sent an urgent message and asked if I could meet him near the Oakhurst entrance to the Forest."

"Did he say why he wanted to see you?"

"I hoped it would be something about my friend,

326

Merridyn. She's very worried about the trial. For all his faults, Pousses sees and hears many useful things. I've encouraged him to learn all he could about the person who'd put poison into Merridyn's potion."

It was now clear why the feline had quizzed Ivan—he was interrogating him.

The cat told him important things, but Ivan felt he should keep the comments to himself until he could prove them on his next trip. Maybe Pousses would give him even more clues.

"One of Simon's soldiers asked if I'd return your saddlebags to you. When I learned you'd be here at the same time as my meeting with the feline, I agreed at once."

"Ah, yes." Ivan lifted his dark eyebrows high. He took the saddlebags from the goddess's delicate hands and draped them over Bounty's rump and thanked her.

"Is Pousses hiding somewhere in the trees?" She glanced above, searching the mass of jutting limbs.

"He was here—just long enough to insult me. The bad-tempered cat admitted he didn't like or trust me."

Anna-Iza's eyes grew wide, and her pink lips parted in surprise. "He often lacks good manners when it comes to visitors." She gave a little laugh. "Lord Graydon should enroll him in a Personality Improvement Class."

Ivan smiled at her remark, relieved after sharing the incident with her. Only moments ago, his heart ached from the cat's biting words. *It isn't the only time I've been offended since entering the Forest.*

"Besides," Ivan added, "Pousses was anxious to leave and have his dinner at the castle."

The goddess threw back her head and laughed. A musical sound he remembered—like a whispering breeze through the leaves, like a river on its way to the sea. "His unkind remarks don't surprise me."

Ivan pulled his shoulders back, bringing air into his lungs. Anna-Iza made him feel brave and strong, and wise. Moments like these, he felt her genuine affection and was sure she cared deeply for him. "May I help you down?" He extended his arms, knowing she must reject his gentlemanly offer. It was forbidden, he knew, to put his hands upon her, and he tried to obey, but...

Her smile disappeared. Ached brows came together. "I-I..." She closed her pretty lips and hesitated.

Then, to his surprise and delight, Anna-Iza leaned toward him, ready to be embraced. She fell into his arms. Ivan eased her small frame from the horse, settling the dear goddess onto the ground, close to him.

"Is it all right to hold you?"

She didn't answer at once, torn between her feelings and actions, considering the consequences.

Ivan was ashamed. It was wrong to take advantage. He'd been warned in the past that he could never have her. She belonged to her sister goddesses, and their peculiar gods in a far-off land. Loosening his hold, he dropped his hands and stepped back. Shame flushed through him. "I-I'm sorry." He hung his head. "I should be more considerate of your rules."

"No...I want you to hold me."

His mouth parted in disbelief. He wavered, wondering if he'd heard correctly—and what had changed. Then, he gathered her into his arms and drew her to him. He remembered her slender neck, the lavender scent of her hair, the dainty curve of her shoulders. Ivan whispered her name over and over, hardly believing his good fortune.

"Are you sure this is okay? I mean, I know you are not to be touched…not by me, an outsider. Though I've embraced you before—even kissed you." His neck, his chest, his arms, felt warm.

"It's all right," she spoke tenderly, "but only for a short time."

His arms tightened around her, and he asked, "Were you punished by your gods for Burtack's brutal treatment of you?" The vicious Black Knight had grabbed Anna-Iza from her quiet time of prayer and threatened her with his knife against her neck. Enraged, and with the help of The Challenger, Ivan slashed Burtack's throat with one swift stroke. He shuddered, thinking of that horrible time not that long ago.

"Nothing came of it. My sister goddesses are too loyal to snitch. There was no one else who saw it that would carry the violation to my gods in the east." Moisture misted her eyes. She laid her head against his chest and released a gentle hum.

He didn't want to make her cry. Leaning into her, he kissed her forehead.

Anna-Iza shivered in his embrace.

"Then what of my affection toward you?" Fearful he would be held responsible for any punishment that might come against her. He held his breath, hoping she wouldn't answer.

"No one reported the incident."

This brought a genuine grin. Ivan pressed his lips against her cheek with a gentle kiss. Her sweet fragrance set his senses spinning. *How can I make her mine forever?*

"Why?" he suddenly asked. "Why did you ignore me that day at the castle's burnt-out stable?"

"I-I couldn't let my sisters, or anyone, know how I felt about you. Only Diana, my Goddess Advisor understands. My disobedience would set a poor example for the other girls."

He stroked her warm cheek and around her delicate ear with his fingertips.

Anna-Iza seemed content to be near him, happy to be held.

"I almost believe Pousses arranged this meeting," Ivan said. "Perhaps the selfish cat isn't so self-centered after all. He must've known when I'd leave the Forest and finagled a way for you to meet me here."

"In that case, I'm grateful." She nestled her head against him and murmured a sigh of contentment.

A memory flashed in his mind. *What of my affection toward Coreena? Why haven't I thought of her during my trip to the Forest? Am I so fickle and blind to these two realities?* A jolt of shame flushed through him, threatening to steal his feeling of joy. *No, I won't think about it just now.*

"My dear Anna-Iza. Last night I had a most curious dream. It was about you and another girl—"

"No." She straightened and put a finger to his lips. "I need not hear about it. I'm sure it was sad, and I don't wish for sadness right now."

"You're right." Ivan gladly let the subject go. It was only a dream, and it didn't mean anything. Nothing at all.

The feeling of guilt faded as though the power of the Forest drew it away.

Bounty gave Moonbeam a long, wide-eyed stare. He clomped toward the great silver steed and raised his head, then shook his fawn-colored mane. Stretching his neck, he sniffed the stallion's feathery wings. In those moments, they must have forged a friendship, for Bounty stayed close, making huffing sounds, neighing lightly.

"That's unusual," Ivan said. "Bounty never likes any horses, much less one with wings."

"Moonbeam is most agreeable. He can find something to admire in anyone—animal or man."

Ivan nodded, appreciating such a fine gift.

Anna-Iza gazed at Ivan, as her blue-green eyes blinked a tear down her soft cheek. "I miss you and think about you all the time."

"You do?" He lifted his face with surprise.

"Yes."

"I think about you, too. You are never far from my thoughts."

Her dainty hands rubbed his back. "I'm so happy, Ivan. I wish we could be in each other's arms forever."

They stood there smiling, holding each other. Joy overwhelmed Ivan. He shifted his stance. "It may be none of my business, but I-I know you had a private meeting with Zephyrus. Sebastian wouldn't share the details. When he denied telling me, it hurt my feelings and made me mad. Will you tell me about it?"

The girl eased herself away and drew her purple cloak closer.

Ivan's arms were empty. The goddess's warmth disappeared from his chest. He wanted to pull her back to him again, sorry he had mentioned the conversation.

She glanced in the distance while a frown creased her smooth forehead. "Well…"

He sensed her discomfort. "As long as I know you care for me, dear Anna-Iza, you don't need to explain if it upsets you."

"I do care…very much." Her eyes met his, and she

inhaled deeply. "I care enough to ask Zephyrus if he would help me."

"What did you ask him?"

"A Request to Withdraw from my gods." Instantly, she covered her mouth with her hand. "It's blasphemy to even speak of it. Our Circle of Goddesses has been in the service of our gods for thousands of years. I've asked Zephyrus to help me break away, and I'm frightened about my decision."

Ivan gasped. "I didn't know it was even possible."

"I'm not sure, either, but Zephyrus said if I were unhappy, he would support my request."

"What does this mean?"

"It means I would be free of my goddess limitations." She blinked rapidly as though beating back her tears. Her hands quivered.

He took her in his arms once more and offered his comfort and strength. "I'll help you, too. Any way I can. I'll be here for you, no matter what."

"You don't understand, Ivan. This official process could take a very long time. My gods won't let me, or my sister goddesses, go easily. They will fight to keep us bound to them."

"It doesn't matter." He buried his face against her neck. "*Forever, I'll wait for you.*"

She sighed and tightened her arms around him. He kissed her lips, a soft and gentle meeting of their love for each other, as he did on his first visit to the Forest. It had been a dangerous time, as the weeks ahead could be dangerous for them. Ivan would do whatever was necessary to keep her safe.

The dogs barked. Canute pawed at Ivan's trousers, wanting to go home. Indeed, time was slipping away.

They must leave, soon. The girl looked down at the beagles and smiled with fondness.

"Anna-Iza?"

"Yes." She tipped her head, meeting his eyes.

"What is Zephyrus's *lofty scheme?* I'd hoped to question Zephyrus about the statement, but Simon kept his attention. "Does it mean him helping you break from your gods?" Though he didn't give Peter's name, he wondered, *how does his brother know of this term?*

She blinked and appeared to think on it for a moment. "I'm not sure. I've not heard anything called that before." She shrugged and sounded uncertain. "I suppose it could refer to a scheme—my plan to break away with Zephyrus's guidance."

Ivan grinned. Happiness rushed over him, and he pushed the worry from his mind. Lifting Anna-Iza's chin with his fingers, Ivan bent close. She raised her arms and wrapped them around his neck, pressing her soft lips against his.

Ivan returned her kiss. Pulling her closer, he kissed her again. This was not a Kiss of Discernment. It was a kiss of love. He knew the difference.

A dark-haired lad will come seeking and find maturity, wisdom, and friendship. He will risk his life for the Forest's survival. The oath of the Forest is to keep him alive.

The Black Book of Pearls. Chapter 77, Verse 7

A word about the author...

In an earlier career, Vicki Thomas was a freelance fashion illustrator in Los Angeles, working for both wholesale and retail fashion houses. After she retired from her business, she taught watercolor classes to young people for about fifteen years. Now she's an active fine art watercolor and acrylic artist as well as a passionate writer of young adult fantasy.

Vicki and her husband live in the lovely Sierra Nevada Mountains, not far from Yosemite National Park. The deer, quail, and wild turkeys come to visit and drink the provided water. This year a couple of newcomers, a big black bear and a mountain lion have shown themselves on the Trail Cam.

http://www.vickithomasauthor.com/
https://www.vickithomasaritist.com

Thank you for purchasing
this publication of The Wild Rose Press, Inc.

For questions or more information
contact us at
info@thewildrosepress.com.

The Wild Rose Press, Inc.
www.thewildrosepress.com

www.ingramcontent.com/pod-product-compliance
Lightning Source LLC
Chambersburg PA
CBHW051135030726
47504CB00004B/883